Under Pressure

From the Casefiles of Detective 'Mal' Malone

Jen Flanagan

Under Pressure

From the Casefiles of Detective 'Mal' Malone
Copyright © 2022 by Jen Flanagan

First Edition: July 2022
This edition was first published in 2022.

Cover design: Haley Tenney
Editor: Moniga Bogza, Trusted Accomplice

ISBN: 978-1-7377499-5-0 (Paperback)
ISBN: 978-1-7377499-4-3 (eBook)

Printed in the United States of America
Published by: Serenity Endeavors Press
https://www.jenflanaganbooks.com/

Contents

Endless thanks to my husband and my sister. They read and re-read scenes and helped me talk through plot points at length.

Thanks to my friend, Kellie, her support and encouragement is one of the reasons I write.

A huge shout out to my writers' group. You ladies make it all possible. Thanks to my friends and family for your ongoing support and love.

To my readers, thank you for having faith in me and waiting around for this book. I hope this has all the twists and turns to satisfy your mystery-loving souls.

Now, turn the page and find out what happens next in our beloved Roscoe Village!

Chapter 1

"There's no security set up back here." Sam's eyes were on the door in front of us, his mouth turned down. "And no surveillance. What's wrong with them?"

"Isn't that a good thing?" I was kneeling, already at work, picking the lock. It clicked on my first try. Triumphantly, I swung it open and stood to collect my bag before heading in. After sitting for the past two hours, waiting for the drop-off, my legs had gotten stiff.

"Well, yes, for us." He huffed, stomping in behind me in his all-black spy outfit. He stopped short when he realized he couldn't see. "But I could have disabled it."

"Of course you could." I hustled past him, my flashlight aimed in front of me. I made a beeline for the front of the store, on the hunt for the new deliveries.

"Wait!" he whispered loudly, switching on his headlamp. He froze as he scanned the building. Light bounced off the walls erratically. "Did you hear something?"

"No one's here. You thermal scanned the place." I held a hand in front of my face to block my eyes from the light. "Careful with that thing. Keep it aimed low. We don't need anyone calling the cops because they saw something suspicious."

"Sorry." He lowered his head, taking a hesitant step forward. "I guess you're right. Unless they have newer technology I missed."

I looked around the dry-cleaning shop, guiding my light slowly around. Beige walls surrounded us with a long rack on one side, a small office portioned off in the back, and a countertop in the front with chipped Formica. "I think we're good."

"If you say so." Relaxing, my unofficial business partner—consultant was the legal term—started poking through things.

"Hang on. Don't contaminate the evidence!" Presenting rubber gloves to him, I held up my already gloved hands. "Just because there's no one here doesn't mean we should be leaving a trail. We need to find it, check it out, and get out."

He and his wife, Suzy, had stumbled into my life when she went missing and I was the private investigator he'd hired to find her. As fate would have it, we got her back, and I'd been stuck with them ever since. They were the friends I never knew I needed.

"We can check it out once we get out. I know someone who can test whatever's on it."

"That's if it looks like evidence. No sense tipping our hand until we need to. If it comes up missing, it'll be a dead giveaway that someone's paying too much attention."

"But you heard it too. The audio came through, clearly stating they needed to drop something off. There was an accident."

"*Something* about an accident. And I'm not sure it was really explicit."

"I'm almost positive he mentioned a little accident." He stuck his gloved hands into one of the bags of unprocessed clothes sitting behind the outdated counter. "Something like that."

A while back, we'd planted a bug in the conference room of a local crime boss's Chicago speakeasy. The same one who happened to have ordered Suzy's kidnapping and death months ago. We'd been following up on any lead we could.

"It may be nothing." I walked over to where the cleaned clothes were hanging, a beam of light guiding my way. They were all pressed and wrapped in plastic. Storage tubs were stacked against the wall behind them.

"Yes, but we're losing battery life. We estimated four to six weeks, but the bar's been busy and we've been recording a lot of audio."

Silence hung between us in the dark, both of us knowing time was closing in on us. Realistically, at this point, we only had a matter of days left. And with the plan we'd hashed to get it planted, it'd be back to square one if we didn't get any solid leads, *anything* to go on to bring us closer to real evidence, enough to lock Fabian Dessi behind bars for good.

"Maybe they're disposing of a body here," he went on, spotting the plastic storage containers. Rushing over to them, he tripped over a bag of clothes hidden in the skirts of long hanging dresses. The bag ripped, sending dress shirts and sweaters flying.

"Hang on, Sam." I rushed to help, trying to locate all the clothes and gather them back together. There was nothing to be done about the bag, but we were able to heap it together without being too obvious. I wrapped skirts around it, hoping whoever found it would run into it themselves and think they did it.

"The containers are a little small to store a body." Sam bent to open a lid. "Maybe they cut it into pieces."

Wrinkling my nose, I joined him, peering in. His headlamp lit up the interior of the box, landing on jugs of chemical solvents.

"Huh."

"The two guys in the sedan we watched only brought a bag."

"This could be where they clean up their crimes, though." He rushed to the next container. "I'll check the others."

"They said their boss wanted it cleaned right away, that it was his favorite shirt." I slowly made my way back through the shadowy storeroom and found the ledger on the counter. Each entry matched a number and a pickup date. "They said they'd be back tomorrow."

The last entry in the book had the number 533026 next to it, with tomorrow's pickup date. The description listed a men's blue button-up shirt. I didn't remember anyone coming in after them. Bending down, I started going through the bags at my feet, looking for a blue dress shirt matching that number.

"Find anything?" Sam shouted.

"Shhhh."

"Sorry."

"Not yet, but I think I have the number of the order." I started going through a second bag. Finding a black skirt marked 533024, I gripped my flashlight between my teeth so I could use both hands. I was close. Sifting between a cashmere sweater and a vest, I saw a flash of blue. As I pulled it out, I checked the tag.

533026. Lamp still firmly clasped between my teeth, I said quietly, "Found it."

Light bounced off the ceiling as Sam hopped across the tiled floor to join me.

When I shook out the shirt on top of the other clothes, the hair on the back of my neck rose and a chill danced down my spine. Dark red spread across the left side. My blood turned cold.

"See!" The would-be detective next to me clasped his hands in excitement, bouncing on the balls of his feet. "It's blood. We can get it DNA tested."

I leaned closer, inspecting the splatter pattern.

"It looks awfully thick. It might be something else." We had to be sure.

He swiped the shirt from my hands and sniffed it.

"Careful!" I semi-shouted, sending a panicked glance towards the front window. "If we ruin the evidence, it's useless."

Frowning at the shirt, I leaned in to give it a sniff. It smelled like oregano and basil. Probably marinara sauce. To be honest, it smelled pretty good.

"I still think it's blood." Sam's chin pulled up, defiant. "They said it was an accident."

Deflated, my body sagged. It was just another in a long line of failed leads. "Their boss, or somebody else, spilled the sauce on his shirt. Come on, let's get out of here before someone calls us in."

"We have to test it to be sure." Holding tight to the garment, Sam's eyes remained trained on the spot.

"If it comes up missing, they'll know something's up. Dessi's already on our case after the night in his speakeasy. We need to lie low until we know something for sure." Gingerly, I eased the shirt from his hands.

"But-but this is it, Mal! This is someone's blood. I know it!" He stared right at me, blinding me with the light before ripping the shirt back to inspect it closer.

"Hang on," I started, but he was poking at the stain with his gloved finger. A bit of sauce rubbed off.

"See?" I tried to point out. "Blood isn't that thick."

Shoulders drooping, he suddenly tensed, sucking in air, and clenched the shirt. "This *has* to be it."

I wasn't sure what he was planning, but it didn't look good. I reached out to take the shirt, but he pulled it out of my reach. Off-balance, I braced myself on the bag of clothes, but they were too soft. Unable to gain purchase on the slippery plastic, I slid, slumping onto the floor.

Sam's eyes were lasered in on the stain as he sniffed and inspected it closer and closer to his face.

"No," I said, drawing back, but it was too late.

Fueled by desperation, Sam stuck his tongue on it.

My mouth turned down in disgust, and I sat back on my heels.

"Huh." He frowned. "Maybe it is marinara."

Rolling my eyes, I started stuffing the spilled articles of clothing back into the bag. Then I held out my hand, waiting for him to give me the shirt so I could add it to the rest and slide everything back where we found it.

"Come on, let's go." I headed towards the door.

Following, he smacked his lips. "I'm gonna need to get that recipe. It's pretty good."

It was a quiet drive back to my office. Sam's unusually silent self carefully packed his fancy surveillance equipment into the bags he had left in the back seat. He always had the best gadgets. It made sense, really, since he owned his own tech company, creating apps, security systems, and stuff.

"We'll get a good lead, Sam." I tucked my small bag in the back with my run-of-the-mill binoculars. I hated to see him lose his optimism. Normally, this discussion went the other way around.

He nodded, fingers stilling over a zipper. "I don't want this to be Suzy's life," he eventually said. "No one should live in fear every day."

I hardly thought Suzy felt like that, but I understood his point. He had been paying Sentinel Security to follow her around ever since he got her back. Wyatt Parker, who owned the security business, had since become a close friend of ours and an accomplice in seeing Dessi locked away.

"But what would Wyatt's guys do if they didn't have you adding to their schedule?" I flicked my eyes towards him to see his reaction. "And how would Wyatt afford that Land Rover without all the work? You've got to account for half of his business."

That got a smirk from my techie-geek friend. "I doubt it's half, but yeah, he might have to downsize some."

My phone chose that moment to ring.

"Speaking of the devil," I muttered, pressing the phone icon on my steering wheel.

"Any luck?" Wyatt's voice came over the Jeep's speakers.

"Not tonight," I jumped in. "Spilled sauce on a favorite shirt. Apparently, that takes two people to correct."

I heard a humph over the phone line.

"Next time," I said, wishing I still believed it.

"Hey, Columbo."

I hummed pleasantly at his reference to the TV detective. *Cute.*

I was just pulling away from where I had dropped Sam off at his car, near my office. Even through my phone's speaker, Rhodes' voice sent a warm wave down my back.

"Hey, yourself." Unconsciously, I fiddled with my auburn waves.

"Any luck?"

"Not this time," I repeated, unable to pull together any enthusiasm this time.

"Next time." He supplied the optimism for me.

"Thanks."

"Want to come over? I can put a pot of coffee on."

The man did say the sweetest things. He definitely knew how to brighten the evening. Coffee was, after all, one of the top three best pleasures in life.

"Actually, Jen asked me to stop by Hungry Brain if I had time. I haven't seen her in weeks." Not since she and I made up, after recently discovering one of my oldest friends had been secretly dating a cheating ex of mine. But it was her choice, and she knew the score. And since he seemed to be making her happy, I was willing to see where it went, for her sake. The bar was a local hangout for cops and a usual for us.

"Oh, sure. Of course." His voice was light, but I could hear a thread of disappointment in it.

"The crew's all there tonight," I said, meaning the team I had gone through the police academy with. It was where I had met Jen and the slimeball also known as Alex Rodriguez. They'd finished training; I hadn't. It wasn't entirely Alex's fault. Let's just say my temper had raged more than was healthy after his indiscretion. Thankfully, I discovered I actually did do better in the less structured private-investigation sector.

"Then you should go. I've had you all to myself these past weeks. Enjoy yourself."

Everything was still new between us, having only recently officially started dating after spending the last few months dancing around each other. But things were starting to get serious. At least, I thought they were.

"You want to come?" I blurted out.

He paused a moment. "Are you sure?"

"No," I answered honestly. "But come anyway."

"Will your ex be there?"

"Probably."

"Okay." He laughed. "What could go wrong?"

It was one of the things I liked best about him. He had the best laugh.

Pushing through the crowd at Hungry's thirty minutes later, I pointed to the back patio with one hand and laced the fingers of my other with Rhodes', who followed behind me. He turned sideways to better navigate his broad shoulders through the small bar frequented by the local cops and firefighters.

It had been a while since I was attached to anyone like this, and the feeling was equally scary and exciting. The last time I arrived here with someone was with my ex. The same one I expected to see tonight. *Awkward.*

"Hey!" Jen's eyes lit up when she caught sight of me on the patio. Her mirth quickly migrated south to create a full-on teeth grin to display her delight when she spied Rhodes. She hurried over to me. "*Omigod!* I'm so glad you brought him. How are you guys?"

"Good," I said, hugging her.

"Nice to see you," Rhodes said, surprised when she angled in for a hug. I had to remind myself that they'd met when I was admitted to the hospital after escaping from Dessi's thugs.

A few of the guys from the academy saw me and headed over.

"So, who's this?" Stevens caught sight of us in the casual space illuminated with twinkling lights strung from the wooden beams above.

I cast an apologetic glance towards Rhodes, tightening my hold on him. It might be the first time I felt protective of a guy. *What did that mean?*

"Marlon Rhodes," he spoke before I had a chance to introduce him.

"This is Stevens." I gestured to the guy giving my—*was he my boyfriend?*—the once-over. Two other officers had now flanked him. "And that's Walker and Bradshaw."

"Nice to meet you." He nodded, shaking their hands. "You all went through the academy together, right?"

"Yeah," Stevens said, rocking back on his feet. "Until Mal left us. Jen was left as the only token female in our class."

Jen laughed, lifting her cocktail to take a sip, but I stalled. It had never occurred to me before. I wondered if it had been hard on her. You'd never know with her perpetually sunny disposition, but still.

"What do you do, Marlon?" Walker lifted his chin, giving him the obligatory once-over.

"He's a fire captain in Bricktown," I said, giving his hand a squeeze.

"Couldn't cut it for police?" He sniggered.

"Well, you know how it is." Rhodes gave him a sideways grin. "*I* could handle the heat."

The guys let out a hearty chuckle, clapping him on the back. And just like that, he had been accepted.

"Mal." A voice behind me made me turn. I took a deep breath in an effort to keep my face straight.

"Rodriguez." I nodded to the detective in question and his partner, George Michalski.

"You made it." Jen rushed up to him and stretched to plant a kiss on his lips, then stilled, looking warily back at me.

I shook my head, waving her off. It was weird, but I was most definitely not jealous.

"Sorry it took me so long," he whispered to her, his hand on her hip. "I had someone in questioning."

Rhodes leaned in. "You good, Malone?"

"Absolutely." I winked at him, turning back to the guys. "Okay. I still don't have a beer in my hands. Who's buying?"

"I gotcha, Mal." George raised his hand, motioning for the waitress.

Rhodes ordered a beer as well, his body at ease with a wide stance. To the casual observer, it looked like he was relaxed, but I knew him better. He was taking in every conversation and social cue in the group.

"So, Rhodes, is it?" Detective Dillhole addressed him. At his nod, he continued. "I hear you're a firefighter."

"That's correct," he answered, not bothering to correct him on his status with the crew.

"Oh, cut the crap, Alex." Stevens slapped him on the shoulder. "We already went through all that. He's okay."

I wasn't sure if he was being supportive of me, Rhodes, or if he had beef with Rodriguez. Accepting my beer, I toasted those around me, hoping my history wouldn't mess up anything in my future.

Chapter 2

"Thanks, Mal," Brian smiled, taking the cup of coffee I handed through the window of the Sentinel Security van parked outside the brick building housing my little PI office in Roscoe Village, a suburb of Chicago that I called home. It consisted of a small lobby and one even smaller office. But it was a home away from home to me.

"Anytime." I nodded, continuing on.

"Morning," Suzy sang out as I pushed through the door and strains of jazz music floated through the air. She was in a good mood, better than usual.

Noticing excitement dance in her eyes, I stopped to consider her. "What did you do?" I paused to take a long pull from my coffee before setting hers down on her desk. I had grabbed the coffee at Grounds, across the street. It was my favorite place for breakfast. The heavenly tasting liquid kind.

"I have something to cheer you up!" My receptionist and office manager waved a hand in the air, ignoring the steaming cup in front of her. "A new case!"

My heart sank. Last night out with friends had been a brief break in my regular schedule. It had helped me momentarily forget we were running out of time on the battery in the audio surveillance in Dessi's conference room. A new case was something different entirely.

"I can't take a new client now. I have to devote all my time to listening to yesterday's audio. There's got to be something there I can use."

I hoped.

"You and Sam need a rest from that. He came home last night and listened to Sunday's all over again."

I winced. "I probably should have checked in on him. He was pretty bummed."

"Tell me about it." She crossed her arms. "You'll either get something, or you won't. You're doing everything you can."

"We *will*," I emphasized. "It's just taking some time."

"In the meantime, you have a new case." She slapped a file on the desk, finally picking up her coffee.

I took the folder and flipped it open to peruse what she had typed up.

"A pet store?"

"It doesn't have a hard-and-fast timeline, so you can look in on it in between things."

"Just as long as it's not another infidelity case." I sighed, sitting to read through it. I could use the extra money. The income from the jewelry case I had just wrapped would only last so long.

"Not unless we absolutely have to." Her mouth turned down. "Those are just depressing."

"You're telling me. So, the pet store owner is worried about someone buying pets?" I frowned, not understanding.

"Not exactly." She fidgeted.

"Who's it for, Suze?"

"Brent."

"And who is Brent?"

"Just the sweetest, kindest, little teenager ever." She batted her eyelashes. "He's worried about those poor animals. And you're going to help him figure out what's going on."

I raised an eyebrow, then sighed heavily, knowing there wasn't any point in arguing with her. It sounded like another pro-bono case. "When is he coming in?"

"He's working today." She turned back to her computer once she knew she had won. "You're stopping by at 2 p.m."

Shaking my head, I stood. "I'll be there."

"How was your evening last night?"

"Good. I took Rhodes with me to Hungry's to catch up with Jen."

"You did?" She looked shocked. She was never shocked. Leaning in, her eyes grew wide, hoping for gossip. "How did *that* go?"

"It went well. The guys gave him a hard time, but he took it well enough. He bantered back and forth with them." I raised a shoulder. "You know guys."

Nodding, she swiveled in her seat. "I'm assuming things are good now with Jen?"

"Yes, no hard feelings. It's not like I wanted to get back with Rodriguez." I frowned. "It just pissed me off when I found out she was doing it behind my back. I don't understand what she sees in him. I mean, he's gorgeous but a cheater. Why would she give him a chance?"

"Maybe her relationship with him is different than yours."

"I think that's true, but still." I wrinkled my nose.

"Many didn't see what Sam and I had when we first got together."

"You guys are made for each other." I pursed my lips, but I got what she meant. To a lot of people, the beautiful brunette was out of his league with her long legs and polished look. But they worked.

"Did you go back to Rhodes' place?" she angled for details.

"Nah, it was going on ten when we left."

She just raised a hand like she was saying, "*So?*" and widened her eyes suggestively.

"It's still new." I let out a laugh, getting her point.

"You've known each other for months now."

"We've been fighting over personal issues for months now."

"And?"

"And it's going well." I struggled to explain. "I don't want to mess things up. We've both botched things up a few times already."

"You won't. He's a good guy, Mal."

"I know it."

"But you've gotta give me something." She rolled her eyes. "Sam's been focused on that stupid audio. I haven't gotten a quiet evening with him in ages. Tell me you at least shared a hot kiss when he dropped you off."

"We met there, but yes. There was a steamy moment when he walked me to the Jeep." I warmed at the memory of him standing in front of me, one hand on the Jeep door, the other braced near my head. Crimson crept up my neck and bloomed in my cheeks.

"Yeah?" She scooted her chair closer, eyes going dreamy.

"And it ended almost as soon as it started. Whistles and catcalls from the patio behind the bar spoiled the moment. They were peering through the slats in the fence to tease us." I shook my head. "There was even some singing."

"Singing?"

"'Mal and Marlon, sitting in a tree.' Like a bunch of kids."

"They were supporting you two."

"They were."

"And how'd it go with your ex?"

"There were a few tense moments, but Rhodes played it cool and didn't react to any of his jabs."

"Were they really jabs?" she questioned me.

I thought back over the night honestly. Or at least I tried. I was biased against the man. "Maybe, maybe not. Either way, we mostly hung out with the other guys. Rodriguez and George broke off to talk to some new officers. Jen flitted back and forth, talking to everyone."

"I'm glad you and her worked things out."

"Me too," I said, breaking away to head to my office and get started with my day.

Chimes from the bell affixed to the door announced my arrival at the nearby pet store. The place didn't smell overwhelmingly strong, but you could tell many types of animals lived here. An iguana placed near the door cast a baleful eye at me. I had never been overly fond of reptiles.

I stepped to the right to give him some space and perused the shelves. Beginner's guides for pets like chinchillas and sugar gliders stood on a revolving wire rack in front of me. A sharp yip to my left caught my attention. Turning, I saw a large crate full of golden retriever puppies. The frown that had marred my face since I heard of this non-lucrative job melted away at the sight of the fluffy fawn-colored balls tumbling around inside. However, concern remained at the thought of the poor pups, likely from a puppy mill. I wondered where the mom was.

"Hey there, sweetie," I whispered, reaching in to scratch under the chin of one of the pups that had waddled over to the side nearest me, giving me an untrusting eye. One ear hung low, making her look a little lopsided. Eventually, she leaned in, her tail wagging hard enough to swat her brothers and sisters behind her. After patting her on her head, I straightened and heard a soft whine when I pulled away.

"That one's a total snuggle bunny," a voice spoke from behind me. Whirling around, I caught sight of a soft-looking young man. It had to be Brent. "You'd have a lifelong friend if you took her home."

"Not quite in the market for a dog," I said, appraising him. "I like them, but I'm not home enough."

"You could consider kenneling," he offered. "Lots of people kennel during the day. The dogs get used to it and like having a safe place while their owner is out."

"I'm out more than the typical nine to five, unfortunately." I cast a look back at the pup, who had lowered down on her front legs in a playful manner, her rear in the air, tail still wagging nonstop. My heart twisted.

"Then, what can I help you with? Cats are pretty low maintenance, but Archie there could use a good home. He's been with us for a few years and is the sweetest little iguana I've ever met."

As I looked over my shoulder at the lizard in question, his tongue darted out to wet an eye and disappear into his toothless reptilian mouth. I barely contained the shudder that rippled down my back.

"Maybe not Archie, then," he surmised.

"I'm actually here to help you." I turned to look at him squarely, sticking out my hand. "I'm Detective Malone. Suzy told you to expect me."

His eyes widened as he pumped my hand, his words pouring out. "I didn't really think you'd come! I'm so glad you're here. Thanks for coming. What a relief!"

I gave him a sharp nod, eventually retracting my hand. "So, tell me what's going on." I had read Suzy's notes but wanted to hear him announce it unrehearsed.

"It's so creepy. This lady comes in every few days and buys pets." He lowered his voice. "I mean, it's not normal to buy pets every few days. What is she doing with them all?"

"Maybe she loves animals. Some people have twenty cats." I shrugged. "Tell me what makes this lady creepy?"

"Well, it started with just mice," he explained, walking to the register and pulling a notebook out from a shelf underneath. He flipped through it to a page and put his finger on a line. "I figured it was for a snake or something. People with snakes get a mouse every week or so, to feed them. I didn't think anything of it until she got the hamster. And *that* wasn't so bad, but then it was a rabbit a few days after. That's not normal, right?"

"Did you tell your manager?"

"He didn't care." He ran a hand through his hair, the thick strands sticking up in its wake. "He said if she's paying for them, why would he care? But who knows what she's *doing* with them."

The guy seemed sincere. I had worried he wanted me to look into a girlfriend who had ghosted him or something, hoping to gain some intel. But no, he seemed legitimately concerned about all those furry little mammals.

"Does she ever buy anything else, like pet food?"

"No. Not even bedding or snacks. It doesn't make sense."

"Do you have an address?" I asked, not sure what to think about it yet. She could be buying pet food from a cheaper store, one that didn't sell pets.

"No." He frowned, tossing his notebook on the counter. "She always pays in cash."

"We'll need one." I studied his notebook. I didn't have time to sit around and wait for her to come by, and follow her home.

"How do I get that?"

"Tell her you have a loyalty program and need to fill out a form. You need her address for it."

"But we don't."

"So?"

"What if she wants a discount?"

"Are you allowed to offer any discounts? Ever? Under any circumstance?"

"I can give them 10% off if a pet dies within the first thirty days."

"Then, if she comes in ten times, you can do that." I shrugged. "We'll know what's going on by then. And if everything's on the up and up, you just tell her they stopped the loyalty program. That not enough people signed up for it."

"Huh." He pursed his lips. "I could do that. It's weird, but it works."

"When is she due back if she follows her previous pattern?"

"Very soon."

"Call me when you get an address," I said, setting my card onto the counter with a snap. This case would be in and out, easy-peasy. And then I could get back to what was really important. I turned to go.

"Thank you!"

I nodded, already stepping to the far left of the aisle to give Archie plenty of room on my way out, regardless of the plexiglass aquarium that separated us.

Later that night, as I was going back over the audio from the day before while chowing down on a salad from Mariano's Fresh Market in my small one-bedroom apartment in Roscoe Village, a mumbled comment caught my attention. It was between Dessi and a firm female voice I assumed belonged to Cynthia, the business manager at Red who had given me a run for my money when I planted the bug in his conference room. I rewound the recording to play it again. Something was being delivered to the video-gaming place in Oakbrook.

It seemed like an unlikely business spot for the calculating crime boss. Dessi probably made a lot of money on gaming machines. That part made sense. But the store had an oddly placed winery in the back room. It was a little low class for Dessi. A strange convenience store/video-game gambling *winery*?

What could the delivery be? I stabbed at my salad. I'd been by once before, with Rhodes, on a date night. Maybe we should check it out again, I considered, chewing.

Pulling my phone close, I dialed Sam. While I was sure Rhodes would be up for a repeat—we had a lot of fun laughing over fries on our first official date night—it would mean more to Sam to be involved. Especially after last night.

"Oakbrook?" he answered, his face filling my screen on the video call.

"Yep." I nodded. Of course, he had zeroed in on the same tidbit.

"I'll pick you up in ten." He hung up before I could object. After shoving my salad back in the bag, I bent to put my boots back on. It looked like we were in for another night of stakeouts. I'd finish my dinner in Sam's Tesla. He'd love that.

"You didn't have time to eat dinner?" Sam said, eyeing a drop of vinaigrette fall from my forkful, paused at his words.

"I didn't have dinner waiting for me when I got home," I said blandly. Then curiosity got the better of me. "Hey, Suzy doesn't leave that much before me. How does she make dinner for you between when she leaves the office and I head home for the day?"

"Suzy's amazing." His eyes glazed over in adoration. "She preps food the night before. Chops veggies, marinates meat. I tell her she doesn't have to. We can order food. Hell, we can hire a chef, but she won't have it. She wants to cook our meals."

"You're a lucky man."

"I am. I just wish she'd let me spoil her a little more often."

"Why doesn't she? Is she just being stubborn?" I asked, honestly curious. I'd seen very few name-brand items in their house. That is, except for Sam's clothes and the wine labels. But I'd bet she did some savvy shopping for those too. "I know you didn't have a lot when you started out, but you'd think she'd relax a little by now. You're rolling in the proverbial dough."

"It's more complicated than that." Sam glanced over at me as we sat outside Lola's Slots and Wine Bar. He was strapping on enhanced-vision goggles, but paused, pushing them up to his forehead to see me better. "After her first marriage—"

"Suzy was married before?" I said with such force that small bits of chewed lettuce and dressing splattered on the dash.

"Uh. I probably shouldn't have said that."

"When was this?" I asked, hastily wiping my mess with the napkin I had brought.

"It's her story to tell, Mal. I shouldn't have said anything." His eyes cast down, then he pulled the goggles back over his face, affixing them in place, and examined the lot. "Hey, what's that?"

Assuming he was trying to distract me, I rolled my eyes before looking out the window. Two men were lifting the metal door of a delivery van that was backed up to the rear of the store.

"This is gonna be it. I just know it!"

"Looks like a delivery." Peering through my binoculars, I saw the guys walk wine barrels to the back of the van, set them on furniture dollies, and wheel them down the ramp and into the building.

"Not just a delivery," Sam said excitedly, holding a large parabolic mic up to the window to amplify the sound, headphones firmly in place on his head.

"What do you mean?"

"See those guys?"

"Yeah." I ducked under the audio stick he motioned with as it swung around the small cab.

"They're ready for serious business. I can tell."

One of the guys lit a cigarette and took a deep drag.

"Yep," I agreed. "Looks nefarious."

"You'll see, Mal. Just wait till they start talking." He repositioned the audio stick and shoved up his night binoculars to adjust a setting on the amplifier.

"Can you hear what they're saying?"

"No. They're not talking."

I took some pictures just in case, but it looked like the winemaker was just getting some sort of wine delivery, probably grapes or something.

We stayed another thirty minutes, but only five barrels were unloaded and moved into the building. Apart from one guy asking the time and letting out a large belch, we heard nothing.

"Should we follow them?" he suddenly said as they prepped to go. Lines appeared between his eyebrows in concern.

"It wouldn't hurt."

"Maybe it's not wine barrels."

"They do make wine, Sam." I looked at him, hating to burst his bubble. It was hard not to get hopeful as well after all of our dead ends. "But you never know. Let's go."

Excitement was back in his eyes as he carefully edged his car out to follow at a distance. As he pulled over across the street, he waited for the truck to choose a direction before continuing. When had he become so good at this?

A short drive later, we arrived at a trucking company. The semi pulled in, driving around to an empty bay. Sam drove past the place and into a lot across the street.

"Looks like a normal delivery," I said after watching them open the bay and go inside to bring out another load.

"Maybe they work with Dessi." He peered through his night goggles.

"Maybe." I packed my binoculars and empty salad container away. It was a long shot, but worth investigating. "We can look into the trucking company tomorrow. I doubt we'll see anything else tonight."

Chapter 3

The next morning, after I had gotten home from my morning jog, I hit the button on the coffeepot to brew before heading in to shower. My morning home brew was just to break my coffee fast in the morning. I considered it just whetting my appetite for the main course, i.e., a cup of liquid delight from Mo at Grounds on my way to work.

As I chugged a little water to rehydrate from my run, I spied the little succulent I'd picked up several weeks back from a friend who ran a newspaper stand down the street. The dirt was looking a little like the concrete outside. Wincing, I tipped my glass over to slosh a little liquid into the pot. Oddly enough, the plant appeared to be doing pretty well. It was the first thing I'd ever been able to keep alive on my own. It seemed silly, but the thriving little plant made me feel like I wasn't doing so bad at this adulting thing.

Shrugging, I glanced at Mr. Bunn, my coffee maker, but he wasn't quite ready. I debated waiting a few minutes to take my morning coffee into my morning shower, but it was already going on eight o'clock. These late-night stakeouts were wearing on me. Turning on my heel, I trudged to the shower sans coffee.

"So?" Suzy said, glancing up at me when I finally walked in, mid-caffeinated and clean.

"Sam didn't tell you?" I frowned, setting her Snickerdoodle Latte down and sipping on my dark mocha, extra foam. "It looked like it was just a wine delivery. But we're going to look for a Dessi connection with the delivery company."

"Not that." She waved me off. Her eyes widened as she leaned forward. "The pet store."

"Oh, that." I plunked down in the chair across from her. "He has no leads I can follow. He doesn't even know where she lives. I gave him some ideas. Hopefully, the next time she comes in, he'll be able to get an address. Then, we can look into it."

"What'd you think about it, though? It's a juicy case, right?"

"It's odd," I admitted. "I have no idea what someone would be doing with all those animals. I just hope it's not something creepy and disgusting."

We both sat with that thought for a minute.

"If he calls with an address, that means she's got a new pet."

"Yep."

"You can follow up on it pretty quickly, though."

"Maybe." I shrugged. "Dessi's my top priority."

"True, but..." her voice trailed off.

"Yeah, I know. I just hope it's not one of those pups." I shook my head.

"Puppies?" Her eyes softened at the thought.

"Golden retrievers." I smiled, remembering the cute little female with the wagging tail.

"I have to go back with you next time." She sighed.

"Is that a good idea?"

"Why not? Dessi's told you himself that he's not interested in me anymore."

"But why risk it? We'll have him behind bars soon enough."

Her eyes flicked to me. "Maybe."

The thought sunk to my stomach. If only I had been able to get information from those goons who kidnapped me, or connected him to Suzy's disappearance, she wouldn't be in this mess. I was a private investigator, for goodness' sake. This was literally my job.

"Besides, I haven't been anywhere but here and home in months," she went on, not noticing the pit I had spiraled into. "I'll drop the idea to Sam, let it sink in before Brent calls with the address."

"You're going to have to convince Brian." I nodded towards the door. "Which means Wyatt too, as you well know." We were all protective of Suzy. She was only ten years or so older than me, but she tended to mom us all.

"You let me worry about that." She winked, picking up her coffee.

It sounded like an impossible feat; Wyatt was a stickler for security, but she had strange powers over people I would never understand. I just hoped I hadn't set up a bad situation.

As I settled in at my desk, I opened my laptop and started clicking through trucking companies in the area, trying to find some connection to Dessi. I attempted matching business license names to all of his known holding companies. Sam would do better at this part, but he sometimes missed illegal connections. He was brilliant, but also just a genuinely good guy, not quite understanding how a criminal would think.

I was getting nowhere and doodling notes when my mind drifted to Rhodes. Maybe he'd be free for dinner tonight. I wasn't much of a cook but was pretty good at throwing food in a skillet or roasting it in an oven. Mariano's might have some stuffed pork chops or salmon that would impress the hunky fireman.

Scrolling through my phone, I resolved to listen to last night's audio after a short call to Rhodes. It's not that I didn't want to find something against Fabian Dessi—nothing would make me happier—but it was getting tiring, listening through some useless static every day with the odd, boring meeting about his speakeasy. When we did get meetings with the crime bosses, it tended to be droll discussions about food and wine as we strained to catch a mumbled word or phrase that could be helpful.

"Morning." Marlon Rhodes' voice came through my phone, instantly lifting my spirit and causing me to smile. The dispatch toners in the background reminded me that today was a workday for him. I had forgotten. It was taking a while to get used to the twenty-four-hours-on, forty-eight hours-off schedule.

"Good morning." I swiveled in my chair like a teenage girl with a crush. *What was happening to me?* "I forgot you had to work today. I was going to invite you over for dinner."

"Is that so? You're going to cook for me?" He chuckled pleasantly. "Well, no way could I turn that down. I'm free tomorrow night if that works for you."

"It should." I hesitated, already thinking about what could go wrong. I hadn't even listened to last night's audio. What if we had a new lead? *That's what I want,* I strained to remind myself, not a quiet evening.

"If anything comes up on the case, I understand," he threw in there, obviously hearing the tension in my voice.

"I'm sorry."

"I'm not. It's your job, and it's an important one," he said with finality.

Warmth spread across my chest. I had never dated anyone like him before. It was why I was so hesitant to open up to him in the beginning. Anyone, really. I thought I didn't have room in my life for a relationship.

"Thanks," I simply said, unable to explain the rush of thoughts and emotions flooding my mind.

"I'm glad you called. I wanted to talk to you about something, too."

"Shoot."

"I'm sending someone in for a new case, an old firefighter's wife. Collins was my captain when I first joined, and he retired shortly after. He's in a nursing home now; Linda couldn't get him in where Gran's at, unfortunately. Sean was telling me Linda's having trouble paying all his bills."

"Does he have Medicare?" I knew firefighters retired young and wasn't sure if he was old enough.

"Yeah. And I would think Medicare would take care of anything his fire pension didn't, but it sounds like his breathing treatments and tests are adding up, exceeding the limit. Linda thinks they're out to get her money and wants to talk to my *detective friend.* That's how Sean put it," he clarified, sounding slightly uncomfortable.

"It's fine," I reassured my—*boyfriend?* I tried the word on for size. It was cute that he was dancing around what to call us, but I understood.

"Apparently, he was telling her about us. So, she's stopping by to see you. I hope you're okay with that. It might be good to have another case to keep you busy during downtime."

"If things heat up, I'm going to have to focus on the Dessi case, though."

"Of course. I appreciate you looking into it."

"Anytime."

"And I'm looking forward to dinner tomorrow night." His voice lowered to a soft vibration that sent shivers down my spine before he signed off.

I took a large gulp of chocolatey-flavored caffeine and shook the feeling off before digging into my drawer for my earbuds and locating last night's audio file on my phone. I didn't want to miss anything important.

The whir of an electric motor announced Sam's entry into my office a couple of hours into the audio file. Or rather, the Sambot 2.0's entrance. Sam worked from his office at PhishNett, an app-and-security tech company he owned. The previous remote-controlled robot affixed with a tablet had been replaced a week ago with a taller version, one I didn't have to peer down to see. One not so ironically resembling the Star Wars character R2D2, with one difference; installed in the front of his domed top was a tablet with Sam's face currently displayed on it.

"Listening to the audio?" he asked through the tablet's phone app. I think it made him feel more like he was in the office with us.

"Yes, did you hear anything interesting?" Hitting pause on the audio, I popped out an earbud and pushed aside my notebook, where I had been taking notes, knowing he had already listened to it.

"Maybe, but I'm not sure." He hesitated. "There was a comment about something being in storage. It sounded like it was at the other end of the conference room, so it was a bit muffled, but it was during a conversation about an antique store or estate sale or something."

"I'll listen for it. Thanks for the tip."

"I looked into the trucking company, but I didn't find any tie to Dessi."

"Me neither."

"I added a notification, if anything comes up online connecting the two."

"Good idea." I tapped my pencil against my desk. "I'll keep thinking of ways to tie him to it. Maybe something will come up."

"Hopefully." The frown was back on his face, but he also looked drained. I could tell he was getting as tired as I was of filtering through vague references for any minor detail.

"Look. Why don't you take a break?" I attempted to reassure him. "I'll finish listening to the audio, and I'll give you a call after. I only have another two hours to get through."

"On the Sambot?" He perked up.

Normally, I just called him on my phone's video app.

"On the Sambot," I promised.

Shaking my head at the full-on toothy grin on the tablet, I watched his face disappear into sleep mode, and the Sambot whirred into the corner to wait. It was a bit creepy, but also incredibly impressive, not that I'd ever tell Sam that.

Before I could hit play on the file, Suzy's face poked into my doorway.

"Yes?" I raised my eyebrows in question.

"He got it." Her eyes lit up with mischief.

"He?"

"Brent."

"Ah, the address?" I clarified. Her excited nod made it obvious she planned on coming with me to investigate. Still not sure it was a good idea, I added, "Did you talk to Sam?"

"Sam said if I had security and you with me, he'd be okay with it. He doesn't like it, but he knows I'm antsy to get out and about."

"And Brian?"

She preened. "He's ready whenever you are."

My eyes narrowed at her, wondering how she had convinced the man to risk the trip out in public. No way would Wyatt be okay with it. "I'm assuming he ran it by Wyatt."

"We're just going in and out." She brushed it off. "It's a short stop across town."

"You talked Brian into keeping it quiet from Wyatt?" I raised my eyebrow.

One shoulder lifted.

"You can deal with the lecture you'll get from him later." I shook my head, resigning myself to the fact that I couldn't stop her. "I have to get through this file first. Maybe three o'clock?"

A high-pitched squeal emitted from her as she jumped up, spun on one foot, and disappeared back to her desk.

I put my earbud back in and hit play.

"It's in storage," a man's voice came through the audio file. I was pretty sure this was the group of organized crime lords. They occasionally met at Red, Dessi's speakeasy. This had to be what Sam was talking about.

"They'll never know the difference," another voice said.

"Doesn't matter. Just have your guys be at the estate sale on Friday night," the first man responded.

I breathed a sigh of relief. Tomorrow was Thursday night, and I wouldn't have to call off my date night with Rhodes.

"It's a waste of time. It's antiques," the second voice replied. I wondered if they were selling fakes, passing them off as antiques. "Nothing will go wrong."

"I've got men to send," a voice I'd never forget as Dessi's sounded off. It felt like a cold hand between my shoulder blades. I fought back a shiver.

"Is it secure?"

"It's in my storage," Dessi's voice responded. "I can confirm it's secure."

He was doing a good job at becoming indispensable to these men. It wouldn't take long before he had the same reach they did. There was one difference; most of these guys kept their heads down. Sure, they did terrible, illegal things. But they targeted larger audiences. Dessi had no conscience, no code of conduct, no honor among thieves. It was all a big game to him, and he didn't care who got hurt, as long as he got to play the best hand.

I finished the audio file before using the Sambot's voice activation to call Sam.

"So?" His face filled the screen.

"Friday night," I confirmed. Who knew what we would find, but it was obvious they were doing something illegal. We would be there, and we would do whatever we could to figure it out.

"There are several estate sales on Friday."

"Only one selling eighteenth-century chairs once owned by Fred Seivers."

"Seivers? I didn't find that name connected to any of the top names in crime locally."

"It's an alias for Petrelli, one of Marchi's guys." They all worked for Pietro Marchi, the top dog of the food chain.

"How do you know these things?" He shook his head, impressed.

"Just time on the job. You'll get there." But then, maybe it would be better if he didn't. "I can take this one if you want to stay home with Suzy."

The light of excitement flickered from his eyes. "But what if you need tech? What if you get into trouble?"

"I can call Wyatt if I need backup." I instantly regretted saying anything. "I was just trying to give you two a night off. I think Suzy could use it."

"Good call." He nodded, looking off-screen at something. "I'll take a break from the audio tonight and tomorrow night. Plan something special." His eyes made their way back to mine, resolve firmly in place. "But I'm not missing out on a clue Friday night."

"I understand." I hoped we found something before he was too deep to disentangle from mafia leads. *Me too*, I thought. If I never took another job that had ties to the mob, I'd be a happy PI.

As I finished up my notes from the file, I added a final one. Look into storage facilities owned by Dessi.

Chapter 4

Meanwhile, in a small fire station in Bricktown,

"Hey, Cap." A firefighter approached Rhodes, holding a newspaper. "They released the names of the people who got shot outside that warehouse."

"Can I see it, Healy?" Rhodes' hand shot out to take a look, coffee forgotten on the desk in front of him. Mal had told him it was one of Dessi's meetings that had gone awry. Bystanders had gotten caught in the blowout. His eyes skidded over the page, looking for the right section, stomach going in knots when he recognized two of the names. "Shit."

"Know them?"

"Yeah." He sighed, looking at it again in case he had misread the first time. Hoping. "Nate and Warren are from Bricktown. I don't know the other two, a husband and wife, just out walking their dog."

"Oh yeah." Healy frowned. "Nate was the kid we picked up with the knife wound a few years back. We've been on a couple of calls to his house."

"Yeah, he's been out of that world for a while now." He handed the paper back. "Joined Warren at the community center's basketball league. His mom got clean, been going to AA, and Nate has been keeping out of trouble."

"I wonder what they were doing out there. It's a little way outside of our district."

"No idea. I honestly didn't think Nate would get back into that. His life was turning around."

"Shit," Healy echoed. "Wrong place, wrong time?"

"Maybe." Rhodes' jaw clenched. This was the second time Dessi had messed around with someone he cared about.

"It's three."

Glancing away from my computer, I saw Suzy standing in my doorway, bag in hand, eyes wide with excitement. *The pet store,* I remembered. "You're ready for your jailbreak?"

"It's no jailbreak!" she protested. "Brian's coming with us."

I cast her a look. "Alright, let's go. We just need to lock up."

"I have the phone forwarded to my cell." She held it up. "If anyone calls, I'll still be able to take it. And I have a note for the front door."

"It's only a couple of hours early. I doubt we'll get a rush on investigation needs."

"Still." She jerked up a shoulder, then waved her hands, ushering me out. "It's my job to keep this place running. I take it seriously."

She was always better at that than I was. *What would I do without her?*

After pausing to press the previously taped note to the now-locked front door, she raised her eyebrows and headed toward the Sentinel Security van parked in front. Brian looked up from his phone at the movement, his body slumping in apparent excitement of our little trip. *Not.*

"3441 W Belmont Avenue," Suzy announced, climbing in and buckling up.

Following suit, I switched gears, getting my mind back on Brent's case. "What did he say when he called?"

"Not much. Just that he got an address like you asked."

"Must have sold another animal to the mysterious lady."

Suzy wrinkled her nose. "I hope you figure out what she's doing with them."

"Me too."

We rode in silence the rest of the way, trying not to guess.

After Brian found what he decided was a good parking spot, he made us wait in the locked van while he checked the store out.

"How do you handle this all the time?" I wondered aloud.

"This?" Suzy questioned, then realized I meant her security. "Oh, I'm just happy to be included in this little field trip. It's my first real foray out, not counting work. If it takes a few extra minutes, so be it. It keeps me safe and Sam happy, especially while Dessi is out there."

I strained to take a deep breath, the weight of responsibility feeling especially heavy on my chest while she sat there, calm as could be, excited even. It reminded me of a hooded hawk, excited to be set free, even for the short flight of a hunt. This wasn't how life was supposed to be.

Her eyes lit up when Brian exited the front and walked around to open the door for us.

"Looks safe enough." He cast a glance back down the street before ushering us towards the store.

Animal sounds greeted me again, along with the faint smell of caged pets. Looking around, my eyes quickly found my scaly nemesis watching me enter. Mouth in a thin line, I made a hard right, winding around the books when I heard a shriek.

Eye-licking lizards be damned. I beelined it back, before the sounds of baby talk registered in my head.

Suzy had found the puppies.

Leaning over their little box, she had all but climbed in with them. Two little squirming goldens were in each of her arms, and her cheeks were getting covered in puppy kisses as they leaped to get closer to her radiant face. I had only seen that level of glow in her eyes once before, when she saw Sam for the first time after her abduction.

As I made it over to her and around the reptile, I heard a little yip. The loner golden with the floppy ear was sitting away from the group attempting to remove all of my friend's makeup. Curious, I stepped closer. She backed up and yipped again, dropping down on her front paws in a playful pounce. It was impossible to ignore the appeal. Dropping my hand to her head, I let it sink into the cream-colored fur, delighted in the velvety softness of it. The pup hadn't jumped into the chaos around her, focusing solely on my hand scratching her ear. I had trust issues too. I could respect it.

"I'm glad you got my message." Brent's voice surprised me from behind. The pup jetted away to the corner to see who had approached the top of the box, then relaxed and plopped to the ground. Stretching out with a yawn, she remained unconcerned by the excitement around her.

"You got an address?" I asked, turning away from the puppies.

"Yeah." His voice rose excitedly. "I did like you said. The fake rewards program? It worked like a charm."

He gestured to his desk in the back, and I followed, pausing when I realized Suzy wasn't behind me. She was still working to disentangle herself from the blonde fluff, giggling hysterically. When she eventually broke, she and Brian followed.

"Lane Pollett." He brandished the notebook he kept behind his desk in the air like a trophy. "541 N Oakley Avenue, Apt 406. I have a phone number too if you need it."

"I'll take everything you have." I took photos to transfer to my notes later. "What's her description?"

"Dark hair, not black but close. About this tall?" He raised a hand to his eyes.

"Approximately five feet, six inches," I noted. "Age?"

"Uh." He scratched his chin. "Twenty?"

"Twenty?" Suzy said, surprised. "I just assumed she was older."

"American?"

"Yes," he answered.

"Caucasian?"

He nodded.

"Is she attractive?" I asked.

"What does that have to do with it?" Suzy asked.

I just shrugged. It could have to do with Brent's assessment of her, or anyone else's response to what she was doing.

"A little." He frowned. "She's kinda harsh."

Interesting. A harsh woman buying cuddly pets.

"What'd she buy today?"

"A short-tailed Chinchilla."

I added the details to my notepad. What in the world could a young woman be doing with that many pets? Were they dying? I tapped my pen, trying to think of anything else important.

"What time did she come in?" Brian asked from where he stood, leaning against a shelf.

"Uh, nine? This morning," the store clerk said thoughtfully.

"Is that when she normally comes in?" I asked, curious. Brian dipped his head, seeing I had caught on his train of thought. She obviously didn't work a typical schedule. It was a Wednesday. Normal nine-to-fivers would have been at work.

"I think so. Usually in the morning, not always that early, though," he added.

"Anything else seem important or strange?"

"I can't think of anything. Except she doesn't seem excited about the pets. That was part of the red flag for me. I mean, if you're going to take a couple of pets home every week, wouldn't you be excited about it?"

"Oh, yeah," Suzy spoke, eyes sparkling.

"I just want to ensure they're safe, you know?" Brent gave us the perfect puppy-dog expression. "Pets sometimes end up in the trash when people don't want them anymore. I don't know what she's doing, but I just want to make sure it's not something like that."

I laid a hand on his arm. "We'll do what we can."

We made our way out of the store and buckled back into the van.

"On to Oakley?" Suzy asked.

"I don't know." I hesitated. "It's getting late."

"It's not that late," she argued. "I'd still be at work right now."

When I gave Brian the go-ahead, Suzy clapped her hands, overjoyed.

Oakley was only a few blocks over, and when we approached, the sun was still up. It wouldn't be easy to case the place. It was a large, brick apartment building stretching over half the block. It wasn't terribly fancy, but not rundown, either.

"Apartment 406 is probably on the fourth floor," I mused aloud, counting up the windows.

Suzy nodded, studying the building herself. "Should we get out?"

"I'll check it out," I said, opening the door. When she moved to follow, I held up a hand. "It'll look suspicious if we both go."

Never mind the big, hulking security guy who would most certainly be in tow.

Thankfully, she didn't argue or appear too hurt. I closed the van door and made my way to the front of the apartment building, and walked in, not pausing to look around like I was casing the joint. Which I was. Sort of.

The inside was lined with bricks, matching the exterior. Only the interior walls were drywalled, having probably been renovated. An office sat to my right, next to the stairs, with a security cam mounted above it. A long hallway traveled down the center of the building, with apartments on either side. It looked like there was another staircase and cam at the other end of the hall. Without a thought, I headed up the stairs to my right, quickstepping it up four flights. My feet beat a staccato in the brick-lined stairwell. At least it wasn't the sixth floor.

I was breathing heavily by the time I hit the fourth floor, and I took a steadying breath before punching through the door. Barely glancing up, I saw twin security cams on this floor as well. Even-numbered doors were on the right, odd on the left. Walking steadily down the hall, I ticked off the doors to my right, 400, 402, 404, 406. There it was, on my right, facing the back parking lot, about a quarter of the way down the hall, the fourth apartment from the end.

Slowing only a touch, my eyes took in the door for anything unusual. I didn't hear any strange noises or any loud pets, for that matter. Breathing in, I thought I caught a lingering scent of the pet store, but that could have been from my clothes. I was sure, however, that I smelled bleach.

I continued down the hall, bypassing the room, passing under the camera at the other end of the building, banging through the door, and back down the stairs. I was out the door and headed for the van a few minutes later.

"So?" Suzy asked when I settled back into my seat.

Brian's eyes were on me in the rearview mirror, obviously interested.

"Fourth apartment from the end," I pointed out the window. "No strange noises, but I smelled bleach. Like someone was cleaning up."

"What do we do next?" Suzy's eyebrows drew together in worry.

"I don't have plans tonight. I'll sit in the lot and see what happens." It wasn't obvious that anything bad was happening to the animals, but we had something solid to follow, at long last. Unfortunately, it was for the less important case.

"Sounds like a long night."

"I can listen to today's audio again. See if I missed anything."

She rolled her eyes. "Always the audio."

When we got out after we arrived at the office, I caught Brian's eyes in the mirror. Surely, he had noticed we had gained a tail on the ride back.

He nodded.

"See you tomorrow, Suze," I said, shutting the door.

"See you, Mal," she replied, barely glancing up from her phone. Her hand raised in a wave.

Brian rolled the window down as I approached to talk. "Are you going to tell them?"

"Yes, of course," he assured me. "Just as soon as I tell Wyatt. He'll probably want to handle the conversation. No need to make her panic."

I gave him a look. *Wasn't there?* It wasn't a flower delivery vehicle that had followed us during our ride back to the office. It was a nondescript black sedan. "Keep me in the loop if anything happens."

"Sure thing." He nodded.

I'd text Sam the plate number once he had been brought up to speed.

An hour later, I was settled comfortably in my Jeep, alternating between yet another salad and a cup of joe I'd picked up from a new coffee place in town I wanted to try, Hexe Coffee Co. I took another sip, appreciating the richness of a regular old cup of drip coffee. I called it dinner coffee, the kind you drink with dinner.

My cell phone rang. It was Wyatt.

"Hey," I said, hitting the button on my phone where it sat in its dash holder. Wyatt's face filled the screen. Unfortunately, he looked mad.

"Hey, yourself." The corners of his mouth pinched tight. "What were you thinking?"

Oh yeah.

"Suzy's little field trip?"

"Field trip," he repeated.

"Brian was with us."

"And you knew how I'd feel about it." The pitch of his voice rose.

"You're mad at me?" I tilted my head. "Suzy chose to go, and Sam knew about it. Brian and I were both with her."

"No." He sighed. "I'm not mad at you. Or Brian, or Suzy."

"Did you unload on them?"

The glower he gave me told me what I needed to know.

"I'm just doing whatever I can to keep her safe. It is kind of my job."

"I get that." *Oh boy, did I get that.* "We all are."

He looked down, a lock of blond hair falling into his eyes. I could hear him scuff his shoes in the gravel outside Suzy's house. "I guess I need to go talk to Brian."

Wyatt was a big tough guy, but he was also a big softie.

"I'm assuming he told you about the tail."

"Black sedan, yes."

"I got the plate number."

His eyes lit up. "Nice."

"Yep, I'm gonna text it to Sam as soon as I get off the phone with you. I assume they know by now."

"Yeah." His mouth went back into a thin line. "Brian filled me in on both things at once. It's part of the reason I blew up."

I shook my head. "Not good news."

"Nope. Dessi said he'd lay off, but"—he blew out a breath—"can't trust that man."

"Mighta been me." I lifted a shoulder. "Maybe it's retaliation for breaking into his offices."

"It's been weeks."

"Or he's just trying to keep me on my toes."

"Maybe."

"Could be entirely unrelated to Dessi at all."

He just gave me a look that said I knew better. Unfortunately, I did.

"Keep me posted," he said. "And, Mal?"

"Yes?"

"I hope you get a break in the case."

"Me too. I'm doing everything I can. That's kinda my job," I said, repeating his words from earlier.

He nodded.

Hanging up, I ripped off a text to Sam with the plate number.

Sam: The black sedan?

Mal: Yep.

Sam: On it.

I took the last few bites of my salad, closed the lid, and looked around the Jeep for a granola bar or something, even though I knew there wasn't anything to be found. I needed a regular meal. I hadn't cooked in days. Or gotten a good night's sleep. What I needed was a break.

Shoving the bag aside, I picked up my coffee and my earbuds and turned last night's audio back on. I looked through my windshield, counting to apartment 406 again. Still no lights on in the place.

I had run a short background check on Lane Pollett. She was enrolled at the University of Chicago and drove a blue Chevy Malibu. There wasn't much on social media, which was odd, but I did get a good pic of her driver's license photo: dark hair, pale, light eyes. She was young, recently turned twenty-one. It didn't sound like someone who would get off on killing small animals. But then again, neither had Bundy.

I yawned. If I could get more of an idea of Lane and her schedule, I could make it home in time to get to bed a little early.

Chapter 5

The ringing of my phone jolted me out of a light doze. I'd *never* fallen asleep on a stakeout, but it had been a while since I had done this alone. So much had changed for me, working with a team. I wasn't even sure how I felt about that.

Rhodes' image filled my screen with a picture I had taken that night at Hungry's. He was saying something funny; his eyes were lit in laughter.

"Hey," I said after hitting the accept button.

"Hey, Columbo." His voice rumbled through my speaker. I loved the effect it had on me. "We still on for tomorrow?"

"So far. There's an estate sale Friday night, though. Sam and I are going."

"A lead?"

"Yes, and dammit, it better not be another dead end."

There was silence on the other line. It made me wonder if he was as frustrated as I was. He had seemed okay with it before, but there was only so much patience any one person had.

"I'm sure it'll work out," I mumbled, needing to break the quiet.

"What time?"

"I think the sale is at six."

"No, dinner tomorrow night." I could hear his smile over the phone.

"Oh, six or six-thirty works for me." I quickly calculated how long it would take to get through Mariano's after work and quickly tidy up my apartment. It wasn't big enough to take very long. "Is that okay?"

"Absolutely. What can I bring?"

"Just yourself."

"A beautiful woman is making me dinner, and I can't even bring anything? You've got to let me bring something, or I'll feel completely useless."

"You didn't let me bring anything when you invited me to dinner." I smiled at the memory. He had made a hearty beef stew and a salad. He had even lit candles for the table.

"That's different," he insisted.

"How?"

"It just is."

"Okay, fine." I laughed aloud. "You can bring a bottle of wine."

"Done," he said, pleased with himself. He stopped short when the toners went off in the fire station. He paused before saying, "It's not for us. How's your day been?"

"Not bad. Suzy lined up another job for me."

"That's good."

"It's mostly pro bono. A pet-store clerk is worried about someone adopting a lot of pets."

"Weird."

"Maybe. Anyway, Wyatt was ticked because Suzy went with me to investigate."

"You broke Suzy out?"

"Not exactly," I explained. "Brian came with us."

"Okay."

"Brian didn't clear it with him."

"Oh, that makes more sense."

"Yeah, and then a black sedan followed us back."

"Shit."

"Exactly." A beep interrupted our conversation. "Hang on, I've got a text."

I hit a button on my phone and read the incoming message.

Sam: *The car is registered to Dessi.*

Mal: *Didn't even bother to hide it.*

Sam: *Looks like he wants us to know he's around.*

Mal: *Got the message.*

Sam: *Be careful.*

Mal: *Always.*

"Sam said it was Dessi." I filled Rhodes in. "The car's registered to him. It was probably one of his lackeys."

"Any idea what he's after? Isn't it a little late to be pissed about that night at his speakeasy?"

"I would agree. Sam thinks it's just a warning, letting us know he's watching."

"Like we'd forget."

"Right," I said, pleased he had said "*we*."

"Promise me you'll be careful, Columbo," his voice broke in suddenly. "I know you're capable, but you're not invincible."

"I'll keep an eye out," I promised.

Toners came through the line again. "Crap, that's me... I'm just worried, Mal. Text me when you get home tonight. Please."

"Will do," I said, hanging up. It was nice having people who were concerned for me, but the thing was, I was starting to worry as well. I took precautions, but he was right. I needed to be a little more careful.

Headlights struck my windshield, then bounced off as a car entered the lot. It looked like a sedan, possibly black.

Shit.

Starting the Jeep just in case, I visually tracked the sedan as it pulled into a space and turned off its lights. A nearby streetlight reflected off it, glinting a blue hue. It wasn't Dessi's car; it was Lane's.

Letting out the breath I hadn't realized I was holding, I turned the engine off and slipped out, locking the door behind me. Lane was struggling with something from her back seat, giving me cover to speed up my step and approach her before she slammed the car door.

She was juggling an armful of books and three to four large store bags. I couldn't tell what was in them. Ignoring her, I headed toward the building entrance, angled to put her in my path.

From the corner of my eye, I watched her hoist her books higher on her hip. She had a short black skirt, black tights, and clogs on. Her hair had been cut since her DMV photo, hanging shoulder length in a straight bob.

I was within feet of her when I pulled my phone from my jacket pocket, fumbled with it, and caught my foot on the gravel, my elbow jutting out to send her books to the ground. Shocked, she stumbled, arms flailing to catch them, and the store bags slipping from her elbow to her wrists, jerking to spill open.

"Oh, no," I said, righting myself. "I'm so sorry!"

Moving to catch her bag, I pulled one from her hand, causing the rest to match the fate of her books as she dropped to gather them, her face pinched.

"Just leave it," she shouted, shoving her hair behind one hear and looking up from her crouched position. "And look where you're going from now on."

"I didn't mean to," I lied, my eyes dropping to take in the contents of the bag. I saw a big bottle of bleach, gloves, and a brush. An orange rolled out of one of the bags on the ground, coming to a stop at my boot.

"I said just leave it." Her voice boomed, and she snatched the bag from my hands. Her eyes had narrowed into little slits.

"Okay." I held my hands out in front of me, backing off. "I was just trying to help."

Stuffing the orange into the other bag, she gathered the remaining handles together and straightened with her arms loaded once more.

"Want me to get the door for you?" I offered, trying once more.

Instead of answering, she huffed, stomping towards the building.

Staying in the lot, I watched her enter the building and waited for her to get to her apartment. I wanted to make sure she had given us the right number.

As I stuffed my hands in my jeans pockets, I felt the summer air lift the ends of my hair. It was cool, but not chilly enough for a jacket. Within minutes, the light flicked on inside 406. Jackpot.

Pleased, I turned to leave, but halted at the sight of a black sedan parked in a space between my Jeep and me.

Panic slid up my spine, ice-cold now, pinching behind my ears. I had left my baton in the glove compartment. Headlights were aimed at me, preventing me from seeing inside the car. I eased my phone from my pocket, where I had stuffed it after the fake stumble, and slowly made my way to the right, putting as many vehicles between us as possible. If they had guns, there wasn't much I could do, but I could try to use another car as cover.

The black car slid forward out of the space but didn't roll down a window or open a door. I had made it between the rows, crouching down to keep steel between us. It turned down another row, heading for the exit, and I shot out from my spot behind a car, making a beeline for my Jeep and pivoting around it instead of exposing my back to the sedan.

I entered through the passenger door and locked it behind me before thumping over the center console and ungracefully flopping down in the driver's seat. My eyes still firmly trained on Dessi's car, I kept missing the keyhole until I realized it was because my hands were shaking. The vehicle continued out of the lot and turned to drive in the other direction. Dropping my forehead to my steering wheel, I steadied my nerves and tried again, finally getting it to start.

What had I gotten myself into?

A hot shower and a whiskey later, I was starting to feel some reprieve from the fear that had crept in and taken root inside me. I had grown up with a cop for a dad; it took a lot to shake me. I could count on one hand how many times I'd felt like I needed to clear my own home, room by room, to ensure no one was hiding, waiting for me.

Funny how all but one of those times were in the past few months. The previous time was when I was fresh at the academy and we were first learning about home invasion and tactical progression. It was the same week I'd swapped out my door chain for a swing-bar lock.

Swiveling my head, I glanced back to the door, triple-checking that the bolt and bar were in place. Satisfied, I flicked through my phone to let Wyatt know I saw the sedan again tonight and that it looked like I was the target of their attention, whatever that meant. It might not have had anything to do with Suzy.

Three little dots popped up, indicating he was texting back, but then they disappeared. At length, I simply got an, "Okay."

As I rolled my eyes, I remembered one more thing. I had promised to let Rhodes know I got home safe. Sighing, I stared at the phone. If I told him what had happened, he'd worry even more. If I didn't, I'd be intentionally keeping it from him. I considered forgetting to text, but that seemed dishonest, especially since I knew he was concerned.

After typing and deleting a few times, I settled with,

> *Mal: Home safe, but I got another visit from the sedan after I hung up with you.*

> *Rhodes: Everything okay?*

> *Mal: Yes. It just pointed its headlights at me. Made sure I knew it was there. Then it left.*

> *Rhodes: I don't like this, Mal.*

> *Mal: I know.*

I tapped my fingernail on my laptop, waiting for his reply.

> *Rhodes: I'm glad you're home safe. I'm assuming you checked the place out when you got home?*

> *Mal: Every room.*

> *Rhodes: Okay, thanks for letting me know.*

> *Mal: See you tomorrow?*

> *Rhodes: Wild horses couldn't stop me.*

I snorted out loud.

> *Mal: Thanks. Hope you can get some rest tonight.*

> *Rhodes: You too.*

> *Mal: Good night.*

> *Rhodes: Night.*

I had better figure out something good to feed the man. He was being more supportive than any other guy I'd ever dated. At least he was now; we had gotten past the part where he reacted badly out of worry for me. I was glad we had passed that point. It's hard being vulnerable with your fears. I was learning too. I made a mental note to ask for Suzy's advice. She had more experience than I did.

I opened my laptop and hit the search bar to see what I could find out about storage units and trucking companies. I'd do a little research, then I'd haul my tired self to bed. I had listened to enough audio for the day. Tomorrow, we would have another file...if the battery held.

I knew Sam would be checking for anything in Dessi's name. He had found some business ties to other companies, shell ones that kept the criminal's name off the license. Still, I wouldn't be worth my investigative salt if I didn't at least try a few obscure locations to find connections.

Making a list of storage units nearby, I noted the current owners. Then I looked through that for anything linking back to Dessi or Marchi. Nothing jumped out at me, but I had a growing record of names of people meeting with Dessi at his speakeasy. Some came from the audio and some from a surveillance camera set up across the street to track coming and going activity. It wasn't complete, but it was better than nothing.

The trucking company was easier; it only had one owner, Jan Kressler. But try as I might, I couldn't find anything connecting Jan to Dessi. He did business with everyone in the Chicago area, inbound and outbound. If there was a connection, it was lost in the shuffle with everyone else.

Running into a dead end with that, I tried to follow the delivery they had gotten the night before. Maybe I could find out what was delivered. Pausing to think, I savored another sip of whiskey when I heard a bump in the corridor. Freezing, I listened for another sound, but heard nothing.

As I gently set the glass on my coffee table, I stood and quietly made my way to the front door, collecting my baton from where it lay by the entry. The scrape of a foot on the other side shot adrenaline through my system. Placing my hand softly on the handle, I leaned in to peer through the peephole, straining to control my breathing.

But as I looked through, the tension slid out of me. My neighbor Noelle stood in front of my door, anxiously looking back and forth.

Flipping the lock and deadbolt, I swung the door open.

"Can I help you?"

"Um." Her eyes went wide, like a deer in headlights.

I waited.

"I wanted to apologize," she eventually said, staring at the ground. "I shouldn't have let Eddie spy on you."

"Probably not a good idea to let people spy on others. You know, people without badges." It was a good life lesson.

"But in my defense, you are a little odd." Her nose scrunched up. "I mean, you come and go at odd hours of the night with ripped clothes and bloody lips. What about that time you came home with your face all black and blue? It wasn't that big of a stretch to think you worked for the mob."

I winced at the memory; it had hurt like shit. "I'm a private investigator."

"I know that *now.*" She flung a hand in the air.

"This is a crap apology." I jutted out a hip to lean against the doorjamb, my arms crossing across my chest.

"I know." She deflated. "I meant to just stick with I'm sorry."

She genuinely looked it. The poor thing had probably been through hell. And part of it was my fault. Eddie Leeman, who worked for Dessi, had talked his way into her life and apartment to keep an eye on me. Unfortunately, she had actually fallen for the guy.

"How are you holding up?"

"I'm okay," she said quietly after a pause. "Eddie's in jail."

I nodded. "As he should be."

"I know it wasn't real." Her lower lip trembled. "But it felt like it."

Oh hell, there goes my "early to bed" plans.

I stepped aside. "Want a drink?"

Noelle raised a hand to wipe a tear away and shuffled in.

Chapter 6

A rubber band pinged against my door, landing on my desk. Suzy.

"Yes?" I called out to the lobby.

"Are you expecting someone?"

"No?" My mind quickly ran through the past few days. I had just gotten into the office. Who could be stopping by at this time? *Oh, right.* "Older lady?"

"Yes," she said. "She's coming up the stairs to the building."

"She's a retired firefighter's wife." I filled her in, standing to walk to the doorway between my office and her space, suppressing a yawn. Noelle had been over until well past eleven the night before. "Rhodes' uncle sent her our way."

"That was nice."

"Yes, except we've already got our hands full."

"I'm sure you can fit her in." She beamed up at me. "I have faith in you."

"I do too." Sam's voice came from the tablet set up on Suzy's desk.

I jumped back in surprise, and I heard Suzy giggle.

"Is he always on that thing?" I took a deep breath, steadying my nerves.

She just shrugged, eyes still twinkling in mirth.

I shook my head at her but had to stop mid-shake. The door opened, sending a jingling sound through the office space, heralding the arrival of one small, hunched-over woman. That was odd; the jingling sound, not the woman. I didn't remember having a bell on the door. It also sounded oddly electronic. Squinting, I saw a blue light at the top of the doorjamb. Curious, I turned to Suzy. One side of her mouth tilted up as she attempted to ignore me.

Sam.

He had installed a sensor on the door. Of course, he had. Probably an alarm with a door-chime during the day to announce visitors.

"Mrs. Collins?"

The woman paused, her tensed face softening for a smile. "Are you Mal?"

"I am." I stepped forward to greet her.

"I've heard so much about you." She reached out her hand sideways, more to hold onto me than for a shake.

"Don't believe a word of it, Mrs. Collins." I gave her a wink. "Why don't we go into my office?"

"Thank you." She shuffled forward. "And please call me Linda, dear."

"Yes, ma'am."

After helping her to a chair, I took my seat across from her.

"Can I get you anything to drink?" Suzy piped up from my doorway.

"Oh, do you have any water?" She turned to look at my receptionist.

"Sure thing." Leaving, she sped off to our water cooler.

"How can I help you?" I asked, folding my hands on my desktop. I had an idea of what she wanted, but it was good to hear it from her.

"Well." She patted her short, curly hair, making sure everything was in order. "When Sean told us about little Marlon's detective friend, I thought you'd be the perfect person to help me out. See." She leaned in and lowered her voice. "The people at the nursing home are out to get me."

"They're out to get you?" I questioned, hoping she wasn't dealing with a bout of paranoia.

"Yes!" She brought her small fist down on the chair's arm. "They think I'm just an old lady and don't know when I'm getting swindled!"

"What exactly have you noticed?"

"Well, thank you, dear," she said to Suzy, who handed her a cup of water. She paused to take a sip. "My Doug worked thirty-two years for the city, thirty-two hard years, mind you. He fought fires and handled medical calls for the good people of Chicago. And we had the city's insurance for all of that time, until three years ago when he went on Medicare. It's supposed to cover us."

"I think they do have some limits to their coverage," I offered. I'd hate for her to expect them to cover all the costs.

"Oh, I know that." She waved it off. "But his pension should be enough to handle anything left over. At least, that's what Doug always says. He's in a home now."

"He's not at the same one Miss Ellie is at, right?"

"Oh, no. Unfortunately, no. I had hoped to get him in there, but there's a wait, you see. He's at Weston Assisted Living."

"And you feel like you're getting overcharged at Weston?"

"That's correct." Her chin jutted out. "They're already expensive as it is."

"Do they list their fees so you can verify them?"

"Yes, but it's not their housing and meal fees I'm concerned about. It's their medical care fees."

"The ones you expect Medicare to handle?"

"That's correct. Every few weeks, I get a bill for tests, or medicine, or lab work. I ask them if they're billing Medicare, and they say they have. That the bills are more than it would cover, so I'm getting the remainder of them."

"Is Mr. Collins having a lot of medical concerns?"

"Some, yes." She hesitated. "The job isn't easy on a firefighter's body, Detective. But I just know something isn't right. Medicare should be paying more than this. I'm getting bills every month for a few thousand dollars. That's *over* the set assisted-living fees."

My eyebrows raised. Maybe she *was* getting swindled. "I can look into the billing at Weston, but I'll need you to sign paperwork allowing me access to your records. I don't need access to your bank's financials, just your records at Weston. There will likely be medical information included. Are you comfortable with that?"

"You're a friend of Sean's and Marlon's." She shrugged her shoulders as though that was enough for her.

"I appreciate that, Mrs. Collins. But you should always be careful with people looking into your financial or medical records. Unless they have a license." I pulled out my private investigator license and set it on the table. It didn't hurt for her to see my card. Hopefully, her trustful nature wouldn't get taken advantage of in the future, someday.

"I have some bills from the last few months if that helps." She pulled papers from her large purse and handed them to me.

"Definitely."

I reviewed my standard paperwork with her, making adjustments for the type of records and information I would be looking into. It covered my butt if anyone questioned me digging into her details, and it made it easier to access the records. Not that Sam couldn't get ahold of anything he set his mind on.

Mrs. Collins went over the papers and signed them. "Do you need me to leave you a retainer?"

"I can bill you after the fact." I wasn't hard up on cash at the moment and was already worried about having the time to look into it. I'd drop this case if I got a good lead, and I didn't want the guilt of her retainer sitting in my bank account.

"You can leave your card on file, though." Suzy's voice floated in through the doorway. "Just to make it easy to bill you after it's closed."

"Oh, that's a good idea." She dug around in her bag and presented a card to Suzy, who had walked in to take it.

That woman was always a step and a half in front of me. If it weren't for her, I wouldn't be collecting on half of my cases. Of course, if it weren't for her, I wouldn't have half of the pro-bono ones I had. So, I guess it was a wash. Still…I felt better at the end of the day. And it was hard to get mad at Suzy.

Paperwork and payment settled, I stood. "I'll see what I can find out. I have a couple of other cases going right now, but I should be able to fit yours in between."

"That's fine, dear. I've been dealing with this for close to a year now. There's no definite timeline, but it's not going to sort itself."

"I understand." I moved to help her as she stood to leave. "I'll give you a call within a week with an update."

"That will be just fine."

Taking her nearly empty cup, Suzy handed her a copy of her papers, with one of my cards stapled to it.

"Have a good afternoon, Mrs. Collins."

"Thank you, dear." She nodded, opening the door to leave. "And remember, it's Linda."

"Will do, Linda." I held the door open for her.

She seemed like a sweet lady. I hoped I'd be able to help her out. It was an interesting case; I'd never looked into insurance before.

"Mal?" Suzy interrupted my thoughts.

"Yes?"

"Sam's calling."

Suzy must have hung up when Mrs. Collins arrived. I hadn't even noticed the beeping sound coming from my office, R2D2 beeping noises, that is. It would take some getting used to. Why couldn't he just use the phone?

Completing the eye roll I had started before Mrs. Collins came in, I made my way back into my office, collected my coffee, and took a slug. My mouth turned down at the now-cool coffee.

"Hi, Sam."

"Hey, Mal!" His face displayed in the Sambot 2.0's round chest—I refused to call it R2D2, even in my head—his eyes lit with excitement.

I settled into my chair and pushed the coffee away. "What's up?"

"Did you hear?"

"The mention of the sale tomorrow night?"

"Yes! We were right." He pumped his fists in the air.

I nodded. It was something. Hopefully, *the* thing. "We were right about it being an estate sale and Friday night. I'm pretty sure I heard them mention 6 p.m., so it looks like we were on the money with the Fred Seivers alias."

"I know! What could be up with those chairs? Maybe they have a hollow leg and a flash drive with stolen information or evidence against someone on the inside, like blackmail."

"We need surveillance equipment. With a shot like this, we have to get it on camera." I had no idea what we'd find, but I wasn't going to chance it.

"Don't you worry." The corner of his mouth rose, and a devilish gleam lit his eyes.

I could only imagine what he had planned.

"I looked into the storage unit comment, but couldn't find any owned by him or any company associated with him. Did you have any luck?"

"None."

"Dug around info on the trucking company. Came up empty."

"Me too." He dropped his head for a microsecond. "But, hey, we can keep an eye on it, too."

I hated to waste time, but who knew what would pan out. At this point, I had to stay on every possible clue. "We can."

"I'm serious, Mal. I think there's something there. It's a gut thing. Maybe something's in those wine barrels."

"I agree. I'll think of something." I promised. I'd try to find a way to look into it further. It was just that, at this moment, I couldn't think of another angle.

He let out a breath. "So, after the sale, Suze wants to have everyone over. To talk about plans."

"That's a good idea." We didn't have much time left, and everyone knew it.

And now I had a curious pet buyer and possibly an insurance overbilling issue to look into. I rubbed my temple, then out of habit, reached for my coffee cup again and took a sip before I remembered it was no longer warm. At this point, it was downright cool. *Ew.*

"Pick you up at five tomorrow night?"

"Five?"

"I have to get you suited up."

"What?"

"You know, surveillance equipment."

I wasn't aware of his plans but knew there was no point in arguing. "Five is fine. See you then."

"Bye!" He beamed at me before his face disappeared.

My head dropped to my hands. I had so many things to look into at the moment, plus last night's audio to listen to. Sure, Sam would listen to it, but I couldn't let him down.

Sighing, I weighed my priorities and to-dos and picked up my phone. Some undercover work was better done without the risk of being caught on camera.

"Hello?" a young female voice answered.

"Yo. This is Jo from J & Sons. I'm calling about the delivery you received Wednesday night," I rattled off in a strong Chicago accent. "We're calling to confirm the delivery. We had some issues with a couple of them in the last few days. New guys, whaddya do? Anyways, can you confirm your delivery?"

"Um, we got a delivery Wednesday night. Is that what you mean?" She sounded a little unsure of what I was asking for, but I needed more detail.

"That's great, yes. Can you confirm what you received?" I was pushing it, and I knew it, but hopefully, she was young enough to go for it.

"You want me to look in the barrels?" Hesitation had entered her voice.

I wasn't sure if it was because she was uncomfortable with the request or because she felt she shouldn't be sharing it. I debated how far to push her.

"Just the number of items and description will do."

"Oh, I can do that." Her voice eased. I could hear her moving around the room. "We got five barrels of grapes, about rib high."

I bit back a laugh. "So, the barrels are around four-foot-high?"

"That's about right."

"Thanks, hon." I couldn't help the smile. "That'll do." Then on a whim, added, "So's, the boss-man makes wine? In a slots place?"

"Yeah." She snorted. "He actually does. Names it for his wife, Lola."

"S'it any good?" I lowered my voice.

"Not so much."

"Thanks." I chuckled and hung up.

It wasn't much, but at least we knew the store clerks thought they were getting grapes, and it sounded like they actually made wine. Well, the store manager did, at least. If something illegal was going on, it wasn't out in the open.

I wiggled my mouse to wake my computer from hibernation and typed in Weston Assisted Living. I could start some basic research on complaints against the place while I listened to the previous night's audio.

Multi-tasking. That's how I would work on three cases at once. Something would pan out.

Chapter 7

Meanwhile, on a noisy and crowded basketball court in Bricktown,

"Hey, Marlon!" A thin, lightly graying man made his way around the basketball court. The pungent scent of adrenaline and testosterone floated through the air like in a high school locker room.

"Hey, Teddy." Rhodes stuck out a hand and clapped the older man on the shoulder in greeting. "How's it going?"

"Fine, fine." He rocked back on his heels to get a better look at the fire captain. "It's been a while since we've seen you. You're getting old."

Laughter rumbled through his chest in response. "We can't all age as well as you, Ted."

"Like fine wine."

"Something like that."

"So, what brings you to the center?" He turned back to the court, his eyes tracking the players. "You here to show these youngsters how it's done?"

"Ha! Hardly." He watched the kids cut across the court, shoes squeaking on the heavily waxed and buffed wood floor of the Community Outreach Center's indoor gym. One tall kid leaped into the air, sending the ball toward a basket. It was almost like he was in slow motion. The ball barely made a sound as it slid straight through the net. "They'd wipe the floor with me."

"Probably." He shrugged. "But it's good for them to relate to other adults in the community."

Still watching the game, Rhodes let out a sigh. "Fine, I'll join the next game, but put me in against Nate."

"You sure about that?"

They both watched as the tall kid in question stole the ball, weaving in and out of the players, only to send it through the air again. Another perfect basket. Nate Hastings was a force to be reckoned with, on and off the field. A red line marked his left bicep, oddly matching the red of the Chicago Bulls jersey he wore. It looked like they had not only gotten mixed up in the crossfire as bystanders, but he also took a bullet. Luckily, it looked like it was just a graze. Nicely healing, too.

He didn't have a chance in hell, but why not? He knew how to take a butt whoopin' with grace. Considering his T-shirt and jeans, he dropped his head in a short nod. "I'll throw on some shorts."

In long strides, he exited the community center and walked back to his truck. He'd just left work that morning, so he had his gym bag with him. He hoisted it over his shoulder and headed back to his impending demise.

Fifteen minutes later, he stood on the side of the court, stretching out his quads. He wasn't that old, but compared to these kids, he was ancient.

Nate was standing with Warren, not quite meeting his gaze. He'd heard the kid was doing better since he joined the team. He hadn't gotten into any other trouble, no arrests, no hanging around with those getting arrested, but he still looked standoffish. His body language wasn't exactly friendly.

"You really gonna join us, Marlon?" Warren approached with the ball. He did a little fast step to the side and bounced it.

"You *betcha.*" Rhodes grinned. "You know how to play with that thing, or do you only know fancy moves?"

The kid's laughter rang high and cheerful. Nate cracked a smile. Barely.

"Oh, I can play." His eyes sparkled. "But can you keep up?"

"Let's see." He winked at the kid.

Teddy waved his hands, whistle in his mouth. Taking his position on one side of the court with several other kids, Rhodes watched Nate and Warren ready themselves across from him. No way he was as fast as they were, but hopefully, he wouldn't completely embarrass himself.

As he nodded to Teddy, he heard the peal of the whistle. The ball went up into the air. He and Nate were nose to nose. Nate's hand shot a foot higher, coming in contact with it before him and deflecting it towards a teammate. Rhodes hurried to guard him, trying to maintain a few feet in front of him while the taller kid jetted to the left and right.

Someone from his team stole the ball. Changing tactics, he tried to shoot out from behind Nate, but the younger man created a wall in front of him he could barely get around. Stepping back, he raced around the field, creating an opening. Catching sight of him, Nate flew over the floor to block. The ball was passed to Rhodes. He took aim, steadying his breath, and let it fly. It was a perfect shot, its trajectory straight to the basket.

A mere second after it left his fingertips, Nate's hand appeared, sending the ball to the side, right into Warren's waiting hands.

Letting out a whoop, he danced across the floor, passing and zig-zagging around to get the ball again. Rhodes picked up his step, keeping up with the guys and angling for Nate again.

One of the players on his side stole the ball once more and dribbled it down a few feet before Warren blocked him, trying to get it back. When he looked around to pass, Rhodes put his hands up to signal he could take it, but Nate charged towards him, leaping into the air and setting himself right in front of him. Shooting Rhodes a goofy grin, he turned and blocked him from the pass.

The game went on for a half hour, with both sides taking a few points, but Nate and Warren's team steadily held the lead. Finally, Rhodes had an opening. He signaled for a pass, his eyes meeting Nate's across the court. No way he could make it to him in time. The ball flew through the air. He caught it and took aim, not wasting a second, but Nate was already bounding past players, attempting to block it. Releasing, he watched the ball, eyes wide, as it sailed through the air and right into the basket.

He wasn't as fast as these kids, but he had spent more time on this court than they had. He'd had years on them, from all the time his uncle Sean worked at the fire station. It had kept him out of trouble in his youth. He hoped it would do the same for them.

They got their points, and the ball went back to the other team. Doubling down, Nate and Warren tag-teamed it down the court and almost immediately got the next basket.

A whistle pierced the air, and Teddy waved his hands to announce the end of the game. The last basket had given Nate and Warren's team the points they needed to win. Out of breath, Rhodes leaned over to put his hands on his knees. His legs were shaking, and he had a stitch in his right side. He hadn't expected to win but was glad he hadn't gone down in the middle of the game. It had been quite a while since he was in a pickup game.

"Right on," Warren said, smiling wide. He put up a hand to high five Rhodes, still bouncing on his feet. "You did good for an old guy."

"Gee, thanks." He was still breathing hard and noticed the kids around him were barely out of breath.

Nate nodded in appreciation at him. "Not bad."

"I think we've earned a water break." Rhodes angled his head off the court.

The kids followed.

"Looks like you two are putting those other kids through their paces," he went on, trying to start a conversation.

"Gives us all something to do." Warren shrugged. "Better than what I was doing."

"I remember those days. This place saved my ass. I was headed towards trouble, for sure.

"You used to come here?" Nate finally spoke. "As a kid?"

"Yep." Rhodes dipped his head. "If it weren't for Teddy and the other guys, I'd have ended up God knows where, getting roped into working with scum like Dessi. I'm just grateful this place is still here. You guys have to stick together, support each other so you can keep your grades up and make something of yourself."

Warren beamed. "I've got all B's, except for two A's."

"No shit?" Rhodes tilted his head. "That's better than I got. Congrats, man. How's it going for you, Nate? I know it's tough to stay on this path, but it's worth it."

Nate cast his eyes down. "It's okay."

"I heard Dessi's been poking around the area, trying to pick up cheap help. He's not bugging you guys, is he?"

Warren cut his eyes to Nate, his mouth in a thin line.

The taller kid shrugged, rubbing the healing wound on his arm. "Maybe there was a little work."

"You get that at the shooting?" Rhodes lifted his head. "I heard about that. When Dessi's involved, nothing good happens."

"I told you that." Warren nudged his friend. "Sounds like Dessi's bad news."

"It was nothing major, honest." Nate focused on his shoes. "I got in a little trouble over it, but I'm hoping it'll blow over."

"At the shooting?"

"Yeah." He kicked at the ground, his shoes squeaking. "Somehow, they knew I was involved. Some lady who works for the head guy asked me to find them a warehouse to meet in. Make sure no one was around. Gave me a few bucks. You know the drill. I did, and I let them in. It was nothing."

"And you were there too?" Rhodes looked at Warren, who cast a sideways look at Nate.

"Warren had no idea what was going on. Honest. I shouldn't have, but I dragged him along with me just in case things went south."

"And it did." Looking back and forth between the kids, he recognized himself in them. Trying to fit in, trying to be included in something bigger than themselves. But this wasn't the way. "Did you get into trouble too, Warren?"

"Nah. Nate explained things. They believed him."

"Would you be willing to talk to someone?"

"I mean…I'm no snitch. Besides, these guys… They make problems go away, and I don't have a death wish, ya know?"

"I'm not asking you to put yourself in danger, but you may be able to share things that could help us out. Either way, I may be able to get some legal advice for you."

"Really?" The kid looked up. "I've got a court date coming up next week. That'd be great."

"In the meantime, steer clear of Dessi. Take it from me. I know firsthand. He's got his fingers in more illegal pies than I can count. You gotta stay clean."

"I will." His head hung low.

"Then, it looks like you'll be spending more time around here."

"Maybe you could stop by again."

"Yeah, Pops." Warren jumped in, winking at him. "You got all those muscles, but you gotta stay fast."

"I could probably use some cardio." The fire captain rubbed his flat stomach. It wasn't soft, but it didn't have the definition it once had. "We'll see."

Knocking the ball out of his friend's hand, Nate faked left and zoomed off to the right. Warren's face split into a grin, and he sped off after him, leaving Rhodes standing by the water cooler alone.

The careful ease in his body dropped, and he crushed the paper cup in his hand. A nerve in his left eye twitched. Dessi was going after the kids in Bricktown. His kids. His turf.

It was personal.

A whiff of his own sweat hit his awareness, and he wrinkled his nose, making him headed to the locker room to clean up before going home to figure out what to do next.

"Everything looks in order here," Suzy said, standing in my doorway. She had offered to look into Mr. Collins' bills for Weston. "I mean, nothing's obviously inaccurate. But you'll need to verify what's gotten billed to Medicare to see if it's correct."

"I'll check with the assisted-living facility," I promised. At some point, when I had the time. I had already listened to a full day's worth of audio and had very little to show for it.

"Good plan."

Exhausted, I stretched. I really should get up every once in a while. Sitting in an office chair for hours sucked. I itched to be out on the streets instead of being cooped up indoors. At least I had gotten through the day and could go home to relax.

Suzy walked back to her desk and grabbed her coat. "Any hot plans tonight with the fireman?"

I froze. "Oh no. He's coming over for dinner!"

"Tonight?" Her eyes rounded.

I nodded.

"What time?"

"Six-ish?" I winced, head whirling. What was I going to do? I had been consumed by my job. I couldn't let him down.

"You have an hour, tops." Her lips pursed, eyes off in the distance like she was going to find the answers written on my brick walls. "Salmon and vegetable gratin."

"Gratin?" My mouth made an "O" shape. "I don't know how to make that."

"It's easy. I'll talk you through it." She waved me off. "It's basically vegetables with cheese. I'll text you the ingredients and the recipe. You'll have it in your phone by the time you hit Mariano's."

She knew me so well.

"Suze, you're a lifesaver." If only I could pull this off.

"I know." She shot me a wink and sauntered out of the office, texting as she walked.

Racing, I gathered my laptop and keys, stuffed my earbuds into my pocket, and headed towards the door, barely remembering to lock it behind me.

Sure enough, by the time I entered Mariano's parking lot, my phone had dinged. Suzy had saved the day. The only problem was, I was worried she had overestimated my cooking abilities. Sure, I had roasted salmon before, but the gratin thing sounded like a stretch. Maybe I should just buy something from the deli. They had a broccoli salad and an interesting pasta-salad thing.

But I was trying to show Rhodes that he meant something to me and I could make time for him.

Panicking, I slung an arm through the handle of the store basket and headed to the cheese section, scrolling through my phone to find Suzy's text.

Flour. Could I do flour? I had some, but I didn't often use it outside the occasional chocolate-chip cookie. I frowned, collecting the shredded Swiss and heading for the frozen-vegetables aisle. The recipe called for fresh broccoli and cauliflower, but that wasn't happening tonight. Luckily, Suzy had made a note that I could use frozen ones to save time. *Definitely doing that.*

Quickly, I grabbed the frozen bags from the freezer, tossed them in my basket, and headed for the fish.

"Can I help you?" the guy behind the counter asked.

"Salmon." My eyes scanned the fish behind the glass. "I just need salmon."

"All out." He folded his arms.

"Of salmon?" My voice raised an octave. "How?"

"Well. People came in today and bought a lot of salmon. Must be a run on salmon."

"Of all days." I slumped. "I'm making dinner for my boyfriend tonight." My God, it sounded weird, calling him my boyfriend. Like we were kids.

"We've got trout? If you were my girlfriend, I'd be happy if you made me trout."

I frowned, looking up at him. What was that supposed to mean? Was trout some sort of date-night food? I considered it. *Fish was fish, I guess.* "Wrap me up a pound and a half of that."

Nodding, he grabbed a large filet and set it on the scale. His eyes slide to the basket on my arm.

"Broccoli and cauliflower? Are you going to get some lemon? It's so good on trout."

"Sure." My plans were already thrown off-kilter. "Just squeeze it on after it bakes?"

"No, cut it in slices and lay it on the trout. Lemon and a bit of thyme. A good bit of salt and pepper. Plenty of butter. Fresh parsley if you have time."

"Fresh parsley," I repeated dumbly. "Probably not, but the lemon I can do."

I thought I had some thyme in the cupboard as well. Taking my package, I hurried on.

"Good luck!" The clerk shouted.

I waved a hand in thanks, already headed to the front of the store to grab a lemon on my way to check out. Maybe tonight wouldn't fall apart, after all.

Chapter 8

Holding my breath, I carefully slid the cookie sheet holding the trout into the oven. It looked pretty good, lightly seasoned and decorated with lemon slices. A knock at the door jolted me in shock. My body jerked, and I nearly lost the trout, spilling it out onto the vegetables baking on the bottom rack. The fish slid to the edge of the pan as I balanced on the balls of my feet, slowly rocking back until I caught myself. That would have been just what I needed, falling headlong into the oven. Taking a deep breath, I slid the pan in, quickly rearranging the meat on it before shutting the door and pushing a chunk of loose heat-frizzing red hair behind an ear.

I had been rushing around the kitchen for the past half hour, trying to figure out the roux Suzy believed I could figure out. I thought it resembled the cheese sauce it was supposed to look like, but it was a little lumpy. Maybe it would smooth out in the oven.

"One minute!" I yelled in the general direction of the door as I quickly washed my hands and opened it, totally forgetting to check the peephole. Luckily, it was my newly titled boyfriend. The instant Rhodes caught sight of me, his face lit up and he grinned at me like a little kid. "What?"

He stepped over the threshold and held up a hand to my cheek. "You have a little flour on your face." Taking the towel hanging limply in my hands, he gently ran it over my cheek and forehead, smiling warmly at me.

"Oh, oops." The tension slid out of my body. His soft touch slowed me down. I had been in such a hurry since I left the office, I didn't even think about changing my shirt or sprucing up my hair. The curls were probably out of control. I ran a thoughtful hand over my head.

"You look great."

He looked great. Fitted T-shirt over worn jeans. Flipping the towel over his shoulder, he placed his now-empty hand on my hip. This close, I could smell the woodsy scent I had come to associate with him. My face flushed.

"You do too." My hand landed on his broad chest, and I looked into his eyes, which were lined up directly with mine due to our similar height. He watched me closely, that slight smile still on his lips.

He leaned forward and hesitated a moment. This was still new for us. When I met him the rest of the way, my lips touched his in a soft, gentle kiss.

Then I remembered my fish. I had forgotten to set a timer. Spinning away, I hurried back to the kitchen to rip open the door. It was only beginning to warm, the top not even white or flaky yet. It couldn't have been more than a few minutes. I may not know how to make much, but I knew fish didn't take long to bake.

"You actually cooked."

Turning, I saw him glance over my shoulder at the vegetable baking in the oven. He looked very pleased. Blushing—*since when did I blush?*—I stammered, "It's just veggies and cheese…Suzy gave me a recipe."

Like I was blaming it on her. What was wrong with me?

"Smells great."

I blew out a quick breath. "Thanks. Sorry, it's not quite ready yet. I kinda got a late start at cooking. I should have stopped by the store yesterday instead of today. They were out of salmon."

"Salmon?" An eyebrow went up at my onslaught of words.

"Yes, I had to get trout."

"Trout works." He held up a bottle of wine. "Is red still okay? I wasn't sure what we were having."

"Definitely." Relieved to have a distraction, I took the bottle and got to work uncorking it and pouring it into the only two wineglasses I had in my house.

"Busy day at work?"

"Very." I handed him a glass before walking into my tiny living room to sit while dinner finished cooking.

"Any good leads?"

"Nothing new. We heard another mention of the estate sale tomorrow night. They're planning something. We're just not sure what."

Nodding, he swirled his wine and took a sip. It felt like he had something on his mind, but he wasn't sharing.

"How was your night? Busy?" Maybe he'd had a rough call the night before.

He shrugged. "Not really. We ran two calls. Car wrecks."

"Anything bad?"

He shook his head. Something was undoubtedly on his mind.

We made small talk until the timer went off. He had gone to see his grandma, Miss Ellie, today at the nursing home. I let him know Mrs. Collins had come to see me and that I was helping her look into the situation. I didn't feel comfortable sharing more than that. She could tell him and his uncle what she chose, but he wouldn't hear it from me. Confidentiality was important.

"This looks amazing." Rhodes took his plate in with an approving eye, then looked up with a smile. "Thanks for this."

"Of course." I sat down with my plate. It felt weird, cooking for someone and having him in my place. It had been a long time since I was with anyone who meant this much to me. And back then, I absolutely wouldn't have taken the time to cook for him.

But Rhodes had cooked for me first. It was a fact I appreciated. He made the first moves and put himself out there way further than I ever had. This didn't feel like I was going overboard in a domesticated way for a man. If anything, I was playing a little catch-up. It was a good feeling.

I tasted the fish, hoping it was okay. It was flaky and cooked well, but it didn't taste like the salmon I had been hoping for.

"The trout is good." He lifted a fork. "I like the lemon."

"Thanks. The clerk at the shop gave me pointers."

I poked at the vegetables. It was still a little lumpy but tasty. Good thing the whole thing was covered in cheese. I was a little disappointed, but he was making an appreciative humming sound, so I let it go. Besides, Domestic Goddess was Suzy's thing, not mine.

"So." He sat, staring into his glass of wine after we had both finished eating. "What are your plans for tomorrow night with Sam?"

"We're taking surveillance equipment, and I'll have backup just in case, but basically, we're planning on trying to get evidence of whatever they're doing. Try to catch them doing something illegal. If we can get a video of it, paired with the audio proving they were planning the illegal act, maybe it'll be enough to arrest Dessi."

"What if Dessi's not behind it?"

"Dessi's undoubtedly behind it. He's the one speaking in the recordings, though they're still being vague."

"I agree, but what if you don't get him on video, just someone else or one of his men?" He frowned.

"I don't know. Maybe we can use whatever it is to dig in deeper. Find more evidence." I stopped toying with my wineglass. "The guy is running all sorts of illegal activity in Chicago. At some point, he's going to slip up, and I'm going to get evidence to use against him."

"You need something strong, though. He's going to just blame it on whoever you catch doing the deed."

It was my turn to frown. Did he think I couldn't do this? "It's not like the cops are getting any closer. No one is going to push as hard as we are right now."

"I know."

"Technically, not everything we're doing is legal. But neither is what he's doing. That's the point. We're doing things the cops can't. I know you might think that's immoral, but it's what needs to be done to get him off the streets."

"Mal." He set his wine down and looked at me straight on. "I don't have any issues with what you're doing."

"Then what is this?" I tossed my hands in the air.

"I'm just worried he's going to continue to walk."

"You and me both." I watched him fiddle with his hands. "What's going on?"

"Fabian Dessi is dangerous." His expression darkened. "If we don't get him, he's going to ruin more people's lives."

"We?" It was the first time he had talked about my objective as something we shared. I knew he cared about Suzy too—who couldn't?—but he'd never projected this type of passion towards it. Unless he just wanted me done with the case.

"We." He met my eyes, and I could see anger simmering there. "I'll do whatever it takes to help."

"You want to help?"

"I do."

"Is this because you're worried about me?"

"Of course I'm worried, Mal!" He exploded up from his seat, eyebrows furrowed. "You're chasing after a deranged criminal. And he's on to you! He's got his guys following you around town, watching your apartment. You're focused on Suzy, but it's like you're totally forgetting you're not safe either."

I sat there, stunned. Maybe I shouldn't have told him about the sedan following me, but I wasn't going to start lying in the relationship. "I'm sorry this is so hard for you, but this is what I have to do. This is my job."

"It's not your job." He held up a finger, correcting me. "No one is paying you for this."

"Well, maybe not a job. You're right. No one's paying me, but if I don't do this, he stays out there…doing illegal things, hurting people. Is that what you want?"

"No!" He turned to pace the room, rubbing his temples.

"Then, what's the problem?" If he wasn't going to be able to handle this part of my life, it was better that we figured it out now. "It's a sticky situation, but it's one I'm in. I'm sorry you're coming into my life at this point, but this is me. You said you'd be able to handle my job. It's not the safest, but it's what I do. Like yours. It puts you in harm's way. We *both* have dangerous jobs."

I shrugged, attempting to make it look casual. Inside, my stomach was twisted.

Crossing to me, he took my arms in his hands. "I can handle your job. I don't like you being in danger, but I can handle the job. I get it. I get the need to take care of others. That's why this is so incredibly *difficult* for me. The problem is that this man, Dessi, isn't just a run-of-the-mill bad guy you're trying to prove is stealing, or assaulting a local shop store owner, or even an embezzler. He's the head of a crime syndicate, Mal. A kingpin."

"Technically, Marchi's the head guy." I lamely corrected him. The severity of it wasn't lost on me. And lately, I had been parading around like it wasn't any different. Like he wasn't any worse than one of the cheating spouses I'd spied on. "I know what you mean, though. And you're right, but it's easier not focusing on the fact that he could pull my feet out from underneath me any time he wanted."

"I'm terrified, Mal."

"I know." I did know. He was a protector, and he couldn't protect me. "And I'm sorry about that."

We both stood there, unsure what to say or do.

"Will you be able to be with me? Knowing you can't keep me safe?"

"That's why I want to help." He looked up. "Can I?"

I shrugged. "Possibly. I don't know exactly how yet, but more people on the cause can't be a bad thing. Tomorrow night, we're all meeting up at Sam and Suzy's after the sale. Do you want to join us there?"

"What about at the sale?"

"What do you mean?"

"You said you had backup. Are they going to be waiting?"

"Wyatt will have someone in the area, ready to head over if trouble arises."

"That's not immediate backup." He ran a hand over his head. "What if I sit in the parking lot? I can be in there in moments."

"That's not a bad idea. I could have Sam suit me up with a mic and an earpiece. You could practically be with me the entire time."

"That sounds much better."

It was my turn to take his arms. "But you're going to have to let me do my thing. It might be much harder to see me in potential danger than just hearing about it after the fact."

He managed a tight nod. "I'll do my best."

"Okay, then." My stomach was still in knots. I wasn't sure how this would work, but he was right. We were taking more risks than we needed to. I could meet him in the middle, but I wasn't abandoning my goal. "I'll call Sam and let him know about the change of plans. You can come with us to their house and be in on the rest of the meetings."

"I'd like that."

I picked up our plates and took them to the kitchen, needing a break from the tension and unsure where to take the conversation now that we had settled the main issue. When I came back into the room, he was still standing where I'd left him, looking down at the table and his empty wineglass.

"Would you like another? We can sit out on the balcony. It's nice out tonight." It was true; the hot August day had cooled down nicely in the windy city.

"I think I should head out." He turned to look at me, his eyebrows still drawn. "I'm not much company right now, and I think it's better if I go home."

Disappointment flooded me. It wasn't the evening I had hoped for. We'd hardly had any time to ourselves, any time to really enjoy each other. I crossed an arm over my chest. "If that's what you want."

"I honestly am sorry, Mal." He closed the distance between us. "Dinner was great. It was so sweet of you to cook for me. I just need some time to think. I'm not angry with you, but I'm worried I'll take it out on you. I don't want to treat you like that."

"Okay." I understood that, at least. It's not like I was good at letting things go when I was deep into something.

I should be glad about it, but regret at the loss of our first potentially romantic night still pulled at me like a heavy coat. "I'll let you know when and where to meet up tomorrow."

"Sounds good. Thanks for letting me be included." He hesitated in front of me, taking my hand. "I do care about you, Mal. More than I expected to."

"Me too." It was true. A little frightening, but true.

Leaning in, he gave me a polite peck on the cheek and turned to leave.

Staring after him blankly, I wondered what in the hell that meant. Did he feel more like a brother to me, or was he too irritated to be romantic? I had no idea what to make of it, but I was vacillating between sadness and anger.

Instead, I poured a half glass of wine, locked the door behind him, and headed out to the balcony. By myself.

Chapter 9

"Hi." I pasted on my best smile. "I'm trying to find a place for my grandma. Can I talk to someone about Weston?"

The receptionist at Weston Assisted Living gave me a sharp glance. "I'll see if our business manager has time to see you. Please have a seat."

As I sat down in the plastic chairs in their waiting room, I kept a friendly look on my face. It was easier to get flies with honey, and all of that. But it wasn't a complete facade, because it felt good to be out in the field again, instead of stuck behind a blasted desk, listening to audio for hours on end. I hated sitting around all day. It was why I had left the police academy. Well, one of the reasons.

I knew I should have gone to the apartment building to poke around there instead, but I wanted to get a feel for this case and see how difficult it would be. It was possible it would be a one-and-done meeting. If I had time, I'd swing by there before going into the office for the day and listen to last night's audio.

The customers at the speakeasy had probably had a better evening than I did. My leg bounced with pent-up frustration over my failed date of the night before. It wasn't just about the dinner; it was more that it took so long for us to get past our differences and give a relationship between us a go. It seemed as though we were doomed to have things come between us.

"Can I help you?"

Shoving my thoughts aside, I resumed my friendly mask and stood, sticking my arm out to shake hands with the woman in front of me. She was in her mid-forties, with a bored expression and light-brown hair pulled back into a clip.

"Hi! How are you today? I'm Marina." It was a cover I often used. It kept me from slipping up. "I'm looking to find a place for my grandma. She's getting dementia and needs more care."

"Weston is a full-service assisted-living facility."

"Would you be able to give me any information about the fees? She has Medicare, but we're just trying to figure out what all this is going to cost. I mean, it should pay for everything, right?"

A frown passed over her face. "That's a common misconception. It pays for a lot, but there's a limit. Honestly, it's surprising it doesn't pay for as much as you'd think. I have some brochures that have our daily rates on them."

"Does that include everything? Or do they get billed extra for things like food, cleaning, medical stuff?"

"It covers room and board, but not medical care, of course. Everyone needs a different level of care, so we can't offer a one-size-fits-all approach. Follow me to my office. I have some papers I can give you."

"Thanks."

Leading me down a hallway, she made her way to a small office, around the desk, and sat down, then pulled out brochures from a stand in front of her and handed them to me. Two small chairs faced her desk, so I claimed one and waited patiently.

"These are our standard rates and all the amenities we offer." Turning to a file cabinet behind her, she pulled out forms and laid them on the desk. "These are some forms to get you started. We have an application fee, to run a credit check, but you're in luck. We do have room. There's no current waiting list."

"Ms..." I looked down at the sign on her desk. "Helen Thompson. I'm just starting to look. I'm not quite ready to fill out an application."

"Well, you can take it home with you and look it over. Do you have power of attorney?"

"Yes." I lied. It would be easier if she thought I could make all her decisions.

She stood, ready to have me leave if I wasn't filling out paperwork.

"What about the medical fees?" I said, still sitting, looking at the brochure. "It only has the room and board listed here."

"It's all standard." She waved a hand. "Depending on what tests or medication your grandma needs. We take care of it for her and bill her insurance or Medicare, if available."

"It doesn't get a markup?"

A pinched look crossed her face as she managed a tight smile. "We add a small fee for providing medical care, much like an office visit. It's all very standard, I assure you."

"How much is it?"

"It depends on the care your grandma needs."

"So, you don't have a set list of fees?" I kept pushing her, trying to keep my teeth unclenched. It was no wonder Mrs. Collins was having so much trouble with her accounts and this woman.

"Ah. Of course, we do. It's just that it's all in the system."

"You could print them out." I couldn't tell if she was trying to be difficult or if she really didn't have fees. Maybe she just made them up as she went.

"It's in the billing program, not easily printed."

"You could print the screen."

"It's too long. I'm sorry. I'd like to make it easier for you, but you'll find the same situation wherever you go. It's honestly small fees, just added onto the medical bills."

"I'll tell you what. What if I go over the last couple of medical expenses from her doctor and have you look them up? You could type them into your computer and give me fees on those specific items."

She set her jaw. "There may still be some variability, depending on the differences in treatment, costs from the doctors, and the labs. But I can take a look at it."

"That'd be great, Ms. Thompson." I stood with a flourish. "I'll be back soon with a list."

"Great," she said blandly.

Heading past the office my Jeep kept avoiding, I cast a longing look towards Grounds and my second cup of coffee. Apparently, I was going to kill two birds with one stone today and check out the apartment again. Besides, it was barely nine o'clock, and it was a beautiful day.

Scanning the lot, I didn't see Lane's car. Maybe she was in class. It was too bad she was on the fourth floor. It was too high to sneak a peek inside her apartment. Getting out of my Jeep, I halted and leaned back in to grab my expandable baton before tucking it into my waistband and clipping the holster to the top edge of my jeans. I wasn't going to be caught without it again. Smoothing my V-neck T-shirt over it, I turned to inspect my work. It wasn't too obvious. Satisfied, I walked towards the building to get a better look. There were bushes under the windows, so I couldn't use a ladder. The area was too exposed to the main road anyway and was well lit.

Entering the building, I found the office on the main floor and knocked for the landlord.

After nearly a minute, I raised my hand, ready to knock a second time, when I heard rustling on the other side.

"Just a minute." A muffled voice hollered from behind the door. It opened to reveal a man in his mid-fifties, mouth opened wide in a yawn.

"Good morning."

"Is it?" He cast me a squinted smile, scratching his balding head.

"I'm just apartment shopping, and this place is so conveniently situated from work for me. I was wondering if you could show me around."

"There's only two apartments open right now. Everything's single bedroom." He blinked and shook his head, trying to wake up. "If you give me a few minutes to freshen up, I can show you one."

I nodded and turned back towards the hallway while the guy shut the door to change and, hopefully, brush his teeth. I eyed the cameras at each end of the hallway again. It was smart but made it difficult to poke around.

Pulling out my phone, I sent a quick text to Suzy, letting her know where I was and that I would be a little longer than expected. She sent me a thumbs-up, and the door behind me opened along with a blast of cologne and, luckily, a little minty freshness. Or was that Bengay?

"One of them's right on the main floor," he said, heading down the hallway, keys in hand.

"Where's the other one?"

"On the fourth floor."

"Can we look at that one?"

"Why?" His mouth turned down. "It's up four flights of stairs."

"Yeah." My brain searched for a reason to want a more inconvenient apartment. I shifted my weight from foot to foot. "I don't like ground-floor apartments. They're too easy to break into. And it's harder to peep into windows on higher floors."

His eyebrows raised.

"I had an issue with a Peeping Tom at my last place."

"Whatever." He marched to the stairwell, sighing deeply as he headed up the first flight.

I hopped up the stairs behind him, waiting as he continued his ascent. This was going to take forever.

When we finally made it to the fourth floor, he stopped for a breather before going to the second door on the right of the hall, 402. Only two doors away from Lane's and on the same side of the building. Unlocking the door, he swung it open, standing aside to let me pass through first.

It was a small apartment. The living room opened straight into the dining area and kitchen, separated by a peninsula. A short hallway from the living room led to a bathroom and what I assumed was the bedroom. The wall at the end of the apartment was brick, probably part of the original building, and framed two large black-trimmed windows in the dining area and a smaller one in the kitchen. Flat white drywall covered the rest of the living area. It had an industrial look and feel, except for the newer-looking smoke detector on the ceiling. It was actually very nice for a college student. I liked it.

"The open floor plan makes the place feel larger," I noted out loud, walking to the windows to look out onto the parking lot below.

"You'd need a crane to peep at anyone up here." He huffed. "Or binoculars from the library across the road."

Finding the building on the other side of the street, I took note of which direction it faced. I had forgotten the library was on this side of town.

"And every floor has a camera at the end of each hallway. I monitor them mainly in the evenings, occasionally during the day, but I have them stored for six months or so. So, if there are any issues, I can pull them. We don't often have security problems."

Turning away, I picked around the kitchen a bit before heading to the hallway and apparent bedroom, attempting to make my walk-through realistic. If it had a balcony, I'd honestly consider the change. This place was awesome. It was probably more money than I was paying at the moment, though.

"How much for this place?" I walked back out to where he was standing.

"I'll give you the rate sheet downstairs."

I nodded and waited for him to lock up behind us and then followed him back down.

We returned to his apartment, which seemed to double as his office, and I waited in the hallway. He left the door open as he riffled through a filing cabinet near a desk tucked into the side of his living room. Having found what he wanted, he came back to the doorway and handed me a piece of paper.

It had the floor plan for the listed apartments, as they were all the same, plus information on grocery stores and gas stations nearby. This was my neighborhood, so I already knew all that. The monthly rate and down payment were also marked and, unsurprisingly, out of my current budget. It covered water, trash, pest control, and any regular repairs. I raised my eyebrows, impressed. Too bad the nursing home couldn't offer anything so clear and concise.

"What about pets?" I asked, looking up.

"No pets." He shook his head.

"None?" I frowned. "Even something small like a hamster?"

"No pets." He repeated.

"Okay." I folded the paper and tucked it into my back pocket. "I'll run the numbers and let you know if I want it."

"Sounds good." He headed back into his apartment and shut the door.

Walking back into the sun, I considered how she could be getting pets inside if they weren't supposed to have them. Maybe she brought them in another container. Or maybe they were for a friend. Or many friends. Maybe she was a pet gifter. *Probably not.*

Checking my phone for the time, I made a quick decision and went back to my Jeep to grab my tote bag. There was a little traffic, and I lightly jogged across the street, looking up at the side of the library to get my bearings. As I entered the main door, I found the stairs and took them, winding up to the fourth floor. The brass plaque noted that this was the non-fiction section. Early on a Friday morning hopefully meant not a lot of people.

Wandering around, I walked between stacks towards a wall of windows. The apartment was directly across the street; only the parking lot separated it from my spot. I looked down and found my Jeep. Turning to look around me, I found a couple of college-aged kids sitting at a table going through laptops. *Why would you sit in a library if you were going to be in front of a screen? Didn't that kind of defeat the purpose?*

As I scanned the rest of the room, I saw an adult perusing the stacks, but he looked pretty consumed with what he was looking through.

Counting the windows from the left, I found Lane Pollett's apartment and reached into my bag to produce my binoculars to see what I could find. It would have been easier if the apartment was closer; the lot added a good chunk of space. Frowning, I concentrated on identifying the right window. I recounted my way up the building and over, and when I spotted the apartment, I refocused. The light hadn't shifted too much, and only the top right of the window was blocked by a glare from the sun.

It was dark inside her unit, but I was able to make out a kitchen table and some kind of wire-framed cabinets against the wall. It looked like cages. I couldn't see into them, but it sure looked like she had found a way to get cages and animals into her apartment. Whatever she was doing, she was keeping them alive. At least some of them.

Pulling away from the window, I tucked my binoculars back into my bag and turned to go. The two kids were watching me closely, grinning like idiots.

"What?" I lifted a shoulder. "I lost my car and thought it'd be easier to see from up here."

"Sure," the one on the left said, wagging his eyebrows. "Want my number? I can give you the *real* thing. In person."

Rolling my eyes, I headed out.

Chapter 10

Meanwhile, in the most delicious coffee shop this side of heaven,

Uncertainty crossed the store owner's face as Rhodes entered Grounds. Just because he was friends with Mal didn't automatically make him friends with the barista, but he was hoping he could still ask a favor of him.

Stuffing his hands in his back pockets, he took two small steps to the counter. He'd hoped, at this time of the afternoon, it would be less busy, and he was right. But given his current discomfort level—he hated asking for favors—he would have taken a little distraction.

"You're Mal's friend, aren't you?" Mo looked over the large gleaming commercial espresso machine he was polishing. "Rhodes?"

"Marlon Rhodes, yes, sir." He shuffled his feet.

"Can I get you a coffee?"

"Sure." He blinked in surprise, almost forgetting it was a coffee shop and normal to purchase something. "Just a small drip coffee, please. Dark roast if you have it."

"I have a Papua New Guinea I think you'll like." Laying a hand on a mug, Mo raised his eyebrow. "For here?"

"Yes, please." He edged one of the barstools out and took a seat. He could feel the older man's eyes on him. "I was wondering if I could ask you a question."

"You can." He cocked his head. "But if it's about Mal, I'm not sure I'll be able to answer. I don't make it a habit to disclose people's information. Must be the environment, I guess. People tell me all sorts of things here."

"Oh." He held up his hands, exhaling in nervous laughter. "It's not about Mal."

"It's not?"

"No. It's more of a legal question."

"Are you in some kind of trouble, Rhodes?"

"Not me, exactly." He took the cup of coffee Mo had slid across the counter. "There's a community center near my fire station in Bricktown."

"I'm familiar."

"Back when I was a kid, I spent quite a bit of time there myself. You could go as far as to say it saved my life." He stared into the inky depths of his mug. "I was spiraling down a bad road."

"Rough childhood?" His eyes softened as he leaned against the bar counter.

"No one's fault but my own." He shook his head. "I spend a little time there now. Keep an eye on the kids in the neighborhood. I see them often enough on the job anyway; it's a good way to stay in touch. Anyway, one of the kids there, Nate, who's been making a lot of effort to get on a straighter path, got into a little trouble recently."

"That's very noble of you to want to help. But if he's still saying yes to the wrong things, he may need a little more time before he's ready to walk the right path."

"It's nothing more than anyone else there has done for me. Less, though, in so many ways." He sighed. "But it's more than that. He was approached by one of Dessi's flunkies."

"Dessi's involved in this?"

He nodded. "A pretty Asian-American female approached him. I'm guessing the business manager from his speakeasy, from Nate's description of her. Cynthia, I believe, is the name. And you know how persuasive Dessi can be. Imagine what kind of people he employs."

"I don't have to." His jaw worked. "I know the type."

"The kid found them the warehouse for whatever business deal they were doing."

"From the shooting?" Mo stood up straight.

"Yes."

"Does he know what they were doing there?"

"No clue. He didn't ask questions."

"Smart kid."

"Not smart enough to steer clear of Dessi."

"Hopefully, he's learned that lesson."

"I certainly hope so. He got caught in the crossfire when things went bad." At Mo's concerned look, he held up a hand. "Nothing bad, just a graze, but I think it scared him good. And I tried to add to that…as much as I could."

"May be a blessing in disguise."

"Maybe," he admitted. "Anyway, the cops got involved. He was questioned. And in the flurry of it all, with the ambulance and the hospital, he admitted his involvement. I'm just worried about the kid. He said he's going to keep his nose clean, but he's got a court date coming up next week."

"You know I don't work as a lawyer anymore."

"I know that." Rhodes slid his coffee cup from hand to hand. "I'm not asking you to do anything like that. I just came here to see if you'd be willing to talk to him. Maybe, you could give him a little advice about the public defender they're going to give him. And possibly, maybe, make sure it sounds serious, even if it isn't that bad? I just want him to leave that life behind for good. I'm worried about him."

"You want me to scare him." Mo's eyes twinkled.

"Would you?" He looked up at the man, eyebrows drawn together imploringly. "I could bring him here some afternoon, when it's quiet like this. You wouldn't have to go out of your way."

Slowly, the man nodded. "Bring him by."

"Really? I mean, thanks, man. I truly appreciate it." He stood to shake Mo's hand. "I won't forget it. And I hope you don't think I'm the type to ask for favors all the time. It's just that it's this kid, and he's tied to Dessi. It's all getting personal here, and I want to do whatever I can to reset the balance that man has thrown off in this town."

"Don't worry about it." Mo patted him on the shoulder. "It's a good idea. And a good thing that you're doing."

"Thanks."

"So, tell me how things are going with Mal. I haven't seen her in a few days."

Rhodes grimaced.

"Uh-oh." He picked up his polishing rag. "Lay it on me."

"That's enough tape." I winced, slapping Sam's hand away from my bra strap. He was mic-ing me up for the evening's estate sale and attempting to adjust my bra straps to fit around the excess of tape he was securing to my skin. At this rate, I would need to stand under a hot shower to get it all off without removing an epithelial layer.

I noticed Rhodes standing in my living room, studying the knickknacks, books, and movies in my entertainment center. He had been quiet since he arrived at my place. After last night, I wasn't sure where we stood. It wasn't a warm reception, but it wasn't exactly chilly either.

"I think I'm good, Sam. You mentioned a camera?" I pushed past him to rummage around the items strewn across my kitchen table. I didn't have time to worry about my potential boyfriend at the moment. It would have to wait until later.

Leaning around me, the techie geek stuck a hand in the pile and emerged with a large crystal pendant. "It's in this."

"Seriously?" I took it from him, studying its murky dark-blue and gray surface. As I turned it over, I could see an embedded mechanism.

"It's glass. It's only thick enough to disguise the camera."

"Cool." I slipped it over my head, settling it within the deep V of the flowy top I was wearing. I would forgo the usual long pearls I wore to dress up an outfit. I still wore stretchy tight-fitting trousers that were built much like dressy leggings. Reaching up a hand, I made sure the curls I had added weren't messed up by the necklace. It seemed ridiculous to curl curly hair, but it was the only way to tame them enough for a polished look. That and an unhealthy amount of hair spray. Sam, on the other hand, looked ridiculous. "You know estate sales aren't formal events, right? This isn't an auction at Christie's."

"So?" He smoothed down the lapels of his James Bond-esque suit, moving to check his initialed cuff links. "I'm undercover as one of Chicago's wealthiest."

"Sam, you are one of Chicago's wealthiest. You made the Forty under Forty list last month."

He waved me away. "I'm doing okay. It's still light-years away from those schmoes on Michigan Avenue. They're crazy rich."

I executed a perfect eye roll, turning back to the table. "What's the rest of this for?"

"It's just good to have on hand." He picked up a few items—pens and mini magnifying glasses—and started storing them in the pockets of his suit.

I wasn't sure what he expected we would be getting into, but apparently, he thought we needed to be prepared for anything.

"I'll be right back," I said, padding barefoot across the room, towards my bedroom, to get shoes. Staring into the closet, I considered my boots. After the night I was kidnapped, I swore I wouldn't wear dress shoes again. They were only flats, but even so, I hadn't been able to gain footing when I was abducted and had

had to take them off when I ran. Obviously, not an ideal situation.

Still, I had backup tonight. Sam would be with me, and Rhodes would be in the car waiting outside. In an attempt to push past the fear, I leaned over and grabbed the flats, sliding my feet in them and walking out before I could change my mind. I had stretched emotionally this year. Hopefully, it wouldn't bite me in the ass.

"You look nice," Rhodes said at my reentry to the living room. It wasn't quite as warm as I was used to, but maybe it was an olive branch to get past the tension. "Your hair looks nice, but I still prefer the wilder curls."

"Thanks." I smiled, struggling not to touch my hair like a teenager. "So do you."

That got me a smirk. He ran a hand over his shaved head. "I worked really hard on my hair today. It took an hour to look this good."

"Totally worth it." I flirted back. This felt much more normal.

"You two ready to go?" Sam broke into the conversation.

"Sure," I said.

Rhodes nodded. "I think it's a good idea if we take my truck. Dessi's guys aren't familiar with it."

"Probably a good idea." I considered it, but this wasn't just my stakeout. "Sam?"

"Okay with me."

After gathering the rest of our things, we headed out the door.

The sale was thirty minutes away, in Oakbrook, at the home of a wealthy elderly lady who had passed a couple of months previously. Sam and I wandered through the house, keeping an eye out for key players. We had gone over the DMV photos of those we knew from Dessi's speakeasy. It wouldn't be good to misidentify anyone.

Tables were piled with belongings from closets and cabinets. The lady had more teapots than I'd ever seen a person have. Old British porcelain ones, authentic Chinese clay ones, Turkish ones, although those may have been coffeepots, and an interesting hand-painted one was marked as Polish. The desk in the study was filled with Tiffany lamps—real ones—but we had yet to see the chairs or anyone we knew.

"I'm going to split off and look in the bedroom," Sam said. He turned to move past a few people near the door, looking exceptionally overdressed against their T-shirts and jeans. They each carried a teapot. Apparently, you just carried around whatever you wanted and paid near the door, unless it was a large item. For those, they gave you stickers upon entry.

I caught myself fiddling with my necklace and reminded myself it wasn't just a piece of jewelry and moved on as well. The chairs were probably in the dining room, but the living room was packed, and I had to move with the flow to get to the other side. Going through the kitchen, I was able to slip through a throng of people milling around the dining room door. A large, stately hutch took up one wall at the far end, and an exquisitely hand-carved mahogany table set on display in the center.

Along the back room, however, stood a pair of armchairs with upholstered backs and armrests on closed-sided upholstered walnut frames. Fitted into the seat was a puffy red-and-gold tailored cushion. Even from across the room, I could read the large sign that stated they were bergères from the 18th century. These had to be them. I knew from the sale posting that they were advertised as having once been owned by Fred Seivers, a well-known businessman in Chicago. Of course, I knew him as an alias for Petrelli, one of Marchi's other big wigs.

We knew they had planted these chairs into the sale, but we didn't know why.

"Is that them?" the whisper from behind me sent the hairs on the back of my neck on end.

Jolting, I spun around to find Sam over my shoulder. I had to fight the urge to chew on him for sneaking up on me.

"Is that them?"

"Yes, I haven't been able to get closer yet, though."

Together, we edged along with the room as the people moved clockwise, taking in everything. As we got closer, I could make out the price on the chairs. Even though many of the items in the house were very exorbitant, these took the cake at $30,000.

"Holy crap, that's expensive!" I leaned into Sam to whisper.

"Extremely overpriced." He considered the chairs. "Even if they're real Louis XV gilt bergères, they shouldn't logically be priced over $18k."

Turning, I stared at him, my mouth agape.

"What?" He looked affronted as he touched his tie. "I know things."

I snorted.

"I did some research." He shifted his eyes, looking sheepish.

Cracking a smile, I leaned over to examine the chairs we had finally come even with. I made sure the necklace camera could pick it all up.

"We just mark it as sold if we want it, huh?" Sam asked.

"Seems so."

"That's weird."

"Why?" I said, fiddling with the tags they gave us.

"If they're here so someone special buys them, it doesn't seem very safe."

"Maybe that's why they're overpriced?"

He shook his head. "Some dumb schmuck may not know how excessive that is. This is Chicago."

Bending over, he picked up the chair cushions one by one, turning them over, and prodding at the upholstery. It all looked secure. I knelt and ran my hand down the carved legs. They didn't look to be glued together anywhere.

"Maybe it's something small, attached underneath." I touched under the chairs but only found wooden bottoms, not even a felt lining behind which something could be stashed.

"Then, why choose something as large as a chair?"

"Surveillance. Maybe it's easier to keep track of something larger."

Scooting back, I checked the fabric covering the tall back. It appeared undamaged. I poked along the seams, seeing if there were any loose spots or places that looked like they had been cut and reattached.

It looked like they were just chairs. Fancy chairs, but just chairs.

Standing, I turned to scan the room. I still didn't notice anyone out of place, but right before I turned, the back of a head and a gait pricked my memory. I'd recognize that swagger anywhere, and the suit, probably his customary three-piece that somehow never looked out of place on him. *But why would he be here? Why wouldn't he let one of his goons handle this?*

"I think that was Dessi." I bent down to Sam, who was twisting the legs gently, trying to get them to unscrew. He stuck a hand into his pants pocket to present one of the pens he'd stashed there, before clicking the end of it to expose a tiny, slim knife. "Careful. You don't want to have to buy it."

"That's actually a good idea." He looked up at me, completely serious. "We'd have more time to examine it."

"Let's take a break, move around the room a little," I suggested, stressed out at the thought of Sam paying thirty thousand dollars for some chairs, even if he could resell them. "If they're planting this here to be bought by someone, we'll see what's going on."

"But what if someone takes it?"

I tucked one of my "Sold" stickers in the cushion of a chair. "If someone gets too close, we'll let them know we saw it first, but it won't be too obvious."

"Okay," he said, slowly moving away, reluctant to leave them.

We circled the room again, watching anyone who paid attention to the chairs.

I broke off to examine a small, carved Dutch table near the windows and caught sight of two men who were chuckling and speaking under their breath. A box of Tiffany lamps sat at their feet. They were watching a couple who had approached the chairs to appraise them. Sam was swooping in, ready to defend his purchase if need be, so I moved to overhear the men better.

A few minutes later, I noticed Sam vibrating in anxiety at another couple's attention on the chairs. I worked my way back over to him.

"Do you think that's them? The buyers?" His eyes were wide. "Do you think we should tell them they're sold?"

"I think they're just overpriced chairs Dessi's unloading for Marchi," I whispered. "It's a bust."

"What?" He turned to face me, eyebrows drawn.

"I was listening to those two over there." I pointed to the men gathering yet another Tiffany lamp. "Fred Seivers is running some kind of scam to get people to overpay for what he's identifying as 'elitist taste.'"

"I'm buying them anyway." He set his chin. "Maybe we'll find something."

"Seriously, Sam? You'd just be funding the mafia."

"You're probably right." His shoulders sagged in the custom-fitted suit.

"Come on, let's get out of here." I slid an arm into his and headed him towards the door.

It was another fail. I wasn't sure how many of these we could take. Surely by now, one lead should have led somewhere. That *was* the definition of a lead. We were running out of time. How many more would we even get?

As we were filing out, a figure heading into the kitchen, holding a large painting, caught my eye, but when I turned, the lady behind me blocked my view.

Quickly, I stepped around her to see Dessi's suit-clad shoulders and slicked-back hair. I jumped back and out the door, hoping he hadn't seen me.

We could look up the painting online to see if there was anything interesting about it, but we'd reached the end of our trip. We needed to get out of here.

Chapter 11

It was a quiet drive to the Mennons' house. We had dropped Sam off at my place to get his car, and now Rhodes and I were following in his. I felt for Sam, but it was hard to brighten his mood when mine was scraping the bottom of the barrel as well.

"I went to see Mo today." Rhodes' knuckles turned white for a moment as he clenched the steering wheel.

"You did?" I said, surprised.

"He's a good guy."

"He is." *Where was this going?*

"A kid from my fire district, from the community center, was one of the bystanders in the warehouse shoot-out."

"Is he okay?"

"Yes, thankfully." He glanced at me, and one side of his mouth kicked up. "But he helped Dessi secure the spot, for Cynthia."

"Crap." Maybe that's why he had been preoccupied.

"Exactly."

"Oh, so you were getting legal advice."

"I was." He looked at me again. "Do you mind? I should have asked."

"Not at all." I shook my head. "Was he able to help?"

"He's going to talk to the kid." He bowed his head.

That sounded like Mo. "I'm glad you talked to him."

"Me too," he said, still pensive.

We pulled into the drive. "So, are you ready for this?" I asked, attempting to switch gears.

"Should I be worried?" The corners of Rhodes' eyes crinkled in mirth. He looked up at the stronghold Sam and Suzy called home. "It is a little much, huh?"

"Not to Sam. The place could withstand a missile strike. Or so he claims." I waved at Jim, who was parked in the Sentinel van outside, as I jogged up the steps. Brian must have the night off.

Wyatt answered as I raised my fist to knock. Outdoor cams took away the element of surprise.

"Hey." He nodded somberly. Sam must have beat us here. I wasn't sure since he parked in his garage.

"Hey, yourself." I walked in, and Wyatt leaned in to shake Rhodes' hand.

"Hey, Mal." Suzy's voice came from the kitchen. I headed around the corner to greet her.

"How bad is Sam?" I asked, wrapping an arm around her for a hug.

"He's a bit bummed, but he'll be okay." She shrugged. "How're you?"

I raised a shoulder. "I'm okay. I just feel like I haven't gotten anywhere. It was a big buildup for nothing. It's getting frustrating."

"But, hey." She raised her eyebrows excitedly. "You're well underway on your other two cases. Lots of good leads there."

"I guess." She had been so pleased when I filled her in on my investigations earlier that afternoon. Or maybe she was just happy to see my excitement. "But now I feel like I shouldn't have wasted my morning. That I should have been thinking of another way to scrape up dirt on Dessi, maybe follow up on that sale or on Fred Seivers."

"You're doing what you can," she assured me, patting me on the shoulder and moving to greet Rhodes as Sam came down the hall. "I'm so glad you could join us tonight."

"Thanks for including me in the Scooby gang." Rhodes offered a light smile.

Sam's eyes lit up for a moment, and Suzy giggled. "You'll fit in just fine."

"Come on." Wyatt tapped his fingers on the table where he sat, waiting for us.

"What? You got a hot date to get to?" I teased despite the late hour.

His eyes flickered, but he recovered quickly.

"What's this? A date?" Suzy pounced on the juicy topic but only got a look from the laconic security professional. It seemed not even she could spur additional information out of him.

The sound of pens and watches hitting the counter had everyone turning their heads back to the kitchen. Sam was emptying his pockets of all the gadgets he'd thought would be useful in our undercover work. His tie hung loosely around his neck.

"I didn't even get to use the laser cutter," he mumbled.

"Maybe next time," I offered.

We all looked around the room at each other at that thought. Hopefully, we had a next time.

"I have something to try," Suzy piped up, disappearing around the corner for a moment before emerging with a wine bottle and opener.

"Good idea," I said. Maybe after a glass, the crew would be in better spirits, me as well.

She smiled at me, manipulating the opener and pulling the cork out. "Grab some glasses, Mal. This isn't just a drink. It's investigation!"

She turned the bottle for us to see the label, and I read aloud, "*Sin*fandel," and, "Lola's Fine Wine. Is that from Lola's Slots?"

She nodded enthusiastically. "I thought we could try it. This one is a zinfandel, obviously."

The name didn't do much to dispel my doubts that a decent wine would come from a winery inside a video slots lounge and convenience store. I crossed the room to collect glasses and brought them to the table where we were all gathered.

Giving everyone equal pours, Suzy split the bottle between the five of us. Lifting her glass, she toasted, "To seeing Dessi behind bars!"

We all lifted our glasses and took a sip. And as one, our mouths turned down. It was worse than I had imagined. Wyatt spit his back into his glass, pushing it to the middle of the table.

"It's not very good, is it?" Sam tilted his head, then took another test sip. At our appalled look, he opened his eyes wide. "What? I was trying to give it a second chance."

After abandoning our unwanted glasses on the table, I got to business. "So, tonight was a bust, but we did see Dessi at the sale, buying a painting. Since we didn't see him mingling, my guess is he was there just to get the painting. We need to look into what it was. See if there's a lead there."

"I already looked it up when I got home." Sam pursed his lips. "The ad included the name and artist. It looks like an upcoming New York talent who happened to be at the sale. The value of the painting is raising, so it was a smart buy, but I didn't see any ties to anyone local."

"But why would he go personally?" Rhodes wondered aloud. "I don't really know much about his habits, but that feels strange to me. He employs people to do things for him."

"I would agree," I said. "Sam's got surveillance on his bar and occasionally picks him up on the city's video cams around town. Based on that activity and the conversations we listen to from his conference room, he does run some of his own errands, but mostly, he sends someone."

"Maybe it was something personal," Rhodes said thoughtfully.

"What's our next move?" Wyatt asked.

"We're still recording audio for the moment." Sam raised a finger.

"I think we're going to need to start tailing him," I threw in the ring. I didn't like it, but it was the only idea I had to take this to the next level.

"He's going to notice that. I'm not sure that's a good idea," Suzy said worriedly.

"We can take turns. Keep our distance." I fleshed out the thought. "Maybe if Sam installs cams along some of his normal routes, we can break off near them and pick up in other locations. He wouldn't have a constant tail that way. It'd be harder to notice."

"I still don't like it. The moment he feels threatened, he'll react."

"We have to do something."

Everyone looked around the room for feedback. Rhodes didn't look very happy about the conversation, but true to his word, he didn't say anything. And it was hard to argue my point. We were circling the drain and needed something to give.

I tried another angle. "We also know there's a storage facility somewhere, but we haven't been able to locate it. Could be their records aren't online or he's using a pseudonym we don't know about."

"It *could* be a storage facility." Sam held up a finger. "He could also be referencing storage at Red or at his house. He may just have implied he had a facility to sound important."

I grimaced. He was right. It was entirely possible, but it was one of the few facts we had to go on. "Our other options are tailing Dessi's goons and the other bigwigs meeting with Dessi."

"That doesn't sound any safer." Suzy pulled a face, probably remembering being drugged and locked up by one of those goons.

"We could go in and see what's in those barrels," Sam said. "To know for sure."

"We could do that." I agreed. "My only other thought is to find someone to go undercover with Dessi. Someone he doesn't know."

"It would have to be someone new," Rhodes said.

"There's too much of a risk that he knows about you." Wyatt shook his head. "It would have to be someone new, with zero history in this town. Let me think on it. I might know a guy."

Even though we hadn't gotten very far, the hovering sinking-ship mood and lateness of the hour were weighing heavily on everyone, so the topic fell away, and we broke apart. The beeline Wyatt made for the door did a lot to confirm my guess that he did, indeed, have something he was trying to get back to, even if it wasn't a date.

I didn't have the energy to needle him any more about it. Tomorrow was another day.

Rhodes drove me home, stifling a yawn himself.

"Want to come in for a cup of coffee?" I asked when we parked outside my apartment. I couldn't handle anything else. I'd fall asleep.

"I don't think I can, sorry. I have work tomorrow, 7 a.m." He turned to me and put a hand on my arm. "I'm sorry for the way things have been going lately."

"*You're* sorry?" I laughed. "I'm the one who's been dragging you through this case."

"I mean with us."

I sobered, unsure what he meant. My heart tightened.

"I'm going to try to work on my attitude." His voice was soft. "But just so you know, it comes from a place of caring. About you."

"Thanks," I said sincerely. "I like having you around."

He winked at me, making me blush, and leaned forward. I met him over the center console of his truck as his hand slid over my cheek and his mouth met mine in a soft kiss. He pulled back to rest his forehead on mine and gaze into my eyes. "I think you're pretty special."

"Back at ya."

I set my phone on the charger and climbed into bed. My fingers itched to check the audio recording from tonight. It wouldn't be completed until 2 or 3 a.m., but given the tensions today, I was anxious to have something to go on.

Heaving a big sigh, I clicked off my bedside lamp instead and scooted down, pulling my blankets up over my shoulder. I willed my brain to stop spinning.

Just as I was starting to relax, my phone buzzed. Jolting up, I grabbed it. It was a restricted number.

"Hello?" I clicked the light back on.

"Mal. It's been too long," Dessi's mocking tone came through the line.

I scrambled to stand up, shoving my feet into my boots and locating my baton on my bedside stand. I whipped it open; somehow, it made me feel more prepared. "What do you want?"

He chuckled. "Did you think I'd forgotten about you?"

"If I had, the car would have reminded me. Why are you following me?"

"If I were following you, you wouldn't know about it," he preened. "I sent the car to say hi. I wanted to make sure you hadn't put me out of your mind."

"As if I could."

"So kind of you to say. But it seems I shouldn't have worried."

"What does that mean?"

"As if I wouldn't notice you at the sale. You're hard to miss. However, I've got to hand it to you. I'm impressed you knew I would be there."

"Did you get what you wanted?" I asked, refusing to give him anything.

"I was killing two birds with one stone, as it were."

"Care to elaborate?"

"And what fun would that be?"

"Sorry if I don't share your idea of fun."

"Hmm, if you didn't, you wouldn't have picked your current route."

"What does that mean?"

"I just mean, you would have stayed on a more law-abiding path. Like your father. But it's more fun on this side of the law."

That got my attention. What did he know about my father? "I'm not on your side of the law."

"You veered off the enforcer path a long time ago."

"That doesn't mean I'm a criminal."

"You hang out with the likes of Domenico Poggiali."

I blinked. *How did he know about that?* Dom was Marco's uncle and the competing side to Marchi, the top dog in Dessi's chain of command. We had become friends after I proved Marco's innocence in an embezzlement case months back. As much as you can be friends with the head of a Chicago mafia ring. Which probably, truth be told, meant mildly acquainted, but from a positive perspective. Somehow, even though what he did was illegal, he seemed to have more standards and honor than Marchi's lot.

Of course, I was probably splitting hairs.

"Maybe that's why you couldn't cut it, though." He went on, ignoring my silence. "Even with the family connection, you couldn't make it through the academy."

It burned. I felt like I was constantly fighting for a place in a man's profession, but I set my teeth in silence. I wasn't in the mood to play.

"Fine," he continued. "Goodnight, then. And, Mal?"

"Yes?"

"I'm glad to see you're back in the game."

A foreboding feeling slid down my back, its icy fingers closing around my heart. If he only knew how closely we'd been listening to him go on about the other members' business, praising them, and offering to help out. Unfortunately, he was careful about what he said, even in the confines of his offices. It said a lot about his trust in his audience.

I knew I should call Sam or Rhodes, but it was late. I'd catch them up to speed in the morning. There was nothing to be done tonight anyway.

Clicking my light back off, I kicked my boots off but kept my baton tucked in with me. Thoughts whirled around in my mind, and I struggled to calm them.

Giving up, I switched the light back on, picked up my phone, and scrolled to the audio recording in process. Maybe if I listened to a little from earlier in the evening, I could sleep. It was boring enough.

Within moments, I had Dessi's voice in my ear again, although this time, he didn't know I was listening.

"What makes this time different?" a voice asked.

"Those sellers were idiots," Dessi said blandly. "I took care of them. These guys know how to handle a deal."

"When?"

"Next week, Monday night."

A chill skittered from the top of my head to the back of my neck and down my spine. This could be it.

"Where?"

"A warehouse near Humboldt Park."

"More deserted than the last time, I hope."

"Hence the Monday night. I've got it covered."

"You had it covered last time."

"I've got it covered," Dessi repeated, his voice tight as though he was speaking through clenched teeth."

I heard a chair scrape and footsteps head out of the conference room.

"Get Cynthia," Dessi said aloud.

And just like that, the audio went dead.

Scrambling, I leapt out of bed and dialed Sam's number. He answered on the first ring.

"The warehouse!" he let out in a yelp.

"Exactly," I confirmed. Of course he had been listening. "And the audio."

"It's dead."

"Shit."

"Shit."

"We need to meet up again tomorrow night."

"Agreed."

"I'll call Rhodes."

"I'll call Wyatt." The phone went dead.

Dialing his number, I sat back down, hoping he wasn't already in bed. I hated calling him, but I knew he'd want to know. Too much had happened.

"Everything okay, Mal?" His voice was steeped in concern. I could hear the sounds of a bed creaking.

"Dessi's planning another warehouse deal, Monday night." I jumped right into it. "I couldn't sleep and cut into tonight's audio. I already called Sam, and we're meeting up again tomorrow night to make plans."

"Shit," he echoed our earlier sentiment. "I'm on the books for tomorrow."

"That's okay. I can update you after the meeting."

"Okay, thanks for letting me know."

"There's one more thing." I had him on the phone. I had to tell him. "Dessi called."

"He called *you*? On your cell phone?"

"Yes. It was from a restricted line. He mentioned having a tail on me. He was baiting me, trying to find out what I know."

"You've scared him."

"I guess."

"That's not exactly a good thing."

"Probably not."

"I'll call in. Take a vacation day."

"You don't have to."

There was a pause. "Unless you tell me you don't want me there, I'm going to be there."

I let out a breath in relief. I had hoped he would offer, but didn't want to ask. My chest felt lighter than it had in days.

"Thanks."

Chapter 12

"We should do a pizza-and-margarita night, like a proper team meeting," Suzy said, tapping her chin with one arm propped up on her desk the next morning.

"It's not a bad idea," I said, perched on one of her lobby chairs, clutching my coffee like the life force it was. Especially after the previous night. Caffeine was my friend.

"And Rhodes is going to make it?"

I nodded. "He had to call in to work, but he'll be there."

"How sweet." Suzy's eyes sparkled in appreciation. "I felt bad that last night was his first meeting with us, and we didn't even have dinner or anything."

"We had the wine." I slid her a look, eyebrow raised.

She executed a perfect eye roll, stealing my signature move.

"Will you pick up the pizza from Mantovani's on your way? And make sure there's one with lots of olives. Sam rediscovered them and just realized they could be put on pizzas."

"Just now?"

"I know." She pursed her lips to control her smile, lightly shaking her head. "He thinks he's discovered something."

"Will do."

"Maybe we can find out more from Wyatt this evening." She wagged her eyebrows. "What he's been up to."

"Only if he wants to talk. You know how he is." She shrugged.

"I need to get those bills Mrs. Collins left with you," I said, switching subjects. It's not like I had audio to listen to anymore. "I want to see if I can get a clearer answer from Ms. Thompson with real-life examples."

"Sam did a little research online on Weston and said they have a reputation for lots of fees. It's possible the place is just expensive." She opened a drawer and handed a file over to me.

"True. I can check with a couple of other places too, to get a cost comparison."

"You could call the place Rhodes' grandma is at."

"I was thinking of that. They were so nice when I went there to see Miss Ellie. Too bad they have a waiting list."

"What's your next move with Brent and the pet hoarder?"

"I'm not sure yet. It looks like she's keeping the pets in cages. Not exactly illegal."

"Yeah, but what is she doing with them? It is a little odd."

"Agreed. It doesn't feel right."

"And from what Brent says, she'll just continue to collect."

She was due to purchase another one any day now, if she followed her previous pattern.

"Unless we can get in there to see what's going on, we can't find out for sure. She already doesn't like me." Maybe I had played my hand too quickly in the parking lot with her. "I'm not sure I could talk my way into her apartment. Especially if she's hiding something."

"I could try."

"She's not even supposed to have pets in the building. I doubt she'll let in people she doesn't know. She's not the friendliest type. I thought of using one of Sam's drones to get a better view, but we already know she's got cages in there. We might not even be able to see much more than that through the window. Unless we break in, I haven't figured another way to find out more information." I chuckled, but stopped at Suzy's expression, eyebrows slanted in, eyes narrowed in thought.

"It's an older building. Does it have those older keyhole locks?"

"Yes, perfect for lock picking, but I'm not breaking in. That's really illegal. We're only bending the rules for the Dessi case because of the situation."

"She's not supposed to have the pets there, in the first place, right?" At my nod, Suzy resumed the tapping on her chin. "I may have an idea."

"Really?"

"Is it legal?"

"Mostly."

At my frown, she laughed. "But we'll need to rope Brian in again."

"Do you think he'll help after Wyatt's explosion?"

"Probably." She smirked.

"Well, you get him to agree, and we'll talk. Otherwise, I'll continue to run through options. I just hate the thought of those sweet puppies getting bought by Lane."

"Why don't you adopt her?" Suzy asked, knowing which one I meant. "I saw how smitten you were with her."

"I don't know. I have a hard time keeping plants alive."

"Pets are a great way to see if you're ready for kids."

I shot her an earth-moving eye roll, securing my position as the champ eye roller. "Totally not ready for that. 'Sides, I don't think I'm the mom type."

"Doesn't Rhodes want any?" Suzy looked surprised at my answer.

"Uh..." I looked dumbfounded. "I have no idea. We've never talked about it. We've just begun dating. And it's not been the most normal or ideal dating situation."

We'd had a rough go of it, lots of stops and starts to get over in the beginning, and now that we were both in it, I didn't know where it was going. Even though last night's talk had done a lot to encourage me, it had been a real roller-coaster.

"Why did you think he wants kids?" I finally caught up with how confidently she'd asked the question.

"He just made some comments about the kids at the center last night. Yesterday, he was playing basketball there with them."

"He did? He didn't mention it to me." *What did that mean?*

"I ask a lot of personal questions." She waved a hand.

"So do I. It's kind of the main tool for a detective."

"Not the same way. You investigate; I prod into people's lives."

I sagged into my chair. "What if he wants kids and I don't?"

"One of you will adjust," she said like it wasn't a big deal at all. "Kids are a blessing."

"It's okay not to have kids. You and Sam decided not to have them."

Suzy's eyes dropped to her lap, her mouth pulled in. "Not really."

I looked at her questioningly.

Studying her hands, she played with the ring on her left one, spinning it. "We couldn't have kids."

"I had no idea. I'm so sorry, Suz."

Tears gathered in the center of her eyes, brimming on her bottom lid. I gave her time to elaborate, but she shook her head tightly, just a small nod to let me know she wasn't ready to talk. Maybe in time.

"It might not matter anyway," I went on. "Things haven't been going all that well."

"Seriously?" Suzy shifted the topic back to me. "But things were going great! What happened?"

"I'm just worried things are moving into the friend zone."

"What happened to the passion? You guys had so much sizzle."

"Not sure. He's being protective. Not overprotective, like an asshole-y jerk, but it's starting to feel more brotherly, and I'm not sure I like it."

"You need to change that."
"Yeah, I know."
"You need to talk to him."
"Oh, joy."

Meanwhile, in a brick coffee shop across the street, filled with nervous tension,

"Your boy here has a bright future ahead of him," Mo said loudly, announcing his and Nate's return into the nearly empty seating area. His face looked serious. "As long as he stays busy and keeps his nose clean."

The younger man shifted awkwardly on his Nikes, his head bobbing in a show of bravado, likely still uncomfortable from their conversation. He'd have to fight his pride if he was going to get help.

They had disappeared into the barista's back office a half hour ago. With Mal at work, Rhodes was able to take advantage of the day off and bring the kid in today. But the wait had wore on him, worrying about how things were going.

"Are you ready to go?" he asked the teen, setting his empty coffee cup on the counter.

"I need to take a whiz first." Nate dipped his head and angled towards the restrooms.

Finding Mo's face, Rhodes searched it for a clue as to how the meeting went.

The man cracked a smile, easing some of his pent-up tension. "I don't think he'll mess up again. He's pretty worried about getting caught up in Dessi's web of lies again. I told him what happened to Jeremy."

"You did?" he asked, surprised the retired lawyer would use the man who had been ordered to kidnap and get rid of Suzy against the kid. After she had gotten free, Dessi had him beat to a pulp. So much so, that the man had willingly turned himself in, claiming he was acting of his own volition, thus keeping Dessi out of the picture.

Mo nodded. "He needed to know what he had in store for himself."

"Do you think he'll get time for this?"

"He's not sharing a lot of information, which isn't great. But they don't have much of a case against him. My guess is he won't see time, but he'll probably get probation."

"His public defender—"

"He doesn't need a public defender," Mo cut in, shaking his head.

"But I thought—"

"I'll call later today to let them know it's not necessary and to get my name on the docket. I'm going to take the case."

"You said you didn't work as a lawyer anymore."

"You're right. I don't do it for pay anymore, but I've kept my license up. I'm doing it pro bono."

"You honestly are a good man, Maurice." Rhodes shook his hand.

"Don't let it get out." He winked.

"I just arrived at Mantovani's. I can pick you up on my way to the Mennons," I said into my phone. There was no sense in Rhodes driving separately; he was pretty much on the way. The pizza wouldn't even have time to get cold.

"Sounds good." His voice rumbled pleasantly through my phone's speaker. "See you soon."

Clicking off, I got out to make my way into the pizza parlor. The familiar smell of yeast and oregano hit me as soon as I stepped in. Attempting not to salivate, I looked for one of the employees. Seeing Marco, I smiled wide.

"Hey, Marco!" I hollered across the room, raising a hand in the air.

He stopped short, turning to locate me in the dim interior of the entryway.

"Heya, Mal!" Walking to greet me, the waiter and son of Dom Poggiali reached out a hand to shake mine. "What brings you in tonight? Another takeout order?"

"You know it." I grinned.

"Let me go check and see if it's ready." He disappeared in the back while I milled around in the lobby."

Reappearing a minute later, he said, "It's almost done. Phil's going to bring it out in a few minutes."

"Thanks, Marco. How's college?"

"Going well."

"That's good. Are you still seeing Marion?"

"Nah." He kicked at the ground. "She moved on."

"Her loss. So, what're your plans after college?"

"I actually have plans coming up shortly."

"You're still finishing college, right?"

"You sound just like my dad." He blew out a laugh. "Yes, I'll probably finish. I just plan on slowing down while I'm opening my new place. This is actually my last night here. They're throwing me a going-away party later."

"Really? That's incredible. Your own place? What brought that about?"

"Well, I had some ideas for Mantovani's, but Uncle Pete wasn't interested in changing. I thought, why not start my own?"

"Is it going to be a sister restaurant to Mantovani's?"

"Not quite." He straightened up, tucking his hands in his pants, his expression turned serious in a way that reminded me of his father. "The place is called Envy. It's pesto pizzas with white garlic sauce and fresh basil. We have Genovese basil, Thai basil, lemon basil; you name it, we've got it. Pine nut pesto versus walnut pesto, lots of unusual varieties. Tomatoes are an afterthought. We have some whole tomatoes we throw on a couple of pizzas to roast until they pop open, but there's no red sauce in the place."

"Wow, sounds delicious. I'm surprised Pete wasn't interested in trying a pesto pizza."

"He said it wasn't Italian pizza, but the thing is, Mal, we're *not* Italian; we're Italian-American. People have to change to grow, and Chicago is my heritage. Well, this is my spin on it anyway."

The passion in the young man was radiating. It was hard not to get excited for him. I couldn't wait to see how he grew up.

"I love it and can't wait to try it."

"We're doing some pop-up tasters around town. Get people excited, ready for more. Our social media drops today and should generate a lot of buzz. Hopefully, that, plus good word of mouth, will ratchet up the excitement until we open, in the next month."

"Where?"

"We've got a place in Lincoln Park we're renovating." He leaned in. "But keep that a secret, 'kay? We're generating demand for it, but not telling them the when and where until a week before, when we open the reservation lists."

"Smart." I couldn't help but smile, the corners of my eyes crinkling in earnest. "Not surprising, considering your business classes and your father."

He swiveled a foot, looking away shyly.

"Are you having news crews on-site for the pop-ups?" I asked.

"Nah." His mouth dropped. "I'm worried Dad's name will get splashed over the news."

"It's bound to get out at some point. The press isn't always kind."

"Maybe. But I'd rather make a go at it this way. Pops always wanted to keep me separate from the business. 'Sides, I want to make it on my own."

"I get that." *Boy, did I get that.*

"If I get a solid reputation and good word of mouth, then it'll have positive implications already. I'm hoping it helps with people's mindset when the connection is made."

"Fair enough." From the corner of my eye, I noticed Phil weaving around the tables, holding five pizza boxes high above him. How he didn't drop them, I'd never know. "What's your name on social media? I'll see if I can catch a pop-up tasting."

"Envy Craft Pizzas. It's a green logo written in script. A play on the saying 'green with envy,' cause of all the basil."

"I love it." I took the pizzas from Phil and handed him money. "I'll keep an eye out for it. I'm glad I saw you tonight to hear about it. Enjoy your party tonight."

Thanking them, I headed out. I hoped he could keep his father's name out of the press.

Chapter 13

"Wow, that smells good," Rhodes said, using the handle to pull himself into the Jeep and swinging the door shut. "Maybe we should just go park somewhere and devour these. Skip the meeting."

"You wish." I glanced at him. It did sound fun. "But Sam would find us within half an hour."

"Pretty sure I could be done eating by then." He considered it thoughtfully, patting his flat stomach.

I laughed, enjoying his levity. "I did get five pizzas. I think we've got enough for you to eat your fill."

"Good call." He nodded sagely. "One for each of us."

"Correction." I held up a finger. "One goes to the van crew."

"Uh." He clutched his chest. "We have to share? The horror."

"Suzy and I won't eat a whole one. We've got you covered. Plus, Suzy always has snacks. If you go home hungry, it's your fault."

"Fine," he teased.

It was a short drive, and I pulled in next to the security van within minutes. Eyeballing Rhodes like I didn't trust him with the food, I made a big show of taking them all with me, parading the boxes to the van to deliver theirs first.

"Yes!" Brian pumped a fist in the air, then leaned into me. "I took this extra shift just to get the pizza."

Shaking my head, I handed over the box. Duri, a newer member of Wyatt's team, was also there. "Two on shift tonight?"

"Wyatt said risks went up, back to two on call overnight. Just in case."

"Sorry, I only brought one for you two." I knew the guys could eat.

"That's okay." Duri lifted a container full of cookies. "Suzy brought snacks too."

"Of course she did." I waved, heading for the door.

"You weren't kidding," Rhodes said, following me up the steps.

"Just wait," I tossed behind me, heading in the already opened door. Wyatt stood beside it, his arms crossed. As soon as I got close, he took the pizzas and headed in.

"How'd it go at the nursing homes?" Suzy asked when I walked into the kitchen and found her stirring a pitcher of her famous margaritas with a long wooden spoon.

"Fine." I leaned a hip on the counter and picked up a carrot stick to munch on. "I got numbers from Omni and Brookside, where Miss Ellie is at, but Helen Thompson at Weston said she needed more time to run them through her billing system." I gave her a pointed look.

"Of course."

"I'll give her a couple of days before I bug her again. Still, it was a nice day out of the office. I can't complain."

"Can you grab the plates?" she asked, carrying the pitcher and the veggie tray out of the sunny, yellow kitchen.

"Right behind you." Swinging open a cabinet door, I grabbed a stack and snagged the paper towels on my way out. Suzy probably would have used her cloth napkins, but it was pizza; they were bound to stain.

The five of us settled in around the table, much like we had the night before. I liked the feel of it, a real team. It was something I hadn't had since I left the academy.

"Dig in," Suzy announced, smiling at Wyatt, who was already on his third slice.

"What?" He looked around the room, his mouth full.

"We eat first," she told Rhodes, pouring and handing him a margarita.

"Thanks," he said, taking the icy drink. "And thanks for having me."

"You're one of us now." She elbowed him lightly. "The Scoobs."

He smiled, crinkling his eyes.

Sam picked through the boxes until his gaze landed on the one with olives. Lips spreading wide, he let out a short cackle, snagging three slices for his plate.

Everything was silent for the next ten minutes, except for the sounds of eating and sighing. Mantovani's had the best sauce; it was rich and garlicky, and the crust had a fantastic chew.

"So." Wyatt leaned back, clearing his throat. "What's next?"

"We need a plan." I took the lead. "Monday night, a deal is going down in a warehouse near Humboldt Park. We need to find it and stake it out."

"If we can find it early enough, we can set up surveillance equipment," Sam piped up.

"Good idea. I can case the area tomorrow and make a list of anything that looks usable."

"I can do an online search of uninhabited buildings," Sam offered, picking a couple of random olives, that had fallen off slices, from the pizza box and popped them in his mouth. "But it may not be uninhabited or listed."

"Agreed, but I doubt Dessi would take the chance of using someone's mechanic's shop, for example, after hours."

"I'll make a list of the few warehouses I know of," Wyatt offered. He probably covered security for some of the buildings in the area.

"If we can find the right place and get set up properly, we should be able to get some video or photographic evidence. I can't imagine Dessi wouldn't be there personally for a job like this. He was at the last one, and it went bad. There's no way he'd miss this one."

"This could actually be it," Rhodes said, trying to be supportive. "We could have him Monday."

"It has to be," Sam said, pushing his pizza crust across his plate.

"What do you mean?"

"It's our last bit of audio," I grimaced. How could I have forgotten to tell him that piece of information? It must have been from the stress. "The audio died right after we heard about the deal."

Suzy already knew, and Wyatt didn't look surprised. Sam had obviously remembered to fill him in.

"We're really under pressure now," Sam said under his breath.

"We're prepared is what we are," I said firmly. "And informed ahead of time. We'll get it. But we'll need your best mic in case we can't get very close. And a few good cameras in case we can set some up."

"I've got you covered."

"Should we call the cops for a raid?" Rhodes asked. "To have backup and gather evidence?"

"We should, and I would ask them, but we don't have evidence for the deal." I wrinkled my nose.

"Sure, we do."

"Obtained illegally."

"But it could be a reliable source," Sam wondered aloud. "Cops have CI's."

"Yes, but they're registered Criminal Informants."

"Can't you be registered?" Suzy asked of me.

"I suppose so, but what if we're wrong? We need them to take us seriously when we need them. You can lose credibility pretty quickly."

"I would advise against it," Wyatt spoke. "If you record it, you should be good."

"But what if they're shooting again?" Rhodes turned to look at me squarely.

"Twice?" I asked. "What are the odds that two deals in a row go bad? Dessi's going to be extra on guard after last time."

"Exactly. And he's scared. He's followed you twice now that you know of and called you to poke around and see what you know. The man's on edge from two different sources. A dangerous man at that."

"From what you said, he made it sound like you're working outside the law." Sam twisted his mouth in thought. "Maybe he's trying to set you up to take the fall for something. He's good about that."

"It's worth the risk. We'll be as careful as we can."

Rhodes gave me a stern look but said nothing.

Sam and Suzy exchanged a glance, then Sam spoke up. "Maybe you should all stay here while we're sorting this last bit out."

"We have extra rooms and would be happy to have you." Suzy reached over and put a hand over mine and Wyatt's, giving a look to Rhodes to include him too.

Wyatt gave a short head shake with a side smile. "But thanks."

"I'm set too." I set my other hand on top of hers, squeezing back. "But maybe if things get worse."

"The offer stands. Anytime you need it. Any of you," Sam said, looking at the three of us, ending on Rhodes.

Rhodes looked down, touched.

The table buzzed loudly from a phone that lit up in front of Wyatt. A female face popped on the screen. Turning my head, I looked at it. She seemed familiar, but Wyatt snatched the phone up before my brain could connect the image with my memory.

"Hang on a sec," he spoke into the phone while heading towards the living room.

I could hear his voice go low as he took the call.

"Who was that?" Suzy said, eyes lit with excitement. "Seems like you were right, Mal."

"I don't know, but she looked familiar." I frowned, still trying to process what I saw.

"Who needs a refill?" Suzy asked, holding the pitcher up and distributing the rest of it among the empty glasses.

Wyatt returned a moment later, his neck rosy with a blush.

"Another hot date tonight?" Suzy asked, but he just looked away, avoiding the conversation.

"I think I'll grab a glass of water." I stood and walked into the kitchen to help myself. On the way back, I admired Suzy's ficus in the corner. If I could keep something that large alive, maybe I would be ready for a pet. If I was home enough, that was. *Maybe it wasn't that great of an idea.* Then it hit me. The plant connected the dots in my memory. I knew where I had seen that face before. It was the gardener at Ms. Lamb's house, from my last case. Ms. Lamb's pathetic excuse for a son had been stealing from her. I stopped short, looking up. "Hillary."

Wyatt's eyes shot to me, going large, then he looked down. His ears were tinged in a pink flush. "So?"

"You're seeing Hillary?" Suzy shrilled. "*How* did I not know this?"

Understanding why he had probably kept it to himself, I winced, mouthing, "Sorry," to him.

He shrugged it off.

"When did this start?"

Knowing he had no choice but to give her at least some details now that she knew, he spoke at last. "I stopped by to check on Ms. Lamb and her security system after Mal's case wrapped. Make sure her kid was respecting her boundaries. Got her number."

"That's just wonderful." She clasped her hands together.

"She seems nice." I inclined my head. "Very protective of Ms. Lamb. I'm sure she appreciated that."

The corner of his mouth threatened to tick up, but he held it down.

"Do we need to get the cops involved at all?" Sam spoke up, still picking through the box for olives and strands of cheese, oblivious to the conversation around him.

"It's not a bad idea," I said, letting the subject shift, for Wyatt's sake. "I'll give Jen a call. I was planning to reach out to her tomorrow anyway. I can let her know what's going on. We can at least have them in the loop in case we need help, last minute."

"I know you probably don't like the idea, but it wouldn't be a bad thing to get Detective Rodriguez in on it, too."

I rolled my eyes at the mention of my ex. "You're probably right. I'll let Jen know she can share it with him. The more, the merrier on this."

"Who's going on Monday?" Suzy asked.

"Sam and I will," I spoke up. "I need his tech."

Sam sat up straighter, eyes bright. "I have lots of new gadgets to bring."

"I'll be backup." Wyatt raised a hand.

"What can I do?" Suzy asked.

"You're staying here under security." Wyatt's raised hand turned to point at her.

Her face fell, and Wyatt looked at me with an "oh, shit" expression.

"We need you to monitor everyone," Sam jumped in quickly. "We're all going to have earpieces and be on a GPS. You'll be mic'd here. You can tell us where everyone's at and watch us on the camera. If anyone stops responding, you can help us find them. I can also have Xavier, my drone, on the rooftop, scanning for body temperature. You can tell us where everyone is. Like, if someone is approaching us and we don't know it. You'll basically be the most important one of all."

Mollified, Suzy gave him a look of pure adoration. I didn't quite understand their dynamic at first, but after I got to know them, I totally got it. They were made for each other.

"I can be backup, too," Rhodes offered. "Unless you need me with you two."

Wyatt nodded.

"As long as we can locate the place, that works best. If we have too many potential places, we may have to station people at different locations, ready to move when things go down."

"I've got other guys we can use if we have too many options."

"Sounds good."

"I'll text you that list of warehouses tomorrow morning." Wyatt stood. "You can check them out while you're there."

"I'll send you what I find online later tonight," Sam said. "I won't be up early enough to get it to you."

"Works for me." I got up to help clear the table. "I'll do a group call tomorrow to update you on what I find."

Rhodes was already collecting dishes, so I snagged the veggie and cookie trays. Suzy got busy loading a tray with the glasses and other odds and ends from the table while Sam walked Wyatt to the door. After carrying the plates into the kitchen, Rhodes set them in the sink and turned on the water to scrub them, then stacked them in her dishwasher.

Cocking her hip to the side, Suzy poked me, gesturing at the firefighter making himself comfortable in her kitchen. Her eyebrows raised in appreciation at the sight. "You sure you don't want to stay here until this blows over?"

Turning, he saw her expression and laughed loudly. "If you're going to bake cookies like that, I may have to reconsider."

After helping them clean up, reassuring Suzy and Sam that we would consider their offer and let them know if we change our minds, we got on the road ourselves.

"Your friends are great," Rhodes spoke from the passenger seat of my Jeep.

"They are." I glanced over.

"They treat me like I belong."

"You do." Reaching a hand out, I squeezed his leg.

Smiling passionately enough to make me sizzle, he put his hand over mine and clasped it. Heat enveloped me, reminding me how much warmth the man generated.

"Still, they went out of their way to accept me. I mean, Wyatt didn't say much."

"Wyatt never says much."

"But he didn't have to. He still included me."

"There was a time when I thought I had to do this all on my own." I opened up to him a little. "Before I met Suzy. I was so desperate to prove I could do it."

"After the academy?"

"Yeah."

"You said Dessi taunted you about your dad." He left it out there, not pushing too hard.

"The man knows how to push my buttons." I tried to laugh.

"Why's that?"

I considered brushing it off again. It was what I always did, but I didn't want a relationship like I had always had in the past. I took a breath. "My dad didn't quite think I could make it in the academy. He didn't want me to become a police officer."

It was the most I had ever shared with anyone. I hadn't even told Jen about it.

"But he was an officer himself. Surely, he'd worked with other accomplished females on the job?" His thumb lightly stroked the back of my hand, where it rested on his thigh.

"You'd think." I laughed, but it sounded more like a croak. "Maybe it was just me."

"Only if he doesn't know you," he said lightly. Then, after a beat, "Can I ask you a question?"

"Sure." *Probably.*

"I've known you for a while now. And you're one of the most capable, competent women I've ever known. You don't really need anyone."

"Uh-oh." I'd heard complaints like that before.

"It's not a bad thing." He chuckled. "A lot of women I've dated needed something from me. You? You're fine on your own."

"I enjoy being with you." I glanced at him.

"I know. You're with me simply because you want to be, not because you need something from me." He gave my hand another squeeze. "I like that."

"Thanks."

"But I'm curious," he continued his questioning. "I just have a hard time believing you'd leave the academy, especially if you were trying to prove yourself. You could say you're a little on the stubborn side."

"Ah, yes." I let out a long sigh, unsure how much I wanted to share. His steady light stroking of my hand had an oddly calming effect. "I'm definitely stubborn…But that's just it. My dad is decorated. He made lieutenant in his precinct across town. Had a handful of large drug busts. Everyone knew his name."

"Big shoes to fill."

"It was." I paused, collecting my words. "After Rodriguez and I fell apart. That was a spectacular mess, by the way. Everyone knew he had screwed around behind my back, probably because I confronted him at the academy one day. I gave him a bloody nose. It was awful. Well, not the bloody nose part. He deserved that."

"I'm so sorry."

"It's in the past now. But I was already at an all-time low, and some of the guys were ribbing me that if I made it through the academy, it was only because I was riding on my dad's shirttails."

"Ah," he said slowly, the light bulb going on. "If you made it in the private sector, it was all on your own."

"Exactly." I nodded. "Combine that with the facts that I might have a small problem with people telling me what to do and liking to do things on my own, and it made sense. When I got called in to explain myself after clocking Rodriguez, I announced my departure. In hindsight, it might not have been the smartest choice in the world."

"But you love what you do."

"I do," I said, pulling into Rhodes' driveway and parking. "But it hasn't been the most stable career. I'm doing okay, but until recently, I've been barely scraping by. And now, I'm not really taking any serious cases, with my priority being on Dessi. I would be making more money on the force."

"But you might have always wondered if it was because of your dad."

"Exactly!" I turned to face him. *He actually got it.*

It meant so much to me that I leaned over my console and kissed him full on the lips without waiting to read his reaction. It was such a relief to have someone finally understand me.

He grabbed my shoulders, surprised, but didn't push me away. In a blink, he had deepened the kiss, turning it into a blazing-hot furnace in my Jeep.

When we broke, he said, "You want to come in for a drink?"

In his eyes, I had the answer to my earlier question. It wasn't a brotherly look he had. And it wasn't a brotherly question. He wasn't talking about just a drink, and we both knew it.

"Yes," I breathed and followed him in.

Chapter 14

The smell of coffee woke me. Stretching, I frowned. The sheets felt worn and soft, but not like my own. And they had a pleasantly woodsy scent to them. Kinda manly. *Hold on*, my brain started catching up. *Who was making coffee?* As I sat upright in a flash, it all rushed back to me. I had stayed over at Rhodes' house.

Pulling the sheet up unnecessarily in the empty bedroom, I looked around. A large dark-wood dresser stood against one wall, and light-gray sheets were on the bed with a denim bedspread. Sheer gray curtains on the windows let in the dawning morning light. Swinging my legs out, I bent to gather my clothes, pulling them on in haste.

I needed to pee. And use a toothbrush. And get a look at myself in the mirror.

I felt oddly out of place. We had never slept together before, and while my memories of the night still burned in my brain—man, could he kiss—I was feeling a little vulnerable about where we were this morning. He'd sent out a few mixed signals lately, even though the night before did quite a lot to confirm his feelings.

I remembered the bathroom was directly across the hall. If I could make a beeline for it, I would be able to gather myself and put a semblance of myself back in order before greeting him. Quietly edging the bedroom door open, I spied the bathroom across the hall and jetted for it, ignoring the kitchen down the hallway.

When I flicked on the light, my reflection didn't scare me as much as I was worried it would. Looking around for a bar of soap, I saw he had set out a new toothbrush and the tube of toothpaste for me. Elated, I popped it from the wrapper and got to freshening my breath.

I scrubbed my face with the bar soap, removing the vestiges of my flaked mascara. I didn't carry a purse, so it was the best I could do. I fluffed my hair, taming down random curls, and considered it good enough.

I could use a shower, but at least my mouth felt clean. I wasn't sure I could have faced him like that. It wasn't like in the movies. That had always bothered me, a couple cozying up and kissing like they didn't have morning breath. *Weird.* Maybe in Hollywood, they were always minty fresh.

Taking one final look in the mirror, I drew in a steadying breath and exited. I planned on being polite and downing a cup of coffee. Test the waters first.

Rhodes looked up from where he leaned against his countertop, cup of coffee in hand. A slow smile spread over his face, heating me to my core.

"Good morning," he said lazily, setting his coffee down and pushing off to meet me. He brushed my hair from where it had fallen near my eyes and gently cupped my cheek as he leaned in for a kiss.

Grateful at his automatic show of affection and acceptance, I leaned in, my hands curling into his sides in a light embrace.

"Morning, yourself." I broke off, setting my chin on his shoulder, once again glad we were close to the same height. Enjoying the warmth he emitted, I wanted to soak in it a moment longer.

"Did you sleep alright?" He pulled back, his eyes searching mine. Maybe he was as unsure as I was.

"I did, thanks." I smiled, giving him another quick peck before turning to the coffeepot. "Can I get a cup of that heavenly goodness?"

"Absolutely." He opened a cabinet door above the pot, selected a mug, and filled it for me. "Cream only, right?"

"Yep." I was pleased he'd remembered. "And thanks for the toothbrush. It made my morning."

He fixed my drink up, stirred it, and handed it to me. "Happy to oblige."

I buried my face in the mug, trying to hide the goofy grin and blush on my cheeks. *What had happened to me?* I was acting like a teenager. Suzy would be so proud. I could barely contain the knee-jerk to roll my eyes.

"Can I make you some breakfast?"

"I have to scout out Humboldt Park today. I should probably head out soon." *And not overstay my welcome.* My stomach growled, however, giving me away.

"Are you sure?" He moved to his stove. "I make a mean omelet."

I couldn't hide my interest in the offered breakfast. "Are you sure?"

"As much as I'm enjoying the dance, you're welcome to stay. I'm happy to have you here."

I let out a strangled bark at being called out, but he only grinned at me. "It honestly sounds delicious," I finally said.

He gave a sharp dip of his head, his lips still tilted in satisfaction, and got to work, pulling eggs, veggies, and deli meat from his fridge and setting them on a large wooden cutting board.

"There's someone in that one, Sam," I spoke aloud towards the phone secured to my dash.

"Are you sure? They don't have any record of Wi-Fi or phone service."

"Did you check electricity service?" I looked through my binoculars at the moving crew who was bringing in tables and boxes into a warehouse he had labeled as uninhabited.

"Why would anyone have electricity and no Wi-Fi?" he muttered, his eyes focused elsewhere while the sounds of clacking keys on a keyboard were audible through my Jeep's speakers. "Ugh, it was turned on this past week."

"In a rush to get to bed last night?" I chuckled.

"I was saving time." He sighed, stretching out his neck. He was in his Jedi robes again. "I'll rerun the rest. Besides, I wasn't the only one."

I froze, surprise jolting through me as I turned to face the phone. There was no way he knew. "Excuse me?"

Then it hit me. GPS.

Of course, the techie rockstar still had me LoJacked. I had totally forgotten.

"Uh..." he stammered.

"Never mind." I wasn't having this conversation with him. He didn't need to know any details of my night, or morning, with the hunky firefighter. I had a salacious thought of him in his fire helmet and shook my head to clear it. I had invited him to run around with me today, but he already had plans to visit Miss Ellie at the home. I told him I'd call if any trouble arose.

"That crossed off one more place."

"Three of the addresses you sent were small apartments on the West Side." I switched back into investigation mode.

"That's right."

"I doubt that's where they're meeting. One of them matches one of the three Wyatt sent. And two of them have bricks caving in and are totally in the open." I drew a line through the unlikely locations on the list I had jotted down earlier.

"How many does that leave?"

"Four." I pulled back into the street, heading to one Wyatt had identified. It was just around the block. "This side of town seems likely. It's mostly deserted and just on the outskirts of Humboldt."

Reading the numbers over the doors, I ticked through them until I found it. It looked boarded up, but I thought I saw movement inside. "This might be it."

"What do you see?"

"Just shadows. But if they're holding a deal here tomorrow night, it makes sense Dessi would have his guys clear the space ahead of time."

"That screws us for setting up cams."

"Unless we do it after they leave."

"They could check it again. And then they'd know they were being watched."

It was a good point. "What if we put the camera on the building across from it? We wouldn't get it all, but we'd get visual of who's going in and coming out."

"That could work."

"We can get better proof with audio when things actually transpire."

"I have a new little remote-control hex bug I'm playing with," he mused. "I rewired it and rebuilt the joints. Added a tiny mic."

"We can bring the mic in after they've already swept for it. Genius."

"There's only one problem. To make it that small, the battery life is pathetic."

"Let's hope it goes quickly."

"I'll work on a second one. Maybe we can send in another if the first one dies."

The warehouse door opened, and a scruffy man with worn jeans and a flannel tied around his waist walked out. He yawned, stretching into the air, his tank top riding high on his stomach. He scratched his head and took a bored look around. "Not Dessi's guys. Looks like squatters."

"Are you sure?"

"Pretty sure." I made a thick line through the location and moved on. The next one was just two doors down, at the end of the street. Pressing the gas, I headed away from the curb and back down the street, to get a better look. "This next one is right here."

"What do you think?"

The entire front was covered in windows, not even boarded up. There was a sign in front. Using my binoculars, I focused in on it. I couldn't quite make it out, but it looked like a security system sign. "I don't think this is it. It's completely in the open. Not Dessi's style."

"Two left."

One of them, I had already driven by. It was a little on the small side, but a solid contender. The space was at the end of a row of buildings but tucked into an alleyway. It was the first one on Sam's list. I just had one more to drive by; Wyatt's third address.

Driving down the street a few more blocks, I made a right. This neighborhood was a little more rundown. There was more vandalism, but I didn't see a lot of people on the streets. Then again, it was still before noon.

"This looks possible too." I parked to get a better look at the rundown building in the middle of the block. It was decently sized for a warehouse. There were few windows, mostly higher up, and several of them were broken but not completely exposed.

"Any sign of movement?"

There were only a couple of cars on the street, but nothing telltale. The only motion I saw was from a stray piece of paper tucked into the corner of one of the broken windows, flapping from the breeze. "None."

"According to Google Maps, there's a building across the street. It might be a good spot for a camera."

"Agreed." With the deal going down the following day, it probably wasn't a good idea for me to poke around on the property. Whatever security measures he'd set up were probably already in place.

Leaving the neighborhood, I took a right and headed back to Roscoe Village before pulling into Holstein Park in Bucktown.

"We should dial Wyatt in and let him know what we found," I said. "And Rhodes."

"I'll get Suzy. She's reading in the other room." He disappeared from the screen.

Finding the buttons on my phone, I dialed Rhodes' and Wyatt's numbers for the group chat.

"Heya, Columbo." Rhodes' face brightened my screen.

I couldn't help but smile, looking away as Wyatt appeared.

"Just following up with the team with news on the warehouse location." I filled them in, composing myself.

Sam and Suzy appeared on Sam's screen. Sam raised a hand, the wide sleeve of his robe flapping happily. "Hi, team!"

Suzy wagged her eyebrow suggestively at me. Wyatt frowned. The corner of Rhodes' mouth tilted up.

"We found two that might be it," I filled them in, patently ignoring Suzy. "I'm worried about going in with cameras this close to the date. Dessi could have security set up."

"True," Wyatt said. "They might sweep for bugs."

"Right. And we don't want to tip him off."

"I'm going to stop by tonight and set up cameras across from the building at least," Sam said. "We can get audio after we set up."

"Text me details, and I'll join you," Wyatt said.

"We don't know when they're meeting, but it's probably after dark," I said. "I'll pack my surveillance bag and set up with Sam around six, Monday night."

"Which location?" Sam asked.

I considered. My gut said the alley was quieter, even though it didn't offer as much protection inside with space. "The one in the alley."

"I'll park by the other location." Rhodes gave a short nod.

"I'll post somewhere in between, ready as needed," Wyatt said.

"I'll be here." Suzy gave a half-hearted smile.

"Directing the crew." I pursed my lips.

"I can drop off the earbud mics when I'm out tonight," Sam offered, "and show you how to turn them on."

"Just let me know when; I'll meet up with you," Rhodes said.

"I'll just find you." Sam waved a hand.

"I don't know where I'll be."

"GPS, duh."

Rhodes' forehead dipped, and his head shot back.

"I mean, um," Sam went on, stuttering. "When you became one of the crew…I kinda, sorta bugged your phone."

"My phone?" he said, surprise evident in his voice.

"Not the microphone part. Just the physical piece of equipment. For emergencies."

I watched Rhodes' reaction. He knew Sam's history with Suzy and me. Hopefully, he'd take it easy on him.

Wyatt watched with interest.

Rhodes' lips pressed together, and he moved his jaw back and forth, considering the new information. Finally, he nodded. "Okay."

Phew.

Later that afternoon, after I had gathered my things, packed, and unpacked them in my duffle bag, I dialed Jen.

"Hey!" she answered on the first ring. "How's it hanging?"

"Hi, Jen. Pretty good. How're things there? You come to your senses with Rodriguez, yet?" Even though it had been a little tense for a while now, I thought it was the appropriate time to tease her about it.

"Haha."

"We should catch lunch sometime, just the two of us." It had been nice to see her with the crew last week, but I wanted to catch up more one-on-one.

"I'd like that."

"Things are moving forward on my case." I gave her the heads-up.

"Do you have anything concrete yet?"

"Not yet. Hopefully, after tomorrow night."

She put the pieces together. "Crap, you're trying to tell me something big's going down tomorrow night, aren't you?"

"Yes. May be similar to the last one that hit the news."

"Mal." Her voice rose in pitch. "You can't run off half-cocked by yourself."

"I'm not," I shut her down. "I have a team."

"A team?" she stuttered in surprise. "Oh-kay, then. Will you at least be careful?"

"Yes, I've got backup, too. That's actually why I'm calling. Are you in the evidence room this coming week, or are you on the streets?"

"Streets. Why?"

"I know you can't officially give me backup unless I have something solid, but could you have a team in the area? Just in case?"

"Who is this, and what have you done with my friend?" She laughed. "Of course, I can, Mal. Anytime. But, um."

"You want to let Rodriguez in on it?"

"Ye-ah," she drew out. "I think it's the best idea. He has experience with this sort of thing."

"I agree."

"You do?"

"I do. Fill him in. I'll text you the details. Once it's over, I'll tell you more over lunch." I crossed my fingers that it would be that simple.

"Okay!"

Hanging up, I poked at the bag on my table. I didn't need to repack it again. Getting up, I wandered to my refrigerator. It was getting close to suppertime.

After some debating, I picked up my phone and dialed Rhodes. He answered on the first ring.

"Wanna get some dinner?" I threw out there before I lost my nerve.

"Definitely," he replied. "But I'm cooking."

"Works for me," I said, swiping up my keys.

"Not so fast." He chuckled, hearing the jingle. "Why don't you grab an overnight bag?"

"A bag? I have work tomorrow." My brain emptied. "Isn't it a little soon?"

"Maybe, but with everything going on…"

"You're worried about me."

"I'm worried about you, *AND* I want you to stay," he clarified.

I bit my lip, thinking. "Give me five."

Chapter 15

The following morning, in a busy little shop serving liquid energy,

Even though the cafe was busier than usual, the chime of the front door still made Maurice raise his head to see who had entered. He made it his business to remember his regulars and offer a level of friendship and support.

The long, shapely legs of the woman walking towards him, however, were not those of any regular he'd ever seen, but he still made it to the register before Chad, today's help for the busy shift. She was a bit younger than he was, but he'd be lying if he said he'd rushed over because he was just doing his job. The woman was stunning.

"Good morning." He put on his most welcoming smile, his eyes lit with interest.

"Morning." Her lips pressed together in pleasure as she flicked her eyes down, then back up.

"What can I get you?"

"I'd kill for a latte," she all but purred, leaning over the counter. "To go, please."

"Coming right up." He nodded, getting to work. The woman actually seemed interested in him. He knew he wasn't a slouch in the looks department; he always made an effort to dress smartly, but it had been a while since he had any serious interest from the opposite sex. Probably because he spent so much time in the shop. "I don't think I've seen you around before."

"That's because it's my first time." She looked around the coffee bar with curiosity. "Cute place."

"Name's Maurice, but everyone calls me Mo."

"Cynthia. Pleased to meet you."

Pouring the steamed milk into her cup, he flicked his wrist with the practiced hand of a barista, creating the perfect leaf. Pleased with the effect, he slid it towards her, watching for her reaction.

"It's on the house. I hope you come back again."

"That's so sweet." She took the cup and raised it to her lips for a taste. A long hum sounded from her throat. "Perfect."

"I'm glad you like it."

The captivating woman leaned even closer, as if she planned to say something privately. Her blunt-cut shoulder-length black hair fell forward to frame her face. Setting down his rag, Mo pressed into the counter to angle in, his pulse kicking up a notch. "It's also sweet of you to worry about that boy."

"Boy?" His head tilted in question. What she was saying didn't make any sense. Unless she meant Nate. But how would she know him?

"It doesn't matter." She canted her shoulder. "He'll still go down. He wants the boy to take the fall, and he will. Don't waste your time."

A familiar sense of manipulation washed over the onetime lawyer. Setting his jaw, he stayed close, his fingertips pressed in firmly into the concrete countertop. "Don't you worry about that. I know what I'm doing."

"I know you do." She raised a fingertip to drip it down the front of his apron. "That's why I'm giving you a tip. As a friend."

Stepping back, he raised his chin. "I guess we'll just have to wait and see, then, won't we?"

"I guess." She flashed him a wolfish grin. "Just a friendly warning. But if I were you, I wouldn't take that case. I wouldn't even see that boy again. He's had a troubled past. You can't save them all."

She raised the latte in a salute, turned, and walked out.

"Two nights in a row!" Suzy's voice pitched to an all-time high when I walked in the door half an hour late. "Tell me *everything*."

Grabbing a mug from the credenza in the lobby, I poured a cup of joe. It had taken me longer to get out of Rhodes' house this morning than expected. I was barely able to hide the glorious smile that crossed my face at the thought of why. Late wasn't my thing, but, well, it had been worth it. So, I had bypassed Grounds for Suzy's brewed coffee. Still a solid choice. I could swing by later for a cup of the good stuff. A snack, if you will.

"Suzy." I shook my head casually. "You said so yourself; I probably shouldn't stay by myself right now, with what's going on with Dessi."

Her face fell. "Please tell me that's not why you stayed there."

Unable to hold back, I let the bland expression fade away, showing my delight. "Nah."

She screeched, raising both hands. "Yes! Now, tell me everything."

"Well, he made me dinner last night. Steaks on the grill. They were delicious."

"And?"

"And he was just wonderful, Suze. I don't know what I expected when I decided to give it a try, but it certainly wasn't this."

"What do you mean?" She tilted her head.

"I don't know." I shook mine. "With Rodriguez, we were always trying to one-up each other. It was highly competitive. But with Rhodes, it's different. He just…"

"Gets you? Supports you?"

"Exactly." I smiled wistfully. *Wistfully?* Honestly, I was beginning to not care.

"I know what you mean." Suzy met my gaze with the same quiet expression. "It was the same for me. I didn't know it could be like that."

"Your previous relationships were bad too?" I asked, wondering if she'd open up to me about her past failed marriage.

She just nodded, turning to find her own coffee cup. Discovering it empty, she got up to pour another.

"Anyway," I said after a beat. Apparently, it wasn't the time. "It was nice."

"Nice, huh?" She looked up.

"Okay. More than nice." Then at her grin, I added, "I mean, have you seen his shoulders? Woah!"

We sat in companionable silence for a minute.

"Rhodes knows how to use his earpiece?" she spoke, breaking the quiet.

"Yup, we're all set for tonight." We had had fun the night before, me helping Rhodes set up his own surveillance bag. I had had brought an extra pair of binoculars with me since I correctly guessed he didn't have any. "You know how to use Sam's command center?"

Her face lit up. "Yes, although he calls it The Bridge." She used finger quotation marks. "I mean, his desk has five monitors."

"What on earth does he do with all of them?"

"Who knows. He and Wyatt got the cams set up in the middle of the night. He didn't get home until 3 a.m. But he said it was better to do it late, when there was less road traffic."

"Makes sense. I'm just glad we have something set up ahead of time." It made me feel like we were at least a little more prepared. Fingers crossed that tonight we'd get what we needed. "I let Jen know. She'll be available tonight too, just in case."

"Good to have friends."

"Isn't it?" I lifted my mug.

"Hey, Mo." I raised a hand, walking into the most perfect place on this earth. I had put in a solid hour of obsessed preplanning for tonight's stakeout with Sam over the phone plus a little research, then spent another half hour, jotting down thoughts on Mrs. Collins' nursing home case, but things still felt off. I needed a break, and besides, I had earned breakfast.

Rhodes had offered to cook for me, but we had been busy this morning with other endeavors. I didn't regret the decision.

"Hi, Mal." He nodded, busy wiping down the counters.

Sliding onto a stool in front of me, I perused the items listed on the chalkboard wall behind him.

"Don't you have it memorized by now?" He snorted.

"You might have changed something to the seasonal menu." I lifted a shoulder.

"Since last week?"

"You never know."

"It's still summer."

"I can dream about the maple-nut lattes." I let my eyes go all dreamy.

Snorting, he went on scrubbing the counter, a little more determined than normal. I had been so anxious to get here, I hadn't noticed how preoccupied he looked. Glancing over at Chad, who shrugged his shoulders over Mo's head, I switched tactics. "Everything good, Mo?"

"Of course." He shrugged, tossing the rag into a bucket in the corner. "Sorry about that. I'm all yours. What's up?"

I didn't believe him, but not feeling the need to push into his personal life, I said, "Lots, but first off, I need coffee. All I've been subsisting on today is two cups of brew."

He had the grace to offer me a look of horror.

"I know!" It was good to be understood so fully. "It's been rough."

"Mocha latte?" he said compassionately.

"You'd better." I sighed aloud. "But make it a cappuccino. Extra foam."

"You got it." He winked.

"And a cranberry-orange scone," I added for good measure. Who knew where the evening would take us? There was no way I'd be able to eat dinner before the night's activities, and I didn't want my last meal to have been, well, last night's meal.

The sounds my dreams were made of—the whir of the burr grinder and the resulting freshly ground coffee aroma, the whoosh of the pressure releasing and dribble of espresso into the cups—lulled me into comfort. Mo poured milk into the frothing cup, and the stainless steel machine let out a bold hiss while he pumped the milk frother, creating the perfect amount of foam. It looked like clouds when it landed in my cup. I wiggled in my seat.

Sighing, I raised it to my lips. Perfection.

"Lots?" He raised an eyebrow while he cleaned the equipment, following up on my earlier comment.

"Don't ruin the moment." I closed my eyes, sipping silently, in pleasure. "A deal is going down tonight."

He waited.

"We're all going. The whole gang."

"We, meaning…?" He left it hanging.

"Suzy, Sam, Wyatt." My eyes shifted to his. "And Rhodes."

He tipped his head in approval. "Things going good?"

"Actually, yes."

"You sound surprised."

"I am, a little." I raised a shoulder. "But it's good."

"I'm glad."

"Me too. Thanks."

"What else?" he asked. "You didn't come here to run your plan by me."

"No, I've got it handled."

"Then?"

"I have a new case." I wasn't sure what to tell him. It wasn't like I had any real questions.

"But you're stuck?"

"Kind of? I know what to do next, but it feels—I don't know—weak."

"What can you tell me about it?"

"It's a nursing-home case." It rattled off my tongue just as it had been rattling around in my head. "The client's getting billed a lot. Possibly, the home is just expensive, and it's running through her Medicare funds, but she's getting loads of extra monthly bills. I'm comparing her billing to other nearby homes, but so far, I'm seeing a wide variety in what everyone charges. I guess I'm at a loss as to how I can help."

He perked up during my download. "Verify with Medicare too. You know insurance fraud is a thing."

"How so?"

"The home could be billing extra fees, things that aren't even taking place. I've seen it before."

"I hadn't even thought of that."

"And call the hospitals to confirm the tests are legit."

"That's what I was wondering." Tiny thoughts in my brain connected into a pattern that made sense. "Maybe the tests weren't even needed."

"Exactly."

When I suddenly stood, I realized my coffee was only halfway finished.

Without missing a beat, Mo reached for a to-go cup, poured it in, and handed it to me.

"Thanks, Mo." I grinned, handing him cash for the coffee, then heading out the door.

"Mal." His voice, more serious than I'd ever heard, had me stopping in my tracks.

"Yeah?"

"Be careful tonight."

"I will, Mo. Thanks."

Chapter 16

"Do you see anything yet?" Sam asked, peering through night-vision binocular goggles attached to his head. He had dressed in a long-sleeve black T-shirt and black jeans, complete with his Batman utility belt. What he had in it, I'd never know.

"Not yet, you?" I asked, surveying the area from our spot down the alley, tucked behind another car. I had rented a vehicle for the night, my green Jeep being a little recognizable. I checked the video feed from the camera on the tablet he had set up between us. Nothing there either.

We were all set up and ready. We had been for about twenty minutes, but we'd likely be here for several more hours. Still, it had been a good idea to get here early.

"Nothing here yet," Rhodes' reassuring voice came through my earpiece.

"Nothing here," Suzy's voice echoed, clear and chipper.

A grunt from Wyatt meant there wasn't anything to say yet.

Fiddling with my binoculars, I hoped against hope we'd get something tonight.

My day hadn't exactly been fruitful. I needed Linda Collins with me to call Medicare and verify what expenses had been submitted. So, after abandoning that route earlier in the day, I called the doctor's office. It had taken a few tries to get to the right person, but she was due to phone me back the next day.

Tired of waiting, I had gone ahead and called Ms. Thompson at Weston, only to hear she still hadn't run the numbers. I told her I'd stop by the next afternoon and hung up. She'd keep pushing me off if I didn't.

After another two hours of waiting and Sam checking with everyone every twenty minutes, we all started to get a little stir-crazy.

"I'm going to step out and stretch my legs," I said, setting down my binoculars and quietly opening the door. I had turned off the door light and crouched next to the sedan to keep my head down. Stepping back, I stretched my legs in a lunge, then switched feet.

"Team," Suzy said, her voice flush with excitement. "I may have something."

"What? Where?" Sam shouted in my earpiece. I could see his arms flailing to grab equipment from his seat inside the car.

"Heat signature. People entered the building. Wait, there's more. I can't tell how many; they're just blobs, but it seems to keep growing."

"Which location?"

"Uh." The clicking of a keyboard sounded in my ear. "The alley location."

Bingo.

"Want me to move?" Rhodes asked.

"Not yet," I said. I didn't want to tip anyone off. "You're not far. Just stay available."

"They're either too far away to pick up audio, or they're not talking," Sam said. I could see him pointing the parabolic mic into the corner of the window.

"What do you see, Suze?" Wyatt asked.

"The heat is gathering in one area."

"Probably a room. The walls won't pick up on the imaging unless they're holding heat, and this place has no electrical service and hasn't had people living in it to generate any," Sam said.

Lights bounced off the gravel as a car entered the alleyway ahead of us. It parked right outside a walkway to the building, and four guys spilled out, all wearing baggy jeans. Two scanned the alley, while the other two went to the trunk and opened it.

"What's in it?" Suzy asked after Sam announced what we were witnessing from our positions.

"I can't tell yet. Hang on. Wait, it's a big box."

"Crate." I corrected. "Heavy. They're carrying it with handles on either side. All four men are packing."

"They are?" Sam peered through his goggles. "How can you tell?"

"They're wearing oversized jackets in August, for one. But look for the bulge under their arms." It was easier to spot on the two carrying the crate. They leaned to accommodate the weight.

"Ah, I see it!" Sam exclaimed.

A collective hush echoed in my earpiece.

"The heat blobs are moving towards the front of the warehouse," Suzy narrated.

"The front door is opening," I picked up the account, peeking out from behind the sedan. "A big man answered the door with a large gun, an automatic. He scanned the alley too, then let the four men in."

"There're a lot of guns inside, then," Rhodes said unnecessarily.

"I wonder what's in the crate," Suzy mused.

"Something Dessi wants," I said.

"Something illegal," Wyatt added.

The Toyota's door opened on the side away from the warehouse, and Sam stepped out. "The hex bug can't make it up those steps. I'll have to set it on the doorjamb. Those old doors don't have a rubber gasket; they're barely hanging on. There's plenty of room for it to make it under it from there."

"What if they're monitoring the door?" Rhodes asked.

"Uh, they moved back to the rear section," Suzy said. "But there's a faint, much more faded blob in the front."

"Could be residual heat." Sam leaned against the car.

"Or a guard," Wyatt warned.

"I'll take it," I said, crouch-walking to meet him. "I want to get a good view anyway. I need to see how close I can get."

"Be careful." Rhodes' voice sounded stiff.

"Which side is the fading heat?" I asked.

"The right side from the door," Suzy answered.

That was good, as our car was down the road, to the left.

"I'll focus on getting audio." Sam reached into the car to get his mic. He looked both ways down the abandoned alleyway and raced across to the nearest building to the left of the warehouse, plastering himself flat against it.

When had he put on gloves?

Staying low, I followed. As I peeked past him, it looked like the coast was clear. Slowly, I circled him, hurrying across the gravel, careful not to make too much noise in my boots. Squatting near a corner window, I stayed on the left side of the building. "Let me know if there's movement inside."

"Will do," Suzy whispered.

"I'm picking up audio," Sam said. "They're just catching up now, with a little boasting thrown in. Now they're laughing."

My heart beat loudly in my ears, and I deliberately slowed my breathing as I stood. Then, in a flash, I leaned in to peek into a cracked window and pulled back. I hadn't seen anyone, so I tried it again, scanning the other direction. Still no one. "I think it's clear."

"They're still in the back room," Suzy said. "The blob is still to the right, but it hasn't faded. Wyatt's probably right; it's someone guarding the door."

Releasing my breath, I stepped up to the window to get a better look around, searching for movement.

"I can't see very far in the dark." My voice was barely more than a whisper. "I need to get closer."

"I'm coming," Rhodes spoke.

"We don't need a ton of people milling about. It'll be more obvious."

"I won't. I'll park a couple of cars behind you, still several buildings down from the warehouse. I just want to get closer, in case."

"I'm moving in, too," Wyatt said. "Standing by."

Working my way towards the front and closer to the action, I found a large hole in the building, where a window used to be. The street lamp cast more light on this side, and I could see a doorway on the street side. I retraced my steps to the empty window.

Reaching through, I leaned over as much as I could and dropped the hex bug lightly on the floor. It would be so easy to hop in and get a better look around. I was tempted.

"I've got the hex bug in motion," Sam said. "It's small, but still might be noticeable if I'm crossing a room. I'll stay along the wall, where it's dark." I could see it crawl towards the rear doorway facing the alley. "There's a man standing near the right corner of the room, but he's on his phone. I'll head to the front."

Ducking, I went back a little farther. There were bushes under these windows, making it hard to get close enough to see inside. However, I could see a doorway with light filling the edges. It had to be the room where the deal was going down. "They must have brought battery-powered lamps."

"I see the lights," Sam said. "And I can hear them opening the crate. They're sifting through it, from the sounds of it."

"Are they saying anything about it?" Suzy asked.

"Could be drugs," Wyatt said.

"No, no descriptions, but I hear a clicking sound."

"Have you made it into the room?" I asked Sam, kneeling under a window.

"Not yet. I'm having trouble making it under the doorway."

I inched back to the open window and peered in to see if I could spot the bug by the door. Squinting, I could barely make it out in the distance. "It's too narrow. I can barely see light from under it. There's a bigger gap on the side of the door than at the bottom, but it's still not wide enough for its legs. I don't think you're going to make it."

"We need visuals if they're not going to talk about the deal itself." His voice was tight.

Without hesitating, I placed my hands on the broken brick and raised myself to the window. The room looked empty. Pulling a leg up, I set a boot on the edge and the other into the room, softly lowering it to the dirty plank flooring. A mouse skittered along the far wall.

In a soft whisper, I said, "I'm in."

I heard a sharp intake through my earpiece as I took delicate steps to the door. Luckily, nothing creaked.

"They're near you, probably just on the other side of the door," Suzy warned. "But no one is moving on that side. There's a little movement on the other side of the room."

At this point, I couldn't say anything else aloud. One hand stabilized on the wall by the door, I peered through the crack. The bright lights around the box made me blink to focus. Three men hovered over it, picking up and examining automatic weapons. *Shit.* I slid a hand into my vest pocket, pulling out the slim camera I used for surveillance work. It didn't make any noise. Holding it up to the edge, I snapped a stream of photos.

"That's not what we agreed on," Dessi's voice came from the far side of the room. I couldn't get a good view of him.

One of the men turned towards him. "That's the price." His face was twisted downward in contempt.

"They're arguing," Sam said suddenly. "About the price."

Dessi raised his arm and shot the man without saying a word.

"Mal!" Rhodes' voice rose.

Snapping a few more pics of the downed man, I slid back to the window, ready to jump out and run if the door opened, but I heard nothing. Under my breath, I answered, "I'm fine."

Seeing movement at the corner of the building where Sam was, I tilted my head out the window. It was Rhodes. I waved him back.

"They settled on the original price," Sam narrated.

"It's okay. I'm getting pictures. I just need one with Dessi in it," I whispered, inching back to my place at the door.

What sounded like a growl came through my ear. It was probably Rhodes, but I was so close. He'd have to trust me.

A man next to Dessi moved into the light, handing a duffle bag to the baggy-pants guys, correction, arms dealers. One of them propped it on the crate, unzipping and riffling through it. Holding one stack of cash in the light, he flicked through it, his eyes cutting to the corner where my nemesis stood. "Is it all here?"

"As promised," Dessi said.

Dammit, he wouldn't leave the shadows! The rest of his crew, three men in total, were still playing with the guns, aiming and shooting the unloaded weapons towards the ceiling.

"Let me see one," Dessi said, setting his personal weapon down on a windowsill next to him to take a gun from the crate. The window had a large crack running down it, and its left side was missing a chunk of pane.

An idea blossomed in my head. If I got the gun with his prints and was able to bullet match it with the wound in the dead guy, it would be better than proof of an arms deal. Spinning as gently as possible, I tiptoe-ran across the floor, vaulting out and letting my knees absorb the shock, then raced around the building to the window with the gun. I had to be fast.

"What are you doing?" Suzy said, alarmed.

Peering around the corner, I saw the black sedan, but no one was in it. Suzy would have said it if someone was waiting out front. "I can get the gun. Perfect evidence. Be ready to go if this goes bad. I'm gonna do a snatch and grab."

"Oh boy." I heard Sam hurrying across the alleyway back to the car.

Staying close to the backside of the building, I bent over to cross under the windows until I came to the opening. Spying the missing windowpane, I straightened next to the wall and curled my hand so it would fit through the hole.

Just as I was sticking my hand through, fingers closed over it and it disappeared. Gasping, I snatched my hand back, blood racing, and I flattened myself to the wall.

"They're moving," Suzy shouted.

Pivoting on a patch of dirt, I sprinted away from the rear door and around the corner. I looked both ways but wasn't sure where they were going. I was pretty sure they hadn't seen me, but the three dealers would be leaving by the alley entrance.

"Everyone, hide," I whispered harshly, scrambling for the bushes under the windows. Wedging myself behind them, I pulled my knees in. One hand pulled my baton from my vest while the other pulled a knife from my back pocket, just in case. My voice low, I relayed, "I'm out of view."

"Me too," Sam's voice was muffled. I hoped he had made it back to the car.

"I'm good," I heard Rhodes.

"They've exited the building. Everyone's out," Suzy said. "They're gathering, I'm guessing, into cars. Large blobs."

The sound of engines engaging carried around the warehouse, but I stayed in place. My chest heaved, and the branches from the bush pricked my face. Better than a gun, though.

After a minute, Suzy gave the all clear. Tucking my weapons away, I crawled out, wincing when my palms hit broken glass in the dirt. Branches scraped along my arms and caught in my hair as I scooted out.

Boots crunched in my vision, and a hand reached down. It was Rhodes.

"You okay?" he asked, hauling me up and crushing me to him.

My breath caught in my throat when a scratch on my cheek grazed his five o'clock shadow. "Yes, just a few scrapes."

"Did you get it?" Sam bellowed in my ear.

My face fell. "No. I wasn't fast enough."

"You've got photos." Rhodes gripped me tightly. "It wasn't worth the risk."

"I hope they're enough." I sighed.

Chapter 17

"I just don't know, Mal." Rodriguez flicked through the pictures displayed on his monitor from my attached camera. "I've seen him get away with more damning evidence than this."

Blowing out a breath, I plunked down in one of his chairs, anger crossing my face. If I hadn't left my post, I might have been able to get better pictures. "But there's a dead man on the ground."

"Yes, and we got to the scene right after you called last night. He's at the coroner's now, getting processed. We recognized the guy; he's local. We might be able to find another connection to Dessi when we look into him. We also picked up the sound of the gun over the ShotSpotter." He sighed, pushing back from his chair. I could see rings under his eyes from not getting enough sleep. "Why don't you leave this with us? This is good evidence. We could use it to bring him in for questioning or put his guys behind bars, but I'd recommend putting it in the locker and trying to gather more for a case. If you can get more, the rest of this will help build that case."

"I don't know how to get any more," I ground out. "That was my last lead."

"Get another lead."

"If it were that easy, *you'd* already have him behind bars," I tossed at him, standing up.

"It's not his fault," Jen spoke from the doorway. "You know how it is. We don't dictate what we spend our time on."

"Yeah, I get it." I crossed my arms. I was just pissed. We had gotten pictures of Dessi's men and the payment itself. We could put his guys behind bars. We even got the dealer they left behind.

Wait. An idea popped into my head.

The gun.

Maybe we could still get his gun. The thought spun in my mind. It was desperate, but possible. Just because I hadn't collected it last night, it didn't mean it was impossible to get.

"We know what he's doing," Rodriguez said unhelpfully. "That's something."

"Uh-huh," I said, heading to the door. I'd leave the camera for safekeeping in the evidence locker; I always had extra ones lying around. "Thanks."

Jen followed me out. "Sorry, Mal."

"It's okay." I paused, waiting for her to catch up. "I just need to blow off steam. I'll call you later."

"Lunch?" Her eyes lit hopefully.

"Rain check?" I asked. I couldn't lose momentum.

"Sure." She nodded. "Just give me a ring."

I headed to the office to call the rest of the team.

"What about the audio?" Sam argued, his face filled with frustration through the tablet in the Sambot. "Between the hex bug and the parabolic mic, we have the argument between them *and* the gunshot."

Rhodes picked up where Sam left off. "We even got them discussing a price, which I would think proves they were buying the guns, especially with the pictures." Luckily, he was able to take the call from the fire station.

Wyatt just grunted, looking away from his phone. It was obvious he knew what I was going to say.

"You're right, Sam. It should be enough. Hell, it *is* enough to put someone behind bars, but even with Dessi's voice on it, it doesn't necessarily mean he was the one who pulled the trigger."

"He'd get another guy to take the blame," Wyatt said flatly.

"He's done it in the past," Suzy stated, standing behind me. She'd had personal experience.

I saw Rhodes sit down wearily on the bench outside his station.

"What do we do now?" Sam hung his head, saying what we were all thinking. He ruffled a hand through his hair, making it stand on end, matching the Wil Wheaton picture on his T-shirt.

"We know what he's doing now. He's bringing guns into Chicago, probably for Marchi." I ran down what we knew. "He's been trying to secure a place at the big boys' table for a while now, opening up his speakeasy to facilitate deals. But the last two sales ended in gunfire, the first because of some issue we don't know about, and this time because the sellers got greedy."

"But the sale was still successful." Rhodes' expression hardened. "Those guns are now on the street."

"And it puts him in a more solid position with the Marchi organization, as long as the legal issues don't cause him any repercussions."

"We could plant a new bug," Suzy suggested.

"I'm not sure we could get away with that again." I shook my head. "Besides, I'd never get into that conference room again."

"What if someone went in undercover to plant it?" Sam asked.

"I doubt he'd let new people in the back. It's too risky." Suzy shook her head.

"What if I told him we had parted ways and I had intel?" Wyatt considered. "That I wanted in on the money."

I shot down the idea. "He'd probably test your loyalty. I don't like thinking how. We would need somebody new to build a rapport with him, or someone at Red."

"Hey, Hillary could get a job as a waitress!" Sam's eyes lit up.

Wyatt physically growled over the phone in response.

"You're right. I'd never send Suzy in." He shook his head, sobering on the idea. "I don't know what I was thinking."

"I talked to my guy," Wyatt said, ignoring his response. "He's willing to go in, see if he can get a job at Red."

"You said he's new in town?" I asked. "So he's not on Dessi's radar."

"Exactly, no history in Chicago. Recently reinvented himself."

"A ghost." Sam's eyes grew wide.

"There's still the gun," I brought up lastly. "It's out there. We can still get it."

"How would we do that?" Sam asked, then said slowly, "You mean, breaking into his house?"

"Maybe. There's still a storage unit we can't locate."

"Maybe that's where he's storing the guns."

"Sounds like we need another plan," Suzy piped up. "Tomorrow night. Let's meet up again at our place. We can all come up with ideas."

It was thoughtful of her. Tomorrow night, Rhodes wouldn't be working.

"Are you sure you're ready to try breaking into the man's house?" Wyatt asked, using more than his usual amount of words.

"I'm ready to finish this thing." I glanced at Suzy over my shoulder. "By whatever means necessary."

"Yes?" Helen Thompson looked up from her desk at Weston Assisted Living, her face falling when she recognized me.

Which was why I had bypassed the front desk when I came to visit, since I now knew where her office was. "Just picking up your billing estimates." I plastered on a fake smile while waiting in the doorway.

Sighing, she dug through the papers on her desk for the one I had given her with the list of expenses. Clicking through her computer, her printer kicked on, and she produced an invoice for me. "It's just an estimate," she warned. "I don't have insurance information to bill or more details on the medical history of the patient. But it should give you an idea of what we would have charged for your grandmother."

"This is great, Ms. Thompson." I held the paper aloft. "It'll help us make a decision on Grandma's care."

I just needed to compare it with what she had previously billed Mr. Collins.

Turning, I retraced my steps back out onto the warming parking lot. It was after lunch, and the heat was starting to set in, marking it as an uncomfortably warm day. As I tugged at the neckline of my T-shirt, I was glad I had only grabbed a salad for lunch. Anything warmer would have sat heavily on my stomach.

Tossing the hard-won paper on the seat next to me, I gave it a humph. Apparently, it hadn't been that difficult for her to gather, after all. Not that I thought it would be.

I turned the hand crank to roll the window down for some fresh air. The Jeep turned a right onto Roscoe street instead of going past it and to the office. She pulled into an empty spot outside HERO coffee bar. *Who was I to question her sense of direction?* Shrugging, I swung out and headed in for two cold brews to take in to work.

"Holy smokes," Suzy said when I walked into the office five minutes later. She was standing near the window A/C unit, her blouse partially unbuttoned, waving a piece of paper between the unit and herself in an effort to coax the air closer. "It's a scorcher today."

"Tell me about it." I held up a cup as the condensing air dripped down the side and formed a puddle around my forefinger and thumb.

She rushed to take the chilled cup and held it to her neck and cheek. "That feels amazing."

"It's even better inside." I laughed, taking a sip. "Cools all the way down."

She took a long pull of her drink and collapsed in her chair to kick her heels off.

I crossed to the air conditioner and tapped on it. "Is it not working?"

"I think it's working. It's just so hot and humid outside. It's having trouble making much of a difference unless I stand right in front of it."

"If you want to work from home this afternoon, you can."

"Not a chance." She sat up straighter. "Brent called. Lane bought another pet this morning."

"What'd she get?" I spun around. Maybe it was the iguana. *Please be the iguana.*

"Another rabbit."

"Why does it always have to be something soft and fluffy?" I considered, silently glad it wasn't one of the puppies. Maybe eventually, it would be. I hadn't had time to figure out a legal way into her apartment.

"We just need the landlord to see she has pets, right?" Her eyes lit with mischief.

"Probably. They're not allowed in the building, so it would at least slow her down on whatever's going on."

"Are you free in an hour?"

"Sure," I said slowly, unsure what she had in mind. She didn't seem to want to tip her hand just yet. Maybe Sam was rubbing off on her, or maybe she just needed some excitement after being cooped up inside. I decided to let it be.

Suzy nodded and returned to her desk, picked up her phone, and tapped on it for a moment. Then, setting it down, she brandished a pair of glasses and slid them on decisively.

"Did you get glasses?"

"Sam bought them for me!" She lit up, tilting her head this way and that, modeling them for me. "They're blue-light glasses, to save my eyes from the computer screen."

"Cute and smart."

Satisfied, she nodded. "Is that the itemized expenses from Weston?"

"It is." I held up the paper I had been carrying. The edge had gotten a little wet from my drink, but it wasn't too worse for wear.

"Let's see how it compares, shall we?" Selecting a file from her drawer, she presented the bills Linda Collins had given us.

I crossed the room and handed it over.

"Hmm," she said, a finger trailing over each paper.

"What is it?" I bent to look.

"They're pretty similar."

"Crap." I had hoped it would have a lot more added fees.

"You haven't heard back from the doctor yet, have you?"

"Not yet. She said she'd call back today. If she doesn't call by lunch tomorrow, I'll try again."

"Could be they're just expensive."

"It's possible," I mumbled, heading into my office. Hopefully, I could get a little research in before whatever Suzy had planned.

Meanwhile, coming out of a retro ice-cream shop across town,

"This was the important stop you needed my help for?" Hillary took a lick from her mint-green dessert.

"Ice cream *is* important." Wyatt gave her a wink as they found an empty table outside to sit at. He scraped up a large spoonful of the dark-chocolate scoop from the cup in front of him. "And I couldn't just go get ice cream by myself. It's a social treat."

"It is?" She shot him a grin.

"It is," he said soberly, putting the spoon in his mouth. The rich flavor exploded on his tongue in chocolatey goodness as he studied the slightly nerdy, completely adorable gardener across from him. It was rare that he ran across someone he enjoyed spoiling more than himself. Sure, he was a nice guy, but he'd never made this much of an effort for a woman before. He'd never wanted to before Hillary.

"Then, I'm glad I got to help you with such an important errand."

"Me too."

Bells from the shop next door chimed. The man who walked out looked familiar, and he searched his memory for a recollection.

"Um, can you excuse me for just a minute, Hillary? I won't be long." Sticking his spoon in his cup, Wyatt stood to follow him to the parking lot. It was the bartender from Red. Mal wouldn't like what he had in mind. It was too risky, but he'd seen the look on the man's face when he'd caused the scene that let Mal slip into the back to plant the bug. He wasn't comfortable with what he was doing for Dessi. Not entirely. He was familiar with the feeling.

"It's James, right?" he said, slowly approaching the man, but keeping his distance so he didn't appear threatening.

James stopped and looked up. His expression darkened when he recognized Wyatt.

"It's alright." Wyatt held up his hands, keeping a light smile on his lips. "I don't want trouble. I just want a short word."

"Okay."

"Obviously, that evening was staged."

"Obviously."

"We both know who you work for."

"Everyone knows Fabian Dessi owns the speakeasy. He owns several businesses in town." James toyed with his keys.

Wyatt just raised an eyebrow. The bartender knew what he meant. He slid a card from his back pocket. "If you ever want to switch sides, it would be good to have an inside man."

"I don't think that's a good idea." He took a step back.

"Is what you're doing a good idea?" Giving the other man space, he went around him, sticking his business card under the car's wipers. "Call me if you change your mind."

Turning, he jogged back through the lot to his date, whose eyebrows were drawn over a pert nose adorned with a green dot of ice cream.

Chapter 18

"Are you ready?" Suzy appeared in my doorway, eyes vibrant with excitement.

"As ready as I can be for something totally unknown to me." I stood to stretch.

"You said you needed a way into the apartment."

"That's correct."

"I've got one." She spun away to gather her bag and keys, leaving me to follow her out the door. After pausing to lock it, she taped a little note to the door, saying we'd be out, and hustled me out of the building and toward the van waiting at the corner with a nervous-looking Brian inside.

"Hey, Brian." I walked up to his window.

"Hey, Mal."

"You good with this?" I waved at Suzy, who laughed me off.

"Yeah, we're just going into the building and walking by the apartment. That's right, Suzy, isn't it?"

"Pretty much." She wagged her head and climbed into the passenger seat.

"Works for me," I said, walking around the vehicle to take a seat in the back. She'd obviously left something out, but I trusted her. She was smart enough to be safe.

It was a short drive, and Brian parked in the lot behind the apartment. We all piled out and followed our fearless bookkeeper toward the door, her straight hair swishing back and forth with each step. She paused at the entrance.

"Mal, can you lead the way? Brian can bring up the rear; he's the tallest."

"Sure." I opened the door and entered. The first floor was nearly empty, with only one person at the end of the long hallway, walking to their apartment to enter. The landlord's door remained shut. "Anything else?"

"No." She pulled her bag off her shoulder to hold it in front of her chest. "Just stay close and walk in a single-file line. When we get to the apartment, hug the wall kinda close but keep walking. It's apartment 406, correct?"

"Yep, on the right," I said, heading towards the stairs as I watched Brian's lean frame bring up the rear, towering over Suzy's average height. Our feet called out a staccato on the stairs as we fell into a rhythm.

On the third flight up, our pace slowed. The fourth-floor door was directly in front of us. I opened it, walked through, holding it behind me for Suzy, and waited a beat before continuing, so they could follow closely. Number 400 was on my right, and I edged closer to that side so the wall was within a few inches of my shoulder like she had asked.

The hallway was clear, and I continued to 402. It was a good thing I trusted the friend behind me because as soon as my shoulder reached the door to 406, I heard a metallic scraping sound directly behind me, followed by a short hiss.

"Don't react," Suzy said in a low tone. A sharp intake of breath from Brian behind her was all I heard after that.

I braced myself but kept walking. Nothing happened. I wasn't sure if anything was supposed to. *Maybe I should have gotten more details.*

Just when we reached the end of the hallway and the adjacent stairwell, an alarm went off.

"Oh, no!" Suzy feigned a loud, surprised voice. "What's happening?"

Apparently, we were in the reaction part of her plan. Turning, I took in her eyes, large like saucers but full of mirth. Brian's eyes, which I could see over her head, were flicking back and forth, unsure what was going to happen next.

Doors started to open, their occupants pouring out into the hallway, confused and worried. Several remained shut; among them, number 406.

"Could be a fire," Suzy spoke loudly, moving back towards the apartment in question.

We both followed, curious to find out more. *What had she done?* But just as we reached the other end of the hallway, thundering footsteps preceded the emergence of the landlord onto the fourth floor. Gasping for breath, he took in the hallway, frantic to find the source of the disturbance.

"I think the sound's coming from there." My friend pointed a worried finger towards the door.

He lunged for it, fumbling with a large set of keys.

Suzy leaned in to Brian and me to whisper, "Lane's in class right now."

"How do you know?" my voice pitched low to match.

"Sam found her college class schedule online."

It took the landlord three tries to find the right one. He stopped to wipe his forehead before swinging the door open.

Right in the center of the living room sat a half-burnt incense stick. Shocked, I found Suzy's eyes, which were twinkling. It wasn't the solution I would have come up with, but it got us in.

Spinning back to the exposed room, I took in the space. Cages lined the wall, spanning the living room and dining room. Smaller ones were stacked on larger ones, all perfectly lined up. A plastic tarp sat under them, and air fresheners were placed at either end and elsewhere around the apartment. A fan sat near the front door, pointed away from it. Suzy had been lucky the incense stick hadn't rolled in front of the fan.

"What's going on here?" he shouted, taking in the rest of the room. "Someone call the police!"

"The police?" Brian asked from the doorway, where the three of us stood.

"Yes, she's broken her contract and will need to be evicted, but also, this doesn't look legal." He looked at us in confusion. "Does it?"

"It depends on what she's doing with them." I stepped inside to get a better look. Some of the animals had shaved patches of fur. I saw the big bottle of bleach I had knocked out of her hand, but alongside it were bottles of things I didn't recognize. Her kitchen was set up with all sorts of test tubes and beakers.

"Hey." The landlord stopped to take me in. "Don't I know you?"

"Yeah, I was considering moving here." I examined the items on the counter. "I brought my friends by to see the building. You're right. That's a good idea. This does look curious. Might be worth a call to the cops to find out what's going on here."

"Oh." He looked at my friends. "Yeah, can you call? I left my cell downstairs."

"Already dialing." Brian's long fingers tapped over his phone.

Suzy's face no longer wore the affected surprise. She grinned broadly back at me. Shaking my head, I pulled her out of the room. "The firefighters will be here soon."

"They'd have brought the cops regardless." She preened. "Saved by the fire alarm, yet again."

It was how she'd escaped from her captors months ago. Using hot water steam to set off an alarm in the back bathroom of the betting parlor where she was being held. Impressed, I nodded. She'd used what she knew.

It was a good idea. It wasn't entirely legal to set off a fire alarm, but it had worked.

The other residents gathered around to see what was going on. Brian didn't like the crowd and ushered us to a spot outside the stairwell to give us space while still being in view of the apartment to watch.

"So, why did you have Brian stand in the back?" I asked.

"He's taller." She shrugged. "Blocked the camera better from the rear."

Several minutes later, the place was swarming in uniforms. Firefighters and cops inspected the space, and a few broke out to ask those around us questions.

Just when the stir of people started to calm down, a thundering noise came from the stairs. Lane

Pollett emerged, arms wide in alarm as she pushed her way through the throng still surrounding her doorway.

"What's happened?" she stuttered.

A female officer turned away from the others to address her. "That's what I'd like you to tell us."

Taking a stumbling half step back, her head whipped right and left, her short dark hair fanning out around her. "Uh."

"Why don't you take a seat"—the officer gestured to the couch, her hand resting on her radio—"and tell me what's going on here."

Realizing she was out of options, Lane dropped down onto the cushion, heaving out a heavy sigh. "I was only doing labs."

"Please elaborate."

"Well, it's for class. I'm a student at the University of Chicago." She raised her hands like that explained everything. "The teacher refuses to hold effective labs to practice our chemistry. I had to find a way to get my answers."

"What kind of answers?"

"Toxic and caustic solutions. It's easier to validate the efficacy of a chemical neutralizer if I can accurately measure the caustic levels of the solution."

Suzy gasped next to me, her eyes flicking to the rabbits and chinchillas. They didn't look that bad, but I had no idea what she had done to them. I seemed to remember Sam had said she was a science major, but I never imagined anything like this.

"You do realize testing on animals is only legal in an approved testing facility?" The cop's composure hardened.

"It's so ridiculous." Lane rolled her eyes. "This is *science!* Besides, well-behaved women rarely make history."

"I think you're missing the point of that saying." She stood and tipped her head to another officer. "Read this woman her rights."

My cell phone rang as soon as we walked back into the office. Suzy headed to her desk to gather her things.

"Hey, Mal," Detective Rodriguez announced through my phone. "I have updates on the body."

"The body?" Still processing what we had found out at the apartment building, it took me a moment to switch gears.

"Calvin Meister. He's a local guy, got a rap sheet that would make Dessi blush."

"Any evidence to tie him to Dessi?"

"Not outwardly, but we've got the bullet. Should we get the gun, we'd be able to link him to the shooting."

Adrenaline spiked my system. All the signs were pointing to a little B&E in my future. This time, it was mostly due to panic and less to excitement, though, considering the person we were targeting.

"We could arrest his friends." His voice dropped, and sounds of shuffling indicated he was changing position. "We have enough corroboration of the sale with their photos and some audio, but if we do, it'll tip off Dessi. I think it's best if we work together on this one. Save the evidence and try for a bigger bust."

It's what I was hoping he'd say. Even so, I felt disappointed that I was having this conversation with him. It meant I had to deal with him on the case, possibly making concessions on my investigation. I also didn't like feeling grateful to the man who had betrayed me years ago.

There was also that.

"If we do this, Rodriguez, I call the shots."

Also, I wasn't going to keep him in the loop on everything we were doing. No freaking way would we get away with what we had planned, even potentially.

He waited a beat. "Okay. For now. But, Mal, if things go too far south, we're going to have this discussion again."

"Fair enough." I could use his help if things went south. And I'd be careful what I told him in the meantime.

"Let me know what you plan next."

"Sure will," I lied, ending the call.

"Everything go okay?" Suzy asked, standing by her chair, her bag still in hand.

"Yep. All under control. We now have backup at the department." I kept the rest of it to myself. "It's getting late. Why don't you head home?"

"Okay. Are you sure you're alright tonight?"

It would be my first night at my place in a while. Rhodes had already offered to let me stay at his place, but it still felt weird without him there. It was too new, I guess.

"Nah, I'm good. Promise."

"You sure? You could stay with us." She fiddled with her bag strap. "We have plenty of room."

"I'll be fine. Sam's got a tracker on my phone and my car. I'm sure he's got some way to keep an eye on me even when he's not around."

"That's true." She laughed, then caught my expression. "I mean, probably. Okay, well, promise to call if you need anything at all. And feel free to come by if you change your mind, even in the middle of the night."

"Will do." I bent to hug her. "Good thinking earlier today. Looks like you've got some investigative skills."

"Heck no." She waved her hands. "I'll leave that to you and Sam, unless it has to do with numbers or smoke."

"Still a little illegal, though."

She held up two fingers a hair's breadth apart, gave me a saucy little smile, and headed out to the Sentinel van waiting outside.

I walked back to my office, packed my laptop and notebook, scooped up my keys, and followed her lead.

Just as I was pulling my door shut, my phone rang again. Frowning, I set my bag on the floor to pick my cell out of the side pocket.

"Hello?" I said, not recognizing the number.

"Detective Malone?"

"Speaking. Who's this?"

"Doctor Sharon Niles, from Northwestern Hospital."

"Oh, hi! I'm glad you could return my call."

"The nurse explained what you were looking for," she preempted me. "I understand there are a lot of difficulties regarding patient care and insurance, especially in a nursing home, but I won't be able to give you any medical information for Mr. Collins."

Of course. "I understand, but I was just wondering—"

"I can't give you information on Mr. Collins," she interrupted me, "but I can give you information about the medical procedures and tests you detailed, from a strictly medical standpoint."

Interesting. Typically, I had to push a little to get that much help from medical personnel, HIPAA being so deeply entrenched into their training. It was a good thing, from a privacy standpoint, less so from an investigative one.

Sam had gotten what he could online, which wasn't much more than what Mrs. Collins had already provided me. Breaking into a patient's records was something even he felt uncomfortable doing. Of course, he'd been very clear that he *could* do it, just that he *shouldn't*.

It was nice to know even Sam had some morals when it came to privacy.

"That'd be great."

"Medically speaking, those tests aren't related to the testing procedure you described. Unless the patient has other underlying issues a doctor is looking for, they wouldn't be combined."

"Okay." My mind clouded with possibilities. Mrs. Collins had said Doug had a lot of medical issues. It was something I could follow up on. "That helps a lot, Dr. Niles."

"Can I give you a little advice, ma'am?"

"Yes. Please."

"Patients information is private, unless you have power of attorney, such as a caregiver or a loved one."

"Right."

"They could take a minute and call the hospitals to verify what tests are being run."

"You mean to say that those—"

"I'm not saying anything." She stopped me yet again. "I've just encountered a few issues in the past. It's not a bad practice to call and validate what you're being billed for with what's been performed at the hospital."

She was very carefully, indirectly, giving me a major clue. I read her loud and clear.

"I appreciate your help, Dr. Niles. And I'll pass along that advice to my client."

"Please do, Detective."

Hanging up, I stared at my phone. It sounded like I needed to have a chat with Mrs. Collins.

Chapter 19

Locking up, I considered going home to make dinner, but I couldn't remember what food I had in the fridge. I hadn't been there in the past three days, other than a short stop to get clothes. I considered running through Mariano's deli, but as I stood on the brick steps in front of my office building in the blissfully cooling evening air, my eyes drifted across the street. I had missed out on a proper coffee today. Since I knew good nutrition was important, I texted Jen to see if she was free for dinner, slid my phone into my back pocket, and headed across the street to feed my soul. If she was free, I could feed my stomach later.

Between the police office, the trip to Weston's, and the discovery at Lane's apartment, it had been a busy day. The scents of Grounds greeted me as I pushed through the door, blowing my concerns away. The place was starting to clear out as it edged toward the dinner hour, and I saw Mo behind the counter, refilling things and wiping down, prepping for the after-dinner crowd. Perfect timing.

At a coffee shop, these quiet moments between crowds were like magic. The baristas weren't stressed. The atmosphere was calm. You could ask for off-menu items and sometimes got to try new seasonal syrups and grounds. It was my favorite time to stop by. Because of that and getting to talk to the owner, who happened to be one of my closest friends.

Plunking down on a stool at the coffee bar, I hooked my bag under the bartop and propped my elbows on the solid wooden slab, resting my chin in my hands. My shoulders released whatever tension was still harbored in them. It had been a while since I just sat and chatted with Mo, I realized as I watched him buzz about behind the counter.

"How's it going?" he said, wiping his hands off, stuffing the end of the rag in his back pocket, and coming to stand in front of me. "Haven't seen you around this time of night for a bit."

"I've been busy with cases," I said, pushing my phone around on the bar.

"Just busy with cases?" He tipped his head.

"That, and I've been hanging out with Rhodes for the past few nights." How did he always know when something was going on?

"Ah." His eyes twinkled. "I guess that's going well, then?"

"It is." I twisted on my barstool.

"I'm glad to hear it, Mal." He put a hand on the counter. "Now, what's for dinner?"

Grinning, I looked up at the board. He always got me. "How about a Cafe con Miel?"

He gave a short nod and turned to the back counter to press the grinder button to shoot grounds into the coffee basket. Giving it a good tap, he used the tamper to compact the grounds into the perfectly pressed espresso puck.

My phone pinged. Jen was in.

"How's work?" Mo twisted the basket into the espresso machine, the stainless steel gleaming as it shook to come to pressure and shoot the pressurized water through the coffee grounds.

"Pretty good." I hooked my heels onto the bar under me. "I've got three things going right now."

"Including the ongoing job?" He raised an eyebrow, meaning Dessi.

"Yes."

"That's a lot."

"It is." I sighed. "Especially since one of the other two isn't paying."

He turned to look at me, surprised.

"Pro bono via Suzy."

It was all I had to say. He let out a short laugh and bent to retrieve milk from the cooler under the counter.

"That one's wrapped as of today, though. Well, nearly. I have to fill in the client."

"The nursing-home case still ongoing?"

"Yes, and I just had a break in it. I need to call the client to go further, though."

"HIPAA laws?" He smiled knowingly, glancing up from pouring the milk into the coffee, creating perfect latte art. After setting the cup down, he wiped his hands and picked up the cinnamon to tap it lightly over the top, before sliding the mug across the bar.

"Unfortunately." I sighed. "Or fortunately. I don't disagree with the laws, but it does add an element of difficulty while investigating."

"Agreed, on both accounts." He cleared his tools, dumping them in the sink to wash.

I wrapped my hands around the mug, taking a big breath of the coffee-and-cinnamon perfume rising from it. I lifted it and let the taste overwhelm my tongue. Yep, this was manna for my soul.

"Hey, Mo?" I asked when my thoughts drifted from the coffee back to the case.

"Yes?"

"What would happen if I was able to prove the nursing home was doing illegal things, billing for extra tests?" I was worried about exposing it. Not because they might be doing wrong, but because of the residents.

"That depends." He paused. "Did they run it through insurance?"

"Yes."

"That makes it worse. They'd not only be stealing from their tenants but from the insurance companies, which would be the government if they're billing Medicare, as a nursing home would."

"If they are, should the tenant sue?"

"They are entitled to, but the insurance company will as well. They may be able to get a refund for the money due them. It's really up to them."

"Will they shut down?" I looked at him over the steaming mug. My eyebrows creased.

"It's possible." He stopped, noting my worry. "You're worried about the others."

It wasn't a question, but I nodded regardless. There was already a shortage of nursing homes in and around Chicago. This was the only one Doug Collins had been able to get into without a waiting list.

"If they're not making enough money to handle the court cases and refund the money they stole, they will. Some people won't be able to leave, even with the reimbursement."

"Due to the shortage of homes out there."

"Exactly." He frowned. "Or someone else will buy it."

I nodded.

"Let me give you the name of a good lawyer. Just in case." He tapped the counter before walking away and disappearing into his office in the back. When he returned, he had a slip of paper with a name and number scrawled on it. "She specializes in medical cases."

"Thanks, Mo." I took the number and slipped it into an external pocket of my bag.

"How're things going with that ongoing case? Any leads?"

"We had one, but we'll have to chase it down more to get where we need to be with it."

He nodded. "You know these things can go upside down quickly."

"Oh, I know it."

"Watch who you talk to. A guy like him has ties in places we can't even imagine. Just be careful."

"I will." I lifted my cup to salute him. "Thanks for worrying about me."

He chuckled, and the bell on the door jingled, announcing a visitor.

"Are you having fun without me?"

Turning, I saw Jen, her chin-length blonde hair clipped back, revealing her high cheekbones. "Hey! You made it."

"Of course." She bent to give me a side hug before sliding onto the stool next to me. "I got out quicker than I thought. Alex had a case to work on late, so this worked out perfectly!"

"Can I get you anything?" Mo asked.

"No, I can't drink caffeine this late." She scrunched her nose.

I widened my eyes in mock horror. "We can't be friends!"

"I could get you an herbal tea," Mo offered.

"I'm good. We're going to grab dinner soon anyway, but thanks," she said.

I nodded, finishing my drink. "Mexican sound good?"

"Yes!" she said emphatically. "*All* the chips and salsa."

"Okay." I paid Mo, thanking him for the advice and friendship, and we walked out into the encroaching dusk.

"I heard about your bust today," she said, taking a right down the sidewalk. There was a Mexican restaurant just three blocks down. "Ropa vieja?"

I nodded, lifting my head to feel the breeze. "And, yes, it was quite the event. That place was crawling with cops."

"I was across town on another call. I was disappointed I couldn't make it." She kicked a loose stone on the sidewalk. "I can't believe all that was going on in that apartment. And that little college kid seemed so young to be doing something like that. How terrible."

"I know." It felt good to put an end to it.

"I mean, where's she going to go from there?" She held up her hands. "College and then jail? I hope she gets some help."

"Definitely." I tucked my hands in my pockets. "I just can't figure out how the little mad scientist got all that into the building."

"Apparently, she brought it all in disassembled and put it together in the building."

"Yeah, that makes sense." I looked at her. "But how'd she get all those pets in there?"

"She brought them in take-out boxes."

"What about the big ones? No way could she fit a chinchilla in one."

She blanched and leaned in. "Fried-chicken bucket."

"Ugh."

"Yeah. And she bleached any surface area they were around every day to get rid of the smell."

"I figured that much. I saw the containers on the ground. Who's got the case?"

"Alex." She beamed at me, deliriously happy. "He's still compiling all the evidence. There were a lot of testing documents."

"Are the animals okay?" I said, unable to shirk from the warmth of her smile. I was pleased she was so happy, even if it was because of a man who had brought me a lot of heartache.

"It seems so. For all her unremorseful ways, I don't think any of them were too badly harmed. They're at a local shelter now."

"Even the small ones?" That was surprising; most shelters only took dogs and cats."

"I'm not sure what they'll do with them, but yes."

"I might know someone who would take them on."

"That'd be great." She stepped onto the stoop of the restaurant and pulled the door open to release the smell of cumin and chili peppers. "Naahh-chos!"

She faked passing out in pleasure. Laughing, we piled in to fill our stomachs with corn chips, guacamole, and salsa.

"Detective Malone!" Brent's voice coming in through my phone sounded as though he was happy to hear from me.

I let the rubber band with a paper clip cleverly attached to it fly towards my open office door. It made a satisfying *ping*. *Ha!* Suzy's head appeared moments later.

Proud of myself, I put Brent on speakerphone and waved her in. She'd been anxious for me to call since I walked in the door this morning. "I have good news and bad news."

"Uh-oh."

I smiled. He was a good kid. "Lane Pollett has been arrested for performing illegal testing on pets she bought from your pet store."

"No!" I could hear the stress in his voice. "Are they okay? I shouldn't have let her have them. I should have stood my ground."

"Hang on." I stopped him. "They're okay. At least, I think they all are. When we get a list from the police, can you confirm the animals with your store records to see if they're all there?"

"Definitely."

"Thanks. It looks like she was doing some routine chemistry tests on them, but none of them looked to be worse for wear than a patch of shaved hair and a little reddened skin. They're at a shelter now, getting care from a vet."

"Oh, good." He breathed a big sigh of relief. "And she's been arrested, so she won't be back?"

"Correct. You saved them, Brent. Who knows what would have happened to them if it weren't for you."

"Oh, I, uh," he stammered. "'S not a big deal."

"Sure, it is. Those pets are free of her now. There's just one thing." I hooked the worm and sent it through the air. "We need to find homes for them. I was wondering if you could help me out with that."

"You want me to take them?"

"They've been purchased from the pet store." I gave him the option. "So, you could just place them back there for adoption, but I wondered if you'd take them on."

"I'm not sure I could keep them all."

"I figured as much." I glanced up to see Suzy grinning at me. "You could foster them, though. And since you care about them so much—fought to save them, in fact—you could create a Facebook ad to find them good homes. You could even screen the potential new owners."

"Huh. That's an idea." I heard his brain whirling.

"You could even create a foundation for pets in need. Offer to foster unwanted pets so they don't end up in the dumpster."

"I like that idea!" I could hear him get excited. "But I'm not sure I know how to do that. I mean, I can do the Facebook part, but not the paperwork part."

"Funnily enough, I've got a friend here who would be more than willing to help you out with that."

I watched Suzy wiggle with joy in her seat. "And you've already got a small donation for seed money, should you agree to do this."

"For real? That's amazing. I'm so glad I found you two detective chicks."

Suzy and I had to bite our tongues from laughing out loud at the kid.

"I'm glad you found us too. Together we were able to save some animals."

Telling him I'd give his contact information to the detective running the case, I hung up. I leaned back in my chair, propping my hands behind my head. "You've got your hands full for the next few months with that."

"Yeah." Satisfaction settled on her face. "I'm okay with that."

"Want me to grab pizzas again for tonight?" I asked, switching gears.

"The guys would probably form a riot if you didn't." Meaning the Sentinel Security guys.

"Good point. I'll place the order."

"And don't forget the olives."

I rolled my eyes.

"When are you meeting Linda?" she asked, having heard me call earlier that day.

"Tomorrow. Mr. Collins has a doctor's appointment today. She's stopping by so I can help walk her through the call to the doctor's office."

"Let me know if you need any help with that."

"Will do."

"Want a refill?" She stood to leave and gestured to my now-empty coffee cup.

"Always. Thanks."

Scrolling through my phone, I looked for Mantovani's Pizza. It would be strange stopping by without Marco there. Tapping my phone, I got an idea. I scrolled past the M's to the P's.

"Mal! Got another hot tip for me?" Paul Whitfield, content writer for the local paper, Insideonline, answered on the first ring. He'd helped me once before, and I'd thrown him a couple of good stories in return.

"I think so." I tapped my pen on the table. "But it has conditions."

"Hit me with it." His voice went serious.

"There's a hot new pizza place coming to town. I think you'll want to get in on their opening."

"What's hot about it?"

"It's called Envy. They make green pizzas with pesto sauces, not a marinara sauce in sight. They have a list of all the specialty basils they're using. All gourmet ingredients. Very fresh idea."

"Interesting. Give me more."

"They're exclusively using social media for marketing, and they're holding pop-up tastings around town. You have to follow them on social media to even know about them, let alone find out where they're going to be. The brick-and-mortar store doesn't even have an announced location yet. They're building up for a later reveal."

"That is fresh thinking. I like it. I'm in. Now, what's the condition?"

"The owner is an up-and-coming young entrepreneur, Marco Poggiali."

"Any relation to—"

"Yup. It's his son."

"Huh…" I could figuratively hear the wheels spinning.

"That's the condition. You have to keep the connection under wraps."

He paused. "Mal, it'll come out sooner or later."

"Later means he'll get a following based on his culinary capabilities and unique marketing strategy. If it holds off long enough, it might just get swept under the rug."

"Someone else could run a story on it."

"True, but you'd have already gotten the first hot tip. Get in right at the beginning. He hasn't even posted anything about the pop-ups yet; I've been watching for it. If you're waiting for it too, you'll get to be there for the very first one."

I listened to him ponder the angle through the phone lines. Then he suddenly said, "Green is the new gold."

I chuckled.

"Or something like that." He kept talking. "I've got to think on it for a bit."

"You think all you want. Check him out and see what you think. Give him good publicity. Just leave Dom's name off the article."

"Will do." His voice trailed off, and I could hear clicking. "I found him online. I'm going to do a little research on what he's posted so far. Talk to you later."

"What was that about?" Suzy asked, reappearing with the coffeepot.

Holding up my mug for her to pour, I smiled. I had a fresh cup of coffee and had already checked two things off my list for the day. Things were going well for once.

"Just taking care of a little detail."

Chapter 20

"Which one has the olives?" Sam poked through the pizza boxes, searching for his favorite pizza.

"You wanted olives?" I deadpanned, my mouth slightly ajar. But at the pained expression he sent me, I let out a bark of laughter. "Of *course,* I got you olives. Just keep looking until you find little black circles on the pizza."

Turning his mouth down at me, he kept opening boxes until his eyes lit up. Stacking three slices on his plate, he did a little jaunty dance to his place at the table, dropping his plate on it before sliding into his seat.

"Hey, Columbo." Carrying a tray of Suzy's cookies, Rhodes brushed by me, planting a kiss on my cheek.

Pleased by his open gesture in front of our friends, I shot him a smile. "I see Suzy's put you to work."

"Uh-uh," he disagreed, his mouth full of cookie. "These are all mine."

"I'll fight you for 'em," Wyatt piped up from across the room. He didn't look like he was entirely kidding.

"Gentlemen." Suzy waved her hands. "There's more where that came from! Let's get some real food in your stomachs before you fill them with sugar."

"Cookies are real food," Wyatt mumbled, snatching a cookie from the tray Rhodes sat on the table before loading four slices of pizza, stacked haphazardly across his plate.

Several minutes later, after our bellies were full and we were lulled into companionable silence, I brought up the agenda. "So. Ideas for next steps?"

Sam groaned, having eaten half of the olive-covered pizza. He ran a hand through his curling, in-need-of-a-cut hair. "I need a nap."

"You can nap after. I still think we should focus on finding the gun."

Rhodes looked at me, catching my gaze from his seat next to me. I knew he wasn't a fan of the idea. It was the most dangerous plan on the table.

"I could use the new guy." Wyatt snagged another cookie. "Name's Grady."

"Is he capable of undercover work?" I asked.

He just raised a shoulder. "That's up to him to prove. He knows the risks."

"But if we send him in there without knowing…"

"Can't use someone we know. Anyone else would have a record in the business. Traceable."

"But you trust him?" Rhodes turned to Wyatt, taking one of the few cookies left on the tray.

Wyatt's eyes narrowed on the remaining cookies. "Of course not."

"Then why are we even considering it?" Sam asked, confused.

"Even good people can be swayed," Wyatt elaborated. "But there are no obvious red flags."

"It's a calculated risk." Rhodes bit into the cookie. "But worth it."

"Exactly." Wyatt raised his own cookie.

"How are you going to get him in?" I asked. "Is he going to just go in looking for a job?"

"He could, but I'm working on something better."

"He'll be our inside man." Sam's eyes sparkled.

"Yeah," I drew out the word, not quite getting his meaning.

"This is so cool." He rubbed his hands together. "So, he's going to find out what Dessi's up to?"

"Yes, but I need to tell him what to listen for," Wyatt asked. "I don't want to show him our hand yet."

"Good idea." I thought. "Any big plans that are going down."

"That's a given." Wyatt waved a hand. "But it would likely be inner-circle knowledge, so…doubtful."

"There's a storage facility. He might be able to find out where that is. He could be keeping any kind of random thing there."

"Yeah, not only the guns they bought," Sam added. "Things we can use for evidence."

"Exactly."

"I still think we should get a better look at those wine barrels." He edged the corner of the pizza box up, searching for one more olive-covered slice, regardless of his full stomach. "My gut tells me that's where the guns are being stored."

"They actually make wine there, Sam. It's awful, but they do get shipments of grapes."

"Doesn't mean they're all grapes." He chewed a hunk of crust. "And what do they do with all the empty barrels?"

"The employees don't seem to know anything about it."

"Maybe they don't. Maybe even the winemaker is clueless about it." Rhodes sat up straight. "He could just know Dessi keeps storage in the back. He *is* the owner."

"It could be the storage facility they're referring to." Sam's eyes grew wide.

"Could be." I wasn't so sure. Why would they call it a facility?

"But if we find the guns…" Sam held up his hand, palm up. "We have him, right?"

Wyatt and I exchanged glances. "We'd have good evidence. We're building a big case, but it takes a lot of evidence if it doesn't tie directly to him. Finding the weapons isn't a direct tie. He's just on the deed of the building. We need to prove he knows they're there."

"To avoid what happened with Jeremy Jones." Sam's mouth formed a thin line, his eyes finding Suzy's across the table. "No, we need something more damning."

"We can still look. It's good evidence and not a huge risk."

"It's breaking and entry." Rhodes glanced at me.

"Mal and I can get in without a trace." Sam's eyes shined with pride. "We've done it before."

"Lickety-split." I high-fived my nerdy detective in training. "Except I probably wouldn't share it with anyone outside this room."

"Noted."

"So," I wrapped it up. "Wyatt's going to see where he can get with the new guy. And Sam and I do a little B&E. Everyone good with that?" I knew Rhodes didn't like it, but I also knew it wasn't as dangerous as going after the proverbial—*wait, was it literal?*—smoking gun.

Nods around the room marked everyone's agreement. Wyatt pushed away from the table and slipped the final three cookies into a napkin before tucking them into his front pocket.

"Are you going to start bringing Hillary around?" Suzy asked, causing him to stop in his tracks on his way to the outdoor dumpster with the pizza boxes.

He frowned. Obviously, he'd never thought about it.

"Does she know about what we're doing?" she went on.

"A little. Not everything." He reddened.

"If you decide to bring her in, you can tell her. We trust your instincts."

Considering it another moment, he gave an uneasy nod and headed towards the door in an awkward shuffle before stopping short. "Everyone good here?"

"We're good." I gave him leave.

Everyone else nodded, except Rhodes, who was balefully eyeing the empty cookie tray.

"Thanks for hosting us, Suzy," Wyatt said, finally looking directly at her. A slow smile spread across his face. "Thanks for everything."

Patting him on the shoulder, she winked at him and walked back to the table to clear it. Gathering glasses, she nudged Rhodes. "Follow me. I've got more."

Collecting plates, he followed her into the kitchen.

Meanwhile, in the cab of a white Range Rover parked in front of a house decked out with English roses,

"Sentinel Security," Wyatt answered his ringing phone. He didn't recognize the number.

"Wyatt?" a man's voice replied. Muted bar noises could be heard in the background.

"Speaking."

"This is James," his voice trailed off, lowering significantly. "From the other day."

"I remember." He checked his watch; it was getting late. He'd just dropped Hillary off, but Red was probably still open for business.

"I thought about what you said. You're right. I'm in over my head over here."

"It happens to the best of us, man."

"But I'm not sure what I can do. The man's got a big reach. I'm not sure it's smart for me to directly—"

"I don't need much," he cut him off before he spiraled too far. "Let's just start with one favor. You only do what you feel comfortable doing."

"What's the favor?"

"I have a friend looking for a job. Any way you could get him on staff?"

"Maybe," he replied thoughtfully. "He's always looking for more good guys. Any history in town?"

"None."

"That's good, actually. Does he have any experience bussing tables?"

"Bussing tables? Isn't that entry-level work?"

"Not with upscale restaurants or bars. Cynthia hates it when people break the glassware. We have all this vintage crap. It's cool, but thin as shit."

"He can." Wyatt smiled, writing his resume in his head. "What will they be looking for?"

"Tell him to keep his head down. Be quiet, listen, and follow orders to a T. Absolutely nothing disrespectful to women. No underhanded comments, nothing. Cynthia will toss him out before he gets a chance to settle in."

"He'll be exactly that. I'll coach him." He scratched a few notes on a notepad propped on his console. "One more thing."

"Yes?"

"Be careful what you tell anybody."

"I will. Thanks."

Unable to ignore the ding from my phone, I slid a hand out of the sheets to tip the face towards me.

"Do you need the light?" Rhodes asked quietly, his voice at a low timber. His chest vibrated against my back, pressed against his side.

I felt bad for waking him. "Sorry."

"It's okay. I was still awake."

Checking my phone, I saw it was from Envy, Marco's new pizza place. "Marco's first pop-up tasting is tomorrow."

"Where?" Rolling to his side, he wrapped an arm around me and pulled me close. He snuck a peek over my shoulder to see.

"He's going to post the location tomorrow."

"Short notice." Taking advantage of the position, he nuzzled into my neck, planting a few soft kisses on my hairline. He laid his head down behind mine, tucking loose strands of my curly hair down where they tickled his nose. "But it keeps people interested, I guess."

"I'm sure it will." Abandoning my phone on his bedside stand. I snuggled into his embrace, blissfully content with his show of affection.

"Wanna go?" His voice was muffled by my hair.

"Free pizza? Absolutely."

"Mrs. Collins is here," Suzy called out from her desk the following day.

"Great." I rose to greet her in the lobby, opening the door for her when she got to it. She paused to carefully step over the threshold. "How are you this morning, Mrs. Collins?"

"I'm doing well, dear. Thanks." She took my offered hand, patting it gently with the other. "And how are you doing?"

"I'm fine, thanks." I led her to a seat in my office. Suzy followed with the paperwork we had gathered and set the folder on my desk.

"You said you had news?"

"Yes, but I need your help for the next part. There's a possibility the nursing home is billing for unperformed expenses. I can't call the hospital to verify what's valid, but you can." I laid the previous few month's bills she'd provided out on the table.

"You think they'd do that?" The wrinkles in her forehead deepened, and she hovered a hand over her chest.

"We don't know. But I think it's worth checking, and if you make the call, I can ensure we get the right answers."

She nodded her agreement.

On her way out, Suzy shut the door to give us privacy. I set my phone on the desk between us and dialed the hospital's account information line before clicking the speakerphone button.

"Northwestern," a male voice answered.

"Good morning." I kept my voice cheerful. "I have Mrs. Linda Collins here today. I'm helping her with her and her husband's accounts. She'd like to go over a few past bills with you to make sure she got everything accounted for."

"I can only talk to her about her accounts unless she has power of attorney on her husband."

"I have a copy of it scanned in. Where can I email it?"

As he rattled off the email address, I typed it into my computer to forward the document.

"I've got it," he confirmed a minute later. "This only allows me to talk to Mrs. Collins, though."

"I understand." I nodded to Mrs. Collins. "You can ask him about these bills."

"Okay." Picking up the oldest bill, she looked to me for reference. I pointed at the first one in line. "February eleventh, I have a bill for lab work for a hemoglobin test."

"This year?" he asked, clicking noises echoing through my speaker.

"Yes, sir."

"That's strange. I don't see any record of that."

I nodded for her to go to the next item on her bill. Her eyes widened, and she moved her finger slowly down the paper to keep track.

We went through every medical item listed, me making small check marks beside the valid expenses. When we were done, about a third of everything billed had never actually taken place.

Thanking the account representative, I hung up and gathered the papers.

"What do we do now?" Mrs. Collins sat back in her chair, her hands folded in her lap.

I took a slip of paper next to my computer and set it in front of her. "You call this number. It's the contact of a medical lawyer I got from a friend. She'll help you out."

With shaking hands, she took the paper from my fingers.

"You'll need to notify the insurance company as well. They'll want restitution for what they paid on Mr. Collin's behalf. The good news is it'll free up some of that Medicare money once they know it's not real bills. But talk to her first, for advice."

"But what happens with Doug?" Her eyes were full of worry. "I'm not able to get in anywhere else yet. If we sue Weston, won't they kick him out?"

"That's why you'll want to talk to your lawyer before you do anything, but from what I understand, they can't just evict him."

"But what if they go bankrupt from all the illegal happenings?"

"There are several possibilities. That's why you need a lawyer."

"Okay."

"Make sure you talk to her first." I pointed at the paper.

"Oh, I will." She stood, her eyes glistening with unshed tears. "Thank you so much, Detective."

"It's my pleasure, Mrs. Collins." I walked around the table to take her hand and let her lean in for a hug. I lightly patted her bowed back.

Seeing us through my window, Suzy opened my door to offer Mrs. Collins a tissue and a paper cup of water.

"Oh, thank you." She accepted the cup, took a sip, and dabbed at her eyes with the tissue. "I'm going right over there to talk to this lawyer!"

"Good idea."

We waved as she left.

"So, they were adding expenses to the bill?" Suzy asked once we were alone.

"Yep. About a third of them. And what was left was overcharged in the first place. They're definitely more expensive than others in the area. Probably why they still have empty rooms."

"It's crazy there's such a shortage of homes.

You'd think a city like Chicago would have plenty of space."

"You'd think."

"They even ran the fake bills through her insurance?"

"I believe so."

She gave a low whistle. "That's insurance fraud, even more illegal. They're going to get into major trouble. I hope that lawyer helps her figure this out so Mr. Collins has a place to stay."

"Me too."

The Sambot, tucked in the corner between the filing cabinet and the brick wall, lit up, Sam's face filling the screen. He had on a yellow-and-black blocked Star Trek shirt.

"Hey, babe." Suzy waved.

"Hey, yourself, Sweetcheeks." He blew her a kiss, virtually speaking. "I thought we could talk about tonight's felonious ingress."

"Word of the day?"

"Yes!" He lit up.

She contemplated it, one finger to her chin. "I like it. Sounds less illicit."

"That's another good one," he said, wagging his eyebrows appreciatively.

"Thanks." She made a sassy dip.

"Well, let's get working on it, then." I broke their chain of attention. We'd be here all day if I let them continue hashing back and forth.

I headed into my office, the Sambot on my heels. As I sat in my chair, I noticed Suzy hung back in the lobby. Leaning around my desk, I raised my voice, "You aren't coming?"

"Nah." She wheeled over so I could see her. "I've got to bill Mrs. Collins."

Guilt crept into me. "Should we be doing that?"

"Of course, we should, and we will." She tipped her head to look at me over her blue-light glasses, the picture of a youthful granny giving me a dressing down. "You've performed a service, which in turn, will be saving her a lot of money. She'll get her money back; it just may take a while."

"True."

"It'll be okay. Besides, you don't need me for tonight's planning, and I don't need to know the felonious details." Done with what she had to say, she scooted back to her desk.

Chapter 21

Meanwhile, in a smelly, trash-filled alley between two tall buildings,

"A busser?" Grady asked.

Wyatt handed him a resume he had previously prepared. "Read it. Get familiar with it. You worked as a busser at a fancy older restaurant downtown."

"If they check it?"

"They won't." He shook his head. And if they did, he had that covered. James did all of Cynthia's grunt work. "Just keep your head down and follow orders."

"I can do that."

His medium build, blondish-brownish hair, and average features made him perfect for this sort of work. He was completely forgettable. Wyatt hoped he'd be trustworthy. He'd love to have him on his team.

"Anything specific I'm listening for?" he asked almost too intently, too interested. The kid would have to take this more seriously if he was going to work.

"Just basic intel. Give me a call the next morning, assuming you don't screw this up and actually get hired. Report out anything you hear." He gave him a pointed look. "No matter if it sounds interesting."

Grady glanced up at him, raising his chin. "I got it."

"Cynthia is smart and successful. She'll be able to see through any bullshit you throw her way. You'll be dropped quicker than shit," he warned him.

"I got it," he repeated more firmly, his eyes darkening.

Wyatt grabbed his collar and twisted it in his fist. "Don't flirt. Don't try to get her to like you." Grady's eyes widened, so he let him down slowly. "The absolute picture of servitude."

"Will do." He swallowed audibly, shifting his eyes away.

"Head down. Zero sign of interest. Less words. More work."

"Got it." The younger man shuffled his feet.

Maybe this would work after all.

Watching the kid walk away, he climbed back into his vehicle, dialing James.

"Hello?" a sleepy voice answered.

"My guy's coming in tonight. Name's Grady."

"Okay."

"He's been prepped and is ready with a backstory of working for Donnelly's a while back."

"That's a good idea. I'll vouch for him if needed."

"Do it subtly. Indirectly."

"No kidding."

"No, I mean, he doesn't know about you. He's new."

"Gotcha. Still getting proved out."

"Exactly." He paused. Now that he'd gotten him involved, he may be able to coax a little more out of him. "Ever heard anything about a storage facility?"

"I've heard him mention one," he said slowly. "But I'm not sure where it's at."

"But is it an actual facility, not just storage somewhere?" he pushed a little, unsure if the guy was telling the truth or covering.

"I think so. Look, I honestly don't know."

"No problem, man." He let him off the hook. "And thanks again for helping out with Grady. With any luck, we can clean up these streets a little."

"Sure thing," he said, then paused. "But I can keep an ear out."

"That would be great, James."

Bingo.

The glow of Edison bulbs strung through trees in the Printers Row Park lit the pathways that wove underneath. Rhodes and I had taken the Brown Line to Belmont, then the Red Line to Printers Row so we wouldn't have to find parking. It was nice to be on foot, walking the streets of downtown Chicago, more like a tourist than a resident of one of the suburbs.

His hand tightened around mine as we crossed under the trees, the ambiance setting a romantic mood. A guitarist sat on the edge of the old fountain, a wide-brimmed fedora on his head and leather straps on his wrists, strumming out acoustic versions of modern songs.

"This is nice," Rhodes said, taking in the area.

"It is. And it's the perfect weather to be outside tonight."

The green space to be hosting the pop-up tasting was on the smallish side, and I was surprised by the turnout. Spying Marco through a curtain of leaves from the tree between us, I watched him gesture to a few other workers, who were all decked out in vibrant-green aprons emblazoned with a large basil leaf and the word "Envy" scrawled across the top in black writing. "CRAFT PIZZAS" was written in small block letters underneath.

Each had a flat box in hand with the same logo printed on the cardboard. As they moved through the crowd, I watched them open them to reveal single-serving pizza slices rolled from the crust to the tail. The tip was pinned in with a green toothpick to form like a pizza croissant. The sides were striped dark green from the pesto, and bits of white cheese oozed out. They looked delicious, and the scent of basil permeated the air. It seemed stronger than what the pizza boxes would be giving off.

Looking around, I noticed a dark-green insulated box tucked behind a tree, almost obscured in the dusk. Beside it sat a fan with rows of fresh basil tied to the wires. Appreciating Marco's ingenuity, I approached a server. He handed Rhodes and me each a rolled-up pizza on a green napkin before moving on to the next person milling around.

I spied Marco across the park, talking to Paul. He stuck his hands into his pockets and danced from foot to foot, full of nervous energy as the columnist peppered him with questions, his cameraman taking footage of the event.

Not worried that the writer would leak Marco's heritage, I turned away, leaving him to figure his way through this media encounter. It would be the first of many if his attention to detail carried over to his final storefront.

Moving to wrought-iron benches stationed at the edge of the park, we sat down to bite into our reimagined pizzas. Basil and garlic exploded on my tongue, olive oil and baked cheese followed up, and lastly, earthy, meaty mushrooms finished out the flavor. An appreciative moan came from the fire captain next to me. Glancing over, I watched him chew on the yeasty hand-tossed crust while nodding his head at me.

"Good crust, too," he eventually said.

"Very," I agreed. Nice and chewy. It was one *helluva* pizza. I had to give it to Marco; he'd done his homework on both food and marketing.

Wiping his hands after we had finished our tasters, Rhodes looked around. "I'm still hungry."

"Me too."

"Want to walk a bit, see what we find?"

"Sounds good to me." I stood, slid my hand into his, and we walked up the street. I had another couple of hours before bed. I had to turn in early tonight to get ready for a 3 a.m. rendezvous with Lola's video-slots bar.

Walking by Marco, I raised a hand in greeting. His eyes lit up when he saw me, then he glanced back at the reporter before returning to give me a sideways smile that apologized for being busy. I waved him off, understanding the need for good publicity.

In between jotting down notes, Paul also noticed me walking by. He nodded, his eyes lighting up at Rhodes and me walking hand in hand, then he turned back to Marco. The pizza maker's eyebrows drew together as he pieced the fact that Paul and I knew each other. His face relaxed, and one corner of his mouth ticked up in mirth.

Unable to help myself, I gave him a little wink as I walked on by.

Meanwhile, in a glitzy, art deco-inspired speakeasy,

"Tables are filling up, and I've got my hands full at the bar," James said, entering Cynthia's office in the back room, bar rag in his hands. Wyatt's guy was sitting across the table from her. At least, he figured it was Wyatt's guy. "We're going to need help on the floor to clean up in the next half hour. Want me to pull someone from the line?"

"Yeah, they won't like it, but they'll manage." She frowned, not looking up from the resume in her hands. "I'm working on getting more help right now."

"Another busser?" He leaned against the doorjamb, feigning interest. "Any experience?"

"Donnelly's." She glanced up, her brow raising at the bartender, lifting the black twenties-style headband where it adorned her forehead. White feathers spread out of it on one side, contrasting starkly against her black hair. "Ever heard of it?"

"Yeah." He nodded, then addressed the man. Definitely Wyatt's guy. "Was Hanley still there when you were?"

"Hanley." He huffed. "Yeah."

"He's a bear to work for, isn't he?"

"Totally." Wyatt's guy blew out a sigh. Then, noticing Cynthia's frown, he raised his shoulders. "But I don't mind hard work. It helps the day go by."

"Hanley ran a few businesses around Chicago when Donnelly's was open." James raised a suggestive eyebrow at Cynthia to imply there was more he wasn't saying, giving her the impression he'd had his hands in some shady dealings. He hoped she would take it as an indication that the guy could keep his mouth closed.

"Why did you leave?" Cynthia narrowed her eyes, watching the young man intently.

"For the job in Indiana," he answered, nodding to the resume. "My sister needed some help with her son, so I moved there for a few years to help out."

The story sounded true. Either the guy was a good liar, or he'd done his job at creating a believable backstory.

"I thought the bar was full." She suddenly turned to him.

"Yeah." He shook his head, dropping his arms. "I'd better get back."

"You wait here," she directed to the new guy, then turned to James. "Check in on things, pour a few drinks, then get him new-hire paperwork."

James nodded and turned away, waiting to see if she had any more orders.

"When can you start?" he heard her ask the kid.

"Anytime."

"Then you start tonight." Standing, she brushed past him. "I'll be on the floor."

"Is Sam picking us up, or are we picking him up?" Rhodes asked from the doorway of his bedroom.

Looking up from repacking my duffle bag on his bed, my head shot back in surprise.

"Us? We?" When had he gotten the idea he was coming with us?

He crossed his arms, his jaw clenching together at my reaction. "This isn't a simple stakeout, Mal. You're breaking and entering a building. Illegally."

Feloniously, I thought, but I wasn't in the mood to correct him. "I know that."

"You're not going without me. It's too dangerous." He shook his head as if it was decided.

Raising my eyebrows, I set my teeth. "Oh, I'm not, am I?"

I'd been doing jobs like this without him for a long time; I doubted he'd appreciate it if I inserted myself into his jobs, no matter how dangerous they were.

He crossed the room, stopping a foot in front of me, almost too close.

I stood straighter, matching his height, but not his width. If he thought he was going to intimidate me, he had another thing coming.

Tension ticked across his face, then he blew out a shuddering breath, his expression softening. He simply said, "Please."

It took the wind out of my sails, seeing the pain and fear behind his eyes. He dropped his gaze, raw and burdened with the blatant need to protect me.

Reaching up, I touched his face.

"You have work in the morning." My voice, softer than before, made him meet my gaze, searching for my understanding. "And if you have calls all night, you'll have two nights in a row without rest."

"I'll sleep when I'm dead." He kicked up one side of his mouth in levity, but his eyes still held a silent plea.

"Extra backup could be a good thing," I said after a beat.

"I can drive," he offered, obviously struggling to reign in his control. "Keep watch from the truck."

"Sam's driving, but you can keep watch from the car. I'm sure Sam won't mind if you come along."

Relief flashed across his face. Pulling me close, he wrapped his arms around me. "I'm sorry. I'm trying to let go and not take command. It's your scene, not mine, and you're doing great. Honest… It's not easy, but I'm trying. Please be patient with me."

"I know," I said, enjoying the feeling of being engulfed in his arms. He pulled away a little too soon, and I looked into his eyes, trying to be as open as he was. "Just ask next time, instead of assuming."

"You're right. I should have."

"Otherwise, it makes you sound like a jerk," I said, even though I knew he'd only acted out of fear.

"Fair enough." The grin he shot me met his eyes this time. "Meet me halfway?"

"Definitely."

The stress relieved from the room, he sat on the bed to watch me check through my pack one final time.

I hefted the crowbar, giving it a playful swing with my wrist. "I'm gonna need this baby tonight."

"Which is your favorite tool?" he asked, inspecting the items.

Wrinkling my nose, I scanned them. "My bolt cutters, obviously." I pointed. "Those have gotten me out of more than one scrape. Heavy, able to cut a padlock or through a bar. Plus, they double as wire cutters if I need a quick exit."

"Move in with me," he suddenly said.

Freezing, I looked up, shocked and, to be honest, terrified. I'd only stayed over four nights. It's not like we'd been dating for months.

"I know you're here right now because it's safer to be together than you staying in your apartment on your own."

It wasn't the only reason.

"But I like having you around." He shifted on the bed to face me better. "I'm awfully fond of you, you know."

"Me too." I meant it. I just wasn't ready for this. "It's fast."

"I know." He picked up my baton. "It's scary being in a relationship with someone as independently strong as you. But I have no doubt it's right, this thing between us. I think it's good for me to get a break from being in control all the time."

"Oh, I can take control." I gave him a wicked smile.

He laughed out loud. "I'm okay with that, too." He paused, fiddling with the baton, then set it on the bed. "In the past, it was all too easy to find people who were more than happy for me to take over. But now that I've had you in my life, that's not what I want. I want a real relationship, the give and the take. The messing up and learning to grow…You're more than I ever hoped for, Mal. And I'm ready to take this to the next level. When you are."

I nodded, adding the baton to the duffle bag. "I'm not here just because of Dessi, you know."

He raised his eyebrows.

"I'm here because I want to be." Zipping the bag shut, I sat down on the bed. I was set. "I like being with you too. It surprises me how much. But I'm not sure I'm ready to move in. I might still need my space." Which was funny, because he worked a twenty-four-hour shift every third day, but he knew what I meant. Moving in was a big deal, giving up an exit plan for whenever I might need it.

And I *always* had an exit plan. Then again, I'd also never considered living with anyone.

"The offer stands," he said, rising to his feet.

"Thanks," I said, meaning it. I set my alarm for 2:30 a.m. and pulled the sheets down to climb into bed. I needed a little rest before our little excursion. And a few minutes of quiet to let myself think through the idea of living with someone.

Chapter 22

I jolted awake when my phone went off. Groggy, I searched for it on the side table to silence it, only to realize it was Sam, not my alarm. And it was only 2 a.m.

"Sam? It's a full hour before pickup time."

"Someone's in your apartment."

"What?" I sat up straight.

"What's wrong?" Rhodes followed suit.

"The motion detector caught it when they broke in."

"Someone's in the apartment," I reiterated aloud, tossing the covers off, jumping out of bed, and stuffing my feet into my waiting boots. "Call the cops."

"Already on their way."

"Me too." I ended the call before grabbing my bag and my baton, and clipping it to my waistband.

"I'm coming." Rhodes paused mid standing and turned to look at me. "Can I come?" he stumbled over his words, twisting to get the right ones out.

"Abso-freaking-lutely." I planted a kiss on his head and jogged into the bathroom for a quick mouthwash gargle, and I was ready to leave.

Red and blue flashing painted the road outside of my apartment. After parking along the street, Rhodes and I piled out, jogging to meet the cops gathered on the lawn. I bit back a groan; Rodriguez was on site.

"Malone." He broke from the other officers to approach us, glancing back and forth between Rhodes and me arriving together in the middle of the night. "The intruder was gone by the time we got here."

"Shit," I ground out, turning to scan the neighborhood as if I could find the perpetrator in the shadow of the night.

"It doesn't look like they took anything," George said, flicking through a notepad. "No drawers were opened, and nothing looked damaged."

Well, that was something. But it might also mean what they were after wasn't there.

Me.

"Did Sam get a visual?" Rodriguez asked.

"I don't think so." I struggled to remember. "I think he just had a motion detector installed."

"You don't think so?" he questioned me, causing Rhodes to stand close beside me.

"He handles my security." I left it at that, walking away from the detective to see for myself.

"Mal." Jen broke out of the crowd of officers to rush over to me and pull me close. "I'm so glad you're okay."

I patted her on the back. "I'm good, Jen."

She pulled back to look at me, her eyes strained in worry. She shook her head lightly, her shoulders drawing in as she looked back at my building. "I'm glad you weren't home."

"Me too." Giving her shoulder a reassuring squeeze, I stalked towards the throng at the door.

"I don't know if they're done in there," George's voice raised to stop me.

"They're done." I knew I'd get more from whatever Sam likely had than from these guys. Whoever had done this was no longer here, and they'd already had a chance to look the place over.

My phone rang. It was Sam.

"Gone by the time we got here." I paused halfway across the lawn to tell him what he wanted to know.

"Double crap."

"Exactly. Did you get a visual or just a notice that there was someone here?"

He lowered his voice. "Well, I'm not on speakerphone, am I?"

"No."

"After the heat-signature reader I had on your roof picked up the intruder last time, I replaced your doorbell with a motion-detecting camera. There's one on the sliding glass door on the back, as well. I didn't want to break into your apartment to set anything up, so I settled for the exterior."

"I think I would have noticed if you'd have replaced my doorbell with a camera one."

"I didn't," he said smugly. "I added a camera to the existing one. It's custom."

"I feel so secure," I said, only half serious since he had set up surveillance devices without my knowledge. Well, I kinda knew…

"Thanks!"

Eye roll.

"So, there's a video?" I prodded him along, pushing past an officer at the door to stomp up the stairs.

"Sort of," he hedged. "It's dark, and he's got a hood pulled over his head."

"He?"

"I mean, whoever it is. Kinda looks like a he, but I can't be sure. It's grainy, and all I got is a bit of a nose."

There were officers in front of my doorway, still inspecting the bolt lock. Had I been home, I'd have had the swing bar lock in place. That would have stopped them. Unless they had come prepared with bolt cutters. *See? They had so many uses.*

"This your place?" asked an officer I didn't know.

Nodding, I bent to inspect the lock. Light scratches, only visible with the flashlight they were shining on it. Definitely picked, but not by an amateur.

"Hey, Mal," Stevens said, his face full of concern. "Doesn't look like they took anything."

Rhodes laid a supportive hand on my shoulder. I reached up to touch it in thanks, sliding through the doorway to get a look around. I raised the phone back to my ear. "Whoever it was definitely got in, right?"

"Unfortunately," he confirmed. "That's all I know for sure."

"Thanks. I'm going to look around here for a minute. I'll meet you as planned."

"Are you sure?" he stammered.

"Definitely." My mouth curled down in anger. "He's not getting away with this."

Turning in a circle, I took in my surroundings. I didn't leave a lot sitting around, so it was easy to see what had been moved. Not a lot, really. And most of it was probably by the police checking things. I walked to my bedroom, pausing at the light switch. I could have been in here when he entered. The thought of it sat in my stomach like bad food.

I could feel Rhodes come up behind my back, giving me space, but still nearby, offering support. Leaning slightly into his chest, I let him take the weight for a moment. He wrapped an arm around me, and I was grateful for it. I knew if I stayed in this position much longer, engulfed in his comfort, I would break down, so I pushed the feeling down, at least temporarily. Flicking on the light switch, I stepped into the room, surveying it with a practiced eye. I'd have time to work through the emotions later.

While sliding drawers open, I ran a hand over the comforter. It was slightly rumpled. I hadn't left it that way. The contents in the drawers looked to be out of order. Someone had rummaged around. I shut them and moved to the closet. A couple of boxes looked to be touched, so I pulled them out. Nothing appeared to be taken, but the invasion of my privacy, especially of my closet, gutted me.

I shut the door, turning to see Rhodes watching me intently.

"I'm okay," I said. "For now."

He nodded, following me out of my room.

"Are you guys done here?" I asked. They were packing things up and heading out the door.

"Yeah," Stevens said. "Detective Rodriguez is writing up the report right now. You can get a copy from him."

I locked the place back up, even though it felt pointless, and made my way out into the oddly bright night lit by flashing lights. I knew Sam would sweep the place for bugs for me.

"Anything taken?" Rodriguez asked.

I shook my head. "Not that I can tell."

He glanced at the man at my back, then flicked his eyes back to me. "You're not staying here, right?"

"Nope."

It looked like he wanted to say something, but he kept his mouth shut. Smart. Instead, he handed me a sheet of paper. "Your police report if anything comes up missing."

Taking it, I scanned the paper as he went back to his car.

"You okay, Mal?" George said, walking up. He put a hand on the side of my arm.

"Yeah, just not having the best night." I gave him a flat smile.

"I can't imagine how that feels." He shook his head sadly. "We see this all the time, but it always strikes me as being so incredibly violating."

He was right. That was how it felt. "Thanks, George."

"Michalski," Rodriguez said, reminding him they were at work.

"Gotta go pack up." He patted me on the back and headed to follow the impatient detective.

I spotted Jen standing with Stevens. It looked like they were going over his findings. Raising a hand, I let her know I was heading out.

Getting back into Rhodes' truck, I sat silently, staring at the report in my hands. We needed to get moving if we were to make it back to his house to meet Sam by three o'clock, but he hadn't yet started the engine.

I looked up. "We should go."

"Do you want me to call in a vacation day for tomorrow?"

"No, I'll be alright."

"Will you please consider staying at Suzy's tomorrow night?" he said, watching me.

As I opened my mouth to argue, I thought about staying in my apartment the following night by myself and halted. That swirling pit in the bottom of my stomach still hadn't gone away. In fact, it felt more like melty, overly wilted lettuce. I shuddered. Maybe I didn't have to be so incredibly stubborn.

"Or at least stay at my place?" he went on since I hadn't said anything. "It doesn't have to mean you've made a decision about moving in. It'd just be temporary."

"Okay."

"Honestly?"

"Yeah. I'll stay at Suzy's for the time being while you're at the station."

He drew in a long breath, then let it out.

Reaching out, I slid a hand onto his thigh as he turned the key in the ignition. "Let's go."

By the time we'd pulled back onto Rhodes' street, we saw a little silver sedan parked in the driveway. We drove up to see Sam sitting in the front seat.

I opened my door. "Did you rent a car?"

"Nope." He grinned, showing all his teeth. "It's Suzy's. It hasn't gotten out of the garage in months. I thought it'd be less conspicuous than the Tesla."

Probably.

"I'll go grab my bag." I jogged up the steps to meet Rhodes, who was unlocking the door for me.

Settled into the passenger seat of Suzy's car, I struggled to keep my focus on the night's task.

"We're just going in, checking the wine barrels, and looking for any other storage rooms inside," I counted off our goals.

"And taking photos!" Sam said.

I held up another tiny camera from the bag on my lap.

"And not getting caught," Rhodes offered from the back seat, where he had elected to sit so Sam and I could talk. "How do you know they won't have any video surveillance?"

"I'll scan for that." Sam waved it off.

"Didn't you say it was harder to scan for if it was hardwired?"

"True. They may be old school." He paused to consider the idea. "We'll take long-distance photos to inspect the area first, see if we can locate them. Then we'll go in and clip wires if necessary."

"I've got that part. I've done that before." Giving him a half grin, I added, "Old school."

"And we're sure the timing is good?" Rhodes asked.

I wasn't sure if he meant because I had just had my apartment broken into or due to the time of night. Maybe it was a little of both.

"They quit serving liquor at one, and the video slots shut down at one-thirty," Sam rattled off. "The workers should have cleaned up and left by now."

"It'll be secured," Rhodes went on.

I wasn't sure if he was trying to dissuade us or if he was just running through details since he hadn't been on the call when we planned it.

Sam flexed his fingers and wagged his eyebrows. "I've got that covered."

True to his word, minutes after we'd arrived and scouted out the security, he was bent over the opened electronic keypad. Wires clipped into it from a handheld device he was busily tapping on with gloved hands. A single streetlight hovered a block away, casting us in a shadow at the rear entry of the building.

"That should do it," he said, cutting an eye to Rhodes, who stood behind us. A light bar lit up green on the keypad. Without taking his eyes off Rhodes, he leaned into it and turned the handle. It opened with ease.

"Show-off." I rolled my eyes, taking a long stride in front of him to edge the door open. I scanned the ceiling and saw no other wires. "There's a security pad inside. The alarm is set."

"I've got it." He pushed past, pulling another device from his black utility backpack. It had a card attached to a cord. Sliding it through the reader on the side of the pad, he punched numbers into the keypad

until the readout changed to
"****DISARMED****READY TO ARM."

"We'll be quick." I turned and planted a kiss on Rhodes. "Let me know if you see anything. We have our phones."

He grabbed my arm to give it a squeeze. "Be careful." Then he jogged to the sedan to wait for us.

I caught up with Sam, then I trailed behind. He had his headlamp back on since we knew the place was empty. There weren't any cars in the lot, and I doubted they'd have the alarm set if anyone was still here.

We were in the storage room, having entered through the same doorway where the delivery drivers had wheeled in the grape barrels.

"I think there's something back there." He pointed into a darker corner, his headlamp shining on boxes and, after that, barrels stacked in a corner.

Hurrying to the barrels, I tried the clasps on them, my own gloves firmly in place. They slid off easily. Damn, I would have liked to use my crowbar.

Sam gasped when I lifted the lid and he cast his light into it, searching the illuminated center of an empty barrel.

"Crap."

"There's more." I reattached the metal ring, edging it back down where it had been and moved to the next. The four stacked in the corner all turned up empty.

Sam's watch beeped. "It's been five minutes."

"We need to split up." I cast my flashlight into the dark storage area. There was more here than I had anticipated, with a wall splitting the space in half. "You want the boxes or to keep going?"

"I'll take the boxes." He set to work, going through them.

Keeping my light trained on the floor, I worked my way to the other door. It had a bar across it, secured with a padlock. Old school. I liked that.

Bending down, I slipped a few metal lock picks from a case in my bag, my flashlight set between my teeth. Holding down the lever with one pick, I used the other to slide the tumbler over and around until it clicked. Bingo.

After I stowed my tools away, I removed the lock, flipped the bar open, and hooked the padlock back into the empty ring, letting it hang while I explored. Shining the light into the room, I saw it looked very much like the first, with more wine barrels stacked against one wall.

Maybe this was it. Placing my gloved hands on the closest one, I gave it a light shove. It didn't move. My heart pounded in my chest. This one wasn't empty.

It could be grapes, though.

As I tried the metal strap across the top, it didn't budge. *Crowbar time.* I dropped my bag onto the floor, pulled out my tool, and set to work. By the time I got the strap off, a light hit the barrels next to me.

"Nothing out here."

"May be something in here." I wiggled the wooden top, lifting it.

Sam's headlamp landed on the inside before I could swing my flashlight around, and it glinted off metal. Three Glock 19s sat on top of straw. Shifting through it, I could feel more weapons stored below. I bet all of the barrels were full of guns.

"We found the firearms from the warehouse sale," he whispered, amazed.

I nodded, almost surprised we'd caught a break. Bending, I sat the lid down and grabbed my camera. "Let's take the lid off two more and get good photos of the guns. We don't have much time."

"Are you sure we can't just call the cops?" Sam shot me a hopeful look.

"Sure, we can, if that's what you want to do." I stopped for a minute. He had more skin in this game than I had. "It might set Dessi back, but I doubt it'll put him behind bars."

Sam's face scrunched up, his eyes narrowing. "I hate that man."

"Me too." I nodded, getting to work on another barrel lid. "Let's get this evidence secured and to the cops. We'll eventually get enough to shut him down."

Setting his teeth, he tore into the other band, shoving it back and forth to maneuver it up and over the barrel.

Moving quickly, I took hundreds of photos of the number of barrels and the exposed guns. I even got the serial numbers of a handful on top.

My phone dinged, sending my heart racing. My fingers reflexively went to my baton, clipped to my side.

"What is it?" Sam asked, freezing, hands stretched over a barrel to reset a lid.

Clicking my phone, I sighed in relief. "It's Rhodes. He's just seeing if we're alright. It's been twenty minutes."

Sam slid to the floor, sitting flat on it, his legs straight out in front of him.

"Are you okay?" I rushed to him, kneeling on the cement.

"Yeah." He panted. "It just scared me."

"Let's get out of here." I stood, slinging the bands over the barrels and hammering them in place with the end of the crowbar.

By the time I was done, Sam had gathered himself and was ready to exit. I scooped up my bag, slung it over my shoulder, and retraced my steps. I swung the door shut behind me, locking it, and scooted a couple of boxes back where they had been before we entered.

Sam punched a few keys, and the alarm read "ARMED." As we exited, we pulled the door shut, and he removed any vestiges of our entry, removing the wires and screwing the box shut. He carefully set his tools into his backpack, zipped it up, and slung it over a shoulder.

Backing away, I gave the building one last look. I hoped Dessi wouldn't move them before we could get him in a compromising position with the guns. Maybe we could catch him picking them up. If Sam set up surveillance of the street, we could monitor activity.

"Everything good?" Rhodes got out to open my door for me.

"Yeah." I slid in. "Let's go."

Sam got in, handed me his bag, and pulled back into the night.

"I hate to ask," Rhodes said. "But were they there?"

"Yeah," I breathed out, still in shock. I twisted in my seat. "We found them. Guns from the sale."

"Shit," he breathed out. "You got pictures?"

"Yeah." Sam's eyes focused on the road. "And we're going to take them to the cops tomorrow."

Chapter 23

I dropped my bag on the floor in front of Suzy's desk.

"Good morning." She looked up from her computer, then leaned over to see my bag. "Where's my coffee?"

Rolling my eyes, I collapsed in one of the lobby chairs, setting my little succulent plant on a side table. No way I was leaving that baby.

"Wait, is that for? Does this mean?" she went on, her eyes as wide as saucers. "Oh, thank the Lord you're not staying alone."

I pushed off my chair and to my feet. "I'll go get your coffee."

"No, no, no." Leaping up from her chair, she raced to me, wrapping me in a hug. "I thought you'd play it off like it wasn't bothering you. Are you alright?"

"I'm okay. I've definitely been better, but I'm okay." I patted her back.

It hadn't been easy, packing up my things, not knowing when I would be back in my own place. I had gotten enough clothes for a week, figuring I could wash them when I needed to. I was glad Rhodes had offered to take me, that morning, on his way to the station. I wasn't quite ready to be there by myself just yet.

Afterwards, unable to go into the office yet, I had driven around town for a while, just thinking, until

Brian brought Suzy in to work. I needed to drop the camera off at the station, but I wasn't in the mood to be around that many people with that many questions. I hadn't even had coffee yet.

"Did you get any sleep last night?" She sat down beside me.

I shrugged, not sure I wanted to talk about it. After we got back to Rhodes' place, we had lain down for a while, but neither of us was able to sleep for the hour or two we had left. Once I was safe in the shelter of his house, in his arms, the events of the evening had washed over me, and I'd cried deep, heavy sobs for the first time in a long while. He didn't speak. It was exactly what I needed. And something I'd never shared before with a man.

"He asked me to move in with him," I said suddenly. That, I could talk about. "Obviously, it's too soon. But...maybe someday."

Suzy's mouth popped open, then shut immediately. She tilted her head, her eyes soft around the edges. "Is it?"

"We've only been dating for what? A month? And things have only gotten serious in the past week or so."

"Serious?" She gave me a sweet, patient smile. "You mean physical? You two've been dancing around each other for more than a few months now. Just because you took your time getting to know each other doesn't mean you weren't seeing each other."

I frowned. "We weren't dating."

"Fine. You were non-dating."

I rolled my eyes."

"You weren't dating anyone else."

"No. That would have seemed wrong."

"Exactly." She wiggled in her seat, delighted I had proved her point. "Hey, if you move in with him, you could have that puppy! You'd have a backyard."

"I'm *not* getting a puppy! I rarely even cook for myself. I run through Mariano's half the time."

"You cook in a skillet and in the oven."

"Sheet-pan food. Not casseroles, not stews, not slow cooker stuff."

"You're right. How could you feed a dog if you can't cook for him?"

"Her," I corrected. Then wrinkled my nose when she laughed.

"Rhodes cooks stews and casseroles and slow cooker stuff, doesn't he?"

I raised a shoulder. He did. It was really nice.

"In a relationship, each person works to their strength. It's what makes Sam and I work so well. It's what makes *any* relationship work well."

"I've never gotten to that part." I picked up my little plant to examine it.

"I'm not going to tell you what to do here." Suzy turned in her seat to face me directly and leaned onto one elbow, propping it on the armchair. "But I'll tell you what I see. You two are both alphas."

I frowned.

"Hear me out." She held up her hands in defense. "You are. You're both very strong personalities and leaders, but you're also both very good at switching roles, trading off where it suits you best."

"Like you were saying." I set the plant back down, giving her my full attention.

"Exactly. It's why I think you two will work." She gave me a soft smile. "That's not to say you won't struggle or argue over who's in charge at times."

Yeah, I knew that all too well.

"But," she went on, "I don't see any red flags. And I know you, Mal. You wouldn't be happy with a guy who didn't challenge you a little."

I thought about what she said. It was similar to what Rhodes had said to me. That he was glad I challenged him.

"But how can he just jump in with both feet like that?" I still didn't get his reasoning.

"Cause you're a planner." She grinned. "He's an activator. In his job, he has to be decisive."

"So do I."

"Not in the same way."

"Maybe."

It was true. Even when I had to change directions, I already had plans B, C, and D ready and waiting. Sometimes even E. Plan E had saved my ass more than once.

"Take your time. Make your own decision. But I hope you don't just run from this." Suzy's voice shifted. "I almost did with Sam. It would have been the worst decision of my life."

"Because you were afraid?" I kicked my legs out, leaning back in my chair.

"Yes. And because I didn't trust him."

"Sam?" I laughed. "He's the most trustworthy person I know." Then I sobered. "Except when it comes to your personal privacy. But he'd never use that to hurt someone who wasn't hurting others."

"True. It's one of the things I love about him. But it took me a long time to see that."

"You'd been hurt before too."

She nodded, crossing her legs. "Badly, and it made it hard to believe someone like him could be that good and honest with me."

She'd mentioned it before, but never elaborated. I let it hang in the air, unsure if she was ready to talk about it or not.

"I didn't trust Sam when he said he was okay with not having kids."

I knew they couldn't have kids, but I wasn't sure why.

"You said you weren't able to?" I asked gently.

She raised her chin. "I was pregnant once." She stopped, emotion rising within her, staining her face. "And I was married once before. He was an abusive asshole."

Guessing what she meant, I was unable to remain seated and shot to my feet. But I didn't know what to say.

"The last time he laid hands on me"—tears filled her eyes, threatening to spill over. She clenched the edges of her seat—"I lost the baby. If I hadn't gone to the hospital, I would have died. I never went back to him after that."

"Oh, Suzy." I rushed to her, crushing her head to my chest.

She wept against me, lost in the memory of her grief. Brushing aside her hair, I held her close to me, this friend who had invaded my life at a time when I desperately needed one.

"Okay," I said, doubled down in my resolve to wrap up this mess. "Sam and I found what we were looking for last night."

"The storage unit?" Wyatt asked, his face looking impressed on his square in the Sambot's display.

"No, the other thing." I knew Sam habitually scanned our lines for taps and our offices for bugs, but it didn't feel right, speaking so outright about it. "From the warehouse."

"Ah. So, you left them?"

I nodded. "Took photographic evidence, including serial numbers. I just got back from dropping them off at the station to store with the other collected evidence. It's good, very good, but we need something solid to tie it to Dessi."

"I hope he doesn't move them too soon." Rhodes' face on the tablet looked worried. I was glad he'd been able to join the call from the station.

"If we could catch him trying to move them, that would be the ticket, but I'm not sure when they'll move. Or if he'll be present."

"I can set up surveillance," Sam suggested.

"We now also have a man inside," Wyatt said.

"We do?" Sam said in awe.

"I ran into James, from the speakeasy, a couple of days ago, gave him my card. He helped get my guy, Grady, hired."

"A job?" I asked.

He nodded. "As a busser."

"He'll be able to listen," Sam said.

"That's great. We now have two additional routes to help us." I shifted the conversation. "But I think it's time to use the other plan. We can't rely on just one path anymore. We've got to hunt down every avenue for proof."

"The smoking gun?" Sam's eyes went round.

I nodded. "It's the only way to attach him to the murders, the sale, everything."

"What if it's not registered to him?" Rhodes asked.

"It's a good point, but it would still have his prints on it." He hadn't worn any gloves; I was watching.

"Unless he wiped it."

"His personal weapon? That he stores in his house?"

"You want to break into that madman's house and poke around until we find it, hoping we don't wake him?"

"I do."

"What if he has it on him in his bedroom?"

"Then we'll overpower him. We have more manpower and the element of surprise. He'd do it to any one of us." I set my chin.

"Correction," Wyatt spoke. "He'd send goons to do it."

I held up my hand to say "see?" I knew Rhodes didn't like it, but I had no better options. Nothing that would end this.

"Do you think he'll have personal security?" Suzy asked.

"It's possible," I admitted. "But Dessi's biggest weakness is his pride. I don't think he'd ever consider anyone would attack him at home. He'll have security, but Sam can see to that."

"I'll also use my thermal-imaging cam to make sure there's no one else around close by. It'll give us some clue as to what we're getting into," Sam added.

Everyone soaked in that for a minute, watching everyone else's reaction. Even Suzy, who'd pulled up a chair next to me, was seriously considering it. We'd all come to the end of our ropes.

"We'd have to find his house," Wyatt said, breaking the silence.

"We don't know that?" Rhodes said, surprised.

"I've looked, but there's no real estate owned by him directly." Sam's mouth turned down. "Or any of his subsidiaries. Or attached to his businesses. Nothing that looks remotely residential."

"We couldn't even track his car parked around town. He has a driver who frequently uses different vehicles. The man's smart; I'll give him that," I said. "We'll have to follow him as he leaves Red. And we can assume his driver will be trained to keep a careful eye for a tail."

I could see the muscle in Rhodes' jaw tick. He knew he wouldn't like the plan.

"Everyone has to agree," I continued. "We're going to need everyone's help on this one."

"In," Wyatt threw out.

"Suzy?" Sam turned his eyes to his wife, waiting for her input. She nodded slowly. "We're in."

"I've got your back," Rhodes said.

"Okay, let's do this." I was grateful for everyone's consensus. "I have a plan."

Was it risky? Sure, but no other action would put a nail in the problem as quickly as this one. I just hoped that nail wouldn't be in our own coffins.

Meanwhile, outside a smallish, historic, single-truck Chicago fire station,

"Cap." One of the guys leaned into his office. "Someone's here to see you."

Rhodes' chair scraped against the tile as he stood to go see who had stopped by.

"Mo," he said, surprised at seeing the barista standing in the open apparatus bay. He walked forward and shook his hand.

"I hope I'm not bothering you at a bad time."

"Not at all. I'm in between calls and already have dinner prepped in the slow cooker."

"Gotta love efficient meals." The older man's eyes crinkled at the corners.

"Especially when you never know when a call's going to come in." Gesturing to the outdoor bench, he led the way over to take a seat. "I'm assuming this isn't a social call. Everything okay with Mal?"

"Oh yes, at least as far as I know." Mo gave a half laugh. "I wanted to let you know how Nate's court case went yesterday. He told me it'd be okay if I shared the ruling with you."

He shifted on the seat, nervous to hear what had happened. Whatever they had decided would change the kid's future. Forever. "And?"

Glancing down, the other man folded his fingers together. "He got probation."

"No jail time?" He could hardly believe it.

"None." Mo gave Rhodes a stern look. "But that doesn't mean he's got an easy path ahead of him. Probation is still serious. And he's going to have to take it seriously."

"I understand. But, hot damn, this is great news!" He threw a muscled arm out to pat the ex-lawyer's back energetically. "I appreciate this, Mo. More than you know."

The kid had a second chance at life.

"I was happy to do it. But honestly, I think you should keep an eye on that kid," Mo warned, dousing his fire. "He's smart, and I think he could go far if he can just stay on track for a little while. We just have to keep him clean."

Sobering, he considered his words. "I can make a concerted effort to stop by the center and let those kids drag me around the court."

"It's little things like that, that make the most difference." He tilted his head down. "As you well know."

"I do." It was true. As he'd shared with Mo, his mentors at the center had changed his life.

"He asked a lot of law questions." Mo cracked a smile. "By the time we got into the courtroom, he understood the basics and was following the conversation volley back and forth. I think he was enjoying the process."

"That's great."

"It is. He was interested in learning more. I have another friend who would be happy to have him around, but to be fair to her, I'd want someone to monitor their interactions for a while, to make sure he's taking it seriously and not wasting her time, at least at first. Would you be willing to do that?"

"Yeah," he said, excited at the idea. If Nate had a mentor like that, it would be even better than just his friendship and coaching on the basketball court. It could mean a real career. "Absolutely."

Nodding, he gave him a business card. "Just give Ms. Tomlinson a call. She works in medical law, but there are always criminal elements to keep him interested. And if he does well, she can suggest another mentorship in a field more appealing to him."

"This is amazing." He studied the card, hope welling in his chest. He was determined to help Nate however he could.

"There's one other thing." Mo's face dropped. "Another reason I'm worried about him."

"What happened?" That didn't sound good.

"That woman who works for Dessi? Cynthia?" He made sure Rhodes knew who he meant. "She was present at the hearing."

"She was probably trying to see what he was going to spill about Dessi." He hoped.

Mo shook his head. "When we left the courthouse, she followed us. I took him to Grounds because I wasn't sure what she'd do."

"That's not good."

"I doubt she'd try anything at his house. He doesn't live in the safest neighborhood, but I'm worried about what she'll do when he's out and about."

"That's why you want to keep him busy."

"Partly. But I also believe he's smart enough to be a prosecutor if he can keep believing in himself and puts in the work."

"Now, she knows where you work, though." He frowned in concern. If Cynthia came after the coffee-shop owner, it would all be his fault. He'd brought Nate there.

"She already knew about me." He waved off the concern. "She came by to warn me off the case a few days ago. As if that would stop me."

Dessi's hooks were getting deeper. "I need to tell Mal."

"It's probably a good idea that she knows."

"Wyatt's guys are typically on Roscoe Ave during the day. I'm sure they'd be happy to keep an eye across the street, too."

"I'm not as worried about Grounds. Dessi will do what he wants. I'm more worried about Nate and him staying the course."

That, he understood, but it didn't mean they couldn't do something else to help out.

"Thanks for letting me know. I'll update the team."

Mo gave him a pleased look. "You've certainly become part of that, haven't you?"

He wasn't sure what to say to that. They were still Mal's friends, but yes, he was starting to feel like part of the crew. They treated him as such. "I'm very fortunate."

Approvingly, he nodded, patted Rhodes on the knee, and stood to leave. Coffee aroma lingered in his wake.

Meanwhile, in the leather-covered back seat of a rich black sedan,

"I'm telling you, Dad. She set that up for me," the voice came through his phone. "She made a deal with the journalist or something to leave the Poggiali name out of the article."

"I hope so." He wasn't so sure. He'd hate for his son to be disappointed. Especially when he was trying so hard and doing such a great job.

"I know Mal. She wouldn't sell me out like that."

"She might not, but I know the news. It's a juicy story, a connection like that." He felt bad, stomping on his excitement. "All I'm saying is don't get your hopes up."

"The story comes out tomorrow. Paul told me," he said excitedly. "You'll see then."

"Okay, son," Dom said, letting it rest. "I'm sorry I didn't go to your tasting last night. I was worried about being spotted. But Bobby brought me a sample, and boy, was it good. I do love pesto!"

He chuckled. "Told you so. We had a good turnout. And so many social media posts! This is actually going to work. Especially with that news article."

"Have I told you lately that I'm proud of you?"

"About a dozen times, but thanks, Dad."

Hanging up the phone, he considered paying a visit to Paul himself. If the reporter was considering a spin on the Poggiali connection, maybe he could impress upon him the error of that idea.

Tucking his phone in his breast pocket, he decided to let it play out as Marco had asked. If the detective had actually done that for him, it would be pretty impressive.

But why would she do that? Did she need something?

Chapter 24

"Good morning," I said, walking into the Mennons' kitchen in search of coffee. I'd slept better than I thought I would at their house. The bed was exceptionally soft, and the linens were scented with lavender and chamomile. Leave it to Suzy to make a guest feel pampered.

"Morning," Suzy said cheerily from behind a refrigerator door. Closing it, she returned with half-and-half in a small glass jug and carried it to the countertop separating the kitchen from the dining room. After selecting a carafe from the cabinet, she set out coffee cups on the counter. "Sam should be out in a few minutes."

"He doesn't have to get up on my account." I slid onto a barstool, pulling one leg up underneath me. I didn't want to be rude, but I really wanted Suzy to pour the freshly brewed nectar of the gods into that carafe so I could have my first cup of divine goodness for the day. The first of many. My eyes tracked her movements.

She turned, pulled a bowl from the cabinets, and set it down in front of her flour canister. After measuring out the ingredients, she whisked together flour, sugar, and a few other things. My eyes flicked to the coffeepot. Maybe I could just hop on over there and steal a cup while it was brewing.

"Whatcha making?" I said.

"Pancakes," she tossed over her shoulder, her face beaming.

"You don't have to go to all of that trouble." My gaze was firmly attached to the coffee. It smelled amazing. Then again, didn't it always?

A shuffling sound got my attention. Looking behind me, I saw a zombie approach. On second thought, I realized it was Sam. Hard to tell with his hair sticking up and his mouth open wide in a yawn.

"Rough night?" I asked, sliding a coffee cup to him. Maybe he'd go fill his, and then I could get a cup.

"No, just waking up." He rubbed his eyes, plunking down on a barstool.

Crap.

"Sam's not a morning person." Suzy danced around me to drop a kiss on his cheek. Smiling, he made a grab for her before she could go back to her breakfast prep, but he was too slow.

Laughing, she got out a skillet and turned the stovetop on to heat it. The doorbell rang.

Sam sat up straight. "Who's that? The guys out front didn't call."

"It's Rhodes. Can you get it, honey?" Suzy said, adding slices of bacon to the pan. Sizzling noises filled the air. "I already called and let the guys know. Jim's on watch today."

"I'll get it," I said loudly, sliding off the barstool and going to the door to see Rhodes standing outside, smiling. *He probably already had a cup of coffee.* "Good morning. You didn't have to come pick me up. I can still drive myself."

"I called him to stop by for breakfast," Suzy shouted out from the kitchen, overhearing me. "And Wyatt."

"Wyatt?" I hollered, heading back.

"We have a plan to go over. And pancakes to eat."

Stopping midway, I leaned into Rhodes, sighing heavily. I whispered under my breath, "You didn't bring me any coffee."

"I figured you'd have some." He pressed a kiss on my forehead.

"I haven't gotten coffee yet. It's over there, brewed, taunting me. The situation is getting serious. Maybe we can call Wyatt to bring some."

"Why don't you just ask?"

"I don't want to be rude."

"It's Suzy."

"I know." I leaned so I could see her in my peripheral vision. "But still. Isn't it rude? It's not my house."

"I doubt it." He chuckled, prodding me towards the kitchen as he walked in with me.

"Can I do anything to help out?" I asked out loud, eyeing the coffeepot. Maybe I should have brought Mr. Bunn from home.

"No, I've got it, but thanks." Suzy grinned.

Plunking on my barstool, I dropped my head in my hand. My leg bounced on the footrest.

"Oh, for goodness' sake." Suzy turned, laughing out loud. "Get yourself a cup!"

"Really?" I perked up, sitting stock straight, one foot braced on the floor.

She rolled her eyes.

I nearly stumbled around the bar, snagging the glass carafe and dumping some of its contents into my mug. Sliding it back onto its warmer, I lifted my cup to my mouth, pausing only barely to breathe it in. I took a sip. *Heaven.* This was heaven. I moaned.

"Does she do that every morning?" She watched me like I had grown three heads.

"Yup." Rhodes grinned. "Best part of my morning."

The doorbell rang again while I came to my senses. I filled Suzy's warming carafe and started another pot of coffee. "That was super mean, Suz."

"It was your fault for treating me like a stranger." She stuck out her tongue. "We're friends. Friends who share their houses and their coffee."

It was sweet. I couldn't stay mad at her. I mean, who could?

"Thanks." Leaning in, I gave her a little one-sided hug. Her hands were busy, full with messy pancake batter and tongs for the bacon.

"It's Wyatt," Sam said from the door.

"Is that bacon?" Wyatt said, following his nose around the corner.

"Sure is." Suzy wiggled at the stove, thrilled to be cooking for a crew.

"We're going to go over the plan." Sam made finger quotes around "the plan." "Should we have our *inside man* in on this conversation?"

"I can make more food," Suzy said from the stove at the prospect of having more guests.

Wyatt shook his head. "I'll let him know to pay attention to his schedule and text me when he's getting ready to leave for home. Didn't you say you wanted to try for Monday?"

"It makes the most sense." I finished my coffee and poured another. "His schedule is too fluid on the weekends. Less predictable. He usually leaves Red around six on weekdays, doesn't he?"

"Yeah, unless he has a late meeting," Sam supplied. "Which he's had before on a Monday night."

I remembered. While I didn't miss having audio to listen to, I did miss the hope that we'd catch wind of a good lead any day. One that didn't involve this level of risk. "If we miss it on Monday, we can try again on Tuesday night."

"Better chance he'll be fully asleep when we try to gain access on a weeknight. Less chance he'll be up late," Rhodes guessed.

"Probably," Wyatt said.

"I'm working on improving my infrared thermal sensors." Sam was finally waking up, with the help of the caffeine. He'd almost gotten his hair to lie back down.

"It's strange that we can't find any record of him owning a house, though." Rhodes frowned. "Isn't it?"

"Kinda, yes," I said. "We have legal documentation of all his other businesses. They're either in his name or a corporate business name he owns. I'm wondering if Marchi owns the place and is letting him live there as a favor for doing business."

"He has been trying to weasel his way up the ladder," Sam added.

"Speaking of weasel," Rhodes said. "Mo's gotten a threat of his own."

"Mo?" I said, spinning to him. "As in my friend and favorite coffee creator, Maurice? The owner of the best coffee bar in the world?"

"The same."

"What happened?"

"Nate, the kid I told you about." He paused, to bring the rest of the team up to speed. "He was one of the bystanders from the first warehouse job."

"Is he okay?" Suzy stopped mid flip, her nostrils flared.

"He was grazed by a bullet, but he wasn't exactly just a bystander." He took a long breath. "Cynthia talked him into helping out, and he found them the warehouse. I think she's trying to get Nate on Dessi's payroll."

"Oh no," Suzy said.

Wyatt shook his head, his mouth in a thin line.

"I know him and a friend of his he took along with him to the warehouse."

"They're kids from his community center near the fire station," I added.

"I spent some time there as a kid," he explained. "Anyway, I asked Mo for advice. He helped him avoid jail time."

"Is the kid on a better path now?" Wyatt asked.

"I believe he is. He wants to be. And I'm trying to help him."

"But how was Mo threatened?" I asked, getting back to the immediate risk.

"Cynthia wanted Nate to take the fall, redirecting attention from Dessi. She wasn't keen on Mo helping him out or how things were ruled. She visited him before the hearing to try to dissuade him. Then, followed him and Nate afterward."

"But she didn't do anything?" Sam asked.

Rhodes shook his head. "I think she was just trying to scare him."

"I hope that's it." I didn't like the idea of Mo getting involved in this. It felt like everywhere I turned, people I cared about were being threatened by Dessi.

"Are they safe now?" Suzy asked.

"I've got a few people watching over Nate." He turned to Wyatt. "I was hoping your guys could keep an eye on Grounds. Just while they're at the office, you know. It's across the street."

"Done."

Our plan had to work. We must all have been thinking the same thing, as we all went quiet, sizzling grease filling the silence.

"How are you planning on pulling this off so he doesn't see us tailing him? He knows all of us by now," Wyatt finally spoke, shifting gears.

"Food first." Suzy carried a plate full of pancakes in one hand and another full of bacon and fried eggs in the other. "Plans after. Wyatt, can you grab that carafe?"

He stood to follow. "I told Hillary about all of you."

"You did?" She set down the plates on the table. "Did you want to include her today?"

"Not for this." He shook his head. "But maybe another time? After all this is over."

"That sounds wonderful." She beamed. "I'd like to get to know this woman who's got your attention."

Clearing his throat, he nodded, pulled out a chair, and sat down to shovel bacon onto his plate.

"Are you sure you don't mind me hanging around?" I watched Rhodes carry a load of laundry out from his bedroom and head into the utility room.

"Of course not. I like having you around." He stopped in his tracks. "I'm not ignoring you, am I?"

"No." I laughed. "Not at all. It's just weird, you know?"

Dropping his laundry basket to the ground, he came over to the couch where I sat and took a seat next to me, putting a hand on my knee. "I just want you to feel comfortable here."

"I am." It was nice being in his space, but things were still new. "I just feel like there's something I should be doing."

He gave my knee a squeeze. "Is there anything you need to do? I can give you space if you need it. I've got a study you can work in if you want. It's not much, but it'd give you some privacy."

He was nicer than I deserved. Scooting over, I planted a kiss on his cheek. "Nope, I'm good. If I go over Monday's plan one more time, I'll go crazy. I'm all set. Actually, I'm not used to having this much free time. Feel free to do whatever chores you need to, or put me to work. Honestly. I'm happy to help out."

"You just relax and enjoy your time off. I just want to get my shift clothes from last night washed up." He wrinkled his nose. "They need it."

"Busy night?"

"A fire down on Damen. In the basement. We were worried about it getting to the gas line." He closed his eyes and rubbed his temple. "I had to make it through the crawl space to help a man. He got tangled in the lines under the house."

"That's scary." I didn't like the thought of him crawling around, literally under a burning building. "I'm glad you didn't get stuck as well."

"I did." He exhaled briefly. "I was actually worried there for a minute. It was pretty cramped down there."

I shuddered. "How'd you get unstuck? Did someone get you?"

"They were busy with the fire." He shook his head. "I had to unclip my pack and wiggle out of it, then push it out in front of me. Helped my guy do the same."

Looking at his broad shoulders and thick chest, I couldn't even imagine someone with his build, scooting out of a pack, stuck, under a house on fire. He didn't even seem fazed by it. How could anyone become so at ease with something so terrifying?

Tendrils of fear snaked around my heart and clenched. My fingers curled into his leg at the thought of losing him.

"Hey." He edged my chin up with a finger. "I'm okay. I made it out."

I nodded. This time.

All those instances when he was afraid for me because of my job made a little more sense now that I was facing the thought of him in that situation. I didn't like the feeling.

"Thanks again for helping out with Monday and taking the day off for it. We could have pushed it to

Tuesday."

"I don't want to waste the opportunity, and I want to be involved." He set his chin. "Let's get this over and done with."

"So, what are the plans for today?" I shifted topics. "What would you have done if I weren't here?"

"Probably some chores." He shrugged. "Or go visit Gran. See how she's doing."

"We can do that," I offered.

"We don't have to."

"It sounds like fun." I pushed to my feet. "And I can help out with chores."

"You're not doing chores." He laughed, pulling me back down for a kiss. "I'm spoiling you a little on your rare day off. You get to do whatever you want."

"How about you go put those stinky clothes in the wash? Then, we can try out that new coffee shop on Diversey and stop by to see Miss Ellie."

"If you honestly don't mind. I didn't get out to see her last weekend."

"Done."

"We can stop by Mariano's to find something for dinner."

"How about this?" I had an idea. I hadn't had a quiet evening in for as long as I could remember. "Since you're letting me stay here, I'll get dinner tonight. We can go get noodles at that Asian place on Roscoe after we visit Miss Ellie. Then, we can come back and have a movie night. Totally relax on the couch with takeout and an action flick."

"An action flick?" His eyebrows rose. "And takeout on the couch with a beautiful redhead? I'm in."

"Cool." I jumped back up. "I'll go get my things while you deal with your laundry."

"Sounds good." He got up and headed back to scoop up his basket. "But I'm paying."

"Oh, don't get me started on that. It's the twenty-first century." I wagged my finger, then headed back to his bedroom, where I had left my phone and wallet. My ringtone sounded.

Moving quicker, I hopped into the room and scooped up the cell, still laughing. "Hello?"

"Bugsy."

My playful mood chilled. Only one person called me that.

"Dom. How's it going?"

The crime lord had never threatened me, but he wasn't exactly a good guy, either.

"I read an interesting article today."

Crap, I hadn't even checked to see what Paul wrote. No way had he screwed me over. Had he? Or maybe Dom was upset I got involved.

"And?" I let it hang.

"You did my boy a solid," he finally said.

"I'm happy to help Marco out. He's a good kid and has great plans."

"I do appreciate it." He paused. "I've heard your name thrown around. Word on the street says things are heating up for you."

That wasn't good. *What had he heard?*

"Anything I need to know?"

"Nothing concrete. Just that you and a certain common enemy of ours are pissing each other off."

"I'm trying to keep my nose clean, but he's making things difficult."

"Do you need a favor?"

"Um, I don't think so." It was tempting, but I didn't. Who knew how I'd have to pay it back. At one time, he'd offered me a job. No way was I getting more involved with this life than I already was.

Then it hit me; he thought I'd done the favor for Marco to earn one from him. "That's not why I did it, Dom."

He was silent a moment.

"I meant what I said. I was just helping a friend. It's not related."

"I know what business he's getting into," he said, meaning Dessi.

"So do I." Luckily, I didn't need to accept that favor in return. I already knew about the guns. "And when I'm done with this, I'm hoping to put an end to that."

"That's a lofty goal."

"The only way to get out of this game."

"It might be." He waited a beat. "I hope you succeed. Not just for you, but for Chicago. What he's bringing into town isn't going to do anyone any good."

I didn't know what to say to that, him being on the same side of the law as Dessi.

"Does that surprise you?" He chuckled. "I suppose it would, but I've been in this business a long time. The people of this city don't need any more help harming each other."

"I'll do what I can." I wasn't promising him anything.

"Listen, if you need the favor, just let me know."

I didn't say anything. It wasn't a good idea to be trading favors with the mafia unless I absolutely had to. Just having this conversation made me uncomfortable.

"You could use it," he went on, "for whatever it is you're after."

"I don't feel right taking it, not for this."

"Okay," Dom said, satisfied. "Good luck, Mal. And be careful."

"Thanks."

I'd need it.

Chapter 25

"Mal." Miss Ellie smiled. "It's so wonderful to see you, dear."

I bent to give her a hug. "It's good to see you as well, ma'am."

"Now, you sit down and tell me all about those big cases you've been solving."

I looked over at Rhodes. It's not like I could tell her about Dessi.

"Gran," he said, coming to my aid and wrapping her up in a big hug. "She can't tell you about that. She has confidentiality clauses. She doesn't even tell *me* details about her cases."

He gave her a pitiful look that made me roll my eyes in response. What a ham.

"Oh." She waved a hand in front of her chest. "I didn't think about that. It makes sense, though. She's a professional."

"I can tell you that this one"—I pointed to Rhodes—"can eat a whole plateful of cookies."

"Hey!" He attempted to look hurt. "Your confidentiality clause doesn't extend to your boyfriend?"

Boyfriend. The word caught in my chest.

It still felt weird, but kinda good too.

"Alas, it doesn't. It's a work-only kinda thing."

"I hope that doesn't mean you share everything." He gave me a wolfish grin over his grandma's head.

"My friend makes the cookies," I rushed onward, trying to ignore him and the blush creeping up my neck. "They're the best."

"Do you do much baking?" She smiled. "I love to bake."

I winced. I wasn't the most domestic girlfriend, and right then, the fact made me feel like I was coming up short, even though Miss Ellie hadn't insinuated anything. "Unfortunately, no. I'm more of a single-skillet kinda cook."

"Mal's generally busy, running her own business." He took a seat next to me, laying a hand on my knee and giving it a squeeze. "Not a lot of women like her."

The look he gave me made my heart melt. It was full of tenderness and warmth, and something more I wasn't yet ready to explore.

Miss Ellie's door burst open, and Rhodes' uncle Sean waltzed in, arms up in the air. "There she is! The woman of the hour!"

Rhodes and I shared a confused look.

"What's going on?" he asked.

"Hello, Ellie." Mrs. Collins propelled her way into the room behind Sean, pushing an elderly man in a wheelchair in front of her. This had to be Mr. Collins, the retired firefighter. She located me in the room. "Hello, dear!"

"Hi, Mrs. Collins." I rose to greet her. "How are you?"

"I'm doing well, thank you." She patted my arm, then turned to look at her husband, adoration evident in her face. "This is my Doug."

"Pleasure to meet you, sir." I shook his hand.

"You as well, young lady." His hand was age-spotted, and his knuckles were knotted, but his grip was still strong. He fixed his gaze firmly on me. "I can't tell you how much I appreciate your help."

"Oh, no worries," I brushed it off. "All in a day's work."

He held onto my hand. "Linda knew something was wrong, but you were able to get to the bottom of it. I'm grateful someone listened to her."

"It's a team effort, sir. I can't take all the credit for it on my own."

Rhodes was watching the exchange, that fondness still in his eyes. He mouthed, *"Thanks."*

I gave him a wink.

"You're here to visit Miss Ellie?" I asked Mr. and Mrs. Collins.

"No!" Her eyes lit up. "I haven't had time to call you yet. Just this morning, I got a call from Brookside, letting me know they had space available for Doug. Isn't that great news? The timing couldn't be more perfect."

"It really is."

"So, we hot-footed it over here." She wrinkled her nose and pumped her slim arms. "We had just finished checking out his new apartment and were on our way to see Ellie when we ran into Sean. I gave him all the news on our case and told him how you helped expose those charlatans."

That explained Sean's reaction.

"I'm glad it worked out."

"Well." Miss Ellie clapped her hands firmly together. "Looks like we have a regular party going on in here! Boys, go make some lemonade for our guests."

Rhodes and Sean jumped up at the order and collected glasses from one of her two kitchen cabinets, bumping into each other to reach the pitcher and lemonade mix. However, I suspected some of the shoving and elbowing was on purpose, and not due to the tight quarters and broad men.

After posting Doug next to the small couch in Miss Ellie's living room, Linda made her way over to give her friend a big hug. I couldn't help but wonder if our little group would stay close, like this, so many years later. It warmed my heart to see the friends, happy together.

"Oh, and I met with that nice lawyer you suggested," Linda said, settling on the couch next to her husband. "She's going to try to work a deal with Weston so the residents can stay while they pay off their debt. She said if she approaches them with a deal and they agree to it, they may be able to avoid an arrest."

"That's great news." I was surprised at that. Of course, that only worked if they had access to the money. But maybe they'd be able to pay it over a longer time. "So, she doesn't think they'll have to sell the place?"

"She did say something about that." She frowned, trying to remember. "They may have to, to pay off the debt. I don't like the thought of that. I'm worried they won't stay responsible for what they owe, but Ms. Tomlinson said she had some ideas. What a sharp cookie!"

It sounded like it. I'd have to thank Mo when I saw him next.

"You did good," Rhodes said, taking a seat next to me on the small love seat. He handed me a glass of lemonade.

"Thanks." I took a sip. It was awfully sweet but very refreshing in the heat of summer. As was the break from our typical plotting against Dessi.

I had hoped Ms. Collins would tell him about the case, since it didn't feel right to share it with him even if he and Sean had been worried about Doug. It was incredibly rewarding to be able to share the win with someone like him, who meant so much to me. I liked the feeling. It was new, but good.

I just hoped it would all work out. I couldn't imagine Weston had the funds to pay off debt of any magnitude, unless they were only scamming a handful of residents. But criminal behavior was like mouse droppings; once you found evidence, you already had a problem.

Meanwhile, later that evening, in a red-and-black decorated office in a prominent speakeasy,

"Monday?"

Grady nodded. "When you leave to go home. I'm supposed to text him to let them know."

Dessi toyed with a Montblanc on his desk. Money always did the trick. Offer enough of it to new, well-placed employees who were paying way too much attention and had interested eyes, and you earned so much in return.

Cash was king.

"Excellent job, Grady." He poured the two of them some of his cheapest whiskey. He wasn't wasting the good stuff on the young man, who wouldn't know the difference anyway. "You keep this up, and you'll be able to afford things like this every day."

The man's eyes lit up as he took the offered glass like it was liquid gold. After a sip, his face flushed with pleasure.

It might have been better than any whiskey he'd had before. At one point, he hadn't known the difference either. But that was a long time ago. He'd reinvented himself since then.

"Thank you, sir."

"Any idea why they want to follow me home?" Keeping his voice light, he studied the young man. He leaned back in his chair and tugged on his vest to set it into place. He wasn't worried about the detective and her friends. They were inferior pawns in the game. He had hoped she would be an interesting opponent, but the idea that she could get a mole past him without him noticing it? Amateur.

"I think they're planning on breaking into your house." He sat forward as if sharing news.

"Yes, but to what end?" He swirled the ice in his glass. Obviously, they wanted in his house. A thought occurred to him. "You mean while I'm there?"

He nodded. "You have something they want."

The laughter bubbled out of him, turning from his well-trained, blue-blooded chuckle to a more maniacal one. Whatever they thought he had, they were idiots to think he'd keep it in his house. He had a storage unit for that.

The PI thought she could break into his home? Hadn't he taken her game piece every time she made a move?

Maybe it was time to shake things up for her and put her in her place.

"So, what should we do today?" Rhodes asked me the next morning, standing by the sink, next to the coffeepot. "It's not going to be as hot this afternoon."

"Thank goodness," I said, blowing on my cup of coffee where I sat at his breakfast bar.

"We could throw something on the grill." He pushed off the counter to stand across from me. "It'll be nice enough to sit outside."

"Sounds wonderful." I didn't exactly want to eat out two nights in a row, but I also didn't know if I felt comfortable enough to cook in his kitchen. And I wasn't allowed to have a grill on my little balcony. It was barely large enough for two little chairs.

It was one of the reasons I had been interested in Lane Pollett's nice apartment building. It was still pretty close to my office, but a little larger and nicer than my current quarters. That was also before I had even considered moving in with Rhodes.

Not that I was actually considering it. Yet.

"You know." He tilted his head. "If we're going to fire up that grill and sit outside, we might as well invite the crew. We do have that big deck out back and a long picnic table. It'd be nice to put it to good use."

"You haven't gotten tired of everyone yet?" I teased him. "Or of the planning?"

"The planning, yes. But the people, no. I like everyone."

"Even Wyatt?" I smiled. He took a while to get to know.

"I understand Wyatt," he said thoughtfully. "And he's a good guy."

"He is."

"Besides, it's easier to cook for larger groups."

"Is it?"

"Definitely."

"Well, then." I picked up my phone. "I'll text the team."

"Let them know it's just for fun, not for work. They don't have to come."

"Will do. You know, if we're not talking about the plan, we could invite Jen." I paused thoughtfully. "And Rodriguez."

He cut his eyes to me, narrowed slightly. He seemed to weigh it, trying to find a way to be okay with it. "That may be pushing it a little far."

I collapsed in laughter, leaning over the counter at his earnest attempt. I wasn't serious, but I was glad to see even he had his limits.

That afternoon, I got busy setting up the back patio table with plates and silverware. We'd been to Mariano's, where Rhodes had studied each steak, intent on picking the right one for everyone, plus a few extra, just in case. He'd even pulled out a large outdoor tablecloth to dress the picnic table up. I think he was genuinely excited about having others over for dinner.

"Are you sure you want to use real plates and silverware?" I asked, sticking my head back through the sliding glass door.

He glanced up from seasoning a sheet pan full of beef cuts, his "I like it hot!" apron on over a T-shirt with the sleeves torn off. He seemed at ease in his kitchen with his head freshly shaved and barefoot in worn jeans. It was a good look on him.

"Are you serious?" He raised an eyebrow. "You want to cut steaks on a paper plate? What about all the meat juice?"

"Oh, right." I made an exaggerated sigh. "You like your steaks ultra rare."

"It's called blue." He dropped a kiss on my head as he walked by to take a look at the table. "Looks great, Columbo. You might be good at other things than investigating."

I gave him a friendly punch in the shoulder for the joke, and he pulled me in for a hug, making a move for my neck. Squealing, I danced away, but he had wrapped his arms around me, and I couldn't get away fast enough. Bent over, he attacked my neck in kisses, sending me into a fit of laughter.

A broad smile spread proudly over his face at the win before he let me loose. Gasping for air, I held onto him, nerves still firing from the onslaught of tickles.

"That's not fair," I said, still catching my breath. "You're not ticklish."

"You can try." He bent his head away, giving me access to his neck. "I don't mind."

Wrinkling my nose, I gave him a playful push, resulting in him grabbing me again and raising an eyebrow in threat.

"Uncle!" I finally conceded, rising up on my toes, still giggling.

A ding from my phone broke us up. I gave him a wide berth to retrieve it from the kitchen counter.

"Everything okay?" he said a moment later. "You have an odd look on your face."

"Yeah." I held my phone up. "It's Wyatt. He's asking if he can bring a date."

"A date?" His eyebrows shot up. "Hillary."

"Actually, he said a plus one, but yes, I would assume so."

"Good for him. And see, this is why it's good to have extra steaks. You never know when extra people show up."

I rolled my eyes. "You did *not* know that was going to happen."

He held his hands up. "I'm not saying I did. I'm not saying I didn't."

The doorbell rang.

I checked the time on my phone. It was a bit early yet.

"Let me check." He headed through the kitchen to the entryway.

Following close behind, I slid my baton from where I had left it on a side counter, holding it ready just in case. I watched him open the door to reveal Suzy and Sam, smiles plastered from ear to ear. They were each carrying a bowl and a bottle of wine. Brian stood behind them with more containers.

"Sorry we're early." She pushed in, giving Rhodes a peck on the cheek and taking in the house. "Where's the kitchen?"

Sliding the baton into my waistband, I directed her past me and followed her in. "What did you bring?"

"Oh, it's nothing." She waved her hands, setting things down. "It's just a little broccoli salad."

Sam set the second bowl on the counter. "And a pasta salad with lots of olives."

My eyebrows rose. "We have baked potatoes and corn on the cob."

"That'll go perfectly with this!" She grinned, taking the lids off the bowls.

"And the cookies." Brian easily held the container aloft over everyone's heads as he walked in and set it on the counter beside the other.

Rhodes' eyes lit on the cookies.

"I'll be posted outside," Brian announced, heading out. "Let me know if you need anything."

"Hey." Rhodes stopped him at the door. "I'll bring a plate out when the steaks are done. Want some of everything?"

"Yeah." His eyes glazed over. "Steak?"

He gave him a supportive nod. "I got you, man."

"Thanks." They fist-bumped, and he headed out.

Turning to me, he winked. "See? Extra steaks."

As much as I had enjoyed the quiet time with him the night before, it was nice seeing him animated, joyful, and full of loud, booming laughter. He was genuinely a happy guy when he wasn't worried over people, anyway.

Hillary arrived with Wyatt shortly after, comfortably dressed in overall shorts and a flowery short-sleeved shirt, carrying a pretty ivy plant for the table. We all gathered around the picnic table outside, Wyatt hovering over her. It was a side I'd never seen of him.

"Haven't you gotten enough of us yet?" Suzy asked, a glass of wine in her hand.

"Not yet," he teased her, throwing the meat on the hot grill. Flames shot up to sear them one by one. "Now, how do you all like your steaks?"

Everyone called out their preferences.

"We're taking a night off." I raised my wineglass, stepping back over the bench seat to stand up. "No planning or business tonight. It's just for fun."

A little of the tension in Wyatt's shoulders eased. Maybe he had been worried about Hillary getting wrapped up in the dangerous situation we were headed towards.

"I'm glad you could join us tonight, Hillary." I nodded to the new member at the table. Everyone was eyeing her, anxious to know more about the newbie. "To the team!" I lifted my glass. "May we all remain friends, even after all this is over."

"To the Scoobs!" Sam lifted his glass.

"To the Scoobs," the rest resounded, their glasses lifted high in cheers before taking a sip.

"Now, Hillary." Suzy set her glass down. "Tell us everything about yourself. We've all been dying to meet you. And we can give you all the dirt on Wyatt."

Hillary skimmed a glance over Wyatt, whose eyes suddenly went large in panic. Hers sparkled with mischief. "Ooh, do tell."

"I'll start first." Suzy leaned in, ignoring Wyatt's groan.

Later that night, lying in bed next to Rhodes, we recounted the evening, laughing over Wyatt's doting on Hillary, leaping up to get her more salad or wine.

"It's adorable." I smiled into his shoulder.

"It is." His voice rumbled under my cheek. "You know, I was turned just as upside down when you came into my life."

"Really?" I lifted my head to look at him.

"Really. When you came to visit me at the fire station, my stomach did a major flip-flop. Like, roller-coaster flip-flop."

I grinned. "I didn't admit it to myself at the time, but I used the excuse of looking into the fires to talk to you more."

"Seriously?"

"Yeah, I wanted to see you in your uniform again. I did plan on poking into the fires, but you were the one who drew me to the station that evening, looking for answers."

"Had the fire not happened, we might not have met."

"True."

"I guess I have my job to thank for us getting together. And your curiosity."

"Ha! True."

My head settled back on his shoulder, and we fell into companionable silence, his fingers trailing up and down my arm. Neither of us wanting to talk about our plan for the following day.

"I'm thinking of taking a trip down to Tennessee, to see my dad," he finally said. "He's made the trip here to visit, and I want to return the gesture. See how things go. Once all of this has blown over."

"That's a great idea."

"I'd like you to come with me."

I'd gone with him before, but it didn't sound like he wanted me to go for moral support. It sounded like more, like a girlfriend thing, being taken home to visit Dad. It made me squirm just a bit.

"Maybe. If I have time."

"If you're busy with jobs, I get it." He let me off the hook.

"We'll see how it goes, okay?" I didn't want to say no. I wanted to say yes. Why was this so hard? "If I have the time, I'll go with you."

"Sounds good." His fingers paused on my forearm. "Have you considered doing the same?"

"What do you mean?" I propped my chin on my hand, fingers spread wide over his chest.

"Have you thought about seeing your dad? I had a lot to work through with mine, but I'm glad I did."

I hadn't thought about it. I had so many issues with my father.

"I'm not sure we could come to any terms. I'm a disappointment to him." I felt the frustration and conflict build within myself. "He'd rather have seen me go to college for some sort of business degree, or becoming a lawyer or something, than fight for justice or follow in his apparently much stronger footsteps. I mean, in what world would we ever be on the same page?"

He didn't say anything, his fingers resuming their path along my arms, his other arm wrapping around my back for support.

"You think I should try," I went on.

"At least give him a chance to accept you." He shrugged. "I'm not telling you what to do. Especially not here. I wouldn't do that."

"I hear you." I took a deep breath, appreciating him not pushing me on the topic. I knew he was hoping for the same reconciliation he had experienced. That was the wrong word. They would never be at the father-son level, but they had found some sort of healthy balance. Leaf was still his father. "I'll think about it."

"You do that." He winked at me, reaching over to turn off the lights, then pulled me underneath him and kissed me tenderly.

Chapter 26

Pulling onto Roscoe Avenue the following day, I parked down one of the side streets near my office. It was a slightly longer drive from Rhodes' house, not exactly within walking distance like it was from my apartment, but it wasn't bad.

Stretching my legs, I walked back towards Roscoe. I was about to wave at the Sentinel Security van, but it was empty. That couldn't be good news. I quickened my step, hurrying to look down the street.

I didn't see anything in front of my office, but motion across the street, at Grounds, caught my attention. Jim, one of Wyatt's guys, stood with Mo, who was looking up at his storefront. The big glass window facing the road had a gaping hole in it, with cracks running into his painted logo across the top.

Anger boiled up in me. It had to have been Dessi. Or Cynthia, because he ignored her warnings against being Nate's legal council.

Checking for cars, I jogged across the street.

"Are you okay?" I hurried over to Mo.

His eyes were pinched at the corners. "Yeah, no one was hurt."

I hugged him. "What happened?"

"It's just this." He waved his hand at the window. "Just vandalism. Nothing was damaged inside. It doesn't look like there was any theft."

My face scrunched up in frustration. "It was a threat."

"Of course it was." He pulled his shoulders up and let them down in resignation. "But it's over. I didn't listen, and I got my payback."

"But what if it's not over?"

Picking up the broom he had left propped against the brick exterior, he resumed sweeping up the glass on the sidewalk. "I'm not going to live in fear."

Neither was I.

Meanwhile, later that afternoon, in a mid-sized red truck headed across town,

"How was school today?" Rhodes asked Nate, having just picked him up. He'd promised Ms. Tomlinson he'd have him there right after school since he had the day off to help the team. As promised, he'd stay this week, just to see how things went.

If things went well, the kid could take the subway next week, but he had to claim ownership of his future. It was up to him to make this work.

"Good." He nervously adjusted the backpack tucked between his legs.

"I heard you had good luck at the court hearing last week."

"Yeah. Mr. Maurice is a good lawyer. Maybe the best."

"He must be pretty good." He smiled, but it twisted with pain when he thought about the boy's safety. After this morning's destruction of property, he felt the need to impress it upon the youth even further. "Hey, Nate. I know you're keeping an eye out for Cynthia and working extra hard to keep your nose clean."

"Yeah." The kid watched him with curiosity.

"Just be careful, okay? They weren't able to pin the events at the warehouse on you, and they may not be happy about it."

"I hear ya, Mr. Rhodes. I'll be careful. I have to be." He shot him a wide smile. "I'm gonna be a lawyer."

"Oh, you are?" He gave him an encouraging look.

It was amazing how much the kid had changed in just a week. It was as though Maurice's personal efforts towards him had given him a new view of life. That couldn't be a bad thing.

"Yeah. I'm working on my handwriting and typing skills at the center after school."

"Not just basketball?" He was impressed. They had all sorts of tutoring, but few kids took advantage of it all.

"That's right." He nodded. "I'm gonna be an advocate for others. Defend people's rights."

"You might have to start with filing, though." He tried to contain a grin at the kid's enthusiasm.

"Maybe." Nate tilted his head. "I'll work hard. Whatever it takes."

"Even if it takes a while?" He didn't want him to think it was going to be easy. Being a public defender took years of schooling.

"That's okay. I'm in it for the long haul, like Mr. Maurice said. What else do I have to do anyway?"

"This baby gets twenty-five miles to the gallon in the city," the car salesman said, patting the hood of the used golden Camry, keys dangling from his fingers. He flicked them up and down like it was a fancy trick. I struggled to hold back the eye roll. I had already asked to take it for a drive, and he was delaying my well-thought-out plan.

"Wow, that's great," I said, kicking a tire. "I just want to see for myself how she handles."

"Oh, you're gonna love her." He gave me an overly familiar smile, leaning in too closely for my comfort. "There's even a mirror to check your makeup over the driver's seat."

"Oh, gee. That's everything I ever wanted." It was impossible to keep the sarcasm from my voice. What was he thinking? Did I even look like that sort of person?

"Let's get in, and you can see for yourself."

Oh, hell no. "I think I'm good to test-drive it by myself."

"But I can show you all the bells and whistles." I could smell his aftershave, bitter over overwhelming body odor from the end of a summer day.

"I know." I swiped the keys from his fingers on their next flick up. I affected a sweet smile. "I just don't think I could concentrate with you there."

Glancing at his watch, he hesitated. "It's getting a little late. We close at seven."

Backing away, I edged into the driver's seat. I just needed him to take his hand off the door. "I'm just going around the corner. I'll be right back."

"Okay," he trailed off, lifting his hand.

Snapping the door shut, I started the engine in one motion, hitting it into drive and zipping out of the lot, leaving him to stare open-mouthed in my wake. It was nearly six-thirty, and I was running behind schedule. That is, if Dessi held to his.

Pulling up to the light, I took my phone from my pocket and propped it into the cup holder. I loved my Jeep, but Dessi knew me, and the Camry was more conspicuous.

"That took long enough," Sam's voice came over the speaker.

I took a right onto Clybourn. Today of all days, the traffic lightened up, and I made a right onto Damen. At last, things were going my way.

A *bing* came through the speakers.

"It's Grady," Wyatt said. "Dessi's keeping to his pattern. He's getting ready to leave."

"I'm almost there." I raced a red light, watching for cops. "I'll be there in just a few minutes."

Speeding up a bit, I changed lanes and headed towards Wicker Park.

"He's walking towards the door," Wyatt said.

"Can you make it?" Rhodes asked.

"Yeah, I'm nearly there." I almost sideswiped a couple hesitating on the curb. They headed across after me. *Tourists.*

I made a right onto Bloomingdale and pulled into an alley. "I'm in place. Is everyone else set?"

"I'm in place," Rhodes answered.

"Me too," Sam piped up.

"Me three," Suzy spoke, happy to be driving her car for the few minutes it would take.

"Me four," Brian said.

"Ready," Wyatt said.

The Camry was in park, my hand hovering on the shifter. A moment later, I saw a black Audi pull out of the Dream Time parking lot, the cover for the hidden speakeasy.

"It's go time, people." Letting my foot off the brake, I rolled forward, following the car at a decent distance. "He's turning right."

"I'm headed in that direction," Sam said. "Be ready to move."

"Turning left onto North," I announced, following him onto the street. I kept a car's length between us. "Right towards Old Town."

"Gold Coast," Sam guessed.

"Probably."

Traffic got between us, dropping me back three cars, but I still kept him within my sights. "His lights are on for LaSalle." I needed to back off. I had followed long enough.

"I've got him," Sam said as his Tesla cut me off, still a few cars behind Dessi.

"I'm out." I turned left, heading back towards the dealership. "Everyone else in place?"

"Redirecting towards the Gold Coast," Suzy said.

"You didn't believe me?" Sam laughed.

"I figured Lincoln Park."

"Lake Shore Drive is the best."

"For some."

"I mean it's elitist, for people like him. Turning left," Sam said. "I'm breaking off. The Tesla is too obvious to tail him for long."

"I'm here," Rhodes said. "I've got him. Traffic is tight here, though. I don't know how long I can keep sights on him. Maybe a couple of blocks."

"I'm on it," Suzy said. "I see the little bastard."

As I pulled into the car lot, I spied the salesman pacing in front of my Jeep. Oops. I slid into an open space, got out, and threw him the keys. "The mirror wasn't big enough."

After unlocking my car, I got in, clicked my phone into the holder, and backed out, leaving the guy standing there, still trying to get words out.

"I see him," Wyatt said.

"I'm back in my Jeep. Heading that way," I said.

"No point. I think we have him."

"I'm right around the corner," Brian said. "I can pick up wherever you leave off."

"Let me tail him to the end of this block. I think he's turning. There're some high-rise apartments close by on Lake Shore. It's probably one of those." He paused for a minute. "Okay, he's turning right."

"I see him. I'm on it."

"I'm circling the neighborhood," Sam said. "I can jump in next if needed."

I pulled over to the side of the road. No way could I make it far enough to jump back into the train. I crossed my fingers. This had to work. If he made the tail, he'd throw us off.

"Got it," Brian eventually said. "He's pulling into a garage. There's parking on a side street, half a block away, in view of the building. I'll head over there and keep an eye on him."

"I'm pulling up behind you," Wyatt said.

"Okay, parked," Brian confirmed. "I'm scanning the apartments with binoculars. If he switches on his lights, I can tell which one is his."

"It's not dark yet," I said, wishing it was later in the year. "He might not."

"It's habit," Wyatt said. "He'll switch them on."

"Top-right corner," Brian announced, pleased.

"Got it," Wyatt's voice hitched up.

"I have visual confirmation," Brian said.

Everyone cheered.

"I'll count the windows and send the location to everyone's phone."

I laid my head on my steering wheel, closing my eyes with relief.

We finally had him.

"Setting it for two thirty again?" Rhodes asked.

I looked up from my phone. "Do you think we should get up earlier?"

"We're meeting at the Mennons at three, right?"

"Yeah, you're right. Sam's not picking us up." I edited my alarm. "I'll set it for two. I'm packed, so it won't take long, but I can use the time to get into the right headspace."

I rubbed my forehead. I'd never willfully gone into another person's house in the middle of the night. Warehouse, yes, but not with other people there. And not with the intent to overpower them if necessary, possibly even harm them. We were talking about a killer here, but still… It didn't sit easily in my stomach.

"You good?" Rhodes sat down on the edge of the bed, next to me.

"I'm good. Just ready for this night to be over. And maybe the possibility of getting our lives back to normal."

My phone rang. It was Rodriguez. That was odd.

"Hello?"

"Mal." He sounded breathless. "There's been a theft."

"What happened?" I stood up suddenly. "Is Jen okay?"

"Yeah, Jen's fine." He took a deep breath. "The evidence. Someone stole it."

"Shit!" I exploded. Rhodes appeared in front of me, anxious to figure out what was wrong. I held the phone at an angle to tell him what Rodriguez had said.

"I had it marked under a pseudonym so no one would know what case it was for. I have no idea how anyone knew it was there."

Distrust trickled down in my gut and grew. No one knew about it but him and Jen. And there was no way she would betray me.

He, on the other hand, had already done just that. Our history, once again, raised its grotesque head.

"Why?" I bit out. "Dessi pay better than the force, huh? Wasn't climbing the ranks quick enough?" Then it hit me; he *was* awfully young to be a detective. One of the youngest. I'd only made it to detective because I went to the private sector, but we were about the same age. "How expensive was that detective rank, exactly? Do you have no honor?"

"Mal." He sounded stunned. "If you think I would do something like this, you really don't know me."

My heart went out to Jen. She'd believed in him, had hopes and dreams with him, and had tried to get me to believe in him too.

"I don't think I ever really knew you." I hung up the phone, throwing it into the corner of the room, and let out a savage scream, my hands in tight fists by my side.

Not saying anything, Rhodes came up to me and grabbed my arms. I fought against him for a moment, then collapsed into him, my fingers curled into his back in anger, holding on for dear life.

"How could he do this?"

"You sure it was him?"

"Well, it wasn't Jen." I laughed bitterly. "Why am I so surprised?"

"It isn't your fault he's a lying, cheating bastard. Just like it's not your fault Dessi's a conniving madman."

I knew he was making sense, but the burden of responsibility still weighed heavily on me.

"I have to call the team." I walked over to the corner, still shaking in anger, to my phone that sat, discarded, on the ground. A single crack ran across the screen. Great.

That was my fault.

I didn't want to discourage them, but they had the right to know.

"What's wrong?" Sam said, seeing my face. He looked off-screen, probably motioning Suzy over.

My mouth pinched even further. It was painful to admit I had messed up. I cast my eyes down, feeling the guilt. It had been my idea to turn in the evidence. I waited for Wyatt to answer.

"Yes?" We had everyone.

"I made a mistake." Rhodes frowned at me. Moving to stand behind me, he laid a hand on my back.

"What happened?" Wyatt asked.

"Rodriguez sold us out." I let out a short breath. "The evidence is gone."

"Gone?" Sam's eyes got wide.

"Do we know it was the detective?" Wyatt asked slowly, his eye twitching.

I pursed my lips. "He says it went missing, but only he and Jen knew where it was. He had it under a code name in the evidence locker. Who else could it be? He's not trustworthy. He's already proved that. He was on the case when Jeremy Jones walked. He probably had something to do with that one, too."

Wyatt gave a short nod.

"We have nothing?" Suzy's voice asked from the other side of Sam's phone.

"I have backups of everything I gave him," Sam said nonchalantly.

"You do?" My eyes went round.

"Of course."

"I don't." My gaze slid to the right and down. And with it, my mood. How irresponsible of me not to have done the same.

"We have his voice on the recording, from the parabolic mic. We just don't have his picture."

"We don't have pictures of the stored guns or of him holding the one that killed Calvin Meister, the arms dealer. And if he has those pictures now, he knows we know about them. He'll move them quickly."

"I've got surveillance set up," Sam said. "They haven't been moved yet."

Unless Dessi moved them before Sam got it in place.

"I'm sorry." I looked them all in the eye. "This was my fault. I take responsibility."

"Oh, stop it," Suzy said. "You were giving him a second chance. How could you have known? You were trusting your instincts."

"Not really." I shook my head. "I was trusting Jen's. I still didn't trust him."

Wyatt wasn't saying anything. He knew I was at fault. His eyes flicked down. "I just got a text from Brian. He wants to talk about Dessi."

"Bring him into the call," Sam said.

A moment later, another box appeared on my phone, and Brian's face filled it.

"Hey, boss." He looked around the screen, taking in everyone before waving. "I have news. After you all took off, I stayed to keep an eye on Dessi's condo. A couple of hours later, another black sedan came—a Jag, not his Audi—but the same driver."

He was being extra careful not to be followed.

"I tailed them." He held up his hands at our nervous looks. "I was careful. I nearly lost him three times from hanging too far behind. Followed him to a storage unit across the river, near Bucktown."

"That's not far from here," I said.

"The place is in a rougher neighborhood," Brian said.

"Were you able to see which unit was his?" I asked, hope catching a toehold in my chest.

He shook his head. "I couldn't get that close without giving myself away."

We all let out a collective breath.

"I bet I know what name it's listed under." Sam's eyes twinkled. "I looked up the property records on the condo after Wyatt found the address. Thom Aleksander Kozik."

"Th-om?" I said, surprised.

"I think it's pronounced 'Tom,'" came Suzy's tactful voice. I could almost hear her fighting a grin at her husband.

"What's that nationality?" Rhodes said, curious.

"It's Polish." Sam's eyebrows raised as laughter bubbled out of his mouth. "He's not even *Italian*! I bet he dyes his hair."

"Fabian Dessi isn't even real?" I asked incredulously.

"Oh, that identity may not be real, but it's legal. Apart from the fake part. He's managed to get a birth certificate and all relevant paperwork under the name Dessi. It's a duplicate of his original one, except he made himself five years older, probably to gain acceptance and stature with the local mafia. I don't know how he got a fake identity that well integrated into the system," Sam said, impressed. "but he's done his homework. He's even got driver's licenses and property tax payments registered to Dessi. Thom has very few records within the past ten years."

"Does this change things?" Rhodes asked. "I mean, should we go after the storage unit tonight instead of his condo? Who knows what we could find there?"

I considered the option, but it felt like things had boiled to a tipping point.

I shook my head. "I think it's now or never. I say we go for it. But you all have to agree."

One by one, they all nodded.

"I know you don't normally carry." Wyatt looked directly at me. "But tonight, you do."

I cut my eyes to Rhodes, who was watching me carefully. "I already have it in my pack."

It was a standard 9mm Glock. Perfect for when I needed extra protection.

Wyatt's head dropped in agreement, as did Rhodes'. I knew I didn't need it, but I was appreciative of his approval.

Tonight's stakes had just gotten a little higher.

Chapter 27

Meanwhile, in a glass-and-chrome-filled condo with a prime view of Lake Michigan,

"Excellent work." Dessi smiled, revealing pearly white teeth. He spoke into the phone at his ear. "What was on the cameras?"

"Pictures of the guns in storage and you at the warehouse sale," a voice spoke into his phone.

"And the audio?" His mouth turned down in anger, his teeth set. She would pay for that.

"Most of the sale at the warehouse. Including the argument about price and a gunshot."

"All circumstantial." Dessi tapped his fingers against his black home-office desk, his fingers like little soldiers, marching one after another.

"What do you want me to do with the evidence?"

"Destroy it, you idiot."

"What about the detective?"

"I've got things handled from here." He ended the call.

"You sure it's going to be tonight, boss?" one of two large goons in front of him asked, hovering near the door.

"Why else would they want to know where I live?" Dessi raised a perfectly manicured eyebrow. He pulled down the cuffs on his tailored shirt under his dove-gray vest and checked the time on his pocket watch. "They just lost everything they have, and they now know where I am. Trust me. It'll be tonight."

"Testing," Sam said, cupping his ear. "Everyone able to hear me?"

"You're sitting right next to me, Sam." I gave him a look.

He stuck out his tongue. "I mean through the mic."

"I hear you." Rhodes sat crouched next to me in the back of Wyatt's Sentinel van, his hand on his ear, still adjusting his earpiece for comfort.

Wyatt and Brian nodded.

"You sure you don't mind helping tonight?" I asked Brian.

"You're not doing this one without me. I want to help put an end to his guy as badly as you do."

"You're coming in clear, babe," Suzy's voice came through my earpiece.

Sam crouched across from me, digging into his bag. Taking my advice, he'd traded his all-black getup for street clothes. They were less conspicuous, especially since we'd likely be seen on Lake Shore Drive, even at this time of night. But the shirt he'd chosen was a Batman T-shirt, the yellow bat signal emblazoned on the front. It was possible the all-black spy outfit he normally wore would have drawn less attention.

"The thermal imaging won't pick up through the roof or the sides of his condo, like they did at the warehouse." He pouted. "And even with my modifications, we'll have limited viewability through the doorway, depending on the layout. It'd be easier if he lived in a house."

"Security is better at the condo," Wyatt said.

"I knew it'd be a condo," Suzy's singsong voice came through.

Zipping up his bag, he mouthed back to Suzy like a toddler, knowing she couldn't see him.

"I can see that."

"How?" he said, his eyes searching the van.

"Gotcha." Her laughter twittered through our ears, the levity soothing my nerves.

Lifting the hem of his shirt, Wyatt drew his gun and checked the cartridge. He looked up at me, his eyebrows raised.

Reaching up, I tapped my lower back, answering his unsaid question. He turned his gaze to Rhodes, asking the same.

Rhodes confirmed he was armed as well. I hadn't known he was a registered gun owner. Apparently, a few things from his youth had stuck. I was just grateful he knew how to use it. He wasn't the type of guy who'd own one without any training on the weapon.

"Ready?" Wyatt asked Brian.

"Ready." Pushing open the rear door, Brian scanned the street and jumped out. We all followed behind.

There was one car a few blocks away, moving through the night. Several parked vehicles lined the street. Nearly everyone would be in bed. It was the only time of day when Chicago was quiet. Even on the edges of downtown, the hustle and bustle of the city ceased to exist. It was like time stood still.

We stood at the end of the block nearest to his condo. His building was one down on the right. Sam pulled out a small tablet, set it on top of a covered trash can, and got to work on it.

"I'm in." He clicked a few more buttons then scrolled. The security monitors popped into view on his screen. "Cutting the camera to the front door, first floor, and thirty-second."

"Are you going to put it on a loop?" I asked.

"They won't notice unless they're looking for it. It's just a regular Monday night. The guards are probably half asleep," Wyatt said.

Sam tucked the tablet into his backpack.

Pulling a ball cap down over his head, Brian turned onto Lake Shore, slumping slightly as he headed towards the front entrance, where a tired night watchman stood. He stumbled a step before reaching the man.

Tipping his hat to the guard, he attempted to walk by, instead pitching forward into the man and spinning him away. The night watchman grabbed his shoulders as we hurriedly approached.

"Sorry, man," Brian slurred out, still wobbly and holding onto the shorter man. We were directly behind him.

Sam quickly held an electronic device up against the card hanging from the guard's waist, careful not to touch him, then reached towards the door with a generic card, wired to the device. The light on the security lock clicked green.

Brian lurched over, his body wracking with fake vomit. He spilled a bottle of carrot soup he'd packed into his jacket onto the ground and hacked over and over. Wyatt opened the door, and the three of us slid through, racing down the hallway. He needed to keep up the distraction for just another few seconds until we cleared the floor.

Hitting the stairwell, Sam pressed the newly coded card against the electronic pad and waved us to follow. It lit green, and we poured through the doorway, heading up to the second floor. He paused to click on his tablet. "Second-floor cam is out. We can take the elevator up from here. I didn't want to wait for it on the first floor in case Brian was having trouble."

"I'm clear," Brian said, his voice back to normal. "The guard was nice but glad to be rid of me. Heading back to the van. Let me know if you need anything."

"I sent the electronic code to an extra card in the van," Sam said. "If we need him, he can use it."

"The guard might give him trouble," I warned.

"Maybe, but I could make it if I need to," Brian said confidently. "I'm new. I got lost, and I'm drunk."

"He might try to verify it."

"Still. I'll be on standby."

The second floor was brightly lit and dead quiet. There were only four doors in the short lobby at the center of the building, with large condos spreading out from the central location. The fire-exit stairs and gleaming silver elevators stood out in the richly decorated entryway. It felt eerie, walking across the carpeted hall with no sounds coming except for our feet against the plush threads. We hit the button to go up.

"The elevator cam's off." Sam glanced up from his pad, a finger poised.

The door opened, and we all entered to head up to number thirty-two.

"Did he have to live so far up?" Rhodes watched the readout change with each floor.

"Higher is more expensive. More expensive means better for some." I wasn't impressed with it, but some people's confidence rested on others' perception of their wealth.

I found Rhodes' hand in the elevator and gave it a squeeze. He looked tight but ready. Wyatt was leaning against one wall, his arms lightly crossed, totally at ease. I wondered if he was honestly that relaxed or if it was only a facade. I always felt a fair amount of unease about things like this, but I normally had the law behind me. Here, I was stretching my thinning morals.

The door dinged and slid open. I stepped out first, my hand poised, ready to pull my weapon if needed.

"With any luck, we'll find the gun in a shoulder holster hanging from his dining room chair," I said, my voice low. "Worst-case scenario, it'll be on his nightstand and we'll have to hold him at gunpoint to get it." Either way, we were leaving here with that gun.

Nodding, Rhodes followed me, taking up my back. Sam hurried behind Rhodes, tucking his tablet in his bag and pulling out a couple of gadgets. Wyatt took up the rear, his gun out and ready, spinning to scan behind us as we passed the closest set of doors. This time, our feet left no sound on the carpet.

Approaching Dessi's door, I read the number posted above to confirm it and gestured to my techie friend. Sam dropped quietly in front of the door's electronic keypad.

Gathering around Sam, we watched him hook a device into the bottom of the keypad and the computer process through potential codes. In the silence of the hall, I could make out my pulse pounding over the hum of electricity. It seemed so loud; I felt like everyone could hear it.

Rhodes and I shared a glance and slowly drew our weapons.

While waiting for the code, Sam sat back on his heels, drew his thermal cam out of his bag, and directed it towards the door. He stretched his neck to the right and left to loosen up, then he froze before turning slowly towards us, his eyes the size of quarters and pointed at the screen. Two large red-and-orange thermal blobs filled it, shaped as figures hovering behind the door.

My heart stopped, dread sliding like cold sludge down my back to settle behind my legs, making them feel numb. I mouthed, *"Retreat."*

The door clicked green.

Raising a shaking hand, Sam withdrew the cord from the keypad and picked up his pack. Setting one foot unsteadily behind the other, he backed up. Wyatt quickly traced his steps back to the elevator and hit the button, his gun aimed towards the door. Rhodes and I covered Sam, walking backwards to follow.

It dinged and slid open. We hurried inside, tucking behind the cover of the stainless steel doorway, guns at the ready for Dessi's door to open. I pressed the close button five or six times until it shut.

When it jolted into motion, heading back down, I pressed my head against the cold steel, breathing for the first time in minutes. That had been close. Way too close.

I felt Rhodes pressed against my side.

"There's no way they don't know we were there," I said. "They have to have seen the door click green. By now, they know we've left. We have to run."

Sam watched us nervously for our next steps.

"What happened?" Brian and Suzy asked over our earpieces.

"They were waiting for us," Wyatt relayed. "Sam saw them with his thermal scanner."

"Oh, God," Suzy whispered.

"What if they make it down the stairs faster than the elevator?" Sam asked, sweat beading on his forehead.

"Thirty-two floors? I doubt it. We can make it."

Unless he had people stationed outside, ready and waiting.

The elevator seemed to take longer on its descent. Finally, it came to a stop.

"I forgot to turn the cams back on upstairs." Sam lunged for his bag.

"Leave it." Wyatt grabbed his bag and headed for the opening door, tucking his weapon away as he went.

We all followed suit, hurrying towards the entrance. The elevator doors shut behind us, and the car headed back up.

Hitting the exit, we bounded out, shocking the security guard as we raced back to the van. Brian waited for us at the end of the block, his weapon drawn and pointed down. He'd left the engine running.

I reached our ride first, slid the door open, and hurried everyone in. Brian was back in place behind the wheel and ready to drive away by the time the doors were all shut. As we pulled away from the curb, I saw two goons appear at the end of the block, guns held high.

"Go!" I urged Brian needlessly.

Shots rang out, hitting the side of the van. Rhodes moved to cover me. Tires squealed as Brian floored it down the street, taking a sharp right, then a left. I hoped we could get some distance between us before they made it to their car.

This was not how I saw us leaving this scene.

"How did he know we were coming?" I looked around at the rest of the crew.

"Did you tell anyone?" Wyatt asked Brian. "If you hadn't been with us tonight and saved our asses, I might have thought you sold us out."

Brian laughed before stealing a glance at his boss, the laughter dying on his lips at Wyatt's set jaw. He swallowed audibly. "I didn't tell anyone."

"All the guys have access to our GPS." Wyatt watched him. "Has anyone been asking questions?"

"Not that I know of."

The van was silent. Not even Suzy tried to lighten the mood.

As we stopped into the Mennons' drive several minutes later, we all stayed seated.

"You all have to stay here," Sam said suddenly.

"I don't think—" Wyatt began to argue.

"I don't care what you think," Sam shut him down. "The house is fully secured. The windows are bulletproof, and the walls are steel reinforced. Believe me when I say it's safe."

"I do. But I'm not sure I need to—"

"You do, and you will." Sam raised his head, looking firmly around at all of us. "No argument."

"Okay," Wyatt said, getting out of the van.

Sam looked at me, slightly surprised. I doubted he thought it would go that easily. He raised his eyebrows at us in a less intense question.

"Okay," Rhodes and I said as one.

"Everything okay, boss?" Duri and Jim asked from the security van on guard for Suzy.

The look Wyatt sent in their direction silenced them. He watched their reactions carefully, scowling. They looked nervously back and forth. Exhaling, he turned and walked up to Sam's doorway, waiting for us.

Suzy answered the door, her arms waving us towards her. "Hurry in!"

We rushed in, and Suzy pulled Sam into a tight embrace. Tears streaked her face. He murmured into her ear, running his hands down her long straight hair.

I realized I was holding onto Rhodes' hand tightly, not knowing when I had grabbed it. I looked up at him. I could feel streaks of fear on my face. He gave me a tight smile, moving in to stand a step closer. His chest rose and fell in deep breaths.

It felt like just another one of my failures, but at least we'd made it out alive.

How long would that continue to work for us?

Raising his head from Suzy's shoulder, Sam said to Wyatt, "You should get Hillary. There's no telling what they'll do."

Wyatt paced the room, searching for answers. Then nodded. "I'll go call her." He disappeared into the kitchen.

"I'll go make up the beds." Suzy headed towards the hall.

"There's no way we're going to be able to sleep tonight." I shook my head. "It's nearly four."

She redirected towards the kitchen. "I'll go make coffee."

Finally, something in my life made sense again.

Rhodes pulled me to him, breaking my chain of thought.

"This isn't your fault." He pressed his forehead to mine, his arms wrapped around me.

I closed my eyes. It sure felt like it. It had been my idea.

"Hillary's packing a bag." Wyatt reappeared. "I'm going to go get her."

He disappeared back out the door.

"I should go," Brian said.

"No," Sam said decisively. "You stay, too."

"Are you sure?" He fidgeted with the seam of his jeans. "I'm just one of Wyatt's guys."

"Wrong again. You're one of the team."

We followed Sam into the kitchen.

Thirty minutes later, we were gathered around the kitchen bar, cups of coffee scattered around. Hillary, yawning from her seat, took a giant gulp of coffee.

At least she was a coffee drinker. Non-coffee drinkers couldn't be trusted.

Wyatt stood close to Hillary, where he could still see down the hall towards the front entrance.

"We've got a mole at Sentinel," he said, frustration emanating from his body.

"Are you sure?" I asked.

"I'm not sure who else it could be. Rodriguez didn't know about this."

Hillary watched him closely, but I couldn't tell if she was angry or worried.

Wyatt's phone went off.

"Yes?" he answered.

"A black sedan rolled by," Jim said through his speaker.

"Draw your weapons," he spoke into the phone.

"We're ready, sir."

Wyatt, Rhodes, and I headed towards the door, drawing our weapons as we ran. We stationed ourselves at either end of the large living room windows. Wyatt pulled the corner of the curtain to glance out.

"What do you see?" I asked.

"The sedan is coming back around."

"It's coming to a stop," Jim's voice came through his speakerphone. "We're trained on it."

We all waited for what Dessi's guys would do. The seconds hand of Suzy's clock on the opposite wall ticked loudly like this was a Jeopardy game.

"It's rolling on," Jim said a long minute later.

As one, we released a breath.

"He doesn't want to attack with the team on guard." Wyatt holstered his weapon. "He doesn't have the element of surprise. You were right, Sam. We're safer as a group."

"We're stronger together," Sam said, standing on the outskirts of the kitchen, his tablet still in hand. When we were all back in the kitchen, he addressed me, "So, what's the backup plan?"

"The backup plan?" I shook my head, having trouble finding my way out of my own self-pity.

"You always have one. What's plan B?"

"I think we may be close to plan F by now." I tried to chuckle at my joke, but he was right. I had to rally. I could do this. Of course I had backup plans. I buckled down to the task at hand. "We have the location of his storage unit now and his real name. Next step, we check that out."

"What if we don't find anything?" Wyatt asked. "There's no telling what he's storing there. Places like that don't have the best security. Why would he store anything important there?"

"I don't know, but whatever he's got there is probably personal. Something he doesn't want found."

"And if we don't find anything?"

"I have a backup plan for that." My eyes narrowed as I fleshed it out in my head. I thought of all the ways I was going to nail Dessi to the floor of the jail cell.

Dessi's biggest weakness was his pride. I would do well to remember that.

Chapter 28

"Mal." Wyatt appeared in the doorway of the room Suzy had assigned to Rhodes and me.

Even though none of us was able to sleep, we'd all separated to get a little quiet space. Rhodes and I had spent the last hour, sitting closely on the bed, our legs and hands touching, but not saying much. We were just glad to be alive.

"What's up?" I stood up, reluctant to reenter the task at hand.

His brows flashed downward in a micro movement, telling me something was wrong. "I had a crew canvas our neighborhoods. They went through your place. Broke things up a bit."

I breathed out, feeling a sinking feeling come over me. "What about Rhodes' place?"

"Nothing that they could see."

I looked back at Rhodes, who was still sitting on the bed, and mouthed, *"Sorry."* I hated that I had put his home at risk.

He shook his head as if to say not to worry, then got up and came to stand by me.

"Should I go?" I was having trouble figuring out what to do next. I felt so unlike myself. I'd never considered this scenario.

"The cops are there. Jim's handling it. He said the landlord's going to throw a padlock on the door until it gets fixed."

It was the second time I had felt this violated. And by the same man.

"What about my office?" I asked suddenly.

"Nothing yet." He shook his head, tapping the doorway as he headed on.

Yet.

Was this what my life was coming to? Why had I decided to try to go against someone like Dessi? Jen had warned me all those months ago. She'd said he was trouble. "Bad company" was what she'd called him. Worse than I could ever have imagined.

I nearly let myself get swallowed up in the fear. Then I remembered Mr. Bunn. Somehow, that little shred of familiarity helped me pull myself out of the depression. I couldn't stop now, or else, he'd take everything that ever mattered to me. He'd go after my friends.

Dessi was scared. He wouldn't be launching such an outright attack if he wasn't.

I turned to Rhodes. "He'd better not have hurt Mr. Bunn."

"Atta girl." He winked.

Meanwhile, in a cheery yellow spare bedroom across the hall,

"I'm really sorry about this." Wyatt leaned against the doorframe, his eyes cast down.

"For what?" Hillary said, looking up from the book she was reading, sitting cross-legged on the bed. She set it down and walked over to him. She barely made it to his chin. "For keeping me safe?"

"It's my fault you'reyou unsafe, to begin with."

She dipped her face under his to meet his gaze. "I know I'm not a tough detective like Mal or a smart bookkeeper like Suzy."

"Don't you dare compare yourself to them. You're special."

"I'm not a fragile little flower," she said sternly.

"I know that. I just don't like the idea of you coming to any harm. Especially when I put you in its way. You never should have gotten messed up with me."

"Messed up with you? Is that how you see it?" She tilted her head to inspect him.

"You'd already be out on Ms. Lamb's property this morning, tending to those flowers you love so much, if you hadn't met me." He let out a ragged breath, trying to keep his emotions under control. It was harder than normal. He couldn't cast a blasé statement and sound cool and composed to cover his feelings this time. "I'm going to see you through this and make sure you're safe, and then I'll leave you be. It's the right decision."

"Is that what you want? For me to go on and find someone else to keep me company?"

"Hell no, that's not what I want," spilled out of his mouth. It was more than he could take. "I want you, but I'm no good for you."

"That man you're talking about? Dessi? He's no good for Chicago." She put a hand, so small and delicate, on his chest. "You and your friends are doing your best to get him off the street. The way I see it, you're the noblest man I've ever met."

His heart clenched in his chest. He searched her face for lies and found none.

But it didn't matter. He couldn't live with himself if she ever got hurt.

"I just can't do it, Hillary. My profession isn't a safe one. It's how I live. I thought I could, but I can't."

"Now, you listen to me, Wyatt Parker." She pursed her little pert lips into a rose and stood on her tiptoes, fingers curled in to poke him in the chest. "I may not have the skills your friends have, but I'm no weak little girl. I pull weeds all day and carry around five-gallon pots full of plants. I know a little about handling myself. Do you think I started living when I met you?"

He pressed his lips together to keep himself from grinning at her. She had gumption, that was for sure. And she did have some of the strongest arms he'd ever seen on a woman. Actually, it was pretty hot.

"No, ma'am, I do not." He tucked his hands into his back pockets, watching her. My God, she was everything he'd ever wanted.

"And you think *you're* going to tell *me* who I'm going to see?" She put her fists on her hips. "I don't think so. Now you get out there and figure out your next move."

"Yes, ma'am," he said just before the door shut in his face.

That didn't quite go as planned.

The lock clicked open in my hands. Finally, someone in this city who didn't protect their place up like Fort Knox, with technology. It felt good to be confronted with a regular, old bolt lock. I stretched and turned the doorknob. It swung open easily.

"There are no security wires," Sam said, scanning the ceiling.

"Nope." I gave the interior a cursory glance.

He tsk-tsked, heading towards the office desk in the corner and turning on the desktop computer. "They don't even have their customers listed online. What are they, living in the nineteenth century?"

I stifled my laughter. If it weren't for Sam, I probably would have fallen by the wayside as well. I'd never have learned to crack into an online database. It was so far out of my skill set.

"This thing isn't even connected to the web." Picking up the mouse plugged into the computer with a wire, he shook it, his mouth turned down in disgust.

It was nearly twenty-four hours since our failed mission at the condo. We had run over my plethora of backup plans. I had several, but one was my favorite.

"I found the account book," Wyatt said, digging through the files on the desk.

"Surely, it's logged digitally, too." Sam peered over his shoulder.

Wyatt just shrugged, flipping through it to the K's.

"There's nothing registered to Thom Kozik," Sam said. "I thought for sure we'd find something connected to his real name."

"Maybe it's listed as something else," Wyatt said, still scanning the names. "No Dessi."

"Look for Marchi or some of his other henchmen. Maybe his business name."

"Looking," Wyatt said, busily scanning back and forth.

Turning away, I poked into a filing cabinet.

"I found customer agreements. Maybe he was using a code name in the book." I flicked through, searching for something familiar.

Pulling open another cabinet, Rhodes started his own search.

"Paper copies?" Sam shook his head in wonder, returning to the computer to see what he could find. "What is wrong with them? Don't they know they can scan those into the system and reduce all this waste? They're killing trees here."

Thirty minutes later, we had found nothing.

"Should we just pick a few units?" Sam asked, looking out the window blinds. "See what we find?"

"No." I shook my head. "I say we move onto Plan C."

There was a lot of room for things to go wrong, but if we pulled it off, it would be so satisfying. Besides, it was very likely our last chance.

"Good news, everybody," Wyatt announced loudly during the video conference call with his team the next morning. It was a mandatory meeting with the whole crew at Sentinel Security. "It's just a matter of time now."

We all stood behind him, delighted looks on our faces.

Knowing we wouldn't be able to get into Red again, and undoubtedly not into Dessi's house, we needed another plan. If he believed we'd stolen something from him, something private, we'd be challenging his character and baiting him to come and get it back.

No way would he send a lackey for something that personal. He thought he was unstoppable. Pride was his greatest weakness. And we were using it against him.

"You've got him, sir?" Jim spoke up.

"We found what we needed last night." He smiled proudly.

"Congratulations," Grady said. "How'd you do it?"

"We found his storage unit," Sam announced, wagging his eyebrows for effect.

"What'd you find?" the new guy pushed.

"We're not sharing that just yet." I pasted on a smile, slapping Wyatt's back in congratulations. "We're taking it to the cops in the morning."

"That's why we're calling," Wyatt said soberly. "Once the cops get it and they issue the arrest for Dessi, he'll disappear. He's got someone on the force, I'm sure of it, so there's no way he won't find out about it."

"But the evidence is damning," I said. "It ties directly to him. There's no way he can weasel his way out of this one."

"That's right." Wyatt nodded. "But in the meantime, we could all be targets. I'm sorry, team, but you will all need to get out of town and lie low for a few weeks until they locate Dessi and this all dies down."

The team on the conference call looked back and forth between each other, eyebrows drawn in concern.

"I know, I'm sorry. I know it's not ideal," he continued. "All I can offer you is tonight. Go see your girlfriends, boyfriends, your family, whatever. Everyone gets the night off, and we're going to celebrate our successes at Mal's office downtown. I'll be covering Suzy tonight personally. I've already called the rest of our jobs and let them know we'd be out of the office for a short break."

"We'll have to keep it somewhat quiet, so we don't draw his attention," I picked up. "But for Dessi, it's just another night."

"There'll be enough of us there. I doubt he'll cause too much trouble." Wyatt nodded, his voice commanding and decisive. "If anyone would like to join us, we'll be there tonight around five o'clock. But come tomorrow morning, get the hell outta Dodge. I'll call you all in a few weeks."

Everyone nodded.

If we were going to beat Dessi, it would have to be at his own game.

The con was officially on.

Knocking on the door of the house where I had grown up felt strange. I hadn't been here in years after my dad told me I had messed up by leaving the academy. A dropout was what he'd called me. Apparently, I was wrong to have tried and wrong again when I gave up. I couldn't win and was tired of trying.

"Molly?" Mom's shining eyes indicated she was surprised and elated to see me. We had talked now and then on the phone, but the tension with Dad always kept a distance between us.

"Is Dad here?" I said, resolved. If I was going to do this, I needed to do it now. There was a possibility things wouldn't go well tonight and I wouldn't get another chance.

Glancing behind her into the house, she nodded, her familiar auburn curls bouncing around her face. She still looked so young. "Come on in, honey. We're glad to see you."

"Who's here, Martha?" my dad said, coming into the living room, his tall stature still as commanding as ever. He hung back briefly upon seeing me enter, one loafer-covered foot coming to pause on the dated shag carpeting.

"Hi, Dad." This would be harder than I had thought. I had to jump in. "Look, I know you never really approved of me being a detective."

He cast his eyes down for a moment, before meeting mine.

"I've not always made the right decisions in life or with my career," I pushed forward. "I felt like I had to prove myself, to do something on my own. And I'm proud of what I've built. It took me some time to get here, but I'm proud of it."

He nodded slowly, choosing his words carefully. "It's not that I didn't think you could be an officer. Hell, you've always had the mind for it. I just didn't want it to change you, like it did me. It's a rough road, and not something I wanted my little girl getting mixed up in."

"That wasn't your choice, Dad." I lifted a hand. "Anyway, take it or leave it; this is me."

"I guess it is." He bounced his head, his lips pressed into a line. "Looks like I pushed you away more than kept you safe. You were going to do what you were going to do."

"I'm not saying I was always right." I thought about all the reasons I'd left the academy. "Not saying I was entirely wrong, either. But I needed to find out for myself."

"I shouldn't have tried to take those decisions from you."

It wasn't acceptance, exactly, but it was what I needed to hear. I nodded.

"I have to get back." I turned slightly, partially facing the door. "I'm in the middle of something, but I needed to do this."

He searched my face, the eyes of a detective measuring my words carefully. I saw a flash of frustration in them, then pain. "You got this, Moll?"

Somehow, he must have understood the severity of the situation. But I had friends this time. "Yeah. I do."

"Then, you'll be there if l stop by and see your office next week?"

"I will," I said, hoping it would turn out to be true.

"Be sure you are." His jaw set, and he watched me leave.

"We'll need to play this very carefully," I said, checking the camera's angle. It caught most of the lobby and Suzy's desk. "We need to know when he arrives. We don't want him sneaking up on us. And if things go bad, we need to be able to track him."

Brian was posted at the door, but I doubted we'd see Dessi until later.

"What's the plan?" Wyatt asked. "We can't tail him. He'll be on high alert."

"Sam and I have most of it." I shot Sam a look. He was just making his way back from the corner cabinet where he had installed yet another camera. The man was thorough. "The only thing we haven't figured out is how to kill his cell phone."

"Someone has to get close enough to brush past him with this." He held up a small device. "It'll wipe his phone. He'll have to get another."

"You can't kill it remotely?" Wyatt frowned.

"Not definitively." He shook his head. "I can make it go down, but there's a possibility he could get it back online if he has a techie employee on hand. We need him to get a brand-new phone."

"Any ideas?" Wyatt crossed his arms.

Sam and I shared a quick glance, refusing to let our eyes land on Hillary, the obvious choice. She had taken to pruning our office plants and was currently fussing over them. She had found a plastic fork and was breaking up the soil, something about it needing aeration.

"Well," I hesitated. "Brian could go into Red; he's never been there before. Dessi keeps his phone in his breast pocket; I've seen the outline more than once. All he'd have to do is brush past him when he leaves his office to come here."

"He'll come early," Wyatt said.

I nodded.

"He'll recognize Brian." Wyatt paced the room. "He normally takes the day shift. He's been sitting outside the office most days since Suzy started here."

"Maybe. How about Rhodes? He's been in the place before, but if he orders a beer and sits near the walkway, he should be safe enough. If anything, Dessi will wonder what he's up to."

Setting down the wires he was carrying for Sam, Rhodes nodded. "No problem."

"I don't like the idea," Wyatt said.

"Rhodes is the best we've got. You can't go, and neither can Sam or I. We could try Jim or your other newer guy, Duri." I held up my hands. "If you're sure one of them hasn't switched sides, we could go that route. I trust your instincts."

"This is silly." Hillary rose, dusting her hands off from repotting one of the smaller plants into a short ball vase she'd found. "He probably doesn't know my face. I'll do it."

"No." Wyatt let out a low growl. "Probably doesn't cut it. They may have followed me to your house."

"My house doesn't mean they know my face."

"All they have to do is pull up your real estate records, then your driver's license photo." He looked at her firmly.

"Last time my picture was taken, I had a terrible burn." She crossed her arms. "I hardly look like my driver's license photo. I'll wear a wig. It'll be fine."

Wyatt crossed the room in three long strides. "You don't know what this man is capable of."

"Yes, I do. You told me." She brushed past him to go to Sam. "How do I do this?"

Sam stalled, device in hand. His eyes ping-ponged between them.

"No, you won't."

"Knock it off," she said calmly. "You may look like an angry Viking right now, but you're not going to physically stop me. This is my choice."

Wyatt's mouth fell open, knowing he had lost. He looked at me. "This is your fault."

I just raised my hands. "I didn't bring it up."

"You knew she would offer."

"I think it's the best idea, but I wasn't going to ask her to do it. She proposed it."

With Wyatt having backed off for the moment, Sam hurried to show her how the instrument worked.

"If you cuff her sleeve, you can tuck it in there." Suzy came forward to help fit it into her clothing, rolling the edge up over the slim device.

"What if it comes undone?" Sam squinted.

"Oh!" She whirled back to her desk, pulling out a drawer to rummage around. Finding what she wanted, she held her hand up, brandishing several safety pins. "I'll pin it! Now all you have to do is bump into him or something."

"If she can get within a foot of his phone, the jammer will scramble it and shut it down." He cast me a side look. "It doesn't actually wipe it."

"Whatever."

"You really want to do this?" Wyatt said, having listened in to the interaction.

"Yes." Hillary raised her chin. "I can do this."

"I know you can. But I want you to know you don't have to." He tugged at her sleeves, ensuring they looked normal. "You have to know the risk. This could end badly."

"I know. It could also end badly with Dessi out there, handing more guns out to gangs."

She got it. I watched Wyatt struggle with her decision, just like Rhodes had with mine. Like I struggled with him being under that burning house. It was hard to know those you loved were in danger. But you had to let people be who—

Wait. *Loved?* My brain skidded through my thoughts. I looked at Rhodes, who had a sympathetic look on his face while regarding the exchange in front of us. He caught my stare and hitched up the side of his mouth in a sideways grin that said, *"I get it."*

I nodded. I did too.

"You weren't kidding." Sam chuckled, his eyes trained on his tablet. "That's quite a burn."

We all turned, stunned into silence.

"It was a gloriously cloud-free weekend." Hillary shook her face towards the ceiling as if recalling sunning herself. "And I don't regret it one bit."

We broke up, resuming our tasks to set up for later that night.

Suzy set out wine bottles and cups to set the stage that we were celebrating our win. She even had a big cooler for ice and beer. I hoped she realized we wouldn't actually be drinking any of them.

"You know," Sam said, his face pressed against the brick wall where he had drilled a small hole to set a camera. "The offices next to you are empty. You could take this wall out and expand."

He jumped off the chair he was standing on and patted the brick divider.

"It's a thought." Rhodes walked up behind me. "You put Dessi away. You'll have people banging down your doors for work."

I let out a light laugh. "We'll see."

I'd never thought of it. Maybe when this was all over, I could take some time to think about what I wanted to do next. It seemed so far away.

"How'd it go today?" he asked, bringing my focus back. "You're sure you weren't followed?"

I shook my head. I'd been careful.

"It went about as well as I could have hoped." I raised my shoulders tightly, pulling a face. "I told my dad what I'd been up to and how I felt. I was honest with him. What he decides to do with it is his decision."

"I'm proud of you." He tugged me close in a side hug.

"I think I worked so hard to be just like him, that I never let him know who I really was."

"I think he's an idiot if he doesn't appreciate who you've become."

"Thanks. I know things aren't going to change overnight, but I feel better about it." Even if my dad didn't stop by and nothing came of it, I was glad Rhodes had encouraged me to reach out to him. Speaking my mind and giving myself permission to follow my own path, regardless of anyone's approval, healed a little chunk inside.

"Hey, everyone." Mo appeared at the door, casual in jeans and a button-down shirt with the sleeves rolled up. I guess it was as casual as Mo got. "Brian said I could come on back. Is this where the party is?"

"I barely recognized you without the apron." Suzy laughed, moving in for a hug. "I'm glad you're taking us up on the offer."

"If things go as planned tonight, though, I'm heading back home." He dropped his duffle bag on the floor.

It had taken some persuading, but we eventually got him to agree to stay at the Mennons, just in case. He wasn't too happy about it, but with what was going on with his business, he'd consented.

"That's it," Sam announced. "We've finished the setup. We've set the hook and delivered the tale. It's time for the wire."

"The wire?" I asked, shaking my head in confusion.

"This is the wire. We're drawing him in here, into our game."

"What's he going on about?" I asked in an aside to Rhodes.

"The Sting." Mo laughed, then winked conspiratorially. "Did you get your inside man?"

"He gets it!" Sam pointed excitedly. "We did. But he might be a double-crosser."

"It happens."

"Let's get out of here. I need to get changed for the next act."

We all had places to be for this next part to go according to plan.

Chapter 29

Setting cones along the side of the road, I waved my arms, diverting the already busy traffic down another street and away from the south store. I poked my red hair up into the cap on my head, tugged my construction vest into place, and jogged over to Rhodes, already posted next to the ROAD CLOSED sign.

"I'm ready," I said out loud.

"Ready," Brian answered in my earpiece.

"Ready," Sam said.

"Got my drink," Hillary said, quieter. "I'm ready too."

"Careful," Wyatt warned. "Don't talk too much."

A *humph* carried through the speakers, and I chuckled at Hillary. Wyatt needed a woman like her in his life.

We stood, watching the rerouted traffic. People honked angrily at us. It was just one of Chicago's many sides—road construction and angry driving. It was a small price to pay for the deep-dish pizza, the many coffee shops, the bakeries, and the Chicago skyline. At night, it was the prettiest there ever was.

"Incoming," Hillary hissed. I heard her chair scrape underneath her.

"Shit," Wyatt cursed nervously.

A muffled sound was heard.

"Oh, excuse me. I'm so sorry." I heard the clatter of plates and chairs moving.

"Say something," Wyatt said. "Are you okay?"

"Thank you, sir." Another couple of bumps and a heavy sigh. "It's done."

"It's done?" Sam asked. "Are you sure?"

"Yup," she said softly, taking a loud slurp from her straw. "I got my shoulder right into his chest. Whacked him good."

Suzy let out an unladylike snort from where she sat safely at home. "Go, Hillary!"

"I have him," Wyatt said. He was posted across the street from Red with binoculars. "He just pulled his phone out and is tapping on it. He's mad. You did it, babe!"

"Told ya."

"He's yelling at the driver. And pacing about."

"He's realizing he doesn't have many options. He'll be on his way to the phone store," I said, watching the traffic. "If he comes this way, he'll be redirected to the east store."

There were only three shops in the vicinity with his carrier. He wouldn't chance taking me down without a good method of communication. He'd need to call his goons in to get rid of our bodies.

"Please don't send someone else," Suzy chanted.

"He doesn't have time," I said, crossing my fingers.

"If he heads North, I'll shut down the electricity on the light." Sam's voice was bright with excitement.

If he picked the north store, he'd eventually get tired of waiting in traffic at the broken light and head east.

"You're one scary dude," Wyatt said, relaxed now that Dessi was out of the speakeasy and Hillary's direct vicinity. "And let's get you out of there, Hillary."

Another long slurp came through the lines. "Almost finished. Okay. I'll head over to Suzy's."

Several minutes later, Brian said, "He's coming this way. Heading to the east store."

"Oh, boy!" Sam exclaimed. "Jacob's ready for him."

"We're headed out," I said, pulling off my cap and vest and making my way to my Jeep. "We'll meet you at the office."

Just before I reached my door, Rhodes grabbed my hand. Pulling me back, he kissed me roughly. "Just in case."

I knew he wasn't happy with the plan, but he had my back.

"I'm moving in with you tomorrow," I blurted out.

He stopped. "What?"

"For real. Like emptying my apartment. Moving in."

"Because of this?"

"Because I want to."

"When did you plan that?"

"I didn't." I laughed. "No planning involved. Maybe I'm tired of planning everything."

A grin split his face. "Spontaneity looks good on you, Columbo. Now let's go catch a mobster."

We piled into my Jeep and took off.

A minute later, Wyatt came through the earpiece. "I just got to the east store. His car is in the lot. I can see him through the window, talking to a curly-haired man."

"Told ya." Sam preened. "My cousin is the bomb. I told him to replace it free of charge, that I felt bad for accidentally messing up his phone. He won't say anything. Supposedly, it's a warrantable defect."

Jacob owned that particular location. Sam had provided the brand-new phone to him preinstalled with a GPS-enabled tracker, making him only a minor accomplice.

"Looks like he's set. He's exiting," Wyatt said. "Get in place. Now."

"Just pulling in now," I said.

"Nearly there," Sam said.

"Ten seconds," Sam's urgent voice resounded in our ears. He was monitoring the GPS from his home office. "Five, four, three, two, one."

Everyone had taken additional risks, but at the end, here, where we knew Dessi would be, Suzy, Hillary, and Mo wouldn't be on the ground, staying instead tucked up safely at the Mennons' compound with Sam, even though he'd argued about being here in person. We could put on the show without him.

"Can you imagine the look on his face?" I laughed loudly, holding up a drink. "What an idiot. He didn't even see it coming."

"The way I see it," Dessi said cooly, waltzing into my lobby and waving a gun casually around the room, "you're the idiot for thinking I didn't know exactly what was happening in my town every step of the way. Checkmate, my little detective."

I dropped my drink on the ground, and the cup bounced, splattering red wine on the carpet and across a wall.

Brian and Rhodes held up their hands.

"H-how'd you know?" I stammered. The fear wasn't entirely put on. The man had a loaded gun pointed at us. I was literally shaking in my boots, trying to keep my wits about me.

"I have men stationed everywhere." Dessi sniffed with superiority. He ran a hand down his pinstripe vest, maintaining the impression of a polished businessman, even in this weather. "You thought you could post an inside man under my nose? I know everyone who sets foot on my turf."

Not everyone. He hadn't caught on to Hillary.

"Grady turned on you the moment I offered him even a penny over what you were giving him. Shame, really." He tsked at Wyatt. "You should be taking better care of your men than that. They're not loyal to you at all."

Wyatt's upper lip curled up, but he stayed silent.

"Loyal like Jeremy Jones and Dr. Millwood?" I pushed him. "So loyal you had to beat them up to get them to confess to your crimes? That's not loyalty. That's fear."

A slow smile spread across his face. "Fear, loyalty, what's the difference? I get what I want. They took the fall. That was their job."

His gun's aim turned to Rhodes. "They knew their place—to take the fall. Mo was a good little puppy. Did what he was told, but you encouraged him to make a wrong decision on this one. Nate was mine. You took that from me."

Uh-oh. That's not how this was supposed to play out.

"You always take what isn't yours." I tried to pull his attention from Rhodes. I needed his confession. "You didn't pay those arms dealers. You shot Calvin Meister. And I had pictures to prove it."

"You had pictures of me at the warehouse." He lifted his gun. "With this baby. But where are they now? All that work, and nothing to show."

"But how did you have someone break into the police station?"

"How simplistic." He sighed. "I have a *real* inside man. One who won't turn on me. I've made sure of it."

"Blackmail, more like it."

He lifted his shoulders.

"That's how you got away with putting the hit out on Suzy and with my kidnapping." I let my mouth fall open as if I was shocked by the news.

He preened. "This city belongs to me. When will you understand that? Besides, Suzy had that coming. I had hoped she'd be here. I wanted to put the final bullet in her head myself."

"Asshole." I took a deep breath, forcing my heartbeat to relax. Just a little further. "You're selling guns to the gangs, causing more violence and death. What's wrong with you? Why would you want to increase the danger in this town?"

"You honestly are sophomoric. To think, I once thought you a worthy adversary. I was actually a little pleased when my men didn't find you in your apartment. I thought, how clever of you to know I'd be coming for you and we could continue this little game." He shook his head sadly.

I blanched at the realization that he was going to have me killed, even though part of me suspected it. *Why else would he have someone break in, in the middle of the night?*

"Of course I'm upping the ante. The good businesswomen and men of Chicago are willing to pay extra for protection when their safety is threatened. The more criminal activity, the more fear, the more money, and the more control. It's just simple logic." He trained the gun firmly on me. "Now, where is it?"

"What is it you want?" I blinked, my hands still in the air. I hoped he would tell us what he thought I had.

"What you took from the storage unit." He stepped closer. I could see Rhodes take a few small steps in our direction. "Don't play dumb with me. And you stay where you are, or she gets shot."

Rhodes stopped. The muscles of his jaw pulsed.

"I can't." I took a deep breath. Here we go. "There is nothing."

"What do you mean, there's nothing?" He sneered. Then it clicked.

"You've just confessed on camera. The cops are on their way. You don't have enough men to look the other way on this one." I pointed to the tiny camera light posted in the corner. My nostrils flared in anger, fear, and satisfaction. "Fabian Dessi, it's over."

It felt so good to finally say that to him.

Rage bloomed in Dessi's eyes. Swinging his gun around, he shot the camera and brought the weapon down to me.

"Drop your weapon," Wyatt said, coming up from his hiding place behind Dessi in the hallway, his gun trained on the crime lord.

Thank God. I was worried he hadn't made it back in time.

But he hadn't, not quite. Because one moment, I was watching desperation build in Dessi's eyes, and the next, I felt the bullet hit my chest. I vaguely saw Rhodes jump in front of me, gun drawn, and heard another shot ring out in the doorway.

Then it all went black.

Meanwhile, in a black sedan speeding across town,

"You idiot," Dessi spit out. "It was all a lie. They were playing you."

"No way." Grady shook his head, his hands held out in front of him. "They have something. I'm sure of it."

A shot rang out, and the young man's head went still against the leather seat.

Holstering his weapon, he pulled out his phone. Things were going downhill fast. Maybe he'd underestimated the detective, but he still had things under control.

"Yes?"

"Pietro, sir. I'm sorry to bother you, but I need a favor."

"What's happened now?" Pietro Marchi slowly said in his heavy Italian accent. "Did you screw up again?"

"Now, sir." He started to sweat. "I can fix this. I just need a few resources. Do you have any inside men in the department?"

"You blew the last two arms deals, Fabian. *You're* supposed to be helping *me* out, not the other way around." He clucked his tongue. "I knew you weren't ready for this."

"The last deal went smoothly."

"With a body in the morgue."

"Tiny detail. There's no trace to you or me."

"And where are the guns?"

"I told you I can't move them yet. They're under surveillance. I can get them tonight. I just need some men to help with that."

Marchi let out a disappointed sound. "You're not worth it. I'm cutting ties."

The phone went silent.

"Pietro?" His voice raised an octave. "Marchi?"

He looked over at the dead man beside him. Cutting ties meant no one in the Marchi organization would back him now. The word would be out in minutes. It looked like he would have to go underground. Luckily, he still had a few men to count on.

"Mal!"

My vision swam. Someone was shaking me.

"Don't do this to me, Molly! Please answer me."

I reached out a hand. My head was spinning. If they would just be quiet, I could figure out what was going on. And why was everyone yelling?

"She's awake."

"I'm awake. I'm awake." I struggled to sit up, but had a hard time taking a deep breath. The reason I was lying on the floor flooded back in the blink of an eye. My eyes flew all the way open. I didn't see Dessi in the room. Shit.

"Where is he?" I asked. I pulled at my shirt, trying to loosen the bulletproof vest. It felt like I had hit my head when I fell.

"Oh, thank God." Rhodes crushed me to his chest.

"Hang on, cowboy," I croaked out, having trouble breathing.

"I saw the blood." He choked, sniffing loudly.

"Blood?" I patted my chest. There was no blood. Looking at the floor, I saw the red stains from my dropped wineglass. It had seemed like a good idea at the time. "Just wine."

"Dessi got away," Sam hovered over me.

"Why are you wearing a trench coat?" I said, poking at him. He had a visitor tag, reading "Sam

Spade," stuck to the left breast and a fedora on his head.

"And Wyatt was shot by Grady. He must have come in with Dessi. He jumped out of nowhere to cover his exit." Sam ignored my question.

"Is Wyatt okay?" I struggled to my feet, holding onto Rhodes for support. My head was still a little spinny.

"Yeah, it was just a graze; the double-crosser shot at his head." He sneered, his head lowered, and he peered at me from under the brim of his hat. "Barely got him, but it bled like a stuck pig. By the time I got here, he'd already gotten cleaned up and had a bandage on it. He took off after him."

"Grady took me off guard too. I was shielding you from Dessi when he shot Wyatt. I didn't want to risk following them out and leaving you." Rhodes glanced away, obviously feeling bad for letting Dessi run.

"It's not your fault. You had two guns on you. I think you did fine. Thanks for having my back."

"Always."

"Suzy's tracking him, but we have to go. Can you walk?" Sam hurried to me.

Now that my vest was loosened, I could. I had a *helluva* bruise, and my head was a little sore, but I was good to go. Pulling my weapon from my waistband holster, I headed towards the door.

"Wyatt and Brian are both tailing him."

"Let's go."

"Are you good, Malone?" Rhodes said gruffly, coming up behind me.

"Yeah." I waited for him. "I'm good. We just need to end this."

I pulled Sam's Tesla's door open, then stopped suddenly and turned to Rhodes. "Did you call me Molly?"

He dropped his gaze. "Maybe."

Nervous laughter bubbled out of me in a strange chortle. Nodding, I swung in and buckled up.

"I'll get you back for that one, Marlon."

"I don't have issues with my name," he said from the back.

"Come on, kids." Sam threw the car into gear and peeled out, tires throwing gravel as they spun to catch traction. "Let's go get 'em."

The rubber caught, and we ricocheted down the street, blowing past the red light and through another. He followed the blinking red light on his mounted phone. "Brace yourself."

Pulling his emergency brake, he whipped the wheel to the left, then released it, drifting around the corner without losing much speed. He fishtailed to the right and to the left, then straightened his route. Even though it was getting late in the day, it was still Chicago, and we met traffic within a block and a half, stopping us short.

The blinking red light went out.

"He disabled his GPS," Sam said. "Suzy, send me Wyatt's coordinates."

"I'm headed onto Diversey," Wyatt's voice came through my earpiece. I had forgotten I still had that thing in. "You good, Mal?"

"Bruised, but I'll live. You?"

"Pissed, but I'm good."

"Hold on. That's just...I think I just click here," Suzy said. "Did that work?"

The blinking light resumed.

"Good job, Suze!" Sam pumped a fist in the air. "Who's a rock star now?"

"Thanks, babe." I could hear the smile in her voice. "The cops are at the office. Jen called. They have an APB out on Dessi."

"Good." My eyes narrowed. I hoped Rodriguez wouldn't try anything. It would be dumb. We had pretty damning evidence now.

"He's going underground. If we're going to get him, we're going to have to move fast."

"We lost him heading east on Diversey, but I doubt he's going home unless he's got something there he needs."

"We're taking Lincoln. Maybe we can head him off." Sam made another quick turn. We made it another block before slowing down. He hit the steering wheel. "I wish we had a motorcycle."

"Can you drive one?" I asked him.

"No. Can you?" he said mockingly.

I nodded. "Yes."

"Really?"

I gave him a cocky grin. It seemed surviving a bullet shot to the chest was good for my confidence. "Of course."

Eventually, we made it to Diversey ahead of Wyatt's white Range Rover.

"Any sign of him?" Wyatt asked.

"None."

"No sign here either," Brian said. "I'm at his condo. I thought maybe I'd catch sight of him here."

"He's probably gone underground." Wyatt cursed.

"We have enough evidence to lock him away for a long time," I said. "We knew this was a possibility."

"Yeah, but I was hoping."

If we didn't get him now, we'd all be living in fear for months or years until he was apprehended at last. I had no idea how many friends he had scattered around the country.

"I might be able to catch a visual on the city's cams." Sam's mouth twisted. "It's a long shot, but it's a possibility."

"Let's meet back up at Sam's to try that. We'll swing by the office to get the evidence and meet you there."

"On my way."

"I'm going to keep driving for a bit," Brian said. "See what I can see."

Chapter 30

Twenty minutes later, we pulled onto the side street by the office, hurrying back to Roscoe and into my office.

"Hang on. I got a phone call to make." I hung back. "You go on ahead."

"Are you sure?" Rhodes paused, turning to wait for me.

"Yep, just give me a minute."

Nodding, he headed in.

I pulled my earpiece out, not wanting the static interference in my ear. I dialed the one person I could think of who could put an end to all this. The last person I wanted to talk to. But I had to find a criminal. Who better to find one than another one?

"Bugsy," Dom's voice came smoothly through my phone. "What is going on out there?"

"It's been a *helluva* night."

"From what I've heard, I'd agree."

I closed my eyes, pressing them shut. I had little choice. "I need a favor."

"I thought you didn't want it."

"I know what I said." I hated taking the favor for Marco's publicity. "But maybe I still don't take that favor. Maybe we can swap another way."

"I'm listening."

"You want Dessi off the streets. I can do that for you. I have evidence on him for the arms trafficking."

"And?"

"And we lost him. But I'm sure you can tell me his whereabouts. You've got ears all over this town."

He was quiet for a moment. "You know I can't do that. We have agreements. It would look like I'm taking out the competition. I give you his location, and I'm effectively handing him over to you. Marchi's guys will come after mine. It's not worth the risk."

"Okay, then." I tried another route. "You're doing it for Marco's story. Paul's been working with me since the arson case. I've been feeding him stories. Everyone'll believe it anyway. But between us, it's to get Dessi off the streets. You want him gone as badly as I do, and it has nothing to do with competition."

"That's true." He considered it.

"Tell them I held it against you. I threatened to expose Marco, ruining his chance at a life outside of all of this."

"That would be unwise," his voice dropped.

"I know that. I'd never hurt that kid." I just needed this one favor. "Tell you what, I'm going to take this evidence to the police station. You think about it."

"Are you *sure* you're not in the business?" He laughed.

I grinned, then stopped. I probably shouldn't take that as a compliment.

"Give me a few minutes." He ended the call.

As I headed up the stairs, Sam rushed to meet me.

"The cameras are gone."

"Rodriguez." I slammed through the police-department door, making a beeline for his office.

"Did you get him?" He appeared in his doorway.

"How dare you?" I shoved him in the chest, knocking him back a few feet.

"Hey!" Jen said from behind me. "What's going on?"

"You're a liar and a cheat." I pointed a finger at him accusingly. "I never should have trusted you. Leopards don't change their spots."

Rhodes and Sam hurried in behind me.

"Mal," Rhodes warned. It was assault, and I knew it.

"Hang on." Sam hurried in, his trench coat flapping in his wake.

"Mal, wait." Jen held up her hands, trying to calm me down. Her eyes were drawn with worry. The poor thing had so much faith in her boyfriend.

"Come on, Mal." George came into the room, trying to calm me down. "Let's just sit down and talk about this as friends. I'm sure we can figure out what happened."

"It had to have been you." I ignored Jen and George, pressing towards Rodriguez. "No one could have gotten to my office as quickly as you did, with your close proximity to the station. I trusted you with the evidence. We all trusted you."

"I didn't steal it, Mal." He waved his hands in the air. "You've gotta believe me."

"Mal." Jen tried again to get my attention off the slimebag.

"Then, who did?" I slammed my hand on his desk, demanding answers.

"Hang on!" Sam repeated, presenting his tablet. "If you'd just let me pull it up."

"What are you talking about?"

"The cameras." He punched a few buttons. "The recording."

"I thought you said they were stolen?" Jen said.

I came to a stop and turned. "I never said they were stolen."

"The video was backed up online, duh." Sam rolled his eyes. "See?"

He pressed play. Dessi burst into the room, recounting our entire conversation and his confession. Then after the gunshots and Grady extracting Dessi, Brian rushed after Dessi and I saw Rhodes cry out and fall to the floor, next to me, tears flooding his eyes.

I looked up at him. He still looked pretty shaken up. I had been so centered on Dessi, I hadn't quite realized. I reached out to grab his hand.

Sam fast-forwarded through the video to after we all left. A uniformed officer came into the office, climbing on chairs to retrieve the cameras.

It was Jen. Weight sat on my chest, nearly knocking me down. I had trusted her.

I swung towards her.

She started edging towards the door, her hands held up, eyes wary.

"Mal," she tried.

"What the hell, Jen?" I descended on her.

"If you'd just take a minute to listen." She looked around for help, but only saw everyone's accusing glare.

It was like someone had dropped me into an alternate universe. None of this made any sense. We were friends. She had helped me stake out the speakeasy, for goodness' sake. What was going on here?

Panicked, she backed out the door, making for the exit.

We all barreled out of the office to find her standing nose to nose with Wyatt.

"And what do we have here?" Wyatt grabbed her upper arms. "Is this the rat?"

"How could you, Jen?" I asked, my eyes rimmed with pain.

Even Rodriguez looked hurt as he walked forward. He turned his girlfriend around and handcuffed her. "You have the right to remain silent."

He went on, reading her, her rights. It hadn't been Rodriguez, after all.

"He took Charlie," she bellowed out, the words flowing with tears. Her shoulders hung loose with her hands captured behind her. "The bastard took Charlie."

Rodriguez's face flooded with emotion as he decided what to do with the woman in front of him with whom he had a relationship. I couldn't imagine the feeling. His duty was to arrest her. She'd broken the law, but the look on his face said he still loved her. Even through my dislike of the man, I actually felt bad for him.

"Tell me what happened." His voice remained crisp and even.

"Dessi called Sunday, saying he found out there was evidence being held against him." Her voice broke in heaving sobs. Snot ran out her nose. "His men had just taken Charlie. He said they'd return him once he got the evidence delivered."

"Did he?" I pushed.

"No," she wailed, the tears coming down harder. "He said there was more evidence at your office. And he'd let him go once it was collected and he'd made it to a safe house."

"Did you even call for an APB?"

"I did." She hung her head. "But I-I called and warned him first."

"Shit." I looked up at Wyatt. "It's how he knew to disable the GPS."

Wyatt's entire body was tight with anger at the typically sweet and kind blonde woman.

"Why didn't you come to me?" Rodriguez asked, betrayal evident in his gaze.

"He-he has Charlie," she stammered, begging us to understand. "I can't imagine him being with that lunatic. I bet he's terrified. You know how powerful Dessi is. He's got connections everywhere."

"We could have gotten him." Rodriguez spun away, collecting himself. He ran a hand across and down his face. "We could have done something."

"He'll never be safe," I said, turning to him. "Not with that man on the loose. We have to get Dessi and find Charlie."

It only made her cry harder.

My phone rang.

"Hello?" I stepped back to hear better.

"He's hiding out in a warehouse. I just texted you the location. This makes us even, Detective Malone," Dom said clearly. "Try that again, and you'll regret it."

I knew he was speaking lines, putting on a show in front of others, so they wouldn't know about the favor. Besides, he never called me Malone.

"Thanks." I hung up and opened up my messages. "We've got him."

Breaking away from Jen, Rodriguez asked George to lock her up and called the troops. We all headed out.

Speeding across town, I sat in the back seat of a squad car, stuck between Sam and Rhodes. It wasn't my favorite way to arrive on scene, but it was the fastest. These cars had sirens.

"I'm sorry about that, back there." My fingers threaded into Rhodes'. He held on tight. As much pain as I was dealing with because of Jen, I realized he had dealt with more due to the major threat of losing me.

"Just don't ever try anything like that again." His voice was soft. "I don't think I could handle it."

I smiled. "I don't intend to."

"Good." He kissed my hand. "Are you okay? With all that, back there?"

"I will be." I took a deep breath. "Let's just get through this first."

The car pulled in to park at the warehouse. I got out, glad I still had my vest on. Rodriguez called orders into his radio, pushing us back.

He looked up. "They're circling around back. He won't escape."

Helicopters appeared overhead, spotlights lighting up the broken windows. It was like a scene from a movie.

Rodriguez lifted a megaphone. "Fabian Dessi. We've got you surrounded. Come out with your hands up."

This was the moment I had been waiting for. My fists clenched at my sides. He was about to pay for his crimes. My eyes scanned the scene, searching for motion. Anything.

Gunshots sounded, scattering across the pavement between the line of cop cars and the warehouse. He wasn't going quietly.

"The SWAT team is on-site. I'm sending them in," Rodriguez said into his radio before lifting his hands and gesturing at the team decked out in black, ready, and waiting. As one, they jogged into the warehouse.

More gunshots went off. Then they stopped.

"What's going on?" I asked, straining to see. I couldn't get around the line of officers.

Squatting down, Sam took a seat on the gravel parking lot, his trench coat spread out behind him. Tipping his hat back, he pulled out his tablet and let his fingers fly over it. "Hang on."

"They don't see him," Rodriguez said, holding a headset up to one ear. "But there's no way he got out. He has to be in there."

"He's surrounded, isn't he?" George pulled up a map on his tablet. "What's going on?"

"Send in backup," Rodriguez directed. "He's not getting away this time."

"Wait, there's something here." He zoomed in and pointed at a spot. "Is this an underground tunnel?"

"Got him!" Sam stood up, his tablet lit with six spinning tops. "He made it to the warehouse next door and just headed outside. I've got him surrounded."

"With what?" Rodriguez asked, waving at his team to go before him.

"Drones." A grin split Sam's face.

Pulling his weapon, Rodriguez and George jogged out, following his team to apprehend Dessi. I itched to join them.

Instead, I left it to the men and women in blue. I had people who cared about me now. I could hand his apprehension on to others. Turning to Sam, I gave him a high five. "Smooth move, Sam Spade."

His face turned beet red in pleasure. "Thanks."

"If you hadn't done that, who knows what would have happened."

"I had to get him put away. He threatened my girl."

"Yes, he did." I patted him on the back.

Rodriguez's team returned, hauling a struggling Fabian Dessi in handcuffs. Gone was the genteel man in the suit. I'd never seen him so angry. Or so full of foul words.

I walked over to watch them read him his rights. Rodriguez opened the back of the police car.

"Where's Charlie?" Rodriguez asked.

He just lifted a shoulder. "I have no idea what you're talking about."

"We have your men, too." He leaned in an inch from Dessi's face. "One of them will talk."

Dessi's eyes narrowed imperceptibly. He feigned a yawn. "I'll be out by morning."

"Not this time, Thom," I said, catching his attention.   "*That's* checkmate."

He stilled, his eyes widening. "I thought you were dead."

"It takes more than that to get me."

Rodriguez closed the door, patting the hood soundly. The car took off.

"I just have one question," Sam said, coming up to stand beside me.

"What's that?"

"How'd you get his location?"

"Dom." I said it low, so the officers wouldn't overhear.

"I wondered." His eyes twinkled. "Was it an offer he couldn't refuse?"

Rolling my eyes, I turned away. "Let's go, Sam."

"And check out the barrels at the video-gaming facility," I told Rodriguez, who was taking notes at the station an hour later.

"Barrels? What kind?" He lifted his pen, trying to focus on the task at hand.

"Wine barrels. The place is also a small winery."

He frowned.

"I know. It's weird. And their wine is awful."

Sam had swung by to get Suzy, Hillary, and Mo, plus copies of the evidence he had at the house. He kept the originals, just in case.

The men arrested with Dessi had spilled Charlie's location. The boy was now at the precinct, waiting for his parents to come pick him up. He was safe and sound, if a little scared. He'd hung onto Rodriguez's neck for half an hour before social services arrived to monitor his health and well-being.

"Noted." Rodriguez finished writing the information.

"You'll find what you need there."

"The guns?"

I nodded, looking over at Sam for confirmation.

"They haven't been moved." He shook his head.

"There's also a storage unit." Wyatt raised a finger.

He had brought his whole crew. They were scattered around the station, taking turns writing up their own statements on what they'd observed while working for the Mennons.

"We never figured out which unit."

"Check under Malone." He grinned.

"What?"

"Store it under your mark's name. Why didn't I think of that?" Sam whispered in awe.

"I went back in the hope of talking the manager into spilling. He wouldn't, by the way. That is, until Hillary came in and talked circles around the guy about his bromeliad. He'd practically killed it."

"What's that?" Rodriguez asked.

"It's a plant." Wyatt looked at him like he'd grown two heads, finding Hillary in the crowd behind him. He raised his hands. "Duh."

She beamed at him.

"She showed him how to care for it and the proper way to water the thing. I swear it looked better within five minutes of her touching it. Anyway, she went into this big story about her brother, who had a unit there and had to go out of town. She'd promised to pay for the next month, but couldn't remember what crazy name he'd used. *Brothers.* She rolled her eyes."

He paused to laugh, then went on. "She had him eating out of her hand. Then she showed the guy a picture on her phone, from an online article—she'd zoomed in on his face—and he ID'd the guy from the newspaper photo as M. Malone."

"Classic." Sam nodded approvingly.

"No telling what he's got in there, but he sure didn't want it found."

"We'll look into it." Rodriguez nodded, adding a note. "Is there anything else?"

"Just sleep." I pushed up from my chair. It had been a hell of a week. A hell of a year, truth be told. But it looked like things were finally going to get a little simpler.

"I need you to sign these statements." Rodriguez jotted down a few more things and slid them over to everyone.

We all took turns signing.

"Let me know if you need anything else," I said as everyone headed out.

"You already did everything, it seems. You even found his mole in the department."

I paused, one hand on the doorjamb, and looked back. He sat on the edge of his desk, his hands tucked in his jeans pockets. Sadness sat heavily on him.

"It doesn't feel so good when someone backstabs you, does it?"

"Is this what it was like for you?" His eyebrows furrowed.

"Sort of." I tilted my head. "We didn't have the same kind of history. But you were the betrayer on that one."

"You were so hotheaded," he blew out, running a hand through his hair.

"Don't blame this on me. You were the one who cheated." I paced back into his office, my finger pointing at his chest.

"I didn't think it was serious for you," he said, studying the floor.

Was that actually why he had cheated? He hadn't thought I was serious?

I had always kept my guard up, and I'd admit I was pretty hardheaded back then, with something to prove and an enormous chip on my shoulder. But to think he had no idea I had real feelings for him? That was crazy.

"I spent time with your *family*. I got close to your mom." I shook my head. What the hell had he thought?

"Ma makes good food."

I had to agree with that.

"We just weren't a good match. We were both young and angry." I let out a long sigh.

"We fought a lot."

"That, we did. We've both done much better the second time around."

"You did." His eyes dropped again. "I'm not sure about me."

The touchy subject of Jen had been brought back up.

"Jen betrayed me too." I set my jaw. "I can't fault her for it. Hell, I might have done the same thing in the same situation, but I'm not sure where we'll be after this. I don't honestly know. Her feelings for you were real, though, Alex."

I hadn't used that name for him in a while. He looked up, shocked by my familiarity.

"She'll lose her job."

I nodded. "She will. And when all this is done, she'll need to find another career. She'll need someone to lean on."

"I'm not sure that can be me." He pulled his shoulders in. "I'm an officer, the officer she stole from."

"I know. I don't envy you the decisions you have in front of you. Whatever you decide, good luck."

He looked up at me. "Are we good now, Mal? Truly good?"

I thought about it. I'd said my piece, talked it out with him for the first time. And I'd finally heard his side of the story.

"I think so." I nodded.

"Thanks." He nodded back.

I left.

"All good in there?" Rhodes was waiting at the end of the hall with Mo.

"Yeah. I think it is," I said, actually feeling it for the first time. Only one thing was still bothering me. "Mo, can I ask you a question?"

He paused, having turned to leave. "It's about what Dessi said, isn't it?"

"Yeah." That part hadn't made sense. "What was that about you doing as you were told?"

Casting a glance down the hallway, he shifted his weight uneasily. "Back when I was actively handling cases as a lawyer, I didn't handle civil cases. I specialized in criminal law. I had history with Marchi."

"With Marchi?" I was shocked. I couldn't believe he had kept that from me. "Why didn't you tell me?"

"I'm not proud of it, Mal." His shoulders hung in shame. "I took a case, and boy did I come up with the perfect defense. I marched in there like the cocky attorney I was and shut down the cops who had accused him of misconduct, questioning all their evidence until it lay in shreds at their feet."

It didn't sound anything like the Maurice I knew. "Did you do it for the money?"

"I did it because I could." He pressed his lips together. "It wasn't until I found out what he had done, that the man who took the fall was innocent, that I started questioning everything. He'd only taken the job to pay for his son's medical bills. They found him dead a week later. I hadn't realized I was protecting the wrong person. After that, I took what earnings I had and got out of the game. Opened up the coffee shop so I could make a living doing something that wouldn't hurt others, maybe lend a helping ear when I could."

"You've always been there when I needed to talk." I laid a comforting hand on his shoulder. "You've been a good friend to me."

"I'm sorry if I've disappointed you, Mal."

"You couldn't disappoint me." I hugged him. "You've been the best mentor and friend I could ever have asked for."

He wiped a tear from his eye when we broke apart. "I've been so proud of you this past year."

"So that's why you were so good at pointing me in the right direction." The realization hit me like a bolt of lightning.

A sheepish expression crossed his face. "I guess."

"I'm glad you were always there to let me talk it out and get unstuck."

"It's been a privilege."

When we got out to the parking lot, I saw a black sedan sitting at the end of the curb. My foot stumbled, thinking of Dessi, but he was behind bars. I frowned. There was only one other person it could be.

"Give me a minute?"

Rhodes followed my gaze. "Everything okay?"

"Yeah." I watched him walk back to the Jeep to wait for me, but he stood with his arms crossed, observing carefully. Mo waited at his car door, beside mine.

The sedan rolled down the curb towards me. I stuffed my hands in my pocket and sighed. What did he want now?

The window rolled down. Dom sat in the back seat and put his finger to his nose.

A slow smile spread across my face. Reaching up, I touched the side of my nose in reply.

He chuckled. "Til next time, Bugsy."

The sedan pulled away.

Jogging to the Jeep, I shook my head, waving at Mo.

"Was that who I think it is?" Rhodes asked.

"It most definitely was." I unlocked the door and swung in. "I'll tell you all about it at home."

"Home? I like the sound of that."

Chapter 31

"Over there." I pointed across the lawn.

"That's a large collection of blankets," Rhodes said, impressed.

Six large ones overlapped like colorful sails to spread over the lawn at Millennium Park, right in the heart of downtown Chicago.

"She doesn't like to go small." I shot him a smile, grabbing his hand as we headed over, three pizza boxes balanced in my other hand. It wasn't a team meeting without pizzas.

The park was fairly busy, not surprising for a Saturday afternoon. We were having an uncharacteristically clear day, and several people lounged on blankets at the park to enjoy it.

"I'm glad we got the rest of your things moved out of your apartment this morning. It would have been hard to come here, knowing we'd have to go back and finish packing things up afterward."

"I bet." I elbowed him. "*You* don't have to unpack everything."

"What?" He faked innocence. "It's not my fault I have to work tomorrow."

It'd be the first time he let me out of his sight since we'd succeeded at getting Fabian Dessi, or Thom Kozik, off the streets of Chicago three days ago. Grady had been found dead, and Wyatt's guys were contacted to let them know the threat was gone. Even though we'd assured him it wasn't his fault, he was still struggling with the feeling of betrayal. I understood the emotion.

"It's not my fault where I put things, then."

He just shrugged. "Move things wherever you like."

It was pretty irritating that he was so easy to get along with sometimes. He just laughed at the expression on my face.

"Hey!" Suzy waved, catching sight of us.

She and Sam were lounging on one end of the sea of blankets, shoes kicked off and relaxing in the sun. This close to the lake, a nice breeze was making its way across the park.

Bending down, I set the boxes in the center, slid my shoes off, and found a comfy place on one of the blankets. Rhodes knelt beside me, toeing his off as well.

"Are these Marco's?" Suzy lifted a dark-green lid emblazoned with *Envy* to inspect the green and white pizzas nestled inside.

"There's still an olive one, right?" Sam's eyebrows furrowed in worry.

"Yes, Sam," I answered, unable to suppress the smile. "Marco added some especially for you."

"We have to still get Mantovani's occasionally," Suzy said, worried for Petite Pete.

"Of course." I nodded. "We can go back and forth if everyone agrees."

"The park in Roscoe Village would have been less populated," Wyatt said, coming up behind us, holding hands with Hillary. She'd already divested herself of her sandals on the walk up and was now planting herself on a spot to relax.

"What a gorgeous day." She picked several clover flowers from the grass and tucked them into her french-braided hair.

"That's why we're here." Suzy spread out her arms, inhaling heavily. "Now that we're safe, I want to be surrounded by as many people as possible."

"Is that what I think it is?" Rhodes eyeballed the basket set in the center next to the stack of pizza boxes.

"Of course." Suzy preened.

"Cookies?" Wyatt's eyebrows went up. They both lunged for it, banging heads over the lid.

"I made plenty," Suzy announced. "No fighting tonight!"

"I'll get them." Sam crawled forward, taking the basket from the two men who looked at him, mouths agape. He opened it, pulled out a container and napkins, and set a cookie on each before handing them out.

Both men looked forlornly at the single dessert sitting in their hands.

"Suze." I leaned towards my friend. "Do you think you could get me that cookie recipe? I'd like to try to make it. Maybe take some with us on our road trip next week."

"Do you want me to come over tomorrow? I can walk you through it." Her eyes sparkled with excitement. "I can help you unpack too!"

I had a lot to do the next day, but it sounded a lot more fun with a friend.

"Sounds fun." I looked over at Hillary. "You want to join?"

"For real?"

Suzy and I nodded.

"Well, okay, then." She grinned happily, clapping her hands together.

Sam turned to crawl back to his place next to Suzy, and Wyatt tossed the lid open on the basket to pull out another handful of cookies. He handed a few to Rhodes and sat back down.

Rhodes held one up in mock salute.

"Hey, save me some cookies!" Brian said, looping through the grass in running shorts and tennis shoes. Wyatt threw him one.

"How long are you going to be gone?" Wyatt asked Rhodes around a big bite.

"Just a week," Rhodes answered. "We're visiting my dad in Tennessee."

"That's even hotter than here." Brian collapsed on a blanket, leaning back onto his elbows, his long legs spread out into the grass. He tossed the cookie into his mouth in one bite.

"It's getting cooler. It shouldn't be so bad."

"And there's no electricity." I gave him a pointed look, leaning forward to prop my elbows on my knees.

"No electricity?" Wyatt's eyes widened in disbelief. "Are you two staying with him?"

"We'll stay in town," I answered, but seeing Rhodes' face, I straightened from my relaxed position to question him. "Right?"

"Dad did offer to let us stay on-site. He said they had an old converted bus we could stay in." He shrugged. "But we can stay in town if you'd like."

I pursed my lips. "I guess we could try it out. We can always get a motel if we need to."

His face lit up. "Thanks, babe."

Suzy jumped to her feet. "They're here!"

Turning, I saw Mo head towards us, two small fluffy golden retriever puppies bounding across the lawn on leashes. One tripped in the excitement, face-planting, then rolling back up to hop straight into the air and chase the other.

"What're they doing here?" My mouth dropped open.

"This little man is mine." Suzy bent down, letting one run into her arms. It knocked her over into a squealing pile on the ground. The puppy covered her in kisses, his tail wagging like a blond flag. Hillary scooted over to pet the pup, falling over into the melee in a fit of giggles. "Brent called a couple of days ago and said he got the pets back. All of them. I just asked him for a favor."

I narrowed my eyes. "And the other one?"

"I thought I could use the company." Mo knelt down to fluff the hair on the smaller, more reserved one. "I'm calling her Miel. For the coffee."

"I know what miel is," I mumbled; it was one of my favorite ways to prepare coffee. Her one ear still hung a little lopsided. She was adorable. And apparently, she was Mo's. I was surprised at the sting of disappointment.

Crossing his legs, Mo sat down on the blankets to say hi to Rhodes. The puppy waddled over to me. I patted her lightly on the head. She leaned in, so I scratched behind one ear, and she leaned in farther, falling to the blanket before jumping back up, surprised.

Suzy scooted closer. I was a little irritated she hadn't warned me first. She could have at least asked me if I wanted one.

"Are you upset?" she said quietly, reaching out a hand to pet Miel.

I lifted a shoulder. "A little, but what am I going to do? She's Mo's. I'd never take her away from him."

Her eyes flashed to Mo's, then back to me, a titter escaping her throat.

"What am I going to do with a dog?" Mo threw me the leash.

"I'm not taking your dog!" I tried to hand it back. Even if she was the most perfect puppy in the world.

"She's yours, Mal." Suzy grinned mischievously, grabbing my knee.

I looked back and forth between them, not understanding.

"Mo said he'd take her so you'd know if you really wanted her. Otherwise, you wouldn't let yourself consider it. Now, you do."

My mouth hung open. "You conned me!"

Miel climbed up onto my lap, standing to press her front paws on my chest. Nosing my chin, she licked at my face. She was freaking adorable. I wanted her so damn much.

I turned to Rhodes, who was sitting on the blanket next to me, my eyes pleading. Would he even consider it?

One corner of his mouth crept up. The look he gave me was one of pure affection. "Of course, you can. It's your place now, too. Besides, I love dogs."

"But it's technically your place."

"Not anymore."

And just like that, I realized I couldn't imagine a world without him in it. His silent confidence, his constant support, his loud, raw laughter. It was everything I never knew I needed.

"I love you."

He stared at me, stunned. Everyone went silent.

"Not because of this," I added for clarity. "But just because of you. I just love you."

A smile spread across his face from ear to ear. "I love you too."

Then he barreled into me, kissing me fiercely. Holding me to him in a wave of emotion. The puppy, displeased at being forgotten, yipped and jumped at us, knocking us over onto the blankets, and making us laugh like teenagers.

"Oh, get a room," Wyatt said. But he was smiling.

"You can change her name," Mo said.

"No way." I hugged her wiggly body to me, smiling at all my friends around me. "It's perfect. Now, let's eat these pizzas before they get cold!"

Epilogue:

"Don't drop that turkey!" I laughed, hopping up the Mennons' front-porch stairs to follow Rhodes. I zipped my jacket a little higher. The temperature had dropped yet another few degrees today.

"I'm not going to drop it," he threw over his shoulder.

Miel leaped up the stairs, her nose sniffing the air under the foil-wrapped food.

"Come on!" Sam held the door wide, wearing a sweatshirt that said *Friendsgiving,* with a picture of Chandler, Rachel, and Ross primed to play football. "Suzy's somewhere, buzzing around the kitchen."

"It smells amazing in here." I stepped in, Miel rushing forward to his brother Bogart. They rolled into the living room, taking turns sniffing each other and zooming back across the foyer into the kitchen.

"Suze has been up since seven, prepping." He took my coat. "Did you get that file I sent you on the Petersons case?"

In the several weeks that followed Dessi's arrest, my business had been booming. Rhodes was right; it had gained me a little notoriety. And Wyatt as well. We'd knocked out the wall between my office and the empty space and were setting up shop together. Suzy was running the entire operation with a customized scheduler and advanced communication systems provided by Sam.

"Yeah. Wyatt's guys are going to be pulling an all-nighter tomorrow to stake the place out."

As I headed in, I heard the doorbell ring again behind me.

"Hey, Suze." I rounded her kitchen bar to say hi.

"Hey!" She paused stirring the cranberry sauce on the stove to give me a one-armed hug.

"Wyatt and Hillary just got here," Sam called from the foyer. "And Brian's right behind them."

"When Mo gets here, we'll have everyone." She clapped her hands. "Can you open that wine? I'm a little behind."

I scanned the kitchen. Dishes sat on every available surface. "What on earth? Are you expecting us to eat all of that? Or did you invite others?"

"Haha." She tucked a stray hair into her clip and ran her hands down her holiday-sweater-and-skirt combo. "It's Thanksgiving. We're all supposed to overeat and go home miserable. It's tradition."

"Gee, sounds fun," I teased, moving to the bottles of wine she left out. I opened two and got glasses from her cabinet to set on the bar.

"Pour me one, please," she said, holding out a hand, fingers wiggling.

"Oh, I can use a glass," Hillary said, dropping like a stone into one of the bar stools in front of the wine. "I've been researching all day."

"Ms. Lamb's Monstera's still causing you grief?" I asked, handing Suzy, then her, a glass. She'd been battling a case of gnats for weeks.

"Yes." She took a long sip. "Ooh, is this cranberry wine?" Suzy just cast her a pleased smile. "I've got it quarantined in the guest shower and have been wiping down each leaf every day for the past three days. It's getting too cold to put it outside."

"You'll figure it out," Suzy said, pouring the sauce into a container and carrying it out of the kitchen to the dining room. She spied Brian, Wyatt, and Rhodes hovering over her cookie tray set out on the hutch. "Drop those cookies. Those are for after dinner!"

"We only had one." Rhodes had to hold his hand over his mouth to cover the lie.

She planted her fists on her hips. "I've been cooking all day. You'd better not have ruined your appetite."

He choked on the cookie, trying not to laugh. "No, ma'am. No chance of that."

"Good." She turned, heading back to the kitchen. "And thank you for bringing the turkey. I appreciate it."

"My pleasure." He grinned.

"Did he seriously smoke a turkey that size today?" she asked me quietly as she walked by.

"Sure did," I said proudly. "He got up at 3 a.m. to start the smoker. Brined it for twenty-four hours before that."

She turned her mouth down in appreciation. "Nice."

The doorbell rang again.

"I'll get it," Sam hollered.

"That'll be Mo." I snagged a carrot from a veggie tray and popped it into my mouth.

"Greetings." My favorite barista whipped into the kitchen, carrying an elaborately layered dessert. "It's tiramisu."

"That has espresso in it, doesn't it?" I eyeballed it, getting excited.

"It most certainly does." He leaned in to hug me. "I used my coffee beans."

I pumped a fist in the air. Mo roasted the best coffee beans in the Midwest.

"What took you so long?" Suzy glanced at the clock on the wall, carrying dishes into the dining room. "Everything okay?"

"Yep." He took a sip of the wine I had just handed him. Taking off his jacket, he adjusted the suit he was wearing underneath. It wasn't his usual suspenders-and-dress-shirt combo. "I just got out of court. I have news."

She stopped dead in her tracks. "Did they come to a verdict?"

"They did." He rocked back on his heels.

We all turned to face him, our eyes wide in anticipation.

"Thom Kozik, also known as Fabian Dessi, was found guilty on all ten accounts. He got six fifty-year sentences and four ten-year sentences."

"Can they even do that?" Hillary asked, eyes wide.

He nodded. "He's been held accountable for every grievous act against him."

"That we know about." I snagged another carrot from the tray.

"True, but it's done." He nodded. "None of our evidence had anything to do with Cynthia, except for Nate's experience, but let's hope that now that her boss has been caught, she'll return to more legal employment. What's most important is that Dessi's off the streets for good."

I let out a deep sigh of relief. "And how about Jen?"

"Jen got a hefty fine and very long probation. I was able to get her out on the short sentence because of her history as an officer of the law."

"Thanks." Emotion still churned inside me about the situation. I wasn't sure where we sat about the whole friendship thing, but I'd at least hear her out. She'd been put in a bad situation, but I couldn't ignore the danger she'd caused us, especially with the resources she had available to her.

He dipped his head. "She'll have a long road to go, but she'll be okay."

"What about Marchi?" Suzy asked.

"They're still processing through all the charges against him. He'll probably walk, but this has given him enough trouble to tie him up for a while."

"Will he come after us?" Sam asked.

"I doubt it. Dessi's the one who left Marchi's information in the storage unit with poor security."

"Plus all the intel from his phone," I added.

"Exactly. If anything, Dessi'd better be careful in there. Marchi might send someone in to get what's owed to him. I just wish we could have gotten ahold of his overseas accounts. They tried to make a deal with him for the information, but no luck. It'll probably revert back to the bank once he dies, unless, by some crazy turn of events, he makes it out early on good behavior."

"Nah." Sam shook his head. "Even if that happens, he's broke."

"What do you mean?" I asked.

His eyes lit up with mischief. He knew something we didn't.

"What did you do?" Suzy crossed over to him.

He just shrugged. "Let's just say the Chicago community centers will be getting some anonymous donations over the next couple of months."

"Some of that was Marchi's money Dessi was holding onto for investments," Mo warned. "It had better not be traceable."

He shook his head. "It's not. I was careful."

It was the best news I could imagine on this holiday. But I had even more news to share. And it related to our barista friend.

"Mrs. Collins gave me a phone call today." I looked pointedly at Mo. "She had some interesting news she said I could share. Seems your friend Ms. Tomlinson got several of the other tenants together to form a large case against Weston. I heard Nate's helping her out with some of the grunt work."

A grin split Rhodes' face. "Ms. Tomlinson has him spinning in circles. He's so busy, but dang it, if the kid doesn't love it! I think he's really getting the hang of it."

"Unfortunately, Weston went bankrupt and had to sell the place. She's pretty sure they're not going to be able to weasel out of *all* the liability, but I let it slip that they have a new owner coming on board. One who's already changed their billing process, promising to provide copies of hospital bills to validate. And they're expanding."

"Oh, fine." Mo shifted uncomfortably, pulling his loosened tie over his head to wad it into a ball and stuff it into his pants pocket. "I'll share. I bought the place."

The rest of the room looked at him in shock.

"What?" He held his hands up in explanation. "It's a lucrative business, and there's a shortage in the city, you know. I'm hiring a business manager, but I may need some bookkeeping help, just to make sure it gets set up properly. I did make some mighty big promises."

He cast a very direct stare at Suzy, shifting the attention from him.

"I'd be happy to help." Suzy smiled, hugging him. "Congratulations."

"Congrats." Rhodes came over to shake his hand. "It's a good thing you're doing."

"It's business." He shoved the compliment off.

"It's helping a lot of people who didn't have anywhere else left to go."

Mo stared at the rug. Rhodes slapped him on the back, almost making him lose his footing.

"I'm so glad to hear how well Nate's doing, son," Mo switched subjects. "A lot of that is due to you."

"Thanks." Rhodes gave him a side grin. "But you helped him just the same. You gave him direction."

The two men studied their shoes.

"Come on, guys. Help me carry these dishes to the table." Suzy spun a finger in the air, rounding everyone up and into the kitchen to grab something. "We don't want it to get cold!"

We all hurried to do Suzy's bidding, carrying platters to the table that was already teeming with food. It was amazing our plates even fit around all of it.

"I just want to say one thing." Brian lifted his glass. He had a sheepish, almost nervous look about him. "I didn't expect to be brought into the fold. You all will never know what it meant to me to be included."

"But that's who we are." I lifted my glass. "We're all just a bunch of misfits who've found a group to call a family. I'm happy you've joined us."

Rhodes' hand found mine under the table. I looked up and locked gazes with him. I'd certainly found my family.

Several weeks ago, my dad had stopped by when we were getting things set up, combining our businesses. He'd finally seemed to be impressed with my success. I was glad we were working towards a relationship together, but what he didn't understand was that it wasn't just my success. It was the team's.

"Sam's got some news of his own." I smiled, prodding him on.

"I hired a director of innovation at PhishNett." He physically folded in, a little uncomfortable with the change. "She's going to handle some of the day-to-day decisions at the company."

"And why are you naming this person to share some of your duties?" I prodded him.

He blushed, and the electricity of it seemed to extend to the curly tips of his hair. "She's going to be my second-in-command so I can better split my time between my tech company and investigations."

I beamed at him, proud he'd decided to join us in a more concrete fashion.

"I think we should rename the place, though," he continued.

"What's wrong with Malone Investigations?" I frowned.

"It's all about you." Wyatt shrugged his shoulders, forking a mouthful of turkey into his face. "Sentinel was a security business."

"What about Free Bird Security & Investigations?" Suzy beamed. "Like a bird set free?"

"Or just Chicago Inner-City Security & Investigations." Brian tested the verbiage, then wrinkled his nose. "That's really generic, isn't it?"

Squeezing my hand, Rhodes leaned in, watching the activity around him. "Thank you for bringing me into this."

"You earned your place." I squeezed it back.

"No, it's more than that. You created this, and you included me in it. I appreciate it."

I knew he had his own crew at work, a type of family I'd never be a part of and didn't need to, but I got what he was saying. It was about building your own family.

It had been a hard-won lesson for me. I'd originally left the academy in my desperation to prove myself, knowing I wouldn't be able to shake the distinction of being my father's daughter on the force. Striking out on my own, I'd gained some ground, but on the whole, I had continued to struggle. It wasn't until I had let myself open up to those around me and accepted their friendship that I found my success.

Not by money or fame, but through the ability of accepting love. And I wouldn't have it any other way.

"What about Falcon Security & Investigations, like The Maltese Falcon?" Sam suggested, enthralled by the idea. "Or Firefly Detectives & Security, and I could make a plaque over our offices that says Serenity. That would give our customers some comfort, right? Ooh, or maybe the Scooby Gang?"

I just rolled my eyes.

"Roscoe Security & Investigations?" Wyatt's eyes met mine.

I liked that. It was our turf, where we lived.

"How about it, team?" I scanned the room. Everyone nodded. Lifting our glass, we gave a cheer. "To Roscoe Security & Investigations!"

Taking a sip of the tart cranberry wine, I settled into my hard-earned happiness. I was still excited about what my life had in store for me, but I was also, for once, incredibly content with what I had.

"Hey." Rhodes' knee touched mine. "It's stew season again."

Memories of our conversation of so many months ago and our first date night flooded back.

"Let's do it." I nudged him back.

"Hey, guys." He raised his voice. "How about Guinness stew next weekend at our place?"

"We should make it a game night," Wyatt suggested, his eyes on Hillary.

"Seriously?" Sam's voice raised an octave. "We could play D&D!"

"*Not* D&D," he said firmly. "Some kind of trivia."

"I can do that." He scrambled to find another. "How about Geek Battle?"

A growl came from the end of the room. "Maybe we should just play cards."

Rhodes tipped his head back in laughter.

"I'm glad you stuck around long enough for another stew season," he whispered in my ear, reaching for the mashed potatoes.

"Not half as glad as I am." I kissed his cheek, ready to see what our future had in store for us all.

From the Author:
Thank you so much for reading my book. I sincerely hope you enjoyed Mal and her friends.

If you do, the nicest thing you can do is leave me a good review on Amazon, Bookbub, Goodreads, or wherever you review books.

Connect with me online:
Website: **jenflanaganbooks.com**
Follow me on Amazon
Facebook: **@jenflanaganbooks**
Instagram: **@jenflanagan_author**
Bookbub: **@jen_flanagan**

Please visit my blog at **jenflanaganbooks.com** for upcoming books, comments, and minor musings.

What's Next?

I've got several books in the works: a new series and some notes for another Detective Malone book. You may be thinking, what story is left to tell? Well, stay tuned, we're not done with mysteries in Roscoe Village!

If you like a little cozy paranormal romance, check out my new series Orca Cove. It's a small-town vibe, with found family, romance, and a little magic!

Orca Cove: Small seaside community, tight bonds, and something magical in the water.

She's been alone for far too long.

Free-spirited Willa Daniels doesn't get stressed about much. She has built the life she's dreamed of, an herbalist and yoga instructor in a quiet town in the Pacific Northwest, and is trying to rebuild her community. But she's still missing something.

A mysterious stranger.

A dark newcomer, Nick Ryan isn't immediately accepted by the close-knit town where he's come to start over. He has a lot of secrets and a deep-seated inability to trust. Even he isn't sure what he wants out of his new situation.

Can saltwater truly cure all wounds?

An unusual storm brings forth unlikely abilities to Willa and her friends. When a body is found onshore at a location Nick was seen the previous evening, distrust and fear envelop the idyllic town. Only Willa seems able to believe in Nick, secrets and all. But will her faith in him be strong enough to outshine Nick's dark past and the dangers it brings with it?

Turn the page to read the first chapter of *Saltwater Cures (Orca Cove Series Book One)*.

Chapter 1

Cold rain pelted down around Nick Ryan as he trudged away from his truck and across the pebbled beach. He pulled the bag he was carrying closer to him, tucking it partially under his open jacket to keep it as dry as possible. It was all he could do in this weather.

Thunder cracked down closer than expected, momentarily drowning out the crashing waves to his right. Raising his head, he searched the sky for lightning, finding it ahead of him, towards his new home. The thought of his fireplace sent a shiver of anticipation through him, anxious to get back into dry clothes.

A body crashed into him, bare arms and legs flailing about to retain balance. Shocked, he dropped the duffel bag, catching the arms of the soaking-wet woman who'd run into him, appearing out of the water.

"What the?" The words were taken from his mouth, the wind carrying the sound far away.

She clutched his arms, her eyes sparked, and her mouth opened in silent laughter. She ran a hand over her face, clearing it of rain.

He looked towards the water and back to her, finally noticing the tan strapless bathing suit she wore. Not a mermaid then, he told himself, chiding his imagination. Although, who would blame him on a night like this? Even on this spring evening, the water had to be forty to fifty degrees. It would be extremely cold without a wetsuit.

"Are you okay?" he tried again, but it was pointless over the howling wind.

Another crack of thunder erupted from the sky above them. Shocked, they tightened their hold on each other's arms as they searched the clouds. The flash of lightning was closer the next time, illuminating the water droplets on her eyelashes and the light blue of her cold lips. A jolt ran through him, a strange connection at the sight of her. Her long hair hung wet, its curly strands plastered to her face. He moved to hold her closer, to try to keep her warm, keenly aware of the mysterious woman wrapped in his embrace.

Breaking their bond, she took an unsteady step back, clutching her arms across her chest. He could see her trembling from the cold. The corner of her mouth kicked up in a playful smirk, then she whirled around and ran up the shoreline, long bare legs kicking up sand and rocks. He had to silently command his feet to stay where they were, the urge to follow was so strong.

She paused only momentarily near the grass line to bend down to gather a blanket, then disappeared into the night.

It took him a minute to recover from the shock, finally remembering his neglected bag at his feet. Panic soaking in, he reclaimed it, holding it tightly to himself, his steps faster as he headed back towards the grass line and the parking lot where his truck waited.

Willa Daniels woke up the next morning exactly where she ended up last night, on the floor in front of her couch, still wrapped in thick blankets. That was strange; she never fell asleep in the living room. She frowned at the fog in her mind. It felt cobwebby and slow. Luckily, the candle on her coffee table had burned out safely at some point in the night. Her mug of tea, almost entirely full, now sat cold.

Shrugging the blankets off, she reached a hand up to her still-damp hair, digging her fingers deep into the curls in an effort to shake them out so they could fully dry. Her strawberry-blonde hair fluffed up haphazardly. She'd try to tame it later.

With a sigh, she bent to pick up her mug with one hand, and rubbed her eye with the other, trying to clear away the last dregs of sleep. That had to be all it was. The cold swim must have zapped her strength. The storm hadn't helped. When the lightning started, they got out as quickly as they could, but it sure seemed like it was striking the water. She shivered involuntarily. They lucked out. But who would have guessed? It rained a lot in Orca Cove, but thunderstorms weren't as frequent.

The water on the Hood Canal was still now, she noticed, looking out the double windows of her living room. Calm and deep blue. Her little one-bedroom condo was right on the coast in a long building, so each unit could overlook the cove. It was beautiful and an easy way to connect to life in the Pacific Northwest. Close to Seattle, but far enough outside the Emerald City for some peace and quiet.

Padding over to her kitchen, she clicked on the electric kettle, dumping out the contents of her mug and giving it a quick wash. She rifled through the many containers of loose-leaf teas on the small bookshelf between her kitchen and living room, selecting echinacea, warming ginger, and astragalus root, just in case her immune system needed it after being exposed to the elements the night before. Her hand hovered over the wakame, a seaweed she had foraged the weekend before, known for its high levels of iron, manganese, and other vitamins. She could probably use the extra energy to clear her brain. She added a generous pinch of ginseng for circulation to round out her tea.

Piling her blankets back onto her couch, she made her way to her bedroom, pulling on a long, embroidered wool cardigan that was practically a blanket with arms. She was still fighting away the chill from last night. She poured the now boiling water over the herbs in her tea infuser and stuffed her feet into a pair of boots, leaving them unlaced as she took her steeping tea out to the back deck.

Leaning against her wood railing, she scanned the coastline for anything washed up on shore from the storm. A long, dark mass far off to the right caught her eye. At first, it looked like a large tree branch, driftwood not yet bleached by the sun. But the soft roundness of it made her think more of an otter. No, not quite that small. A sea lion maybe. They often made their way on shore for the afternoon sun, but not typically at this time of day.

Shaking her head again to try to clear it, she sat down on her Adirondack chair. She must not have gotten enough sleep last night.

She took a sip of her tea. It tasted especially good this morning. But then again, hot tea always tasted good first thing in the morning.

The ping of her phone sounded from inside. Sliding open her door, she headed back in, sipping more tea.

"You okay this morning?" her friend Nell had

texted.

"Yes, a little tired, but taking an easy morning," she answered. That was sweet of her friend. Nell had always had the habit of mothering the rest of them. She sipped her tea, slowly waking up, then texted more. "You doing okay?"

"Yes," the answering text came. "I had a hard time waking up this morning. Didn't even make it past my couch last night."

That was strange. Both of them not making it to bed?

"Weird. Me too. The rug in front of my couch, though, for me."

Three dots appeared to show Nell was texting back. Then they disappeared. Willa waited, drinking her tea. The dots resumed.

"Shelby and Maggie too."

What?

"And Duke?" she texted, asking about the last member of the group that took the memorial dip in the channel the night before.

"No answer yet."

Finishing her tea, she wandered back to the deck, looking out onto the cove. So quiet, so still after last night's storm. Cool, fresh air graced her cheeks.

A dorsal fin broke the glassy surface. Willa cocked her head to watch the water. It was black. Could it be? A black and white back broke the surface, confirming her suspicions. They got an unusual number of orcas in their cove. No one knew why, but it was still always a treat to see one.

The orca's blunt nose rose from the water, and it seemed to acknowledge her. For a moment, it seemed like they were looking right at each other. A shiver ran through her, and she tugged her sweater close around her, her mind now completely awake and running at full speed. Even faster than normal. It was like she had recharged herself. She considered her empty mug. The wakame had seriously rejuvenated her.

Turning back towards the water, the orca was gone. She traced the surface for any signs of it, or other sea life.

A seagull had landed on the dark heap down the beach, picking at it. Discomfort pricked along the back of her neck. Not a sea lion sunning itself then, something dead. Hopefully not a sea lion. The dark shadow formed a plaid pattern. Pieces clicked together in her now clear mind. The meager contents in her stomach tumbled. That wasn't something from the ocean. It was a body.

Spinning off the back deck, she launched herself down the stairs leading to the beach, her boots pulling at her feet as they sank into the sand and pebbles. She cursed at herself for not taking the time to tie them. She raced across the sand until she stood over the body, out of breath but otherwise feeling healthy and full of adrenaline.

The corpse of a middle-aged black man lay on the beach before her. His opened eyes and mouth appeared slightly shocked, as though staring sightlessly into the clouds. She knew better than to touch him, even though she wanted to cover him to protect him from the gulls.

It was then she noticed the dark brownish-red spot staining the front of his flannel shirt jacket, disrupting the blue and green plaid. Willa whirled and heaved into the sand.

"You're sure you didn't touch the body?" the chief of police asked gruffly, his hands on his knees where he leaned over the dead body. She'd known him all her life, having grown up in the cove. "You didn't try to resuscitate him or anything?"

"Warner." Willa cocked her head. "He's obviously beyond saving."

"You tried to put that salve on my razor burn last year." He itched at his freshly shaved neck, still speckled with small red bumps.

"Yeah. And it would have helped." She crossed her arms.

"It's razor burn. It just needs some aftershave."

"I'm glad that's working out for you." She smiled sweetly. There was no sense in trying to help people who weren't ready to be helped.

"I'm just sayin'," he muttered. "Not everything needs-"

"I didn't touch the body." She cut him off. "I waved the gulls away, ran inside, and called you."

"Well, okay then." Straightening, he leaned toward one of his deputy officers. "Ronnie, go get the box of gloves from my truck."

"Yessir." Ronnie ran off.

"Did you see or hear anything strange last night?" Warner regarded her.

"You mean over that storm?" Willa chuckled.

"Yeah, it was quite a doozy. Came out of nowhere too. It's a good thing the body is so far up the shoreline, or it would have gotten pulled into the cove. Were you on the beach last night at all?"

"Yes," she hesitated. "The girls and I, and Duke, were out last night."

"I didn't realize you all were still hanging out." His eyes cast downward. "It's nearly been a year since I've seen you all-"

His voice trailed off.

"Well." She stuffed her hands in the pockets of her sweater. "Exactly. It's been almost a year. And last night was his birthday. It was important."

"I can hardly believe it's been that long. Shame. How's Nell doing?"

"Pretty good. Considering."

"What time was this?"

"Eight, maybe?"

"Walk me through it."

"Like you said, the storm came out of nowhere. We all hurried off the beach."

"All?"

"Yes. I was the last off. It was a beautiful storm." She grinned freely. "Wild and unpredictable."

"Did you see anything?"

Willa thought back to the dark stranger she had literally run into the night before. His hair had been nearly as black as the dead man's, with a similar body type, tall and thinly muscular. Had it not been for the darker skin, she'd have thought it was the same person. If she told Warner that he had been on the beach, that he'd been walking from the very direction where they were standing right now, he'd rush off and arrest him on the spot. As soon as he could find him, that was.

Sure, she thought the best of people, but she honestly didn't think he murdered this man. Call it a gut feeling, but she was somehow certain. Her brows furrowed. "I saw a lot of waves and rain, Warner."

Huffing, the older policeman turned to meet Ronnie, tugging on his gloves in frustration.

She hadn't lied, exactly.

<u>Jen Flanagan Fiction Books</u>

Orca Cove Series:
Saltwater Cures
Uncharted Waters (coming 2024)

Books in the Detective Malone Series:
Bad Company
Here I Go Again
Under Pressure

<u>Willa Daniels Non-Fiction Books</u>

Stand-alone books:
The Art of Living Seasonally

The Natural Path Series:
An Introduction to Herbalism
An Introduction to Soap Making (coming 2024)
Home and Cleaning Solutions (coming 2024)
Body and Skincare Solutions (coming 2024)